UNTANGLING
THE WEBS

Joy Pearson

UNTANGLING THE WEBS

JOY PEARSON

The Book Guild Ltd

First published in Great Britain in 2018 by
The Book Guild Ltd
9 Priory Business Park
Wistow Road, Kibworth
Leicestershire, LE8 0RX
Freephone: 0800 999 2982
www.bookguild.co.uk
Email: info@bookguild.co.uk
Twitter: @bookguild

Typeset in Garamond

Printed and bound in Great Britain by CPI Group (UK) Ltd, Croydon, CR0 4YY

ISBN 978 1912362 363

British Library Cataloguing in Publication Data.
A catalogue record for this book is available from the British Library.

Two wonderful people inspired me to write this book.

Pammie, lifelong true friend and soulmate, whose love, loyalty and steadfast belief in my writing urged me on through dark days to use and not hide my talents. This first novel poured out of me once I began.
In her memory — here it is.

Sir Dirk Bogarde, superb actor and writer. Dirk's descriptive writing leapt off the page, deeply drawing me into all of his colourful inspirational stories.

1

'I'll see you on the dark side of the moon' drifted into Alison's brain as shrieks from the bin lorry mechanism disturbed shallow sleep. Uncurling, she yawned herself awake, weak February light from the pavement's plane tree reflecting dappled patterns onto the blue quilt. Not having opened the white drapes when the stranger had left her dishevelled bed earlier that morning, she'd crawled back in, groaning, 'Hell, I've done it again.'

Now awake and hungover, she felt ashamed at her reckless behaviour the night before, brow furrowing at her neediness, asking him, 'Don't go away?' She'd said this to ex Phil and knew then she'd be like a beetle on its back if that happened. He'd looked amazed at her mistrust, protesting she was all he wanted, rather too quickly. Three weeks ago they'd split – pink angora mittens and revealing photographs she'd found in his Range Rover had been the last straw.

Depression from Phil's betrayal, too much alcohol and what she perceived as her sexual addiction, had last night squashed vows to remain celibate. In a heady alcoholic haze, she'd led Stephen, the party stranger, upstairs. Too much heightened passion for preliminaries, frenzied sex had occurred to the sound of Pink Floyd. Afterwards, they'd slid under the duvet, lying like spoons in a drawer, drifting heavily into sleep.

1

Stretching, she began to remember last night, but tyres crunching on gravel and the door knocker's urgent thud arrested her recall. Reluctantly creeping to the window, wrapping the white curtain around her, she peeped to see new friend, Clare. Frowning, slipping on a robe and appearing tousled at the door, Alison let her in. Clare nudged her suspiciously, tilting her head, 'Oh yeah?'

Wearily, Alison shuffled, yawning, down the hall.

'Bet you went to that party then?' Clare asked pointedly.

'I wanted to give my best friend, Julia, her birthday present so went at nine when there'd be more people and I wouldn't be so noticeable,' Alison admitted gruffly, dehydrated.

'You not noticeable?! I'm noticed cos I get drunk and talk Northern. 'Urry up – tell.'

Sighing, Alison continued, 'Avoiding gossips eyeing me up, I saw Julia handing a drink to a tall slim guy, a dead ringer for Laurence Harvey... a British film star, Mum's favourite. Julia opened Anne Summers lingerie excitedly, declaring she'd model it as cabaret. The young male dish sipped his drink bemused, so I nudged Julia to introduce us. She embarrassed me saying, "This is Alison, deserted by a rat. Stephen's a musician and gardener."'

'Oo er, don't stop,' Clare insisted, wide-eyed.

'We landed here for a passionate night, making out to *Dark Side of the Moon* – I didn't say I'd used it before. Fantastic sex, dynamite.'

'No wonder you look shattered.'

'I am, drank too much, stupidly offering myself on a plate.' She yawned again, leaning against the hall mirror. 'Serves me right if he doesn't return, hate one-nighters, insecure enough at the moment and... '

'I like to play the field, me,' Clare proudly interrupted. If that divorced chap disappears, my ex in Norfolk will 'ave me back. Ooh, is 'ee married?'

'No. He's phoning later, says he'll cook dinner for me if I'll let him.'

'Let 'im what?' Clare giggled.

Alison blushed, walking Clare back to the door, bare feet chilly on blue Edwardian floor tiles. With a worried look, she uttered, 'What have I done, spilling a sexual encounter? You can see I'm overwhelmed and half asleep.'

Watching Clare drive away in her yellow Mini, Alison padded through the lofty wide hall, noticing mascara smudged down her cheek. Drowsily climbing the stairs, she had no qualms at occupying the abandoned bed yet again. Telephoning Mrs. Cade to re-arrange a room design appointment, she snuggled under the soft crackle of goose-down, moulding the quilt around her.

Despite Alison's lethargy, sleep wouldn't come. Clare was the last person to trust with such delicate information. Caught unawares, that was exactly what she'd done. Turning on the radio, an uneasy pang stabbed. She'd missed part one of a serial, so tried to pick up the thread. 'Typical, it would concern betrayal.' She recalled the shock of Phil's deceptions, including Liverpool Airport. She'd returned from staying with her son, Leo, near Nice. Drowsy from the early morning flight, wishing she hadn't agreed to Phil meeting her, Alison had failed to spot him, so sat in the arrivals bar to wait.

After half an hour, she'd felt abandoned, pulse heightened. Scanning faces intently from the edge of the café, she'd regretted her forgiveness of his disgraceful behaviour. Had he forgotten landing time?

As she went to the bar for a bottle of water, Philip had wandered towards her, appearing edgy, as if caught wearing odd socks. His hands were a giveaway, clenched tightly, face set like a mask to deceive. She too, had attempted to re-arrange her expression from anxious to happy. Both pretenders embraced. With false body language, they'd walked stiffly to the car park.

She'd thought they'd be alone, but a woman was in the background, mentally between them. He'd admitted to his dalliance with Jenny, the town bike, but not this one. Phil carried on with his act, but Alison had seen through it. He'd usually opened car doors for her, but announced callously, 'What did your last slave die of?' Alison had felt hurt and stupid, hauling herself into the back seat like a piece of luggage. No question of her sitting in front, he'd taken the passenger seat beside the woman driver. Proceeding onto the motorway at breakneck speed, they'd ignored Alison, sharing silly in-jokes. There was, she knew, unfinished business.

Shuddering under the covers, she couldn't erase the image of Phil. Thoughts flitted to why she'd gone to stay with son Leo in Antibes, how it had helped, then damaged by Phil again.

The last night at her son's apartment, she'd awoken a lot with broken dreams, squinting at the cheap clock between their single beds, willing the crude hands on the garish red dial to indicate eight and not four. The little pill had lost its powers, brain overactive. She recollected tossing and turning, stifled by oppressive heat, gagging as she came into full consciousness. Leo slept on, drugged with beer and nicotine. Twice she was aware of his lean blonde figure exiting the hard bed, stumbling to the humming fridge for cooling water. The difference was his ability to resume sleep, flat on his troublesome back, all five foot eleven of him, size ten's once more at one with the mattress. The adored child for whom she'd almost lost her life, a protracted birth twenty three years before.

Mercifully, now the clock signified an acceptable hour – 7.45 a.m. The interminable night had ended. She yawned, stretching to unlock stiffness from the uncomfortable mattress. Trying to recall fragmented dreams, she wandered to why she was in the tiny apartment. Her love life had been one long soap opera – this latest episode a repeat, of a repeat, of a repeat.

The coffee machine beckoned but the tranquillising pill kept its grip. Despite September heat and care from her domiciled son, she was still suffering from Phil's treachery. 'I'm down but not out,' she'd bravely told Leo. 'A man who cheats isn't worth it.' – platitudes tumbled out.

4

Leo, in his capacity as chef/manager of an Antibes brasserie, had taken a rare night off, at last having time for her depressed ramblings. Constantly seeing the tart, and he who'd inflicted the pain, had slowly sent her 'down the tubes,' she'd admitted falteringly.

'Wow, didn't realise it had been that bad,' Leo had sympathized.

'I don't usually flee the country,' she'd tearfully replied.

After wine on her part and beers on his, she'd desperately needed sleep. Alcohol and anti-depressants didn't mix, although she'd only had one wine. Her system ravaged by anger and hurt, nights were virtually sleepless, emotions more acute than by day.

Focusing on a Nice-bound low-flying aircraft had arrested her thoughts. Leo, cocooned in his pit, stirred, sighed, and slept on. Taking her coffee-stained letter from his bedside table, sent when he'd left England six months before, she re-read it.

'You are a real tryer,' she'd put, and, 'I washed all your teddies today, then saw schoolboys pass in a 'croc,' wishing you were their age. Phil's behaving strangely, saying "It's what you need that determines what you do." If there's one certainty, it's that he won't leave me.'

This statement stabbed. Her throat had burned with de-hydration; she'd taken out a cooling bottle of Evian from the humming fridge. Sipping icy liquid, she'd drifted to irrational acts she'd done for love's sake. All those nights she'd woken up to Phil's side of the bed empty. One o'clock, three o'clock. She'd donned a coat over her pyjamas, staggered into her car, trawling through the town. In the hope of… what? With her in a bar, without her in a bar, with friends, on his own, what? She'd pressed her self-destruct button again and again. Finding nothing, she'd returned cold and anxious to bed, feeling him carefully crawling in beside her later.

She hadn't let him know of her nocturnal wanderings, but one morning, glancing at her watch on the table. – 6.10 a.m. and no Phil. Trembling hands dropped the watch onto the carpet. Determinedly pulling on her coat, she'd nervously driven to where she knew he'd be.

The tart, all twelve stone of her, lived in a terraced house at the bottom of a steep hill. Her address known to many local males, gossip viciously suggested she put a sign up, 'We never close.' Alison had winced, thinking Phil could be in between those Leviathan thighs.

Mist had settled on cars in the silent street. Alison had parked in the adjacent cul-de-sac and crept to the corner. She saw what she'd been dreading, the silver Range Rover standing damply outside the scene of the crime. Head swimming, she foolishly ran to the car, although not a soul to view her detection. Within ten minutes she was back in what was once the love-bed, swallowing hot tea to thaw out. Next thing she knew, Phil was dressing for work at 7 a.m..

Of course he'd lied – there'd been a serious incident involving him on the case. 'Then the bloody car wouldn't start. I'll kill that mechanic, just had the damn thing seen to.'

Very convincing! Time to tell him she knew his dirty secret. The resultant row was monumental, full of denials and half-truths. He'd begged forgiveness; she'd reluctantly given it.

Was she dissatisfied no one had been able to give her the unselfish care her late father had? Henry, her holy man did, for a while. Philip, although loud with the crowd, was a gentle giant at first. A retired police colleague of his had warned he'd always been an unfaithful liar, but she'd seen no proof.

Then the crushing blow, telling her casually he needed to 'find himself' on the Scottish island of Bute. Upon his return, Alison had discovered condoms and mouthwash in his sponge bag. When she'd asked to see holiday photographs, he'd said his camera had fallen into the sea from the ferry. The one on his mobile phone had packed up. She'd secretly gone into his Range Rover, in the glove compartment finding pink angora mittens and a throw-away camera, which she took to one-hour processing at Boots. With dry mouth, she'd opened the packet, seeing cattle, sheep and a boat. Then what she'd suspected – the long-haired mistress grinning on the ferry to Bute. When confronted, he'd had the nerve to say she'd looked for a business there. Surely business was booming at home!

Reflections over, she'd noticed Leo peeling back the duvet, with a yawn. 'You all right Mummykins? Is that coffee I can smell?'

Mummykins, the familiar name. She'd smiled, 'No, but soon will be.'

He'd watched her put heaped scoops of glorious grains into the cafetière. Sitting beside him and touching tousled blonde hair, she'd asked, 'Are you OK?'

'Course, but are you?'

'Leo, how precious you are – more than any man. I've got to drag myself out of this. Phil isn't worthy of one ounce of my affection. He said he'd meet me at the airport, but it's false hope. Leo, you're all that matters to me.'

He'd hugged her tightly, saying, 'Come on, 'let's wrap our mouths around that coffee and sit on the balcony. Remember that framed motto at home?'

She did – 'Life is all there is – say YES to it.' She would.

Alison's reminiscences while with Leo ceased as the radio serial ended with a burst of 'Not Fade Away', by the Rolling Stones. Rather apt, the memory of Phil's lies raw. A travelogue through Cumbria began.

'Probably miss most of it, drifting off.' She did just that.

2

Alison was keen to abandon herself to more ecstasy with Stephen, her new drug. She hadn't realized how much she'd missed sex, hoping it wasn't only that. Balloons had a habit of popping unexpectedly, she had no illusions. Vowing to never again begin a relationship with sex, she'd done precisely that.

'Stephen, I love to feel you near.'

He began to make love to her, pleasuring her gently so she caught her breath. 'Come for me.'

She moaned, opening to his touch like a sea anemone, sinking with him. She didn't say he'd made her feel wanted, she'd only met him a few nights ago. As if he'd read her mind, he whispered she'd healed his wounds. Taken aback by his candour, she retracted her resolve, 'You're healing mine. What wounds?'

Stephen kissed her cheek. 'Another time, yours must be raw, Julia alluded to them at the party.'

'Three weeks since my split with Phil, so I'm surprised at my boldness. Until a few night's ago I felt ugly and discarded.'

Stephen kissed her. 'I was unaware of that, but I need a loving relationship. I'm not putting this well but…'

She put her fingers over his mouth, 'Ssshhh, we've only just met. I wondered what you made of my forward behaviour, not

8

something I expected to happen, my fault, poor sleep for weeks combined with too much alcohol. I dreaded going to the party, having to fence Phil questions, intended giving the present, then leaving. Er… you must know I'm older than you?'

'Stop blaming yourself, I was a very willing accomplice. I've had a relationship from twenty-two to twenty-five, and a few flirtations, but at the grand age of thirty, I can take on an experienced woman, a little older than me.'

Alison corrected him. 'A lot older.'

He rolled her over gently, looking into blue eyes. 'I don't care. Only about you, stay with that while I go to the bathroom.'

Alison awoke early through habit. She squinted at the bedside clock – 5 a.m. Stephen stirred behind her.

'Are you OK?' he whispered.

'Mmm, too early,' she grumbled.

He kissed her soft blonde hair, murmuring, 'Yes.'

She curled up into a tighter foetal ball, waking later to Stephen bringing coffee. He sat on the bed, as she inched herself up, oblivious of how seductive she was – hair tousled, breasts displayed for his delight.

'Oh Stephen, you are a doll. I'm dying for it.'

Stephen, blushing and breathless, agreed. 'So am I. God, you're beautiful, look what you've done to me. Alison, I can't begin to tell you how beautiful this is. I think I…'

She quickly interrupted. 'No, let's enjoy each other, no complications…'

'Please don't tell me to stop.'

Alison stroked his face tenderly. 'I don't want to but… oh damn… Mrs. Cade!'

'Ah, I've done her lawns… what about her?'

'I'm due there in ten minutes!'

Alison had the quickest shower, ushering Stephen out. She hurriedly dragged on black slacks, a black and red Jaegar jacket over a cream silk blouse, and black leather boots. Having rapidly cleaned her teeth, she grabbed keys, bag and folder, dashing to her Lexus car. As an interior designer, she had interesting houses to work on, Mrs. Phoebe Cade's no exception. Approaching the rambling Edwardian house in Ryelands, she hoped Mrs. C. had reconsidered ideas of having a 1970s décor in her sitting room.

The woman herself was waiting at the front door. Alison apologised for the delay.

'Oh, better late than never,' she was re-assured loudly. 'I've made herb tea.'

She led Alison through the Forest Green reception hall, disappearing to make stale herbal tea. Relaxation was impossible on saggy, brown dralon chairs, she'd need an osteopath en route home. Spying a mahogany hall chair near the fireplace, Alison perched on that. Somehow she must persuade Mrs. C. to change her mind or this beautiful Edwardian room would be ruined.

From marriage, they'd acquired furniture from the twenties upwards, her nephew re-decorating badly after Gordon's death. Anaglypta wallpaper, already a howler, had been painted a nauseating mauve. The doors had been thickly coated with cream gloss, almost mirrors. A 1950s black paper rack, topped with red and yellow cherries, added to the mismatch.

Phoebe's late husband's portrait loomed large above the mantelpiece, stern British bulldog expression dominating. Alison thought of them in the bedroom, correct and restrained, Gordon stiffly holding her, Phoebe like a Jessie Matthews heroine, responding with shining eyes to his wishes. After the act, she'd wear a wistful look, grateful he still wanted her, patted like an obedient dog. Phoebe, she imagined, longed to slip the leash, but would forever be at his command.

Mrs. Cade swept in noisily with a huge tray of heavy china. Crashing it onto the oak desk, spilling tea and milk, she gushed.

'Whoops-a-daisy! Mrs. Debbins wot does will murder me if I spoil her polishing. Tea first, I've brought cups, you didn't seem to like mugs, left half your drink last time.'

She continued to shout, as usual. 'Ah you noticed – the teaset, old Wedgwood,' she puffed, pouring shakily. 'The best for the best.' She smiled kindly, handing Alison a large, floral cup. 'Alison, wouldn't you prefer an easy chair?'

Alison assured her she was comfortable, saying she'd let her tea cool to discuss the décor. Her hostess lowered her large, tall frame into a squashy chair, sensible, expensive jersey dress riding up above her knees, as the chair swallowed her up. Thin, grey hair was dragged off her round face by brown combs.

'Remind me what we decided. I'm getting Oldtimers disease,' she shrieked, chortling.

Alison thought the disease was no joke, but produced a folder with notes.

'Oh, window cleaner's here. Must pay double this week. Won't be a mo, Alison.'

Alison, with bemusement, witnessed Mrs. C. slide a framed photograph of a labrador on the wall to one side, revealing a safe. Watching Mrs. C.'s activity, Alison was tickled pink, breaking the tension she'd felt at having to dissuade her employer from her plans. Bustling in, Mrs. C. returned the labrador to hide the evidence.

'Mrs. Cade, the seventies décor, erm… '

'Yes, saw it in an old *Vanity Fair*. I couldn't wear colours in vogue then – I was forty and middle-aged, lost my figure having Hugo and Frances, WI cakes and corporate receptions. Our generation kept to solid traditional stuff.

'I liked what young ones were wearing, lime, orange, mauve, shocking pink – what did they call it in the sixties, psychedelic? Frances had minis and maxis, patent platform boots and long coats. I wanted to have a go, but Gordon wouldn't have allowed it; conservative with a capital C! He didn't even approve of

Frances wearing it, and livid when Hugo came home from university for the hols in flared purple trousers and matching swallow-tail collared shirt.

'Once I made, from Family Circle magazine, Navarin of Lamb, in vogue in the seventies. That wasn't approved either, a British bulldog was Gordon, nothing continental about him. So you see, now I can choose. Going on that assertiveness course recently helped enormously.' she boldly proclaimed.

Alison knew she had an uphill struggle. 'The magazine you gave me, the four page interior's impressive, but... this is Edwardian with original features and... it would be a pity, wouldn't it to...'

Mrs. C. cut in. 'That's the point, I've had to put up with all this... stuff... far too long. Most of it's from Gordon's family, my aunt too. My nephew decorated when I wasn't thinking straight.'

She looked humbly at Alison. 'Bit of a state, as I was when Gordon died. On that assertiveness course we had to learn a phrase, "How you present yourself to be treated is how people will treat you." True. I'd put on too brave a face. Good old Phoebe, stoically getting on with things, stalwart of the parish council, solid wife and mother. I wasn't stoical... dead without him. Though he was leader of the orchestra and I was second fiddle in our marriage, it had worked. He made final decisions, I deferred to him, as in our parents' marriages. I was as intelligent, but played the little woman – didn't emasculate him. When he died, I felt like a swan, they mate for life.'

Alison squeezed Phoebe's hand re-assuringly. Despite loudness, Phoebe was open and warm, not a hint of snobbery or rudeness.

'People had seen me as strong, capable, noisy. I am, can't alter m'character, but no-one can see inside a marriage. That's why I've floundered a bit dealing with wills, insurances, even with help from "them wot know." Now I can make my own plans and no-one to stop me,' she announced, noticing Alison's serious face.

'Ooh your tea, you've scarcely touched it. Tell me what you think of that magazine colour scheme.'

Alison sympathized with Mrs. C. wanting to fulfil her wishes. Feeling selfish with what she had to show, she produced sketches of seventies rooms, coloured in toned down shades to put Mrs. Cade off, seeing the disappointed expression.

'Oh I can't have made myself clear! Fed up with drab, here look at *Vanity Fair* again.'

She selected the 1972 June edition from the fifties spindle-legged occasional table. Placing them on top of Alison's folder, she announced, 'What I wasn't allowed then, but can now, cheerful colours.'

Alison replied diplomatically. 'This is not criticism, but with these room settings… well, hessian walls would be fine if they weren't purple, the rug lime green, and pink circles on the suite. This magazine bedroom page – orange candlewick bedspread, patterned walls, mauve carpet – I couldn't get a good rest in there! This is a lovely place, you've raised two children here and… I don't want you to radically change, then regret it.'

Phoebe agreed resignedly. 'Mmm, I do see. Grand memories, proportions ideal for parties, functions, and family. Gordon adored the fireplace, English oak with acorns scattered in relief down the sides. The children did rubbings as they do in churches with brass. That overmantel mirror took some putting up, devil to clean, Mrs. Debbins says. I have to hold the step ladder while she wobbles, polishing.

D'you know there are scratchmarks from our dog's paws – Jupiter, Gordon's dog really. If he'd been away on business, Gordon, not the dog, Jupiter would be overexcited to see his master, thick tail clearing sherry glasses from coffee tables. There'd be feverish leaping, whining and doggy-dancing. Gordon used to sit in that window seat "having a think," when work problems attacked, the lime walk's view so tranquil.'

Giggling at the doggy tale, Alison suggested, 'Gordon's den?

You can go to town with your own style, reflecting the new you. Mrs. Cade…?'

Phoebe beamed, clasping Alison's arm, enthusing, 'You marvellous girl – that's it! Mine, and at the top of the house, what a view! I rarely went in, Gordon was covetous of his own space. They say every man should have a shed, Gordon's pleasure was his den,' she giggled conspiratorially, 'I bet he's frowning at me, wherever he is hey?'

Smiling back at her, Alison hugged Mrs. C., saying they should make plans. Mrs. Cade linked her arm enthusiastically, leading her to the wide staircase.

***

Alison thought Stephen may feel he was entering another man's territory. It had merely been weeks since her split with Phil. Sipping warm milk and honey, wearing fleecy pyjamas and propped up by pillows, Alison reflected on this whirlwind romance – was it though? Early days yet, she reasoned, relationships had a habit of clouding judgement. Most of hers had begun with sex, continued with more, and fizzled out when she'd realised there was little else. Her insecurity made her sell herself short.

She determined to know a man well first. That, she thought, would bring her happiness. Libido and low self-worth constantly tripped her. She was overtired now and couldn't blame this on work. On average, she'd managed five hours per night that week. The first evening without Stephen, she received an unexpected e-mail. Her mind raced, wondering if it was goodbye. She cautiously read it.

'We've been together a brief time but please trust me – lack of it goes deep with both of us. Stephen. xxxxxxxx'

Alison felt gratified he hadn't mentioned sex. Though positive energy surrounded Stephen, she should have given herself time to see who she might become, without another man.

She picked up *The Times*, scanning through for a design article. The dating page loomed, with hundreds of advertisements. A satisfied sigh escaped her, relieved she now may not have to go down that road again. It had been hard work before and after Henry, and before Phil. She hadn't expected it to be easy, but broadsheets hadn't yielded quality.

She chuckled, one chap said he wanted a woman who makes him laugh so much that milk flows out of his nose. Said he smokes, and doesn't get bladdered. There was a photo of him gurning, with a pint, wearing a baseball cap the wrong way round. She'd laughed again at Julia shrieking when she'd told her.

Consummate liars mainly, thinly veiled stories on their important jobs, top-of-the-range cars. She'd chosen a few, replied with brief details, but quality poor. She'd told Julia she'd been pruning neglected roses, woody and hardly alive, rather like men on dating sites. Julia thought it a good analogy, they didn't know what they were missing, and if presented with it, wouldn't know what to do with it.

One had written that although he liked her photograph and description, she didn't like sport, so he was rejecting her. Weird logic. Her father liked cricket and football, her mother had no interest. It mattered not, people either gelled or they didn't. Men weren't honest with her. Some were still married, had a current girlfriend or were seeking a one night stand. Unless men lived nearby, they could lie without detection.

She switched off the lamp, mind wandering to Stephen's last visit, the atmosphere intense, air full of perfume and excitement. He'd delighted in watching her undress, the sight of her arched back sensual. They'd moved into the king size bed, fresh white sheets cool to the body.

'Are you sick of my saying I love you, like a broken record?' Stephen had asked.

Drawing him towards her, she assured him it was wonderful to hear it, believe it. She'd told Stephen she had her period, which would have made some lovers disappear. Not this man, he did seem to genuinely love her, sex or no sex.

The following Sunday afternoon, they'd intended listening to the Radio 3 concert, but after a boozy lunch, had fallen asleep. Beethoven's Ninth, that glorious choral, played on. They'd slept through most of it, until the full tumult of the choir in the finale awoke them. 'Damn I wanted you to hear it all. Karajan's version's the best.' He yawned, 'Must have been tee many martoonis!'

Alison giggled at his spoonerism. 'Not that tiring orgasm then?'

Stephen grinned. 'Listen to the finale, I'll make tea, then you can tell me what you thought of the performance.'

He saw her coyly smiling. 'You already know.'

She watched his lean nakedness exit. Deeply contented, she went over their lovemaking. They'd gone to her bedroom to hear Karajan conduct Beethoven's great symphony. She'd turned the radio on half an hour prior to the broadcast; Stephen was going to explain it. Within five minutes, talk had stopped and passion started. The Ninth symphony had played mostly without them. Hearing the massed voices of the choir, Alison likened this crescendo to her own; powerful, special.

She called. 'Come on, don't miss the ending… oh there you are.' Stephen carried Earl Grey tea in, including dark chocolate.

'Don't you think I've had enough treats?'

Stephen poured tea. While it cooled, he rejoined Alison until the final notes. She took Stephen's silence to be the absolute brilliance of the symphony. He though, was pre-occupied by a puzzling message on the answerphone.

***

16

A proper date – Stephen and Alison had torn themselves from the bedroom to visit an auction. Antiques and household items, Bristol blue glass next to cranberry decanters and Georgian rummers. A spelter dog sat obediently under an art deco globe, chandeliers dripped raindrops onto silver below. She'd noticed, attending sales, boxes of memorabilia going for a pittance, imagining someone cherishing their keepsakes, no one to leave them to.

At Bentley's Salerooms in Higher Birches, Stephen met Alison at 9 a.m. He'd espied a Cremona violin, a damaged modern copy. High on the wall hung a large, Pre-Raphaelite framed print, which captivated Alison. The Wrangling Nobles, by Henry Payne, was of Richard the Third and the Earl of Somerset in a garden of white and pink roses. Richard looked vengeful, but the others depicted were captivatingly beautiful. She read the label, stating the original was in the House of Lords.

Even though they had to wait until lot 375, Alison won her lot for £20. She was thrilled, making the auctioneer smile. Once home, she took down a picture Phil had sketched of her, hung the print, stepping back to examine it.

'Those roses, such vibrant colours. And the men... perfection.'

Stephen replied, with a wry smile, 'Mm, that tells me you like tall, dominant men in the bedroom.'

Alison coquettishly patted the duvet. Stephen joined her, pulling her down strongly. 'If you want to admire the noble gentlemen when I'm not here, you can, but I shall want a full account of how they made you feel, and what you did, bad girl. When I'm here though, one look at them and I'll have to take you in hand. I can be dominant too, although you haven't seen that... yet.'

Alison burst into giggles. Stephen followed suit, flushing slightly at his boldness. 'Dominant, me? Not in my nature. Is that what you'd like?'

Alison looked at him lovingly. 'I don't want you to prove anything. I like our relationship how it is. We've gone overboard on the physical side, but that's how it often is at the beginning. It's more than that for me.'

Stephen felt unconvinced, but said he was pleased to hear it. At four-thirty, he had to reluctantly leave. 'I'm behind with Julia's garden, heavy rain yesterday. Come for supper on Saturday, I'll show you something special, you can use your antiques knowledge.'

Alison was intrigued. 'Meanie, give me a clue,' she cajoled.

'No, Saturday you can examine it and say what you think,' he insisted, walking through the hall.

Alison smiled impishly, hugging him goodbye. 'I've done that – it's perfect.'

He winked at the compliment, promising to ring that evening.

***

In her warm kitchen, Alison drifted to Stephen, hugging herself, feeling lucky. The distress Phil had brought was fading, his infidelity had freed her to be with Stephen, hurt replaced by happiness. Gone was angst, negative demeanour, humour returning. With Henry and Phil, it had been thin on the ground, both too uptight to let themselves go with silly quips or full-blown laughter. Once she was relating schoolteachers to Stephen, telling of Mr. Wainwright, who had a speech impediment and pronounced W's as V's.

One day the teacher had asked – 'Vigglesvorth, vot are you reading?'

'Vind in the Villows, sir,' came the reply.

Stephen had doubled up laughing. If she'd told Henry or Phil, they'd have given her a pitiful look. With Stephen she could relax and be herself. Even so, something was nagging at her. Despite the euphoria of sex, ideally they should have begun as friends. With stress caused by Phil, a brief sexual encounter was not what she required. Depressed when she'd met Stephen, she'd worried the status quo wouldn't remain; expecting the bubble to burst. It had not. Within a short time she was almost sure they were in love, but was Stephen merely dancing to her tune?

Occasionally, she'd traded sex for company, a grave error. She'd been raised a Catholic, but a lapsed one, realising it was a deal made with God by her parents on her behalf. With constraints and oppositions to common sense, she'd eradicated it from her life when she was eighteen. Free to be herself without that pressure, another constriction appeared – being attracted to men who, seeing her neediness, wanted to control. Imagining Phil would be different, she'd enjoyed sex, but falsehood from him had ensued. He was the biggest controller of all, a taker as she was a giver. Her desperation prevented her ending things, with him taking advantage, lying and disrespecting her over fifteen months of their so called 'relationship.' Although Alison saw honesty in Stephen's eyes, she felt insecure.

Bo's furious washing, after her tasty dish of tuna, gave way to stretching up the door, scratching to be let out. Alison moved quickly, the white door was becoming worn. 'Bo, why can't you miaow?' she scolded, letting the oblivious feline out into the spring evening. The cat scampered off, investigating smells en route to her own spot under the damson tree. Noticing the blackbird on a top branch, she slunk down, and with a mad dash, shot up the trunk in a vain bid for pudding. The glossy bird, unperturbed, hopped onto a higher perch, leaving Bo to shin awkwardly down. At her vantage point by the open door, Alison did her imitation blackbird refrain, the familiar bird cocking his head quizzically, trilling triumphantly at his escape from Bo, who scratched a hole in the ground below.

Alison left wildlife behind, closing the door, visualising a bath. Stripping off jeans and pink tee-shirt, she studied her body in the cheval mirror. During Phil's deceptions she'd lost weight, more when he'd gone, but now happy with her reflection. Her five-foot-six frame looked healthier for re-gaining some pounds. She was pleased with her breasts, full and womanly, glad her legs had regained shapeliness. She stroked firm stomach muscles, standing with legs slightly apart to view what Stephen got so excited about. Remembering the bath she was filling, although a wave of wanting to go further arose, she had to delay the pleasure. Pausing to light a scented candle, with *Dark Side of the Moon* swirling in from the bedroom, she climbed into the welcoming water, resting on the bath pillow. Recalling a former young lover and his gratitude when they'd made out, stronger stirrings arose. A passionate week performing five nights in a play, he the ingenue, she the older woman – one performance had led to another.

Spending time reliving the sensually exciting episode, having unplugged the bedroom phone, she heard it ringing downstairs. 'The answering machine's on. Bet it's Stephen.'

Slithering off the bed, she donned her robe, going downstairs. Pressing the replay button, she heard Stephen's disappointed tones, 'Remember me? Perhaps you're in the bath, mmm what a picture. Finished here... call me at Julia's, bye.'

Before she could call back, another message assailed her ears. A timid voice not heard for years.

'Alison... er... I need your help. No right after my dreadful behaviour, but I'd be grateful. Same mobile number. Thanks.'

The caller left no name, none necessary. No idea when he'd rung, she hadn't retrieved messages for days. Unmistakably Henry, what on earth could he want? The kettle clicked off as she thought of the last time she'd seen him six years ago.

3

It had been near the end of their brief relationship, before the Jerusalem project. Whatever had she seen in this gawky little man of God? Henry, friend and sometime lover. He'd been kind, supportive, Alison's drug for a while. Under the duvet on the sofa, hoping she'd sleep off the painful period attacking, Henry had called unannounced, letting himself in. Saying he was 'hungry for her,' he'd looked irritated seeing her clutching a hot water bottle. Sulking, he'd left rapidly, as if she'd had a contagious disease.

The cat's scratching at the kitchen door brought Alison back to the present. Feeling hungry, she smiled, remembering Clare's blankness when she'd explained food dreams signified sex.

'Oh,' she'd asked naively, 'Why don't I dream of food?'

'Cos you get plenty and not allowed to have impure thoughts as a left footer. Remember I'm a lapsed Catholic.' Clare had laughed, saying she lived and breathed sex, never feeling guilt.

Alison walked on the white tiles to let Bo in from her evening adventures, rewarded with miaows and rubbing of fur against leg. She saw the time, ten minutes to ten. Annoyed she'd been thinking of Henry, unease crept in.

'Damn.' she thought, bolting the door. 'I wanted to make

inroads into Mrs. Cade's project. That blessed message. Blessed – a Freudian slip if ever there was one. Whatever can he want? With Mrs. Cade's project on the study floor, she closed the door tightly for fear Bo might choose to sleep there. Cleaning her teeth, she saw she'd picked up the wrong toothbrush. 'Stephen! Haven't returned his call.' Sliding into bed and opening her London book, she rang him from the bedroom phone.

'Alison, I was concerned when you didn't answer earlier.'

Hearing Stephen's voice, Alison lightened her tone. 'Sorry, work. How was gardening?'

'Fine, apart from wrecking a spade. Why can't David do it himself?'

'Julia does everything – she deserves this trip to France with Poppy. He's in Yorkshire on business isn't he?' she replied as chattily as she could.

'Mmm. Shall I come…?'

'No, I must sleep, see you on Saturday.'

Stephen found it disconcerting to wait.

Alison abandoned reading. She thought of approval and acceptance with men, sex becoming her passport to it, but ending in disappointment, not wanted for herself. Although she loved Stephen, she didn't want this affair to go the way of the others. Insecurity had begun to creep in without him. Stephen had said she was precious, but she doubted he had these anxieties. She didn't want to spoil the magic, maybe too early to discuss with him. Thinking of the telephone message, she vowed to find out what the defrocked vicar wanted.

Having a brief Freudian dream of men resembling Henry and Phil turning into rats, Alison resolved to stay awake. She lay thinking how she'd met Henry. An advertisement in the newspaper under Lonely Hearts – 'Professional Male Writer 43, attractive, caring, discreet, seeks romance. I won't let you down.' She hadn't read anything into the word discreet. He'd seemed genuine on the phone and pleasant when they'd met for coffee.

Balding, five feet eight inches, smartly dressed, moustache, gentle demeanour.

He'd said he wrote for a regional newspaper, revealing on their second date he wrote a religious column in a local rag. Producing a book he'd written with a photo of himself wearing a dog collar on the cover, he'd told of his job as a vicar, saying it tended to put women off. He'd mentioned four children, but evasive concerning his ex-wife.

They became friends, then occasional lovers, discussing theology and art. He'd explained the Christian view, commenting on her doubts. Alison was secure in his care, although they spent little time together. He'd stayed overnight once, appearing tense. Waking up to find him gone at 6 a.m. Alison had found a note.

'Last night was heavenly. I thank you humbly for patience with this mere amateur in the bedroom. You'll think I've run off, in a way I have, for a while. This little man is not used to staying out, and became panic stricken. Hope I can concentrate on driving after all that ecstasy! Your grateful disciple Henry. xx'

She'd been mystified at his disappearance and the last phrase was a strange one for a vicar to use. 'My disciple? Henry? I thought I was his!'

Next morning, between work and laundry, she'd traced events since the morning of the note. Something hadn't rung true, an uneasiness, no call coming that day or next. At three-thirty on the third day, she'd rung the rectory.

'May I speak to the vicar please?'

A woman had answered. 'He's getting our children from school. Shall he ring you when he comes in?'

Thrown by the unexpected voice, Alison had stammered her name, not expecting his ex-wife at the rectory when she and the children lived two miles away.

After a month of no calls, she'd guessed he was married and couldn't face her. Analysing their brief relationship, she couldn't imagine what she'd seen in him. Average looks, childish humour, no prowess in bed. They should have become friends not lovers; her heart hadn't been in it, except the first time, turned on by the thrill of a new man. She'd never had to fake orgasm, but with Henry, no choice. He didn't guess; too besotted.

He'd given Alison tickets weeks before to hear him sing Mozart's Requiem with his choir, so she decided to go. When he'd spotted Alison in the cathedral during the interval, he'd pretended not to have seen her. His wife was bossily warning him to stop drinking, and exactly as he'd described, bad haircut, frumpy clothes. Deceptively, the one detail he'd omitted, was still being married. He rang next day.

'Thanks for coming last night,' he'd stressed fervently, confessing how ashamed he'd been, keeping his wife from her, his position in the church making it impossible to divorce. The longer he'd kept up the pretence, the more complicated it had become. 'I need your help though with a project. I can pay you with my advance.'

As a published writer, Henry was working on his fourth book, Christian based, requiring research to be done in Israel. For the five day visit, he'd promised there'd be no sexual pressure. Almost immediately, she'd regretted agreeing.

They'd stayed in the cheapest hotels in Jewish and Arabic areas of Jerusalem and Capernaum. She'd enjoyed the Dead Sea, the weather, and seeing his Jewish friends for a Shabat dinner. They'd visited a Palestinian refugee camp of twelve hundred, appalled at the conditions and how badly they were treated by Israelis, even gunfire was heard. What she hadn't enjoyed was Henry's company. Despite reassurance of a platonic relationship, sarcasm regarding lack of intimacy was rife, mealtimes especially difficult, inane conversation, squirm-making asides. Little social discourse, preferring to remain silent, nodding like a dashboard dog, causing Alison boredom and tension. One evening, to break the silence, she'd told a dry joke.

'On her fourteenth birthday, Elizabeth, the Queen Mother, had been taken by her parents to the London Coliseum theatre. En route home, they told her gravely that World War 1 had been declared that day. Elizabeth replied she would have been content with a pony.' Henry had blankly stared at his hamburger and chips.

Once back, she'd sorted mail and grimaced at bills. Julia had rung asking how things went. Alison briefly mentioned the trip. 'Bought you Dead Sea products, Henry put them into his case, he'll bring them round.'

Not hearing for five days, Alison rang Henry. A stranger's voice answered, informing her he was from another vicarage and Henry's calls were being transferred to him. When questioned, she'd lied, saying she was his cousin. The vicar informed her Henry was on suspension pending an enquiry.

Her face burned, 'Oh my God!' she'd blurted out, aware this wasn't the thing to say to a cleric.

Kindly saying he doubted she'd be a reader of the tabloid, she'd be advised to look at it.

'What is printed is a serious matter for Henry. He's non-contactable at the moment.'

Shocked and scared, she'd thanked the minister. It must concern our affair, she'd thought anxiously, needing to get the newspaper with the alarming reportage. Her cleaner read it cover to cover; Alison, pretending she needed a gardening article, rang. Potato peelings were in it; Alison insisted she didn't mind. When home, she'd shakily spread it on the table, tearing through it. On page fourteen, acute shock, but relief she wasn't featured, enormous; she'd thanked God for large mercies.

'Cheating Vicar Bonks Married Mistress,' the headline declared. Reeling, Alison had scanned the photograph, showing Henry and the woman embracing in his 'Sinwagon.' Others depicted the mistress trying to dodge the camera, and Henry looking shocked in his hall.

She'd read the script, relating his affair with the thirty-six-year-old mother, the reportage full of cheap jibes and misquotes. If they weren't sure, tabloids made it up. Henry wouldn't say, 'I know I'm going to heaven.' It was reported he'd bragged he was highly sexed, filming their sessions. The article named everyone, including Henry's wife, Mary.

'Oh God, Mary and the children!' Alison had frozen at the unholy mess, mouth parched at his stupidity, angry at his lies. It was not as if he'd begun it when Alison and he had ceased a physical relationship, but months before. Her anger had increased. How could he have cheated on her after the ecstasy he'd said she'd given him and love he'd declared? She was angry at herself for making do, for that is what it had been. Discovering he was married, she'd wanted to end things, but had rashly agreed to the Jerusalem trip, needing the money.

Alison had taken the shocking report upstairs. From her studio window she'd witnessed mist hanging over spindly birches at the end of her garden. The church clock, seen from the lofty studio, chimed nine on Sundays, reminding the faithful that they were expected. Blind faith. That's what faith was, had to be blind or it wasn't. She'd shivered; once she'd been obedient, an uphill struggle. Shall I, shan't I? Will I, won't I? Attempting to make sense of life, needing a catalyst. Henry had been it, God's messenger. She'd seen him as omnipotent, a fatal error.

She'd winced, reliving the treatment at the Church Discussion Group, attending twice. She shouldn't have gone more than once but wanted to make friends in the area. Some were outwardly pleasant and had prayed with her when she was low, but weren't genuine. The vicar said they were a jolly bunch. She hadn't expected Ken Dodd, but there was neither jollity nor compassion there.

Her views were met with blank faces. Narrow-minded,

mean-spirited, superior because they could quote the Bible. When Alison admitted depression, they'd recommended casting off the sin of sex. Mortified by their attitude, she'd felt foolish mentioning her mood. She did not answer the veiled invasive query. The group leader asked for God's forgiveness to Alison for offending him. With flaming cheeks at this audacity, she'd kept quiet, giving an Oscar winning performance when the meeting dispersed, knowing she'd never return.

At Julia's, tea and sympathy so lacking at the insincere group, were in abundance. Alison told her she'd leave the group and the church. Julia had responded angrily, 'You're so worthy and they're not. If they were Christian they would have had greater charity towards you. Oddballs – causing extra stress.'

Trying to put all of that behind, she'd tensely thought, 'Oh God, how could I have let it happen? God yes, I should have trusted him, not Henry, the false Messiah in clerical clothes. She'd glanced at her strained reflection in the Victorian oak-framed mirror. Towards the church across the fields. the faithful few trudged to Monday communion up the cobbled path. Five huddled figures – bent ladies in the winter of their lives.

How had the press discovered his secret? Would he keep his job? Would he be de-frocked? How would his wife react? She'd shivered, couldn't imagine a successful outcome. Drinking tea, she'd recalled his silly phrase, 'Come on Henry, you know you can do it!' Not this time he couldn't.

Enormously relieved the article didn't feature her, she'd nevertheless felt betrayed. How could he have been such a cheat on his wife, but her too? Not concentrating, she'd drunk tea before it had cooled, burning her mouth. She'd frowned, mopped up the spillage, and stalked the kitchen, shoulders hunched from the startling shocks.

Alison had worked hard for weeks to put the past behind her. Henry had telephoned, confessing shame for lies he'd told. She'd asked him why he'd needed another woman, and other puzzling

27

questions. He'd answered them as honestly, he said, as he could. 'Honestly?' Alison thought, 'Ha!'

'I was mixed up, depressed,' he'd pleaded. 'Life isn't cut and dried, I'd reasoned, with no frayed edges. Ha, mine's threadbare.'

Alison had enquired what would happen. Emotionally, he'd said he was forced to resign his office, wife and children had moved, the mistress's husband had forgiven her. Alison couldn't resist asking Henry how the tabloids knew.

He'd reminded her two men had attended his church, joining him in the pub one evening, giving him a watch, generous with drinks. Merry from large Scotches, he hadn't noticed them quizzing him. One of them divulged he was having an extra-marital fling. Foolishly, Henry had confessed his. The 'new friends' proved to be the Press with a capital P, following his movements.

Appearing one evening at his front door, Henry had asked them in. Over the threshold, their smiles faded. The woman reporter revealed who they were, details of the affair, no use denying it. A photographer snapped him reeling with shock.

Henry's voice had trembled as he'd finished the story; Alison pitying him.

'Alison, can you forgive me? I've treated you appallingly. My world's in suspense, I live temporarily with a parishioner.' He'd laughed weakly, 'A man, in case you're wondering, don't worry.'

Alison had icily emphasised she wasn't wondering or worrying, nor could she forgive or forget his deceit. He gave her the platitude on God forgiving the sinner but not condoning the sin. Irritated, she'd sharply replied, 'Don't patronize me, Henry. You're lucky I'm listening after your terrible behaviour. Who are you to tell me what God wants or does? You're not fit to be a man of the cloth. It could have been me in that article, you put me in jeopardy by your own vanity and stupidity. I've had enough of this. Good luck, you're going to need it! Keep it in your trousers in future!' she'd spat out, slamming the phone down.

Alison's hands had shaken as she'd poured brandy. Settling

into the fireside chair, she'd reasoned even though she hadn't loved Henry, his behaviour was disgraceful. Swallowing the amber liquid, she'd centred on his deceit, realizing he could have come from mistress to her in the same day! An involuntary shiver had shot through her.

Two days later, she'd received a letter asking her not to contact him as he had too much to cope with. Incandescent with disbelief, she'd penned a reply, relieving herself of anger at his mendacity.

'Henry, How dare you write, after the support I gave you. Despite protestations of love, you sought another, cheating on your wife and me. When you asked me to your house, before I knew you were married, you were willing to risk my being caught there. We were only having a cup of tea, but you were having an affair then, spied on by those reporters. It could have been me in the Sunday gutter press.

'A veil was drawn over everything. Saying your ex lived elsewhere, you couldn't ring because of work. Lies. In Jerusalem I realized you were difficult to live with. Our relationship was finished, but you asked me to help with research there. What a joke! All you did was sulk because I refused sex, which I'd stressed wasn't on the cards. I soon realised you didn't need my help at all.

'When your superior told me you were suspended, I was horrified. You put him in a tricky position and tried to get me to lie to someone else, finally admitting you'd confessed to the bishop. Your own preservation, that's all you care about. You've lied to your wife, parish, me, and mistress. When I spoke to the Bishop, he knew nothing of me, yet you said you'd confessed all. You've had help from the Church, I've had none. The bishop assured me I'm equally important, which I know; he was someone to talk to about you.

'You're a user, an opportunist and a liar. Instead of a reliable honest man, you're a shallow, weak one. Regarding your comments that anything we had is over, it certainly is! Do you suppose I want a man who behaves so disgustingly? What a deceiver you've been to your wife, me, everyone. Those journalists whom you trusted, have dished out a taste of your own medicine. Now you, the deceiver, have been deceived. Painful isn't it?'

Alison returned to the present, sighing. What a long time ago it was, she'd plunged into a flurry of work and dated no one, married men given a wide berth. Until Phil, there was no one special. Memories of how they met resurfaced.

The meeting was in full swing as she'd entered the crowded village hall. Seeking a spare seat, aware male eyes were gravitating towards her, she'd sat confidently against the leaded window, crossing tanned legs slowly and deliberately, knowing what she wasn't wearing underneath the thin purple strappy dress. Placing her handbag on the window ledge, she'd observed who was there.

Scanning the room, she'd noticed middle-aged grey men furtively avoiding her gaze. As soon as they believed she'd transferred her attention elsewhere, theirs diverted to her. She'd listened to the introduction by the councillor, droning on ad nauseum. Aware of someone staring, she'd flushed, returning his gaze.

The councillor had finally introduced the tall, broad, tanned man. 'Inspector George will enlighten us further. He has our interests at heart.'

'I'll bet.' Alison had mused, surprised the handsome stranger was the inspector. She'd scanned the full length of his strong body as he'd addressed his audience. 'Mm,' she'd thought wickedly, 'he can address me any time.'

She'd felt vulnerable as he began his report in a deep, warm voice. His penetrative gaze had settled on her, smouldering eyes piercing her body, capable hands firmly on the table.

'He has the demeanour of a tomcat, but the marks of a Labrador. Wonder which he is in bed? Slow and calculating or vigorous and unrestrained.'

Emphasizing a point, he'd glanced in her direction. She'd flushed, feeling the purple sundress was missing already.

Involuntarily stroking her arm, she'd thought, 'I've been celibate through choice, I can sample the goods mentally.' You can look but you better not touch, came to mind.

Her reactions disturbed her, hadn't occurred for ages, opportunities, but she'd taken none. Male friends, she'd decided, were safest; no pressure. Not to say she hadn't had sexual urges for some, those allowed to stimulate were out of reach, a fantasy. At the ballet with Julia, the principal male dancer fascinated her. Powerful, yet an inner sensitivity. Watching television and curling up with her tortoiseshell cat on a winter's evening, she'd fall in lust with an actor in a serial, looking forward to the next episode. Safer than reality.

'Men never want to go home,' she'd told Julia, her close friend.

'Hmm, mine's a fixture,' Julia had grumbled. 'Under my feet and skin.'

Alison had shivered, relieved no man would cause stress again. She could ask them to leave when she wanted, watch television, play music, sleep in peaceful solitude. An interesting interior design career, reliable friends, no disturbances. Looking in Inspector Philip George's direction, she'd thought, 'Until now!'

With Phil, she'd been too stressed to bother with filling in her diary, but now, waking from dreams yet again of both him and Henry, she'd recommenced. She caught up, smiling and blushing at what she'd written since meeting Stephen.

'Met Stephen at Julia's party. Wow! Spent night with stranger. Bad behaviour. He's thirty, we gel, but I'm vulnerable. Too much sex, too little rest. He's sensitive, sends me mad with desire.'

She began to update. 'Ache for Stephen on evenings alone. Reflection time. Phil – no pain. Phone message from Henry, unforeseen and disturbing. Julia's off to Lake District to escape horrible David's clutches. What a mistake to have married him.'

4

Driving to Cumbria on a squally March day, Julia was glad to arrive at the Victorian small hotel. Booking in, she read the plaque on the mulberry-coloured wall. Beatrix Potter had been a frequent visitor to the original owner of the property. Julia was shown to a floral room.

The view was breathtaking, emerald fields sweeping down to Esthwaite Water. Though rain was heavy and sky leaden, the Langdale Pikes on the horizon stood tall, feeling like old friends. The Lake District from the age of sixteen had been her spiritual home. The first time she'd visited, albeit in basic conditions at school camp, she'd loved it. School camp – ghastly food, latrines, damp clothes, uncomfortable camp beds in draughty tents and constant rain hadn't diminished her love of this glorious area.

Her room was a contrast to the stairway adorned with cracked oils. She inspected the pink floral bedding, curtains and dressing table surround matching, walls cream. Pillows, which she always sniffed, were thankfully sweet smelling. Sometimes she'd covered whiffy hotel ones with a towel, putting up, saying nothing. Perhaps that was why her marriage was in trouble – putting up and not sorting out!

If the weather was less inclement, Grasmere would have been

on the agenda, quieter this time of year, fewer coaches spewing out loud, polyester-clad Americans with random comments, 'Lois, where in the world are we? Is this Beatrix Potter's place, don't see no rabbits? Maybe Wordsworth's den, Shakespeare's buddy.'

Julia took a nap and shower before dinner. Her phone rang at seven twenty.

'Where the hell are you?' David, her husband, the cause of her escape, belligerent as ever.

'I'm in Cumbria – why?' she replied flatly.

'Why?' he angrily retorted. 'Cos I'm your husband. What the fuck d'you think you're doing?'

Julia replied as calmly as she could. 'The last row was the catalyst.'

A raging reply erupted. 'Suppose you're with Alison, joined at the hip, yer couple o' lesbians. Enjoy yourselves while I'm working my socks off.'

Julia was shocked at his outburst. She should have said she came to escape lies, the enigma of their relationship, but didn't want confrontation. The first year had begun well, with shared interests. A few months on, his polite character had evaporated, long working hours and business trips became a blessing, rather than a resentment.

Since then, Julia had struggled to say anything good about David. An inverted snob, if he couldn't have something, he ridiculed it. Julia gardened, cleaned their cars, saw beauty clients, did housework, cooking, shopping. David rarely showered, threw on mismatched clothing. The snoring through booze and excess weight was unbearable, so she'd begun sleeping in her treatment room downstairs. His rages became incendiary, but weren't the only distress. The last few times they'd had sex, it had been rough. One night, he'd announced vaginal sex was boring, crudely stating he wanted it 'up the back'. Before her escape, he'd brutally held her wrists, saying he deserved it taking on her 'brat'.

One afternoon, his overweight six-foot-build drunkenly towering above her, jutting his head forward, he'd invited her to hit him. This she'd done, unfortunately in front of Poppy, her daughter, who'd run downstairs, hearing them rowing. He'd smirked, telling Julia she was neurotic.

Once, David had rung from the office. Poppy had announced, 'She says she's not here.' Julia, annoyed, asked her not to make things up, causing trouble. Poppy had replied angrily. 'Huh, ME causing trouble! I like that! Look at yourselves.' She'd pushed past Julia, knocking into a table, making a vase of anemones wobble, spitting out, 'I hate my life!' slamming the door behind her.

Julia took her jacket in case her sleeveless green dress proved chilly, going down to dinner, admiring the staircase's window depicting a sheepdog and Herdwick sheep.

The dining room was occupied by an American couple, who greeted Julia with a Texan drawl. Sitting at the window table, she admired crystal candle holders containing lemon scented, lit candles. The waitress took her order of local lamb. Julia refused a starter, preferring dessert, to her hips' detriment.

As the American couple were wrapped up in themselves, Julia read brochures. Noticing in the window's reflection she was being observed intently, she brought the Spanish young man into focus. As liquid brown eyes shyly met hers, warm treacle zipped through her, face flushing. With a sultry look, he licked his lips brazenly, walking deliberately over, silently filling her water glass. Boldly sliding thumb and fingers provocatively along the crystal stem, he was willing her to watch him, eyelids cast down, one eyebrow raised as he put the glass into her unsteady hand. A frozen moment, hunger waiting to be fed. He returned from whence he came, re-appearing at intervals with the Americans' mains and puddings. Julia felt ridiculously vulnerable. 'Because a flirty waiter young enough to be my son flashes sultry looks at me. I'm here by myself to return to myself. Stop weaving fantasies – he's what he seems – a gauche foreign boy missing his mummy.'

34

This must be Juan, the waiter, the receptionist had mentioned. He'd been away from Seville for three months, homesick and probably saving wages, but Julia guessed money wasn't the only thing he was storing up. He disappeared while she was eating divine lamb and vegetables. The sweet trolley heaved with temptations, but Julia craved privacy.

She caught his reflection in the uncurtained window. He was behind her at the sideboard, nonchalantly folding napkins, eyes still upon her. The sexual frisson had rapidly waned, so sliding out of her chair, she spirited herself in soft movements into the thickly carpeted hall, picking up three *Country Life* magazines. Jellied legs nervously carried her up two flights to her room. The magazines would make good reading for a sound night, after broken ones. A safe distraction, unlike downstairs. As she undressed and cleaned her teeth, she felt ridiculous.

'Desperate of me,' she frowned. 'A thin, sloppy young waiter who'd be like a bull in a china shop.'

She shuddered, brushing gums rigorously, blood trailing down white porcelain as she rinsed. Checking the door, she sank into bed, wrapping her nightdress around her ankles. For what, extra security? She skimmed the magazine depicting executive houses. Safe, solid, and very expensive, always a price to pay. She realised the first two adjectives used to apply to David. Lashing rain suddenly changed direction, beating menacingly like rice on the window pane.

'I'll switch off the lamp or Don Juan will think I'm expecting him.'

He'd fancied his chances. She hadn't needed encouragement, her marriage a sham and worsening. Nights were lonely in her treatment room at home. Frustration became acute for the loving warmth of a man. Stupidly, when the waiter had winked at her provocatively with the obvious message, she'd nearly fallen into his trap. She caught her breath, realising he could have seen her room number in the register.

Pushing the magazines onto the floor, she turned, facing the door. The room was very dark, but she could see under the door, the landing bright from tear-drop chandeliers. She flinched as a deluge of seething rain punished the glass panes. Normally she'd have welcomed winter noises and impenetrability of the solid house. Not tonight, every lashing howl made her jumpy, preventing her hearing Spanish footsteps approaching. She hadn't imagined the hungry look. Nor could she ignore that shudder as his brown hand had purposely brushed her naked arm, feeling his heat. An anonymous encounter, no strings, an antidote to her real problem a hundred miles off, had thrilled.

With only five hours rest, Julia awoke at seven-fifteen, relieved that knocking twice in the night, Don Juan had given up. He'd knocked at ten-thirty when she was nearly asleep, making her stiff with fear. Four alarming thuds. Angry and upset, it had taken her ages to resume sleep. A second time with him imploring her to open the door, had made her heart hammer. She'd heard him turning the doorknob. Hotly, she'd anxiously gripped the duvet. Several minutes of her in dread and him in desperation, he'd uttered a Spanish curse and slunk off.

Julia packed, deciding to skip breakfast. Not normally prone to cowardice, she wanted to avoid confrontation, plenty of that with David. The bill was paid and an excuse made, saying she had an appointment in Grasmere, the opposite direction to where she was going. With quivering legs, she anxiously tottered to her car, fumbling with car keys to make her escape.

As she drove on pea gravel, she spied him in the rear view mirror, waving madly in her direction, causing her to speed down the chicane, brushing overhanging laurels. Feeling foolish doing this at her age, on the main road she slowed down, pulling into a layby.

'I was desperate. What trouble it almost caused, needing to be held and loved – held, but loved – no. An inexperienced kid.' she mused. The break hadn't been relaxing, but had revealed her vulnerability. In future she'd be choosy. 'Ha, chance would be a fine thing!' She hadn't been wanting a fling, but her situation was becoming unbearable.

Pulling into a motorway café, Julia bought Kendal Mint Cake for Poppy. Spotting a book she'd wanted, she bought that too. *Cosmic Ordering* was written by a woman, who promised that by positively telling the universe what you required, it would be delivered. A simple concept, she'd look at the stars in the night sky, requesting a good man. It warned to be definite, expecting the answer. Little did she know the universe would have to put her needs on hold for a while.

Relieved to be indoors from the M6 chaos, Julia needed a nap to catch up from the previous night's disturbances. Turning off her mobile phone and resolving to visit her mother in the nursing home later, she settled on the sofa, rapidly falling asleep, so deeply she didn't hear the hall phone ringing at five minute intervals.

A burst of sunlight brought her to consciousness. She uncurled, gazing through French windows overlooking the terrace. No Spaniards in sight! Peace in the quiet house, where she'd lived with Guy before their divorce. David had eventually moved into her nineteen thirties Mock Tudor home. Pure Metroland, Alison had called it, like those in forties movies.

Alison had declared it a designer's dream, unaltered and shabby. Guy and Julia had given Alison carte blanche to restore it. Julia had fought a losing battle to keep it tidy, with David and Poppy, no chance of being more than reasonably organised. When Alison came over, Julia was sometimes ashamed at the clutter. Alison's was the opposite – sparkling, and worthy of *House Beautiful* magazine. It had to be when clients visited for interior design advice. Re-assuring Julia she was comfortable at hers, Julia joked hers would be in the 'before' pictures and Alison's the 'afters.'

She smiled at these remembrances, disturbed by the phone

resounding in the woodblock entrance hall. She supposed it would be David or Poppy. It was neither.

A familiar but grave voice spoke. 'Mrs. De Mar, I've been ringing you for over an hour. It's Anne Deeks from Firbanks Nursing Home. I'm afraid your mother has taken a turn for the worse, she won't last the day. Can you come, the doctor's here at the moment and…?'

'Coming now…' Julia breathlessly reeled, rapidly replacing the receiver.

Grabbing car keys, bag and suede jacket, anxiety high, she drove to the nursing home. Although an agnostic, she prayed to whoever might be listening. Prayers for her mother she frantically blurted out, one to save her, one to ease her suffering, one to let her go peacefully, realising the last was best. Her parent had become too ill when she'd left hospital, and had quite cheerfully gone into Firbanks. Dementia had been prevalent for months and she'd weakened, wishing God would claim her, as she missed William, her late husband. Julia had told her that was the spaniel they'd had, her husband was Charles. Her mother had replied blankly: 'Oh was it?' Her weight had dropped as appetite waned, whippet thin, a shadow of the woman she'd once been.

Julia parked her black VW at Firbanks, anxiously pressing the doorbell. When informed her mother was near death, Julia broke down in a succession of sobs. Anne Deeks led her into the room, leaving to make tea. Julia held her mother's frail hand for five minutes, blinking back tears in case her grief was sensed.

'Goodnight, Mum, God Bless,' she emotionally whispered, and thought she felt a slight squeeze to her hand. The next sound was one not heard before, as her mother slipped away.

Julia had been overwhelmed with convulsive grief, much worse than when her father had died three years earlier. Now she was parentless, in her early forties. At the beginning of their relationship, David had volunteered to push the wheelchair, as if it were his own mother. At the funeral he was solicitous to Julia and Poppy, taking charge as she'd rarely seen him. Afterwards, he played mine host expertly, eliciting comments. 'Julia, what would you do without him?' from a cousin. 'David, so capable, good with young Poppy too.' from Aunt Maud. 'You've got a good one there Julia.' from best man Alec.

She'd smiled, concealing how marital arguments had become like long sets of tennis, back and forth. That evening she'd cleared up while David furtively made phone calls, as if having an affair. In the bath, she reflected on the day, pleased to have chosen her mother's favourite record, 'The Fool On The Hill' by Petula Clark played at the funeral service.

Three weeks on at her parents old house, sorting junk from decent, Julia went upstairs to wash. A door was open, a full moon illuminating the room. Dazzled, she witnessed through the uncurtained window, midnight sky sprinkled with millions of winking diamonds. As a child in winter, she'd gazed at sparkling sequins, pondering the baffling magnitude of the cosmos.

'The cosmos! The book, *Cosmic Ordering*. I didn't use it.' she realised.

She knew why. Dealing with death, funeral, sorting oceans of stuff for charities, to bin, to auction. Her mother had let everything go, a massive amount of belongings in the dilapidated property under thick dust. A broken fridge and mower cluttered the musty garden room. Always the reply – 'leave things alone.'

That book said to be precise and expect the answer.

Spending time practising the request, she confidently announced her need. Looking the moon in the face she spoke clearly, 'I need a caring man to share my life.'

She nearly added 'amen' but this process was different to prayer. Thanking the universe, she turned from the magical scene, retracing her steps down the rickety staircase. Enough for tonight. It's twenty to ten.

She must believe her mystery man would appear, or negate the request. Alison had cynically frowned, but seen how determined she was. For once Julia enjoyed a dreamless sleep.

The following week she cleared rubbish and kept treasures, likening it to her life. Bric-a-brac, books and records went to charity shops, valuables put aside for assessment by a recommended antique expert. Alison had met him at a Pre-Raphaelite lecture in Manchester.

One afternoon, Julia saw a dead badger on the grass verge. 'Why do I have the right to order from the universe? This poor brock has nothing,' she thought gloomily, but knew negativity mustn't creep in. Loneliness had escalated when her mother had died. Without parents, she felt a fully fledged adult, but an orphan, no longer anyone's child. Part of her had stayed a child when they were alive, still nurtured. Her twin brother had died at birth, she was lucky to have had a life, in his memory she'd stay positive. In the car, she re-affirmed what she needed. She would not have long to wait.

5

Weeks later, David had removed larger rubbish, the rest she'd have to do, he'd said firmly.

'Hmm, I knew that anyway,' she'd remarked. He'd smirked, chewing gum noisily to irritate.

Julia felt a sense of achievement. Charity shops happy, rubbish gone, furniture and small items ready for Jonathan Merrick, an independent antique valuer. Alison said he was sixty, honest, and had worked for London auction houses before moving to Cheshire for semi-retirement. His honest opinion would matter a lot to Julia.

By Friday, she'd obliterated huge amounts of grime. The wilderness of nettles and brambles, lawn choked with dandelions, roses and perennials swallowed up by chaos of neglect, being too much for Stephen, he'd recommended another gardener.

Julia's relief that Jonathan Merrick would value furniture and effects, arranging a reputable firm to transport them to auction, was immense. Noise of the kettle prevented her from hearing his car. With no answer to his call, and the door ajar, he found the kitchen. She looked up, startled. 'Oh, didn't hear you knock. I'm Julia. Coffee?' she stammered. 'Only instant, I'm afraid.'

'I followed my nose. Yes please.' He extended his hand. 'Jonathan Merrick, valuer of all things bright and beautiful.'

Blushing, she shook his hand. He was all Alison had said, piercing dark eyes, thick black hair, not looking sixty. Over coffee, relaxing on two navy leather club chairs, and after a two hour appraisal, Jonathan confirmed most would go into a fine art sale, the rest into a general. He was impressed with the ceramics, Fabergé animals, an exciting find, would go to a specialist London Russian sale.

Julia explained how the property had been neglected. 'My parents came from skilled working class backgrounds. When I was little, they had a modest rented place, but my father became qualified, attending night school, rising through the ranks to become works manager By then, we owned our house, eventually moving here. It was beautiful before they became elderly and ill. Both began collecting objets d'art when I'd left home. Dad used to say it was my legacy.' Julia hugged her knees, sighing. 'I'd rather have my parents than mere things though.'

Jonathan listened sympathetically. 'Of course. I have contacts for the clocks, they'll make more than auction. I'll take care of your interests.'

Julia blushed again, not used to such protection.

Much had happened in six weeks. Instant attraction and rapport had resulted in further visits. Jonathan had helped wrap fragile items for the carriers, made tea, related his move from Sussex, job, and widowhood. His empathy allowed Julia to offload her frustration re David. Seeing her anxiety, Jonathan had embraced her, resulting in a warm, breathless kiss.

In bed, Julia reflected happily on the whirlwind of their mutual attraction, a frisson from their first meeting. They'd discussed dangers of their liaison, tried resisting, without success. In the first two weeks Julia hadn't accompanied Jonathan to London with the Fabergé, realising where it would lead. She loved London, beautiful hotels and buildings, but he was free to give her everything, she couldn't reciprocate. It was paradise to be with him, compared to the straitjacket of mere existence with David. Jonathan embraced who she was, seeing beyond her anxious state.

Despite wanting him badly and Jonathan declaring love, Julia was content to bask in his company, with walks in the forest and an encounter in his car. Close enough for now. Jonathan had understood her reluctance to embark on a full affair, realising if she went to his house, the inevitable would happen.

'It's hard for me too,' he'd admitted, pulling back from a passionate embrace. They'd collapsed laughing at his double entendre.

She hugged herself, recalling when they'd succumbed to the inevitable. Poppy was with her father for the weekend, David at liberty to be difficult, no one to witness the unpleasantness. He'd found fault with all Julia said and did. She'd ignored his jibes, aware no one can make you feel inferior without your consent. However, drinking heavily on Saturday evening, he'd burst into her room when she was reading. There'd been a tirade of insults and accusations of neglect. He'd discarded his towelling robe revealing an unwashed corpulent body. Leering menacingly, he'd torn the newspaper from her, staggering onto the bed, groping brutishly. She'd struggled to escape, his weight pinned her down, stale sweat assailed her senses.

'You've let yerself go, fat bitch. Still, you're mine an I'm 'avin yer,' he'd snarled, wildly tearing her pyjama trousers.

She'd escaped by doing something she'd never done to any man. With all the force she could muster, she'd freed her knee, bringing it up sharply into his crotch. He'd yelled, curling up in pain. Hysterically, she'd screamed she'd call the police, staggering upstairs to shower his drunken slobbering off her bruised body. Her threat had sobered him up.

At eight-fifteen next morning Julia awoke in her treatment room, worn out tossing half the night, even with her door locked.

Sunday would be even bleaker; she rang Jonathan whispering brief details. He was incensed, insisting she come to him immediately. She'd crept upstairs, packed a bag just in case – of what, she'd no idea. David lay sprawled on his back, snoring thunderously, not stirring when she'd dropped her shoes. She'd tensed in case he awoke before she reached the car to drive to Jonathan's. Falling into his arms with enormous gratitude, she'd related the trauma.

Lawns swept down a hundred yards to a fence, beyond which was a Scots Pine plantation. As his was the sole property on that section of the lane, it was tranquil walking by spring-flowered borders. Julia pointed to a wolf tree, explaining it was one with wild branches, telling him of Stephen, her gardener, who'd taught her a lot.

'He's Alison's partner. Quite funny too; I asked him, when he'd ordered a bird bath, if it was a sunken one. He'd replied, "No, I don't know any sunken birds!"' Julia saw Jonathan's wry smile and began to giggle. 'Hey, it was funny at the time!'

He'd put his arm around her, telling of his career, late parents, and move from a Queen Anne house in Sussex to this not insubstantial one. He'd even mentioned his finances; Julia protesting it didn't matter, she loved him not his money. Loved him, she'd said it!

With that confession, they'd held each other, relieved they felt the same. It was she who'd broken the silence. 'Eleven o'clock, he'll think I'm shopping. I'll have to return tonight, please understand.'

He'd spoken slowly and deliberately 'I'll be here whatever you decide. From what you've told me, there's nothing to salvage, but I won't put pressure on you. I love you and…'

'Take me to bed,' Julia had demanded, drawing him to her with a husky voice.

Their relationship had begun. She wouldn't rush things because of Poppy. Rows had ceased since the incident with

David, he had work and television, seeming to want little else. No apology, but he'd left Julia alone, unaware of her liaison with Jonathan. Daytime meetings were easy, overnight prohibitive, the pretence of her new situation made her uneasy.

***

Birmingham was the venue for a Complementary Therapy Exhibition which Julia wanted to attend for a day. Jonathan had other ideas, a beautiful converted manor hotel in Warwickshire. At dinner Julia had informed David she'd be away. He'd shrugged his shoulders, asking her to pass the pepper – unnerving.

Careful plans were made to facilitate this. When David had left for work, Julia drove to Birches Green. She parked in Jonathan's garage, excited as a teenager going to a pop concert, skipping to his Toyota. Although he lived on a remote lane, she kept her head down until they reached the concrete ribbons of the M6 motorway.

Jonathan had provided everything, newspapers, coffee and music. After a vegetarian lunch at the venue, they viewed stands offering health foods, massage oils, books, relaxation tapes. Both had hand massages and Indian head massage. Julia whispered she'd massage the rest later. They blushed, giggling like conspiratorial children.

Jonathan suggested tea. The nearest café had a queue; Jonathan joined the snake of thirsty customers cheerfully. How different the situation would have been if David had been faced with any length of queue.

He'd have uttered, 'Forget it. I'm not thirsty.'

Once, she'd protested wearily, 'But I am.'

'Be my guest,' was his miserable reply, pointing towards the queue.

Sitting happily, being treated as a lady, alien to her, she thought of the evening ahead. She'd give Jonathan a massage, he'd bought her gorgeous lingerie, admitting he'd be thrilled if she'd wear it. Aware of an attractive woman in a floral dress, holding the third chair at the table, she looked up.

'May I sit here? I'm worn out.'

Julia smiled. 'Yes. My er, husband's getting tea.'

Julia and the pretty blonde called Trudie, discussed the exhibition. Trudie said she was a stress counsellor, interested in alternative remedies for her nervous cat. By adding Rescue Remedy to its drinking water, the middle-aged moggy had become calmer. Julia spoke of her therapies, suggesting elderly cats benefit from massage. Trudie asked for Julia's business card, when Jonathan re-appeared with Earl Grey and muffins.

Julia nervously introduced them as Trudie pocketed the card, saying she'd enjoyed their chat on cats and massage. Jonathan whispered, when Trudie had left, that he was looking forward to his!

Drinking tea, Julia wondered why she'd given Trudie her card, doubtful she'd meet her again. Julia and Jonathan arrived at the hotel, the foyer neo-Gothic, dazzling patterns on walls and furniture; very Pugin. There were several décor periods, even an Art Deco bistro. Their room had a quieter theme.

'Is this to your satisfaction madam?' he asked, patting the bedcover.

'It's enormous!' she exclaimed.

He led her to the gold queen-sized bed. 'Sshhh, they'll all want some,' he teased, making her blush.

'Jonathan Merrick! There's a side of you I haven't seen yet, I know.'

When Julia had made love with Jonathan, she'd received what David never gave; consideration. Jonathan's heart and soul were wrapped around hers. David hadn't been romantic but Julia had been drawn to his willingness to love her, not recognising his deviousness. Sex had, at best, been adequate and quickly over. Jonathan made lovemaking an exciting prelude, passages of ecstasy, and a magnificent crescendo. There was nothing stronger than gentleness; their love deepened, it became increasingly difficult to drive home.

Making beautiful love, the stress of secret trysts and David evaporated. When Julia awoke from a short nap, she saw Jonathan looking at her fondly.

'I've run you a bath like all good butlers.'

She emerged in a black dress, pearls at ears and neck. 'I'm ready,' she announced confidently.

'Beautiful,' he declared, drawing her towards him.

'Jonathan, I'm proud to be on your arm. I feel like a naïve girl on a date.' She stroked the soft texture of his navy suit jacket. Seeing their reflection in the mirror, she thought them a perfect couple, momentarily marred as David's image loomed, producing a cold shudder.

Of two restaurants, Jonathan had chosen the less formal brasserie. Eating Halibut Clarice Cliff and Oeuf a la Neige for dessert, they'd admired Art Deco gleaming chrome uplighters softening charcoal walls, and black and white floor tiles.

This led to talk of her parents effects. Fabergé items had been taken to London for a Russian auction. Although not jewel-encrusted gold eggs, so beloved by European Royal Families, Jonathan promised her items would realise four thousand pounds.

They held hands across the table. Under the emerald tablecloth, Jonathan slipped his shoe off, stroking her leg with his foot, venturing as far as her thigh, making her flush.

Back in their room, with a concert by Jean Michel Jarre on Radio 2, they became lost in each other, reaching new heights, giving and receiving so much breathtaking love. Happily spent, they lay with the moon as witness at the window, its silvery sheen giving their damp bodies an iridescence like Loetz glass.

At breakfast, there was an air of anti-climax, wanting to stay. Jonathan suggested Birmingham Art Gallery to see Pre-Raphaelite paintings. He felt he'd overdone sex and, despite her protests, wanted to show there was more to their relationship.

Each room in the Edwardian building produced gasps from Julia. She liked Waterhouse, Leighton, and Burne-Jones. Jonathan smiled at her spontaneity. He steered her towards 'The Merciful Knight' by Burne-Jones, its powerful depiction of Christ on the cross on Good Friday blessing an armour-clad knight kneeling before him, drew them in. The knight had spared his foe, depicted crouching in the forest foliage. It was the beautiful expression of forgiveness on Jesus' face and humility on the merciful knight's that was so moving. Julia was as transfixed as Jonathan by the overwhelming scene.

Jonathan drove up the M6, reflecting on the paintings, discussing Ford Madox Brown's 'The Pretty Baa Lambs' surreal light in the coastal scene. Jonathan had explained at the gallery, people assume shadows to be black, but that painting proved otherwise. She'd agreed enthusiastically, pointing out variable hues reflected from sheep and whipped cream clouds. Dire Straits was Julia's request in the car, the last track as they drew onto Jonathan's property was 'Local Hero'. She told him he was hers, whispering she meant it, their break had been magical.

'Thank you for taking the risk,' he said, drawing back.

'David knows of the exhibition, don't suppose he's thought of it or me. Chances of being recognised are nil.' She kissed his pensive face. 'We wanted to be together and we were.'

Jonathan waved her off, counting the hours until she'd phone.

6

Julia relived the happiness of being part of a loving couple, a new security. Hiding behind a mask of apparent normality was proving easier than she'd anticipated. David had shown no interest, merely mentioning Alison had rung. Disappearing on Monday saying he'd return on Wednesday, her relief had been palpable.

After letting Stephen in for gardening, she drove to Alison's house. The kitchen, had been re-designed two years since. State of the art nineteen sixties had replaced tatty units. She'd tracked a Sarrinen white round Tulip set, the table had a central plinth and four bucket chairs with scarlet seat pads. Units, cupboards and floor tiles were sparkling white, with a scarlet window blind. The table set was, because of design and rarity, expensive, but useful to display to clients.

When Julia had gasped at the effect, Alison said she'd planned minimalistically, clean straight lines in white to reflect south-facing light, but zested up with scarlet. Julia needed hers updating, but sharing with David and Poppy, not high priority. Alison admitted hers was orderly because she lived alone.

Julia admired the new scarlet kettle. Alison stood, arms folded, leaning against the worktop, gazing hard at Julia. 'Forget kettles, where have you been?'

Julia blushed. 'I went to an exhibition in Birmingham, stayed overnight. Didn't tell you before, in case it went wrong, even turned my phone off in case David rang, spoiling things.'

'You dark horse, you're blushing. Guess you met someone there?'

'You'd guess wrongly, I already knew him, he took me there,' she admitted bashfully.

'What! But... who... when... and... sit down, tell me!'

Aware how untenable Julia's marriage had become, Alison was intrigued, astonished Jonathan was the lover in question.

'I ordered him from that book,' Julia beamed.

'Blimey, I was really cynical,' Alison confessed. If I hadn't got Stephen, I'd try it myself.'

Julia nodded. 'Love, although only a few weeks. I didn't tell you because I wanted to make sure of my feelings. He's gentle and passionate, makes me feel fanciable, not overweight and undesirable. I put pounds on snacking, you know how I've been. From the first time we made love, my complexes evaporated. He wanted me as I was, not a size ten model with perfect thighs. I was size 16 when I met him. Now I'm 14 I fit into my clothes, but Jonathan couldn't care less. I'm so Happppppeeeeee!'

Alison laughed. 'Mmmm, as I can see and hear!' Making sandwiches, she turned, looking worried.

'Julia, David may seem inattentive; but sees what he wants to. Cover your tracks.'

'We're careful, no one we knew at the exhibition or the hotel.'

Alison stopped slicing cucumber. 'If he's suspicious, he may check your mileage.'

'Mm. For two years I tried with David. I wanted us to see a counsellor to sort issues, highlight positives in our relationship, but he smirked and called me neurotic. When I've rejected his advances, he's called me a feminist. Then his attempted rape. Your recommending Jonathan for Mum's antiques valuation has saved my sanity.'

Alison brought tuna sandwiches to the table. 'How strange life's twists and turns are.' She grinned, 'Remember when we took Poppy to the doctor to get injections when she was six. You explained what he was about to do and a shocked Poppy asked, "You are joking aren't you Mummy?"'

They laughed at this sweet remembrance of the little girl. As her godmother, Alison wanted to protect her. Julia appeared anxious. 'Speaking of Poppy, the atmosphere's really affecting her. Resentment manifested in rebellion — banging doors, throbbing decibels of pop music, answering back. Said she's fed up being thin, asked when she'll put weight on like me! David was bloody horrible to her on Thursday evening. Dinner was late and she announced, "How much longer, I'm ravishing." David gave her a sarcastic glare, saying "Idiot, you mean ravenous. Let's face it, you're never gonna be ravishing with genes like yours." He couldn't have hurt her more if he'd hit her.'

Alison groaned, looking disgusted.

'Anyway, before that, two weeks ago I caught her sobbing, supposed to be meeting her friend Emma. She'd joined an internet site saying she was eighteen, and some chap of twenty-five had been corresponding with her for a week. She showed me e-mails, including one where he wanted to see her gooseberry bush, slang for pubic hair apparently, hence the phrase, 'born under a gooseberry bush'. No clue what he meant, and swayed by his offer of a pop concert, she went to meet him, waited ages outside the venue, poor girl, then realized he wasn't coming.

'She'd crept in, red-eyed. Praising her for telling me, I made it clear she was to leave the site and I'd report him. I blamed myself for being unaware she was getting into danger. It's not just teenage behaviour, Poppy's unhappy. Ha, I'd be too if I lived with parents like us.'

'Julia, what a shock, but you're a good parent.'

'Thanks, it's the strained atmosphere making her insecure. She's guessed it's serious, says she can't bring friends round because of David.'

Alison imparted a revelation of her own re Henry. 'Years since we spoke, don't need more stress.'

Julia pursed her lips, baffled. 'So why are you ringing him back? He's caused you pain; a cheek, wasn't worth it then and isn't now, let him sort himself out.' She sighed. 'I can see I'm wasting my breath. Stop playing the Good Samaritan, you have no obligation to him. Don't return his call, if he rings, tell him firmly NO and mean it.'

Alison, eager to change the subject, nodded in agreement. 'Wonder what Stephen would think if he knew of those one night stands and short interludes in my twenties when Mark disappeared. I wasn't in love with them nor they with me, sex and little else, hoping it would lead to commitment, stupid. I should have stayed celibate rather than team up with the wrong men. I won't use this relationship as a plaster for the last, sex is only part of it. Oh, there I go, saying that three letter word!'

Julia kissed her. 'Call it lovemaking. That appears to be what it is with Stephen. Ring me about the outcome with that swine, Henry.'

***

There was no obligation to reply to Henry, but unwillingly Alison did. She'd heard he'd married Collette, an escort girl's name, Alison had thought.

'Alison,' he gushed, '… I'm in a spot of bother. I …'

'Henry, your call was a shock. Is it something you can't share with your wife?'

Henry coughed nervously, tentatively asking if they could meet.

Alison reluctantly agreed. 'Thursday two o'clock?'

He stammered, 'I can't ask you to come here in the circumstances.' His embarrassment was evident. 'It's a shame, you'd like Collette, she…'

'Two o'clock Thursday.' she crisply replied, already irritated.

Regretting her decision, Alison pondered, 'What's he done, why tell me?' In two days she'd find out.

***

Promptly at 2 p.m. Henry appeared with a bunch of dyed garage flowers and a humble aura. He gushingly told Alison she was beautiful. Through entrance hall and sitting room, he tripped twice and sat clumsily on Bo's slender tortoiseshell tail on the sofa. Startled, she let out a feline shriek, hissing. Sighing, Alison saw how aged Henry looked.

He reached to take her cool hands in his hot ones. Not what she wanted, but she knew he'd act as though nothing had happened six years ago. She suggested he relax and tell her the problem.

It had been a rocky road since his major faux pas and subsequent trouble he'd caused. He'd overcome the shame, newspapers, divorce, estrangement from the church, but couldn't beat his addiction. Alison was bemused at the admission. He admitted his addiction to leather and how it had become all consuming. When he met Collette, he'd hidden porn videos and magazines of girls in leather. He couldn't tell his new wife and for a while didn't require his fix. Six months married, he'd needed what he couldn't admit to her.

'I felt awful, when Collette let me … it was me humping, with her unresponsive. Alison, why are you smiling?'

'Humping – hardly romantic.'

He looked sheepish. 'Suppose not. You get my drift though?'

'Go on.'

'I resorted to taking myself in hand over magazines, but it wasn't enough.'

53

Alison squirmed, fearing what further revelations were to come.

'This is how I got into trouble at a teashop. Saw her as she entered – leather clad, red pencil skirt, white polo necked sweater, red thigh boots, an answer to a fetishist's wish. I watched her sidle by, taking in nappa curves, a frisson other diners wouldn't understand.' Henry excitedly related his attraction to the leather-clad woman. A side of him Alison hadn't known, she feared where the diatribe was leading.

'The object of my desire in the corner, Miss Dominant, faced me. I flushed, quickly gazing down. She looked my way but I kept my cool, unclipping my briefcase, rummaging for something to read. Touching it had triggered where I kept my collage. The person who knew of its existence was Imogen, my therapist.' Henry, flushing, continued. 'I emerged from my trance to find the girl had gone. I gathered up my briefcase, wondering who the tempting girl had been, then saw a business card at the tablecloth's edge.

'It read: Miranda, Leathergirl Extraordinaire. Assuring you of a tight leathery welcome. I will stretch you to your limits. Lashings of fun. Telephone… I know you will come – MIRANDA.

I had a rush of pleasure – echoing the images of the models on my collage, visions in nappa leather moulding their tempting bodies, daring me to look, touch, smell, glossy pouting lips full of sultry punishments. I'd told Imogen, my mother confessor, who was wearing my fantasy – a leather suit with a red short skirt and jacket. Her leather shoes were high red stilettos, blonde hair danced over her shoulders. However, since I shared my fantasy, she hasn't worn leather, promising she'd help me break my obsession.

'I confessed I'd telephoned a leather clad mistress who'd ordered me to wear tight leather for her instructions. Discreet, doors locked, a secret across the miles. I had a thin strap underneath to constrict my… you know. She'd instruct me to look at the collage of teasing models laid out on the bed. Then orders to perform as I imagined her in squeaky leather. Commanding me to tower over the models after instructions to free myself from the confines of the strapping, I'd be told to slide my hand rhythmically along my erm… that.'

Alison was uncomfortable, willing Henry's confusing confession to end. Trying not to flinch, she rued seeing him, shocked he'd be so graphic.

'Stern orders given so I could climax. Allowing me to put sticky leather girls away, I was instructed to go. I told my therapist, Imogen, it ruled my life; she was concerned. I've nearly finished Alison…'

Sickened, Alison wearily replied, 'I had no idea of this, can't imagine why you're in terrible trouble. To ring in a state, there must be something else.'

Henry solemnly put down his glass. Hands clasped tensely, he told how his addiction had been worse since meeting Miranda.

'Surely you don't have to see it as an addiction, merely a fantasy being fulfilled.'

Henry gazed glumly into his lap. 'For ages I've been Miranda's client. I mentioned Imogen, my psychologist, attempting to wean me off my dominatrix. Miranda said it was harmless playacting. I was soon hooked on her giving me my fix once a week on the phone. I also visited. All I knew she'd be from seeing her in the restaurant, innocent-looking but a dominant mistress in leather, making me dress in bondage gear. I had to obey or get six of the best with her squeaky leather riding crop. Each whack made me stiffer, desperate for release. She made me wait until she gave permission.'

Alison squirmed. Henry's voice faltered. 'Alison, when I admitted I couldn't pay any longer, she became nasty, saying she wasn't a charity. I confessed I couldn't have straightforward sex, so needed to stop.' Henry's breathing became laboured, distress making him shake. Alison prised his hands apart, holding them in hers, urging him to complete his story.

'She was furious, said I couldn't treat her like that. Nothing placated her, and… she threatened to inform Collette. She'd gone through my wallet in the bathroom for my address. I tried to brazen it out, but she looked as though she could kill me, calling me disgusting names, saying I'd be sorry.'

Alison sighed. Henry, the weak reckless fool, she could not help him.

'Has she carried out her threat?' she managed to ask.

'Not yet, but the leather jacket I wore to the sessions had become torn on the shoulder so Collette took it for repair. Realizing Miranda's card was in the pocket, I went hotter than hell, hoping Collette hadn't seen it. I intended to go to the repairers pretending to search for theatre tickets.'

He sighed, cupping his chin in his hands, 'No need. I found the card exposing my guilt. My wife and I have identical bathrobes hanging on the bathroom door. I keep a handkerchief in mine so reached into the pocket, then knew I'd explored Collette's robe in error. No hankie, only the card.'

7

Stephen had tried to keep his concentration on gardening at Julia's. Relieved David was absent, he could remove trees without crude jokes flying from the door, but still couldn't concentrate, thinking it odd the message on Alison's answering machine hadn't been mentioned. She didn't have to tell him, he shouldn't mind some ex boyfriend ringing. He'd known her a short time, intensity overwhelming, from initial sexual contact to the love they now had. He didn't want to spoil it.

Digging near the berberis hedge, he guessed the apologetic message was from Phil, who'd treated Alison badly. Struggling with elder roots and double digging on heavy clay, he puzzled why Alison had made no mention of it. Indoors he drank thirstily from the tea flask, delaying chopping the widowmaker, a dangerous tree, until tomorrow.

At home, after ringing Alison, he was edgy, sensing she was distracted. Body weary, brain awake with confusion, he concentrated on the following week when he'd resume Chopin recitals in Manchester, Kendal, and Chester.

Next day Stephen spent time felling the widowmaker, lopping and topping branches, attempting to put doubts aside. It was uncharacteristic for him to feel like this, but the mysterious caller's phone call had unsettled him. If Alison didn't tell him, he'd have to admit he knew.

She rang, Stephen told her he was relieved. She hadn't questioned why, merely teasing she'd relieve him on Saturday, and not to damage his hands, it wouldn't do for a concert pianist to have gnarled splintered fingers. She added, 'Forget the piano, keep them smooth for me.' He'd felt reassured, but still concerned about the message.

***

Alison's demeanour was far from sunny. She'd expected Henry for a short while but his bizarre situation had taken ages to tell. Intriguing though his story was, she saw it as a diatribe. Confession was good for the soul, but he could have told his psychologist. He'd been foolhardy and she had no answers to his despair.

'What am I going to do Alison? I've been a complete hedonist.'

'Sometimes the best form of defence is attack, but in this case I don't advocate it, Henry. Couldn't you say someone put it in your pocket for a joke?'

He smiled weakly. 'Good idea, haven't been able to think straight. When I phoned you, it was regarding the addiction and Miranda's threats. Now Collette's seen the business card, I think she's waiting for me to comment. I should have left it in the robe pocket.'

Henry glanced at the mantel clock chiming three-thirty. 'It's decent of you to listen to my ramblings.'

Alison asked, 'Are you a member of any church?'

Henry's lip curled. 'Huh! Church of England? They put me through worse hell than the tabloids. I believe, but church? Hypocrites! I could have made a fortune spilling what I know about high ranking churchmen. There's no one I can trust, creeps, sycophants. That's why I rang, certain you wouldn't judge me.'

He stood up wearily, shoulders bent, shamefaced. Alison

reluctantly gave a brief hug, suggesting 'If you've removed it, she'll expect you to tell her, but wait until she mentions it, brazen it out.'

Henry patted Alison's hand, thanking her for wise advice. 'You're a good Samaritan,' he gushed, awash with gratitude. 'I didn't deserve your assistance, but you gave it, always a better Christian than I.'

Trudging to his little Fiat, Henry turned around, half waving, but his hand flopped despondently with utter regret. Alison shut the door, leaning against it with enormous relief.

***

Alison had been distracted all week, seeing clients and Henry. She awoke on Saturday, happy she could see Stephen. Sinking into the soothing bath, she knew he'd soothe her body further. The previous evening, the more she dwelled on him, the stronger became the urge to transfer thoughts into reality. Remembrance of their first encounter, visualizing Stephen's hungry look tearing off his clothes, slowly turning to reveal a taut, lean body, allowed a powerful orgasm.

She did housework, mowed lawns. Bathed and dressed in a white peasant blouse to show off pretty shoulders, she chose a skirt. Stephen liked feminine women. She'd worn trousers all week, especially when Henry had visited. He was a leg man, so she'd covered up.

Driving to Stephen's cottage near the post office in Lower Birches, Alison decided against mentioning Henry. She couldn't betray a confidence and it would mean explaining the past. The lanes were lush with burgeoning hawthorn, bluebells, blackbirds piping – Stephen called them the Beethovens of the birdworld. Alison had repeated a call one evening, perplexing the bird, causing him to cock his head and cease singing for a few seconds. Mrs. Cade had been highly amused, saying she'd try it with the owl in her oak tree, asking 'what else can one do when one can't sleep?' Alison could have suggested a few things, but Mrs. Cade would have been shocked. Her generation and background, it wasn't discussed.

Passing the village pub, The Turkey Oak, called after the enormous tree on the village green, she spotted her cleaner and husband sitting underneath pink clematis cascading down onto contorted wisteria stems. Betty Valentine waved. Alison privately called her a 'treasure.' Trustworthy, dependable, hard working. Remembering her embarrassment when, driving to Manchester and realising her vibrator was languishing in her bed, Alison had flushed. Betty would have made the bed around it though.

Her previous cleaner, Jill, was the opposite. Alison had been at Leo's, having left a list of jobs. Suspecting Jill read the newspaper, drank and smoked in the house, Julia volunteered to monitor her from the shed, keeping a beady eye on the back of the property one morning. Jill arrived late, smoked, watched television and used Alison's phone. Instead of removing curtains for the cleaners, the deceitful woman flicked them with a duster. No doubt she'd claim dry cleaning money. Julia let herself in after Jill's early exit. It was obvious she'd used Alison's perfume, make-up, washing machine, her own clothes draped over radiators, cigarette butts discarded in a china saucer. Julia, livid, turned off the heating, gathered wet washing, cigarette packet and ends, delivering them to dishonest Jill, demanding Alison's key. Shocked to see Julia, she said nothing.

Approaching the village shop, Alison resolved to make the evening special for Stephen as they'd been apart all week. She'd need to tell him her relationship fears over dinner though before sex was on the menu.

Stephen's cottage was early nineteenth century with a small garden. Impressive how he'd furnished it with William the Fourth period, from auction and car boot finds. Oak tables and ladder-backs had a burnished patina against buttermilk walls, plain white mantelpiece garnished with New Hall tea bowls. An Irish ringed decanter adorned a walnut table. Recently telling Stephen she was equally impressed with his talents in the bedroom had sent them giggling, falling onto the patchwork quilt covering the brass bed. She'd protested innocence, saying she'd meant the décor.

Pulling her towards him, he'd uttered firmly, 'Restraint? None whilst you're here. Talents in the bedroom? Judge for yourself.' Magnetism between them had been overpowering, full of sexual tension, demanding to be released with feverish explosions.

The door was on the latch. Walking past the piano room, Alison called twice; no reply. Rod Stewart was heard belting out Hot Legs. It was apparent as soon as she entered the bedroom, Stephen was in the en suite shower. Wanting to join him, a flash of guilt attacked; she'd been determined to discuss their relationship before any further physical contact. However, dancing to Rod's gravelly voice, she disrobed, anticipation making her tingle. Entering the steamy bathroom, she tapped on the screen, but the water's force and Rod's raunchy track made Stephen oblivious to her presence. Opening the shower door, she knew she'd been set up. Stephen feigned surprise. Alison stepped into the cubicle, breath catching as sharp jets hit her.

Devilishly, he lathered up his hands with soap, giving her a sensitive cleansing. She offered no resistance. Taking the shower head, he adjusted it to a strong fine spray, drizzling it up and down her aroused body. She delighted at the spray between her thighs, throwing back her head, thrusting glistening breasts at Stephen.

'I shan't stop until you come,' he throatily whispered, hanging up the hose so it sprayed them again, making her lose control. She wanted more, for both of them. She touched his hardness, her turn to be in control, kneeling, looking into wild eyes as she grasped the base of his penis, taking the glans to her lips. He was moist from the water as she ran her tongue up and down the shaft, making him moan and twitch. Teasing him so, opening her mouth to full stretch, she allowed him in. He gripped her drenched hair as she sucked him hard, causing his whole body to stiffen, and with a strangulated cry, he came as she drew back to watch his coming. The water rained over them, muffling their sighs.

Lifting her gently to her feet, Stephen led her out of the cubicle, wrapping her in a bathtowel, carrying her onto their bed, slipping into her outstretched arms.

'How I've missed you! Scant phone calls... I dunno, you seemed distant.'

'Stephen, I've been busy, it's equally insecure for me. I trusted former relationships and look what happened. Surely I haven't given you cause to doubt me?'

'So we're all right?' he tentatively asked.

'Of course. Don't forget I have a longer past, more let downs. Let's be happy as we are.'

'I wondered if Phil had contacted you?' he asked tentatively.

Alison frowned. 'Phil? He's the last person I want to hear from. Incidentally, he's had to leave the police force, my cleaner told me, for fraudulent activities. Good riddance.'

'Gosh. Let's get dressed for dinner, or we could stay as we are.' Stephen suggested.

Alison said she couldn't trust herself without clothes and was hungry for food.

When they'd dined on wild salmon with watercress sauce and raspberry fool, they'd repaired to the sitting room for the surprise. Firelight gave a burnished glow to firedogs and irons. Alison snuggled into the sofa, admiring Stephen's taste in lamps, glassware and period colours. He re-appeared with a bubblewrapped object.

'If you can tell me where this object was made and the maker, it will be yours.' He unwrapped an iridescent purple and green narrow-necked vase, causing Alison to gasp.

'Oh it's beautiful! Art Nouveau satin, colour seepage, iridescent tendrils intertwining. It has to be Pallme Koenig, my favourite Austrian glassmakers?'

'Clever girl, the auctioneer gave me the info.' Stephen saw her pleasure, her joy was his.

She put the beautiful object down. 'How clever of you to buy it.' She sat on his lap, squeezing him in a giant embrace. 'What if I'd been wrong? Suppose you'd have given it to another girlfriend.' she teased.

Stephen frowned. 'Hey, I'm a one woman man, no secrets either,' he announced mysteriously.

Alison broke from his embrace, assuring him neither did she. 'Are you sure? I couldn't bear to lose you.'

Frowning, Alison enquired, 'What's brought this on?'

'Something's bothering me. When I went to make tea at your house, I overheard a message being left. A man solemnly asking you to ring; I assumed it was Phil wanting you back. Don't look like that, I couldn't avoid hearing.'

'Stephen…'

'No, it's been weeks, you could have told me, but you haven't. When I rang, you seemed distant and I anxiously feared the worst.'

Annoyed, Alison spoke. 'I'm not in the habit of practising deceit, had plenty of that. I didn't hear the message for days.'

'I guessed it was Phil, but became anxious when you made no mention of it.'

Irritated, she told him, 'Not Phil, I'd never have replied. The caller was someone from years ago, anxious to share a stressful problem; to say he has difficulties is an understatement! I listened, gave him good counsel, sent him on his way. It wasn't easy seeing him, another deceiver.'

With embarrassment, Stephen falteringly admitted, 'I imagined all sorts, forgive me?'

Alison saw his sheepish face. 'I should be pleased you were concerned. I get insecure too, the past can unfortunately dictate the future, we mustn't let it.'

'What do you mean about the past?'

Alison settled on the sofa. 'We haven't discussed partners much, except Phil and Leo's father.'

Stephen said, 'We all have a past. You're bound to have had more dates than me. So what? I love...'

'Stephen, I need to explain something.' Alison saw his concern.

'Mark cleared off. We'd hardly known each other, and I was pregnant. Too young, too soon. Too young to be responsible, too soon to have sex with him. I was lonely, especially when my parents left for Australia. When I met Julia, she minded Leo. I didn't find dates naturally, answered newspaper ads. I sought love but... got sex. Either a one-nighter, selling myself short, or a brief so-called relationship. When things fizzled out, I returned to being lonely but I was that with them. When Leo went to school I studied and began interior design. Meeting clients was fulfilling, valued for my talents. I did, though, miss a relationship. When I met someone, it wasn't long before intimacy. Suppose it's normal these days, but it can cloud vision.' Feeling Stephen's hand tighten on hers, she witnessed his anxiety.

'I'll come to us in a minute. I thought for years I was highly sexed, but I was wanting love. I met Phil, liked his strength, willingness to care for me, ultimately discovering his treachery. When you've been with a partner for a while, things may not be quite right, but you stay out of habit. Seeing each other twice a week, a walk and dinner on Sundays, and used to each other in bed. When you're aware they're secretive, lying, you should clear them off. You don't. Fear of being without the person you're used to makes breaking off difficult. What do you do? Tell yourself you're lucky to have someone, however imperfect. Familiarity seems preferable to aloneness. Even when you're certain they're cheating, you ignore it to your detriment. Senseless.' She saw a very tense Stephen.

'I've told you, cos after Phil I vowed never to begin a relationship with sex. I met you unexpectedly, good intentions abandoned. We began with a passionate night and it's continued, but I thought I'd blown it, resurrecting insecurity. Fortunately, passion turned to love.'

Sensing she was not convinced, Stephen told her, 'What we have is beautiful, it would be meaningless without loving you.'

Alison nodded nervously, getting up to go to the bathroom. She hoped he hadn't detected her uncertainty, not of him but herself. She wanted to tell him that the shower scene he'd set up was exciting, but she'd love him with or without it.

***

Next day, feeling cowardly, she rang Julia. 'Hi Jools, free for a chat?'

'Yes, thankfully David's away. I could do with a break, been sorting out my tax. Who'd be self-employed? Lots of pros, but the finance side is one of the cons. You OK?'

Alison sighed. 'It's Stephen. I… think I made a mistake.'

'Stephen? He adores you, thought you felt the same.'

'I do, but it began with sex as usual. Henry too, but as a man of the cloth, thought he'd look out for me. Reckless, believing his lies, like Phil's.'

Julia was concerned. 'But you're OK, be glad.'

'I am, but I was drunk. Stephen wasn't, but willing to come to my bed. Flattering, but I want to be loved, not just fancied rotten.'

'What, and you think he doesn't? It's obvious he does, and he's told you.'

'Has he said anything to you?'

'No, but you said Phil's infidelity had freed you to love Stephen.'

'But… Julia… I'm confused… I…'

'Only lust? It isn't Alison.'

'Mm, maybe. I'm scared, my fault – insecurity. When we fell in love, I still peppered our conversation with sexual inuendos and play. What I was used to, hard habit to break. I'm repeating my behaviour, afraid my own self won't be enough to keep him interested. He even set himself up in the shower for an erotic scene when I arrived at his cottage, cos he thought I'd enjoy the game. I did, but it made me ashamed of my sexual addiction, through insecurity.'

Julia became exasperated. 'Sexual addiction? You've always been liberated, no hangups. Heavens, don't lose that. Probably liberating for Stephen you're uninhibited, don't discard something beautiful. None of the others could hold a candle to him.'

'I'll be careful. He doesn't complain but probably wonders when I'm going to bring romance into the bedroom. He does that, I'm reticent to express emotions. Sex is easy, love much harder. As always, I'm afraid of loving through fear of losing them.'

'Aren't you happy with him though?'

'Yessss, but the amount of sex scares me. I'm going to insist on a break.'

She heard Julia sigh heavily, warning, 'You'll hurt him.'

'Perhaps he's unsure and can't tell me either.'

'No, he loves you and doesn't feel the need for... separation.'

Alison became exasperated. 'Course he doesn't, hasn't been in my position. For once I'm going to be selfish and insist.'

'You're not sure you love him?'

'Yes. I'm instigating a break, if he cares, he'll agree. Stupidly, I told him yesterday I feel it isn't only sex. Oh why didn't I come clean, you see, that's what sex is doing to me?'

'How are you going to tell him?'

'I'll ring tomorrow, I'll weaken if I see him. If he wants me for keeps, he'll wait. Ha, I sound confident... I'm not.'

Julia's tone changed. 'Now's the time then.'

'I won't string him along. In six months I don't want to sit here wondering if I'm 'in lust' or 'in love' with him. I'm embarrassed at the way it began, through depression and drink that night. I need to desperately miss HIM, not sex. I can miss that with anyone; did with the others, especially Phil. Big error.

I'll miss it with Stephen, but need to see if I'll miss everything else.'

Julia was slow to reply. 'Erm, what if he asks me about this?'

'Stephen's too honourable to pump you for information.'

'Alison, Poppy's coming through the door. Good luck.'

To say that Stephen was surprised was an understatement. Alison hadn't thought he'd be so upset. She'd wished him success on his concert tour of Wales, but informing him gently of her decision, her stumbling words stung. Annoyed she hadn't expressed it when they'd talked, Stephen protested he'd love her with or without a physical relationship. Alison said she'd realised she needed space, apologising for the cliché. Hearing him gloomily accepting her decision of a ten day break made her wince, aware of his hurt, as he expressed hope she'd return.

Alison's diary for eight days, spoke of loneliness, missing Stephen's company, how talented, kind, loving, loyal he was. She hadn't written anything sexual.

'Able to think of Stephen without sexual frustration, only love, wanting him in my life.'

The last entry. 'In Sainsbury's today saw a man in a wheelchair, head lolling. Although his wife appeared strained, her devotion was apparent, affection between them beautiful to witness. Tried not to stare so went to another aisle. I knew that was how I'd love Stephen. An assistant, concerned, asked if I was OK, as I looked hot. I wanted to say I was happier than ever, but that's for me to tell Stephen – in two days time.'

8

Patients held their breath as Leila shuffled into the doctor's waiting room. Her stench heralded her arrival. She'd shamble into the newsagents, with urine-soaked clothes, producing pained expressions amongst customers. Today, patients winced as she slumped down, muttering.

Trudie gazed at a watercolour adorning the beige walls. 'Winter Pansies' by Kate, an original, cheering up the nervous waiting period. Fragile lilac pansies vibrant against pale winter sky, almost leapt from the solid grey frame, directing Trudie's gaze back to Leila, whose anorak had been clean, delicate lilac once. Now no such colour, save a few creases in the arms. The rest was an oil slick. Those stains could be removed with a thorough wash. Trudie's, on her heart, were permanent.

That evening Trudie took antibiotics for the hacking cough, thinking what Leila would be doing in her ramshackled house. Devoted to pupils, community and aged mother, Leila had retired from teaching. Now, reclusive and senile, help was refused. Locals avoided her trudging with carriers of sandwiches and flasks of tea. Children would point and social workers received short shrift.

Trudie shuddered, grateful in her sixties she had good health, apart from winter bronchitis. In a reminiscent mood, she lit the fire and, wearing pyjamas, opened her late father's cherrywood box full of memorabilia. The first letter was written in Arizona, having stayed with a waspish relative after a cousin's funeral. The welcome proving frosty, Trudie had stayed in a bed and breakfast for the last two days. Sitting cross-legged on the fire-warmed rug, she read.

'Laurie, This is a lost land and American dreamers lost in it. Plastic in substance, soulless in content. Superficiality reigns and the dollar worshipped. You and I worship a different God. Under his banner our paths crossed and destinies merged, finding our promised land in each other. We've shared dramatic highs, enhanced by the genius of Mahler, Fauré and Sinatra. Kisses by candlelight mean more than desert skies and the Grand Canyon.

Another day and the silver tin monster will return me from unreal January heat to England's grey shivery skies. Re-fuel me, inject me with liquid maleness, so our hearts dance again.

Gerda, the owner, interrupted my Vitamin D intake on the balcony by another gift. A gold jumper with beaded sleeves. She's so clever, stained glass, wooden carvings, Tiffany lamps made by her. She tells me in broken German, "I don't give zeez presents to all." She's been fantastic. One day I found two exquisite silk shirts on my bed. "For you if you would like?"

I would like. The kindness in her actions would make refusal unthinkable. Yesterday she presented me with a grey leather coat, 'bought ven I voz slim and not have the hyoosh muscles ere and ere from all ziss verk.'

A generous surprise. Gerda has known hardship, but given me empathy with clothing and her best room. She's all heart, despite a cruel childhood. I wouldn't say her bark is worse than her bite, but I've experienced neither, her house is a safe haven in this wilderness.

Sadly, I can't send this directly to you, so will give it upon my return. Trudie. xx'

Laurie Martin wasn't in her life now, but Trudie cherished the memory. A further note, written to Stephen, her son and his then girlfriend, whilst Trudie was housesitting for him. Stephen had read it fondly, saving it for her family file.

'Welcome back, garden blossoming. In hedge is honeysuckle, flowering currant, and rambling rose. By the barbecue daffodils and tulips spurting.

No evidence of Mickey Mouse, plug for sink missing. Tranquil by fire listening to Classic FM. I've taken bedding to wash. Mum. x'

It had been a treat to spend a week in Stephen's Victorian cottage twelve miles from hers in Worcestershire. Jill, his avaricious, selfish girlfriend, had split after their holiday. Trudie wanted his next lover to have life experience, an older woman who wouldn't take advantage of her son's sensitive, generous nature.

Stephen had just passed his qualifications from Royal Northern College of Music in Manchester, renting a flat. He'd spent time teaching in a primary school, then moved to Cheshire, giving music lessons. Once established he'd put a deposit on a Georgian cottage. Trudie had grieved when he'd relocated. He'd been absent studying, this was more final, he liked Cheshire and she'd guessed he'd stay there.

Hearing the carriage clock strike eight, Trudie was hungry, but a letter caught her attention, something she couldn't send to her father. He'd been dead some years; feeling blue she'd put pen to paper. Loss was an ever present shadow so she hadn't read it again, filing it in the ephemera box. Dinner could wait, she'd read it.

'Daddy, Today is your day, for you are with me although I cannot see you. To be sitting here on December 31st, your birthday, is sad. I want to ring you, but you're not there – where are you?

I haven't been entirely happy. I loved a good man, but our time was measured.

I watched *Dad's Army*, wanting you to laugh with me. Two of my cats have died and your three sisters. Cousin Ken collapsed in Birmingham, dying of alcoholism. Dirk Bogarde died in 1999. We used to see his films at the Gaumont. I have his books – a marvellous writer, felt part of me, I miss him.

This pen is from the handbag with Mother's initials on it. There was her 1984 diary in it, hospital appointments written by you. To see your writing is surreal. It draws you close, a part of you that isn't gone, spirited to an unknown place. I touch the slanted script. I kiss the spindly hand. The ache begins. The urge to ring you is overwhelming, 66615 I want to dial, but my emptiness will increase. Some other life will answer in unfamiliar tones. "He is gone" they'll say, and will not know my grief.

Until we meet, your loving daughter, Trudie.'

Eyes damp, Trudie let the page flutter onto the carpet. Her husband dying when Stephen was a toddler, mother and father within a year of each other, and Laurie, whom she'd never imagining losing, vanishing four years ago, huge grief. Having felt a duty to make the most of life in memory of her father, she'd felt hurt she often couldn't. The disappointment of lost dreams had became unbearable.

Shut down, experiencing nothing, the fridge's hum the only sound, her stomach gurgled with hunger, breaking inertia. When she'd put the papers away and walked into the kitchen, the nothing feeling had changed, thankfully feeling everything, a daughter's sadness for a loving father, a normal emotion, making other trials bearable. His suffering was over from immense cancer pain. 'Out of sight, never out of mind.' she thought wistfully.

Enjoying supper and Rachmaninov's Third Piano Concerto on Radio 3, she gazed at her renovated kitchen. Pale blue walls, a scumbled blue dresser and cupboards. There'd been an Aga, old and battered, as she'd been from the relationship break-up. A modern oven, simple to use, was its replacement.

Dull hall walls had given way to lime-washed ones, with a pine beeswaxed cupboard. She'd initially decorated, but limboing under ladders on stairs proved too challenging; a local firm tackled that job.

Thumb latch doors, she'd kept, but resisted a grandfather clock, disliking the heavy donk... donk... of the pendulum, reminding her of time slipping by. To combat the hall's dark stone floor, she'd lightened the walls with Cornish prints of Stanhope Forbes and Lamorna Birch, lifting it with cream rugs and stoneware jugs. The link with Cornwall was Laurie.

Trudie loved her boiler room, it had a ceiling dryer operated by a pulley. On damp days when Trudie hung laundry, Holly, her tortoiseshell cat, was in attendance for a luxurious sleep. Trudie loved her lemon and white bedroom, one wall papered in a Walter Crane print. Her neighbour had remarked, 'So Colefax and Fowler,' which it wasn't, but she'd been too polite to correct her. Wisteria made attempts to sneak in, Trudie pruned whiplash strands to deter creepy crawlies. She'd been raised in the countryside, but feared moths, daddy long legs, and spiders.

Her thoughts during the concerto turned to her conservatory. From the back garden, white bamboo furniture echoed the light outside. The garden was Trudie's passion, previously expended on Laurie. As the moody third concerto surrounded, she remembered introducing it to him in Symphony Hall Birmingham. Her favourite conductor, Sir Simon Rattle, had been in charge; they'd been captivated by his passionate style. The pianist had been Nikolai Demidenko, spot on – a Russian playing Russian music.

In the vast cream and red Art Deco-style hall they'd held hands during the fervour of Simon's conducting, the pianist's expressive face, his brilliant fingers portraying the angst of Rachmaninov at his most depressed. Exhilerated and emotionally wrung, they'd left silently. Laurie had likened the auditorium to the inside of the Queen Mary liner, promising they'd cruise on her one day. They never did.

Trudie recalled how their relationship had begun, on a WEA French course. Their attraction was instant. The third week Laurie had offered a drink after class. He'd revealed his life, including current difficulties. Irene, his wife, enjoyed his position as a lawyer, but wouldn't let go of working class roots. Laurie didn't care what class anyone was, her inverted snobbery defeated him. She was content to bask in his reflected glory as a successful man. Scanning clothes and household catalogues, the kudos of possessing the latest acquisition was her pleasure.

Her repressive fear was a bone of contention. She'd never allowed the children to eat tomato pips believing they'd cause appendicitis, nor pets in case of fleas. Eventually, romance had evaporated. Asking Irene if she loved him, the reply was, 'where would you find a better housekeeper?'

Her social graces were lacking, but she'd refused to budge. Meals weren't eaten at the dining table, unless Laurie pressed. When she complained she couldn't cut meat, he'd advised she stop holding her knife like a pen and there'd be no problem. Irene had angrily retorted, 'I'll hold my knife as I always have, you snob.' If there was conversation, she repeatedly pointed with her knife for emphasis, flicking food. On trays, so food could be eaten in front of the television, there were no napkins. He'd bought cotton ones which she'd ignored as they needed ironing, so he put up with paper, which she'd said weren't needed, unless free from a café, to be used as tissues. Words had failed him at the last remark.

Irene was fulfilled knitting, sewing, and watching the wide-screen TV. Despite trying to include her in his world, she'd shown no interest. Many years without intimacy hadn't bothered her. Saying he should be fulfilled with his job, they had, she'd said, all they needed.

As a last effort, Laurie had arranged a trip to London in an hotel, a musical, and shopping. In their room Irene had slept immediately. He was thankful, but frustrated as the creak of springs through the wall could be heard. Low moaning, muffled groans, a cry, then silence.

The gap had become a chasm. With their children grown up, Irene became more remote. Laurie's yearning to be wanted by a woman of his own intellect became paramount. Someone to share music, books, the countryside and art.

One evening, on a country lane, Laurie kissed Trudie on the lips instead of the cheek, leaving her breathless. 'You smell like roses after rain,' he whispered tenderly.

His emotions were reciprocated by Trudie. Flirtation became adultery, deep love growing quickly. He was attentive, passionate, tender and romantic. She began to feel whole, proud of her sexuality, new confidence as a complete woman, excited to be nurtured by a kind, intelligent man.

If his wife suspected, she kept quiet. Easy for Laurie to be absent, Irene knew he worked long hours. Staying overnight with Trudie, he became adept at deceit. One evening they watched *Secrets and Lies* on television. The phrase haunted, knowing it appertained to his behaviour, yet happier than he'd ever been. Trudie was too, but being with Laurie felt like a loan which would eventually be called in.

Irene was content to live independently within the home. Years before, she'd suggested he move into the spare bedroom, making it plain she'd folded her tent and put it away forever. He told Trudie he was relieved; she'd laughed at the Freudian slip.

Trudie had confided in her best friend Paula, who lived in

Cheltenham. They'd discussed what she could give Laurie for Christmas. Anything hinting at a change of taste was to be avoided, ruling out gifts inappropriate for subterfuge giving. CDs, novels or biographies would have to do. Clothes were out, men liked to choose their own. Laurie collected paperweights so that wouldn't appear odd. This became the pattern for birthdays and Christmas. Caithness paperweights, Jeffrey Archer novels, compact discs and concert tickets. Trudie treasured the first present from Laurie, a crystal Georgian rummer. On the card, he'd written:

> I give you this wine glass
> Drink from it, drink from me,
> Preserve the beautiful balance
> And don't break either of us.

Paula had advised Trudie years before to date again. 'If you've got it, flaunt it, play the field. If one of them treats you shabbily, don't tell him, he'll know already. Don't answer his calls. Drop him. If you find one that's worth keeping, don't make him too jealous. And hey, make him wait a bit for thingy. Men appreciate what they have to wait for, let them think it's they who're doing the chasing, they like to be hunters.'

Trudie had giggled at the word 'thingy'. 'Listen, I've almost forgotten how to do it.'

'Don't wait forever, if you spend too much time inside, outside becomes menacing.'

Trudie had found those words true. Until Laurie. After Laurie. She hadn't envisaged an 'after Laurie' to be on the cards.

Paula and Trudie became confidantes, Paula confessing an affair with Roger, although fairly happily married. She'd told Trudie when they'd met in the nineteen seventies as voluntary counsellors. Every week at Paula's large split-level home, their lives had been discussed, each recognising a soulmate. At lunch,

Trudie had enthused about the lobster bisque. Paula had remarked 'Nearly as good as sex – illicit of course.'

With toddler Penny, Paula's grandchild, Trudie had been party to her sayings. She grinned at her vocabulary. 'Fankoo. More wubbish. Ginger cat and Garma Gacket, instead of the j sound, 'Gorg' instead of George the postman. Cyber instead of spider, which scared her. Paula had put a rubber one in the biscuit tin to deter her from rummaging there. Trudie adored Orbs, Paula's cat. He'd nabbed a giant moth and eaten it, when Trudie had screamed in terror. She'd renamed him Mighty Moth.

The revelation about Roger was a surprise, as Trudie had thought Paula and James, a successful marketing man, had a solid marriage.

'We do,' insisted Paula, 'but you see someone, you dissolve. Married to a corporate man, plodding along, children at school, housework doesn't hold the same thrill as an attentive new man.'

Trudie listened, wide-eyed.

'I was waiting for the bus after the hairdressers, when the heavens opened. Annoyed I had no umbrella with me, desperately I plonked my empty shopping bag across my head.' Paula saw Trudie giggle. 'A Triumph Stag stopped and its young handsome driver offered a lift. A stranger, but I heard myself accepting! I gave him directions, shaking at my nerve and his. I was in a turquoise floral dress so not provocative. I thought… it's only a lift, but heard myself asking him in. Naturally he accepted.'

Trudie was fascinated.

'He was twenty-four, single, in computers, and lived at Evesham. I told him of James and my daughter. He even petted Mighty Moth, saying I looked feline and could he stroke me instead! Gorgeous – like a model in Austin Reed's window.'

Trudie laughed loudly. 'Stiff you mean?' They collapsed giggling at the double entendre.

'Extremely! Empathy was immediate, I had that adrenaline rush from the tantalizing promise of sex I wanted and was going to get. Yes, shocking. He asked to use the bathroom, then stood at the top of the stairs beckoning me. We had the most exciting hour and a half my bedroom had seen. I had no guilt then, nor do I now. He's a beautiful person, I love him Trudie.'

'Paula, I'm pleased for you, but be careful.'

'Don't fret, he comes when James is out. He rings me, so no trace of calls. We were compatible straight away, as though I'd known him before. You'll never guess what he told me? something you said when you met me! That I resembled Barbara Goalen, the fifties fashion model. I was surprised he'd even heard of her, but apparently his mother knew her in London through the modelling agency she worked for. He showed me a photograph of his mother with Barbara, both striking.'

Trudie looked starry-eyed. 'Exciting. How long is it now?'

Paula, doubled up at the question, could hardly reply. 'No longer than when I first saw it!' she spluttered.

Trudie had laughed at her faux pas too and Paula had said her affair was in its seventh week. She'd related compliments from Roger, telling her she was a sophisticated, beautiful, exciting woman. From James taking her for granted, now she was really living. James adored her from afar. They had the same high intellect, he was courteous, a charming host, a good provider, but absorbed in his career. Paula admitted she had to turn herself on when James occasionally made love to her, never spontaneous, always knowing when he wanted her – insincere compliments, suggesting an early night.

'You deserve Roger, but for God's sake stay the same. No new underwear, a dead give-away. How have you coped with James' once a month requirements?'

'First time easy as James was in Dublin for a fortnight, then London. The fourth week he was home. As Friday night loomed I knew the ritual would begin and I'd give in for normality's sake. I went through the motions in bed, never begins anywhere else, one minute start to finish as usual.'

Trudie reeled.

'Until I met Roger, I hadn't been properly awakened. Knows what a woman wants, and does he give it. He must have had previous convictions for ruining a girl's sleep! I coped with James by thinking of Roger, my fake orgasm would have won an Academy Award.'

They smiled conspiratorially. Paula poured coffee.

'No idea where this will lead.' she said solemnly. 'I can't leave James. He's a marvellous provider and loves me. He may seem complacent, but he's proud, I've suffered his temper a lot. It isn't a pretty sight!'

'Be careful.' Trudie affirmed.

'We have to go to Wallingford on Sunday to the in-laws. Don't know why James' stepmother wants us there, she hates us both.'

After lunch, Trudie kissed her goodbye, 'So pleased about Roger.'

'Not as pleased as I am!' came the reply, as Paula waved off her confidante.

Once clear of main roads and the swish of passing traffic, Trudie reflected on Paula's confession. Exciting to hear, but James loved Paula and she'd never had money worries, unlike Trudie. When her husband Richard had died, she'd only a small widow's pension, so had part-time jobs. Struggling with bills was difficult whilst married, worse in widowhood, her bank account oozing money.

The unfairness to James rankled as Trudie meandered through winding lanes, although Paula told her she'd attempted to discuss their relationship. He'd merely offered spa treatments and clothes rather than valuable time. In reality though, when he could have been with Paula, he wasn't working on his career, but something else entirely.

'If I could go into retirement with a lover, instead of so-called independence. Please let there be someone for me,' Trudie would often pray. People would assume loneliness was worse in winter, Trudie felt it more in summer. In winter she couldn't see couples out together. In summer they were everywhere, bursting out of chrysalises like butterflies. When not working, Trudie would garden, if not seeing friends. Stephen lived nearby until he'd moved north.

When he'd gone, it was a testing time. She'd intended joining an improvers course in French conversation. Her accent was excellent but grammar rusty, so instead enrolled on the beginners course. What she didn't anticipate was Laurie.

That night, Trudie yearned for her absent lover, Rachmaninov had seen to that. Those four years couldn't be blotted out, the best but the most complex. Before Laurie, needing to be held and to hold had been a physical ache. With him she hadn't had it; when he'd gone, it returned with a vengeance. 'Better to have loved and lost than never to have loved at all,' she'd think, but would lie in bed, as now, going from that thought to wishing they'd never met. Picnics, concerts, and day-to-day stuff, which sharing elevated to the sublime, became bitter-sweet. He was, albeit in name only, married. Her perfect love, but she'd ignored the red flag.

Going over telephone conversations, she conjured up how he'd looked the last time she saw him, and if she'd known him at all. Life went on, so did wondering – why, where, when, how? She'd acknowledged positives in their affair, not letting his vanishing act spoil what was. Because their love was so extraordinary, having to return to the ordinary was devastating.

As Holly sprang onto the duvet, Trudie's thoughts halted. Curling into a foetal position, the last images were of the stalker!

9

A restless night but Trudie tackled paperwork. In the sun-enriched conservatory she sat at her early Victorian Pembroke table, which took up little space, having fold down flaps and many uses, dining, desk, and playing cards with neighbour, Georgina.

She thought of Paula and their solid friendship, sharing joys, sorrows, moans and elations. Each knew the other's past and present, lovers, pets, everything. No other friend felt like family, nothing Trudie couldn't tell Paula. Gazing out at the garden, she mouthed, 'almost'.

Trudie read a welcome home note from Paula years before. 'Trust weather hot as here. Not wearing much, sexy knickers from M & S. No. is 1811 if you want some. White cotton, high cut with lace around legs. For those special occasions! I began in tee-shirt, shorts, bra and pants. Now I'm just in my 1811s!!!!'

Trudie giggled.

These notes made Trudie feel less alone, she and Paula had shared so much, each other's confidante. Browsing a letter

Paula had shared from a New Jersey friend, Trudie read the last paragraph.

'News disjointed, how I am honey. Getting a computer if I can find anywhere to put it in this clutter. Kisses to Mighty Moth, as Trudie calls the cat. Is he as big as Garfield? Xxxxxxx Jodie.'

The dear departed British Blue had disappeared, aged eleven. Paula and James had been devastated. Seven years on, when James was clearing around the neglected shed, he'd discovered the perfectly preserved body of their cat under bracken and peat, fur intact. James had buried him under the willow tree where Mighty Moth lay on hot days.

A letter from Paula, when Trudie met Laurie.

'Far be it from me to give you advice but I'd say finish it before he does, while he's keen. Vital for your self-esteem, cos it can't last, you must realise that.' What sound advice it had been – if only she'd heeded it.

Slanting rain rattling on the conservatory roof broke her concentration. Staying at Paula's, something distasteful had occurred. The one thing she couldn't share with her. Trudie shivered, enough reminiscing, Andrea was due for counselling.

Trudie saw the chatty copy letter re Andrea's lost confidence. Trudie occasionally wrote letters rather than e-mails, still nervous of computers, having learnt only latterly. Through the alchemy of the internet though, she'd communicated with people all over the world, giving glimpses of each other. Disappointingly, Laurie Martin had not appeared.

'Andrea, I'm in my garden writing a gradual plan. You want to be happy, but caught in a suppressive situation with an antagonistic man. Circumstances don't allow letting go of Arthur now – but they will!! Compromise may be necessary to achieve peace of mind, for now.

Arthur controls you and who is he to do that? He doesn't have your best interests at heart, but you do!! If you take a firmer stand he'll notice. We're treated how we present ourselves to be treated. Your obligation is to be true to yourself remember.

In counselling we explore the problem. Support of a loyal counsellor will help explore goals. I'll see you soon with a detailed plan. Flattening patterns works, but we have to clear out rubbish within. Trudie.'

Seeing Andrea that afternoon, continuing patterning therapy, Trudie was pleased she was taking control, even a new job in Berkshire with horses. Andrea had given Trudie a spontaneous hug, for directing her 'towards freedom' as she put it.

'Pleasure to see your progress, you've worked hard with me. We can talk on the phone, don't hesitate.' Trudie emphasised.

'All I did was angst. You've given me self-belief, letting me rage, acting as a prop. I needed your support and you gave and gave. Your husband's lucky… oh sorry… you were widowed; there's another man though?' she asked, noticing Trudie's smile wane.

'Not anymore, but these sessions are about you, not me. Drive safely.'

Trudie waved Andrea off. Mechanically rinsing and drying glasses until they sparkled, her head was clogged. Laurie's departure for one, then the incident at Paula's with James. Filling the kettle, she heard Holly at the door and post arriving. There used to be romantic cards and notes from Laurie. Discarding junk mail, she lay on the bamboo chaise longue. Gazing up into the shimmering acid green Robinia tree patterning the roof, she visualised their first embrace.

He'd been invited to lunch, they'd discussed their lives and laughed a lot. Following her into the sitting room, kissing her shoulders, he'd whispered he loved her. Submissively, she'd taken him to her, dangerous passion submerging them. With nervous excitement, their affair had begun.

In four years they'd shared everything, illicit though it had to be. They'd discussed Laurie leaving Irene, reasons why he couldn't. He'd said if she discovered his affair, she wouldn't forgive him, but want him to stay for punishment. If the balloon went up though, he wouldn't.

Telling Laurie of her friendship with Paula, Trudie shared what she'd never revealed. 'Paula was the person I could always confide in – not this time. I'd known her for ages, met doing voluntary counselling for parents under stress. She'd moved to Stratford from Harpenden with James' job. We clicked and I popped in for lunch on Thursdays after manning the centre phone. Paula was on Friday duty; beautiful, slim and elegant, called the ladies loo the powder room, old world values I like.

'After six years she moved to Cheltenham. We decided to send cassette tapes once a fortnight, containing news, funnies, childhood stuff, serious stuff, music. I looked forward to the postie. So did she, and James, pleased Paula was more settled, saying he wouldn't go trout fishing if she had no tape to listen to!

'I went to stay at their new house twice a year. He'd ask "Girls, what's your pleasure tomorrow? Shops? Picnic? Bath Abbey? You decide and I'll drive you."

'This would be at a weekend. In the week he'd drop us off, we'd get a taxi back. I questioned why he was so charming, as Paula had felt neglected. His world was the company; their relationship had become stale. He seemed happy but Paula wasn't. I told you of her love for Roger didn't I?'

Laurie nodded, listening intently, feeling privileged to share Trudie's life.

'When James found out, all hell broke loose, Paula suffered greatly at his wrath. Roger lay low, ringing when James was absent, she lived for his calls. Two years on he moved to Hampstead with his job. Calls became fewer, the last one informing her he was marrying his boss! Three years on he rang to say he was divorced, wanting to meet. She must have been strong cos she told him she couldn't go through that again, and difficult to face James when he asked about her day, waiting for her guilty look. Ha! HER guilty look!'

'Oh, that sounds ominous.'

'It was. Years later when Paula was being treated for depression, the psychologist advised the past should be discussed. Paula told James why the affair had happened. His treatment had made her ashamed and she'd been contrite, she'd said. Then he'd dropped the bomb – admitting scores of flings. "There on a plate to be relished. You take what's on offer.' he'd told her lamely.'

'Insensitive swine.' Laurie scowled.

'Quite. It made her condition worse for a while, but it was a watershed. All that punishment re Roger, James had his own dirty secrets. "At least mine was love, not a series of knee tremblers and brief pokes with receptionists, hotel waitresses and staff." she told me.

'Eighteen years ago I was there to stay two nights. On day one, James took us to an ancient inn at Withington, then Burford church. At dinner, he asked me to go trout fishing with him next day so Paula could rest. I said I had no interest; dejected is probably the best word for his appearance.

"Can't I persuade you, Trudie? You won't be bored, do come." he pleaded.'

'Aah, the plot thickens,' Laurie interjected.

'Yes. Paula flitted in and out, clearing the table and doing the dishes.

"Put some dance music on for Troods." she called from the kitchen.

'Laurie, I'd danced, joked, chatted with him before, and that was all. He played cool jazz and slow danced with me. Immediately

I realized there was an ulterior motive as things were growing rapidly in the trouser department! I ignored it with a scold.

"'Naughty, you're a married man!" He pulled me closer – alarming as Paula was nearby. Then the revelation!

"'Silly girl, refusing my fishing offer tomorrow."

'But I'd be bored.' I stressed.

"Fishing? I've booked us into a Cirencester motel. After lunch we'd be repairing to our room for... a bloody good... you sexy girl."

'I was panicky, uttering "You and whose army?" a daft thing to say, but I was thrown. He said, "No partner, you must be gagging for it. I don't get much myself, as you know."

'That did it. I replied angrily, "I don't know anything of the sort, and because I'm unattached doesn't mean I want you. I've NEVER led you on! Don't you realize your wife, my best friend is next door? If you think I'd betray her as you're prepared to do, I'll leave." I told him forcefully, pushing him and his erection away. He wouldn't give up! Landing on the couch, he staggered up, grabbing my breasts, trying to bite my neck, putting his hand up my skirt in a drunken fumble. He slobbered "But I want you, sexy Trudie. Let me ravish your body tomorrow, we'll have champagne in bed. I could lick it off your tits...""

Trudie saw Laurie bridle with disgust. 'With force, I shoved him to the floor. Paula came in seconds later, tutting. "James, take more water with it. Trudie, come and have some girl talk in here."

'We did just that, but tiredness overcame Paula halfway through Trivial Pursuit, so she retired. James tried to ply me with Bailey's Irish Cream, but I ignored him, saying I was going to bed. Bumping into walls, he begged me not to tell Paula, finger on his mouth saying ssshhh far too loudly. Placing a chair against my door, I heard him shambling into their bedroom, then silence.

'Next morning he was nervous with no eye contact at

breakfast. Paula said she was embarrassed at James getting so drunk. I dismissed it but felt sick by his maulings; inventing an excuse to go home. I decided Paula hadn't suspected, but I visited when he was absent. He rang me once, thanking me for not informing Paula. I told him I'd never hurt her, on that he depended. Sent me a letter too when she went into hospital. I replied on the back, Paula was in hospital for a week, so wouldn't see the post, he'd destroy it anyway. I made it crystal clear regarding the situation.'

'The swine, how dare he put his hands on you. Thank goodness Paula didn't walk in on it.'

'God forgive me, I've actually wanted to tell her. I couldn't, too wounding, and if she challenged him, he'd blame me, saying I came on to him. She may have believed him.'

'Not after his antics with other women surely?'

'She wasn't aware then, stayed married to James for security, and might have thought I could damage that. I erred on the side of caution, also actually telling her… I couldn't, that's not friendship.'

Laurie hugged her. 'You handled it well, thank God you didn't have to handle anything else. I'll make hot chocolate, coffee prevents you sleeping doesn't it?'

Trudie's twinkle in her eyes told him sleeping was not an option.

***

The stalker came into Trudie's life two months into her affair with Laurie. He'd asked her where she'd prefer to go for a short break. Like an excited child, she'd asked, 'The seaside? Oh please?'

Trudie adored the English coast, anticipation of that first glimpse of sea over a hedge. With Stephen, she'd beachcombed, watching waves hissing up the beach and sea winds slapping their cheeks.

The day before their departure to Dorset for two nights, arranged with precision by Laurie, he'd been tetchy, hating to lie, but imperative to get the story straight. Asking Trudie to be ready at 9.30, he'd abruptly rung off. Next morning, feeling anxious, she caught herself frowning. Discords were eased by gardening, so she did just that, forking out dandelions around daphnes, reasoning Laurie was bound to be tense until the area vanished from the rear view mirror.

Old Mr. Johnson, Trudie's neighbour, was happy to look after Holly. Depositing the key with Mr. J., Trudie waited for Laurie. By 9.40, she was concerned. By 9.50 she was wringing her hands. At 10.5, she sent him a message. 'Hello, I'm here with bucket and spade, is there a problem?'

Irritated, she watched from the sitting room for Laurie's car. Fifteen minutes on, no sign; a call would have sufficed. Not the behaviour of the man she knew. She took off her jacket, switching on local radio for traffic reportage – negative. She was a fool to have believed he'd be able to come. Moving her holdall, she spotted the car.

At the front door was a very stressed man. Solemnly, he followed her in for the inevitable explanation. 'I apologise for my lateness' he began falteringly. 'I could invent all manner of excuses but they'd be lies.'

Trudie sat beside his hunched figure on the sofa. 'Why couldn't you telephone me? I'm not going anywhere until you tell me what's going on.'

He held her hands, breathlessly saying, 'What I'm going to say isn't a rehearsed excuse. I wanted to spare you, but you should know what's happened this morning has been occurring for weeks. Also to you, but you're unaware.'

Laurie silenced her attempt to interrupt. 'Let me tell you. My married secretary had a crush on me, popping up everywhere. Whether I was shopping at the weekend or jogging, she'd bump into me. Attentive at work in a professional way, I paid no attention to these coincidences, even thought how kind she was sending flowers to Irene when she'd hurt her leg.

Once at work, I discovered she'd taken my shopping, so made a detour to her house. She produced my bags, asking if I'd unscrew a tight lid on a honey jar. While I did that, I heard her go upstairs.

'When she returned, I was shocked, she was dressed in one of those… teddies, white stilettos and a come hither look! Telling her she was being reckless, she a married woman and I a married man and her boss, I gathered my bags, attempting to go. She'd locked the front door and, breathing whisky over me, lunged, saying "You won't want anybody else after me."'

Seeing Trudie wide-eyed, Laurie continued. 'I made her see she was being foolish, but she wept, saying how unhappy she was. I promised to forgive her if no re-occurrence. Her behaviour was OK at work, but silent calls were received at home.

I kept this from you hoping if I warned her, she'd stop. She didn't, so I asked her to leave my employ. Strangely she agreed, saying she couldn't bear not to have me. I assumed that would be the end of it, not so. She follows me like an obsessed hunter, as though I've a target on my back.'

'Laurie how could you not tell me? What happened this morning?' Trudie demanded sharply.

'She was hiding behind my car as I was leaving, informing me she knew of us. If I didn't stop and… transfer my affections in her direction she'd tell Irene. I tried to placate her, said I'd inform her husband. Her car was blocking me in, I steered her towards it but she opened her handbag thrusting naked photographs at me… I angrily said I had to go. She furiously said she knew where. If I gave you up, she'd give up, she said, then sped off. I binned the photos, driving a diverse route to get here.'

Trudie sat mesmerized. She quietly uttered, 'Jean, wondered why she left your firm. She's been keeping tabs on me too?'

'I saw her when we were out of town. You went to the library,

'I spotted her waiting for you to come out, but she saw me and cleared off. When we left the theatre in Stratford I noticed her car, also outside Cranes, when you were buying sandals; she followed you into the store. I kept hoping she'd tire and give up.'

'What of her threat to tell Irene? Should we still go?'

He held her anxious body to him. 'Yes, we'll lose her in traffic. I want to be beside the seaside with my girl.' Kissing her cheek, he picked up her holdall, resolving to deal with Jean upon his return.

The break seemed to draw a veil over the stalker. En route to the coast Laurie suggested practising French lessons in bed. Trudie had giggled, her mirth rubbing off on him. She devised a quiz.

'First question. What does *je te desire* mean?'

Laurie said confidently. 'I desire you – and I do. My turn – *dis moi cherie.*'

'Tell me dearest. Bit harder please,' pleaded Trudie. 'Say something naughty,' she cajoled coquettishly.

'Ooh things are looking up. *Prends moi.*'

'What here? You can *prends moi* when we get to our hotel. I've got one. *Ca dans moi.*'

He lit up. '*Avec plaisir*' he told her huskily.

For two days the weather was kind, a soft breeze ruffling their hair. The hotel above the cliffs was a gem, the beach below sparkling with silica and pebbles. After evenings of dramatic sunsets, turquoise seeping into cyclamen, lovemaking was perfect to Laurie, almost to Trudie. She had a nagging thought, but unable to conjure up an image of what it was. As she felt it becoming clearer, it slipped away. She'd never met Jean but something was puzzling her. On bracing walks along the coastal path, she couldn't recall what it was.

Once back, Trudie made tea while Laurie petted Holly, who'd ignored her for being absent. This was how cats let their owners know it wasn't how to behave to a loved feline.

Trudie leant to kiss Laurie's cheek. 'Thank you, it's been fantastic. No pressures, no work, no stalkers!'

He put down his china cup, stroking the emerald ring he'd bought her one Christmas.

'You mean everything to me. Are you free Thursday evening?'

'I'll get my diary,' she said, moving towards her desk. 'I hide it from prying eyes now.'

'Prying eyes? Clients?'

'No, they don't come in here. Recently, a woman doing a garden survey, wanted information on which plants I have. It was a cold day so I asked her in, taking her through the conversatory. We came in here for the survey, but I took a call in the hall. Needing my diary, I returned, catching her slamming it shut, explaining she'd thought it was a gardening notebook! Seeing my frown, she made a quick exit. Laurie, what?'

'Was she tall, thin, fiftyish?' he asked, stunned.

'Yes, why?' Realisation dawned. 'Oh… it was Jean wasn't it? She saw our break in the diary.' Trudie slumped in the chair dejectedly.

Laurie was furious. 'That's how she was able to collar me as I was leaving for here. She'd have trailed you, then invented an excuse to feed her obsession, the diary was a bonus. Calculating bitch.'

'Stupid me, thought she was just a nosy parker.'

He shook his head. 'You weren't to know.'

'On holiday something was nagging. My brain, with what you revealed before we went, must have blocked it. She's been in here, drunk my coffee, and read my diary! God I could kill her!' Trudie exclaimed, with a ferocity rarely expressed.

10

Phoebe Cade gave instructions to her cleaner never to enter her late husband's den. Although dead four years, it seemed like weeks since Gordon had gone. Because of that, Mrs. C. had left the den's contents. He, if she hinted it warranted a lick of paint, would refuse. If his clutter was moved, he'd never find it. She'd simply shrug saying, 'If you insist.'

'I do,' he'd say decisively.

Mrs. Cade had enough to do with committees, WI, church, to fret over his den. Occasionally she'd dust, but knew not to move objects from their allotted place. One day in her haste to get to a meeting, she'd left Gordon a note. 'I have hovered in the den.' causing mirth in the family. Others were famous, 'gone shoping' and 'taken children swiming'.

'So you've been hovering in my den old girl have you?' Gordon had quipped. When committees met at their home, he jocularly called them an infestation. He'd been a guest at a naval dinner, inventing the phrase 'a wave of admirals.' Phoebe missed his quips.

When the hot spell at the end of May had gone, Phoebe tackled the den after Monday's WI. Her eyes alighted on the Georgian pine chest. Gordon had bought it at auction, stripped, waxed and polished it, leaving carrying handles on. He'd explained it was used by workers to transport their meagre possessions to hiring fairs. She leant the lid against the wall. 'Phew, some job this is going to be.' It was packed with files, photograph albums, pipes, candle boxes full too. She sat on the floor to begin.

The first packet of photographs was recognizeable, Watergate Bay. They'd rented a house near the beach, carpets of marmalade sand surrounding. Phoebe's late brother had adored it. The next packet was Sandwood Bay near Cape Wrath. Breathtaking, cliffs and pink sand.

Gordon's delight was Cornwall, Phoebe noticed packets with Fowey, Trebarwith Strand, Tintagel written on them. Rifling through, seeing the family smiling on picnics, in the sea, on beaches, and inside holiday homes, she'd extracted sixteen packets, cine film in round yellow cases, and tattered miscellaneous others.

Further into the box, she saw a black spider on top of crumpled paper. Phoebe winced, prodded to make certain it was dead. With a tissue, she popped it into the wastebin.

Flattening the papers creases, she saw poems, with a letter.

'My darling, I've just put the phone down from speaking to you. I'm keeping, well hidden, your missives sent to my private post box. *Mea culpa* but you turned me on. En route to London I bought a copy of *Forum* at the station.

A twinge of jealousy when you told me you were going for a massage. I wanted it to be me administering it. As for your admission that you write erotica, I'd adore to massage you whilst you read to me.

Oh, I feel a dose of self-abuse coming on. Until we meet, your boy sends kisses. Huggy.'

Phoebe was unnerved. A letter to an unknown woman from Hugo? Why was it here and in Gordon's possession? She couldn't tell Hugo, embarrassing. He's nearly fifty. *Forum* magazine? Top shelf publication no doubt, she thought. London. When? No date. Phoebe knew she couldn't give them to her son at any age! Even if I put them in an envelope, he may think I've read them – gosh I have.

She pondered on the discovery. Hugo having a private post office box! Probably when he was at London University. Gordon used to tell him to learn from an older woman. I was shocked, but man to man, I suppose it's OK. She pulled out more Wilfred Owen and Siegfried Sassoon poetry with another letter.

'Huggy, lovely to receive the poems. Brilliant for typing them on your laptop. I particularly like the Sassoon one concerning the German mother knitting by the fire, whilst her son sinks ever deeper into the mud. Terribly sad.

Naughty, reading *Forum*. Re the massage, it was the best non-erotic one ever. Yours are special, reaching places others don't. As you're mastering e-mails, we can send them with photographs attached, safer than letters. Without that password, no-one can discover them.

If you were free, we could be together, rather than stolen hours. Love the photograph of us at Tintagel. Barbara xxx

The phrase 'if you were free' stuck in Phoebe's head. Hugo WAS free when at university; these couldn't have been written then, but when he was married! Her jaw dropped. Gazing at the last one, September 25th 1996, to her horror she realized she was correct. 1996, he'd have been, let's see... born in 1958... yes 38.

Phoebe's mouth dried as full realization sank in. Hugo had been cheating with a Barbara. He married at thirty-five, Phoebe had thought he and Diana were happy, incomprehensible Hugo would contemplate extra-marital anything. She put the paperwork into Gordon's desk drawer.

The revelation so stunning, she left the room in a daze.

Downstairs, she poured a measure of Glenfidich. Eating supper, she couldn't concentrate on the TV documentary. In bed, she pondered what had happened to the photograph of her son in Tintagel, no inkling he'd been with a lover, or if Diana, his devoted wife knew. The main enigma was why this was in Gordon's den.

Next day she dragged books and miscellaneous items Gordon had steadfastly refused to throw out, onto the landing. She paused at four o'clock for tea and biscuits. Eight bin bags of what Phoebe considered 'dreadful old tat' joined the landing collection. Aching, she surveyed the den. Stationery, computer and the children's photographs remained, drawers had been cleared, car magazines, painting equipment and cigarette cards had been hauled out. What she hadn't foreseen was a letter stuffed into a candle box. Nervously, she read it.

'Huggy, thank you for the superb time in Cornwall. Clever boy, learning e-mails, easier than whispering furtively on the telephone. Shall expect a message toute suite. Practise transferring photographs from e-mails into a folder, I'll attach us in Tintagel. You've changed your password – wise!!

I agree one can love two people. Jealousy of your wife doesn't come into it. New passion has come late in life for us, which I treasure. I'm wearing freshwater pearls on one of the pictures – beautiful.
Until next week. Barbara. xxx'

Phoebe was further confused. Hugo's in his fiftieth year, not married until he was thirty-five, hardly a long time. Three years, if he was seeing this woman in 1996. How had he met her, what had she got that beautiful Diana hadn't? They'd lived in Surrey, a convenient commute to his London office. When she and Gordon had stayed, there'd been no hint of anything amiss.

Phoebe's normally brisk enthusiasm had vanished. She sat

hunched, hurting. An uncomplicated, old school, upper-middle class life, secure, with Gordon at the helm. Phoebe had been cossetted, problems kept from her; like the Queen Mother, friends had said.

Preparing dinner was an automatic exercise, brain full of the last days' findings. By nine-thirty, she crept, mentally drained, up the creaky staircase, puzzling why her husband possessed the letters. Perhaps he'd volunteered to hide the evidence, but wouldn't have condoned it. Exhausted, Phoebe fell into a confused sleep.

She awoke twice, freshwater pearls on her mind. Gordon had given Phoebe some for an anniversary, perhaps Hugo had thought it an appropriate gift. Not hers, she hoped. He wouldn't have taken her pearls, unthinkable, never done anything to hurt his parents. Mmm, until now. At five forty-five she awoke from dreaming of photographs, particularly the one attached to the letter she'd found.

Rising stiffly from the turbulent bed, she needed a hot drink. Studying photographs, blissful days in picturesque locations appeared, Tintagel too. They'd holidayed there, now Hugo had re-visited. Disgusted at his deceit, tired from early waking, she dozed on the sofa.

The slamming of the *Daily Telegraph* through the letterbox onto the hall floor startled her awake. Squinting at the mantelpiece clock, Phoebe was surprised it was eight forty-five. She made coffee, bathed, dressed in casual trousers and blouse, resolving to find that missing photograph. She attempted the supposedly easy crossword, giving up, discarding it to speak to Hugo at work. She mustn't wade in, but gently probe.

'Ma, good to hear from you. You don't usually phone here. Not ill are you?'

Phoebe re-assured him she was well, but looking at Tintagel photos, wondered if he'd been back there? 'I'm in a nostalgic mood,' she told him.

'Tintagel? Oh Ma, I prefer warmer climes. Gloomy old place, not going are you? Too cold.'

Phoebe hadn't expected such a lighthearted reply, curious.

She explained casually. 'No, I was rather low going through holiday snaps. Hearing your voice has cheered me up.'

'Good. We'll come up soon. Bye Ma.'

Even more mystified, after toast and Fortnums Breakfast Tea, she viewed more photos from the den. The last was labelled Looe Island, inhabited by two sisters in the nineteen thirties. The Cade's had been there by boat to look at wildlife.

The tattered case released a single photograph, cascading onto the carpet. 'They always land wrong side up, like toast,' observed Phoebe, reaching stiffly to retrieve it. It was blurred, the woman less than distinct. The man with her was one she recognized immediately. NOT HUGO. The familiar man smiling at the camera was older – someone she'd loved for over forty years.

Reeling from the worst shock of all, Phoebe spent ages immobile. The clock struck ten-thirty, temporarily arresting anguish. The phone had rung but she'd had no wish to answer. She sighed sadly. For the last two hours she'd been on automatic pilot, performing chores, but not switching off from the shock. Her fatherly husband, Gordon. Barely believing it, but knowing it to be true. Seeing Alison's Lexus, Phoebe put on a brave face, inviting her in.

'I'm having a sherry, won't you join me?' She saw Alison's surprise. 'Suppose it's a bit early. Did you telephone me earlier Alison?'

Alison nodded, sensing Mrs. C. was anything but her ebullient self.

'Ooh, small one, I'm driving. Is everything all right?'

Phoebe trudged slowly to the trolley. Shakily pouring sherry from the Waterford decanter, she sat, admitting quietly, 'I've cleared the den. Thing is, I've changed my mind... Sorry...'

Putting down her glass, Alison moved beside her. 'Is it memories?' Phoebe broke into sobs on her shoulder. 'Mrs. C, Tell me, whatever it is.'

Blowing her nose noisily, she insisted, 'Alison, call me Phoebe. I can't tell you unless you do,' she stammered. 'I've had a dreadful shock, worse this morning.'

Alison stroked her arm reassuringly. 'There's no one else here is there?'

'No, just thee and me. So very shocking,' she admitted gravely, folding and unfolding the tissue, looking crushed.

Phoebe began the sad tale. Alison too, thought Hugo was the deceiver, asking 'Do you want me to search with you?'

'No need.' Phoebe said resignedly. 'I found it this morning in a tattered packet. Not what I was expecting.'

Alison looked blank. 'I see... no... I don't. Was it someone you knew?'

'No, but the woman is immaterial. It was who was with her, looking deliriously happy,' she reported in a clipped tone. 'See for yourself.'

'I think I should.' Alison replied, mystified.

Phoebe lifted her large frame, trudging to the rosewood sofa table to show Alison photographic evidence. It was apparent who the man was. Wide-eyed, Alison shouted, 'Oh my God, Gordon!'

'There was I thinking Huggie was Hugo; bad enough. Then... worse. Alison, you feel you know someone, pillar of the community, loving husband and father. You imagine you're happy because you feel it.'

They discussed the chain of events. Phoebe announced firmly, 'I need what Americans call "closure," by seeing other things on his computer. My hurt's now anger. Alison, I can't do it on my own. Your age know, not mine, we wrote letters, phoned.'

'One big difficulty. Do you have the password to get onto the internet, where the photos will be attached to e-mails, if he hasn't learnt how to put them into a folder?'

Phoebe looked fraught. 'I've never even been on the computer,' she admitted, flopping onto the sofa dejectedly.

'Don't worry, let's go to the den and have a think.'

97

Phoebe sat on the pine box where the evidence had been unearthed. Alison asked, 'Are you sure this is what you want? You've had awful shocks and may incur more,' she said, holding Phoebe's hands.

'Monumental, no denying that. I can't deal with it until I find the rest. Can we see the photographs?' she pleaded.

'No problem seeing them if he's made a folder, don't need a password. If they're joined to e-mails though, the internet password's required. When was this laptop last opened?'

'Frances stayed here, wanting to research something. We knew the password for the laptop, Beethoven, Gordon's favourite composer; neither of us knew the internet password.'

Five minutes later, Alison, using the Beethoven password, accessed Gordon's files. 'Phoebe, it's obvious he didn't get round to transferring the photos into a folder.'

'Oh that's Gordon, modern technology defeated him. Does this mean the only way to view e-mails and pictures inside the... er... internet?'

'Mm, without the correct password, impossible.' She swivelled around. 'Here's what we do. While I pop to the loo, write down words he may have used as a password.'

When Alison returned, Mrs. C. looked dejected, several words on. 'Jupiter, our Labrador, terrible ripper as a puppy, books, shoes, plastic, wood. For months Gordon would declare, "By Jupiter, next time, he'll go!" We ceased calling him Inky and Jupiter he became. Let's try that, Cornish names, classic cars too.'

As a conventional man, Gordon would have used a conventional word, Alison imagined. He was though then, far from that. Mr. Cade – an affair! Phoebe, though shattered, was determined to 'crack the code'.

'Sure? We can stop if you'd rather.'

'Over my supine corpse,' was the definite reply.

Alison read the list. Jupiter, Alpha-Romeo, Morgan, Lagonda,

Bude, Scottish locations. None worked. She suggested family names he may have used.

Phoebe declared, 'I doubt he'd stoop to using Frances or Hugo's name. Still, I didn't know he'd do this. Shall we try them, Alison?'

'We must.'

Alison tapped Hugo in the password box, no joy. A chilling thought hit her. She turned to Phoebe, asking breathlessly, 'Remember why you thought it was Hugo? How were the letters signed?' Her eyes widened. So did Phoebe's. In unison they shouted. 'HUGGY!'

11

When Stephen and Alison had discussed Henry, they felt happier. For the next month Stephen worked on Julia's garden, performed concerts and gave music lessons. He didn't fret if two days passed and no calls from Alison.

One afternoon, Stephen had downed tools from a tiring branch lopping session at Julia's, discarding gardening gloves, he thought of the irony of the situation. He was a concert pianist, hands his livelihood. The last thing he should be doing was digging, weeding, pruning, planting, mending fences. Needing extra money initially, concert dates were now abundant. Soon he'd finish Julia's garden, resolving to do no more.

Soaking in a hot bath later, he recalled asking Alison to The Bridgewater Hall. They'd made love.

'What a performance!' Alison had declared.

Stephen had replied huskily, 'It takes two. Speaking of performance, do you fancy watching me play this Friday lunchtime – my Bridgewater debut?'

She'd nuzzled his neck, squeezing him enthusiastically. 'The Bridgewater Hall!'

'Steady on, it's half an hour, some time before an evening

concert there. Now that would be an accolade, following in the footsteps of Demidenko, Hough, and Kissin!'

'Hey, how many from your college have played there? It's a real coup.'

'Suppose it is. Shoppers, office workers and music fans usually. I'm quite excited myself, especially as you're off to make me a cuppa.'

Bashing him with a pillow, Alison had bowed. 'On my way, your Majesty.'

'Er, my mother wants to visit next week. You won't mind will you?'

'Don't you want me to meet her?'

'I'd love you to,' he'd hesitated... 'I wondered if you'd think it too soon. I don't want to risk our relationship and...'

'Risk, you said she was lovely?'

Stephen had replied, 'She is. I was tentative cos so far it's been you and me.'

'We're fine. I look forward to it.'

***

Alison's week had begun with unbelievable news of Gordon Cade's betrayal. On Friday, Stephen's recital was a triumph, worthy of the loud applause it received. She hadn't mentioned Phoebe's revelations. Poor Phoebe, Alison had stayed until the mystery was unravelled.

'HUGGY!' they'd exclaimed simultaneously. Unsuccessful with internet passwords, they'd both alighted on the obvious one. Alison imagined Gordon would have thought it safer to leave photographs attached to his lover's e-mails within the internet. Clicking the password box, holding her breath, Alison tentatively typed – Huggy. Watching the Yahoo site gradually appear, she shrieked, 'Eureka!'

Tense with anticipation, Phoebe managed a thin smile,

patting Alison's hand. 'We've cracked the code. Go ahead Alison.'

'Ok, it's loading e-mails. Look – 2005 last time he sent one. Not many.'

'He hardly used the computer.'

Alison scrolled back, e-mails received were business and social, advising meetings. 1997 appeared.

'Ah, September 1997.' It proved to be unfruitful, from an old colleague. The next message was May, again not what they sought. An attachment was seen with an e-mail dated January 1997.

'Huggy, back from holiday. You sounded strange on phone. Barbara. xxxxxxx'

Alison observed Phoebe's anger.

'What's that paperclip thing?'

'An attachment Phoebe.'

No photograph, but a Salcombe hotel menu.

'Hmph,' snorted Phoebe, 'somewhere else he's taken her.'

The next e-mails received were from 1996, three business, three Barbara's. December 1996 produced one from Barbara, looking forward to their meeting on December 18th. The two earlier that year were rather graphic, Alison was embarrassed for Phoebe, but told to reveal whatever 'silly rubbish' there was.

Two photographs, one of Barbara in underwear and one labelled, 'Pearls'. Phoebe dejectedly said, 'Freshwater pearls and not mine. I have three rows, hers are one. How original! You'd have thought he'd have given her something different, never did have any imagination,' she scowled, derisorily. 'Is that it?'

'Phoebe, we should look at the Sent file. Are you ready?' she asked sympathetically.

Phoebe sniffed, agreeing.

'Let's begin in February 1996, when he first used the computer and work forward,' Alison suggested.

None sent by Gordon until one to Barbara.

'Darling, clever or what!? You persuaded me to learn e-mail, so no one else could see. Harvest Supper soon, millions of kisses, Huggy.'

Alison saw Phoebe reach into her dress pocket for her handkerchief. 'Oh how could I not have known? I knew he visited Cornwall, but on business I thought. Such deceit.'

'Three more, be brave.' Alison urged.

Phoebe dabbed her cheeks, whispering 'Very well.'

Next was October 1996.

'Barbara, in a few months – Cornwall, restaurants, dinners at your cosy nest. Lovemaking undreamed of by this late middle-aged man. Until Monday – Huggy. xxxxxxxxxxxxx'

'The bloody rotten cad!' exploded Phoebe, shaking. 'You'd think we'd never had a sex life! Thought things were all right in the bedroom, the rat! Can't have been enough.' She quietened her voice. 'Sorry Alison I…'

'No, don't dare be sorry! Let's do the last two. Look November 1996.'

'Barbara, concerning our tiff. You are wrong to suppose I no longer care. I have responsibilities; difficult leading two lives. You don't have to cover tracks. Please forgive our misunderstanding. Huggy. xxxxxxxxx'

'Oh cracks in the affair?' Phoebe remarked sarcastically. 'Responsibilities, fancy remembering those. Next please Alison.'

'February 1997.'

'Barbara, we've been together seven months or so. You're a free spirit, I'm not, having half a lifetime with my wife. She's been devoted, cared for us marvellously.

We have a bond which I've ashamedly broken. Things became heated on Monday, you said wounding words.

Please don't think badly of me, one can love two people, you said that yourself. What I cannot do is keep up the appalling deceit. My wife deserves better. Over Christmas, I contemplated my actions. I'll miss what we had, but we have to cease meeting.

There is another reason. On New Year's Day I went into hospital for three days with a heart condition. Bypass surgery may be necessary.

The stress doing underhand stuff has contributed to my condition. My motivations for ceasing our affair are love for Phoebe and my heart condition. I will live the remainder of my time with her. On Christmas Day I observed her tiredness from her efforts for our family. Seeing her relate to our grandchildren, I felt such gratitude. I'm sorry. Love Huggy. xxx'

Both women read with stunned surprise. Phoebe uttered quietly. 'An unexpected ending. If I hadn't seen that, I'd never have forgiven him.'

'Wait Phoebe, there's a reply below his e-mail... tagged on at the end.'

'Huggy, so upset you have swept me out of your life. It's too painful to look at anything you have sent me during our affair, so am returning all letters to your post office box. I feel used, and want to post them through your home letterbox. However I am not spiteful, but heartbroken. You though, are a coward, our relationship worth so little that you couldn't have told me your decision in person. Your wife is welcome to such a cad. In shock. Barbara.'

'Ah, that explains why his letters to her were in his den.'

Phoebe sighed wearily. 'Gordon Cade having a bit on the side, no one would have believed it. Alison, I don't want to see this anymore, let's have a Queen Mum shall we?'

She saw a bemused Alison, and smiled. 'Oh it's a family saying. The late Queen Mother's tipple, gin and dubonnet, a real dry martini! She was partial to large ones, so am I now! I'll get you a non-alcoholic drink though, you're driving. You close the ghastly affair, let's have drinks on the terrace – it's a beautiful day. Shouldn't be laughing, it was ages ago and I've had worse shocks.' She paused, eyebrows raised. 'Oh no, I haven't have I? Still, I'll deal with things, and as young folks say, move on.'

Alison, as Phoebe trudged out of the den, knew she was putting on a brave face. She knew the 'moving on' would take some time.

12

Without Jonathan's love, Julia would have found it impossible to live under the same roof as David. Upon her return from Warwickshire, though, David had suggested they lead separate lives within the marriage. She'd been puzzled he hadn't asked about her trip.

It then became relatively easy to see Jonathan. His house in Birches Green, a few miles off, was her haven. Only Alison knew their secret. Julia was certain if David found out, the status quo wouldn't remain, the balloon would definitely burst. He took care of Poppy one evening a week, when Julia had supposed beauty appointments. Deceit was now what she practised, like David.

Initial chemistry between Julia and Jonathan was strong, but a bond had crept in. It seemed like commitment but they had no illusions, even though she and David were leading virtually separate lives.

David, though, drove Julia into the village one early September Saturday, dropping Poppy at her Father's, saying he wanted to put on a show of togetherness in front of Guy. Mind games, Julia had thought, puzzled. An unpredictable encounter was also on the cards.

Stephen had invited his Mother to meet Alison, tentatively

mentioning the age gap, but Trudie had confirmed it was his life and she was certain he knew how to live it.

Before leaving her cottage, Trudie gave Holly a 'head flattener'. She'd coined the explicit term, now both she and Stephen used it. For the three days at Stephen's, Georgina would look after Holly, take in an expected parcel and put the dustbin out for emptying on Friday.

Trudie had elected to drive to Lower Birches. Last time was Christmas 2007 on a rainy day, but this September Thursday, autumn was displaying her colours. Wild winds had spattered the windscreen overnight with acid leaves from the graceful Robinia. Wiping them off, Trudie was thankful her journey up the M5 and M6 wouldn't be in deluges of rain. She glanced back, she'd miss Holly, but excited to see Stephen. Wondering what Alison would be like, she set off in bright sunshine.

Trudie had spent day one with Stephen, meeting Alison on the second at her Edwardian house, finding her charming. Conversation had been easy, both having much in common, including tortoiseshell cats. On the way back to Stephen's, Trudie had said she liked Alison.

Stephen had piano tuition to give in Ryelands the following morning. Trudie hadn't ventured out last time, Christmas Eve, the weather hadn't been kind. This Saturday had a cloudless sky and Indian Summer warmth. She pulled on a sky blue leather jacket over white trousers and navy tee-shirt.

Locking the door, she decided to walk the mile to the village, to shed some weight gained from comfort eating. She turned into Church Street to buy a birthday card and visit the fourteenth century church. The town's Georgian architecture had been well maintained, even new-builds were in keeping.

Writing the card at Trinity Tearooms, the cafetiere half full, she was in no rush to leave the aromatic café, with its white bone china and classical music. Reading the *Telegraph* gardening section, she felt contentment.

Julia and David had called at the teashop so Julia could have paracetemol with a drink. The stress of living with his persecutions brought on tension headaches. Grudgingly he went to order while Julia sat down. Engrossed in an article on Sissinghurst, Trudie hadn't seen them arrive. Passing Julia's table to return the paper to the rack, the dark-haired woman seemed familiar.

'Who would I know here except Stephen?' she pondered, seeing the woman nervously fiddling with a teaspoon. This train of thought unlocked Trudie's memory. 'Hello, we've met before haven't we?' she asked tentatively, noticing Julia flinch. Trudie sat opposite. 'It IS you. NEC Exhibition Birmingham. We chatted in the café. Now we've met in another.'

Julia cautiously whispered. 'I thought you lived further south.'

'I do but I'm visiting my son, didn't realise you lived here. You're a beauty therapist aren't you? You advised massaging my cat.'

Julia hoped David was far enough away not to hear. Anxiety grew, realising who she was with in Birmingham. She wished someone would order cappuccino so the machine's volcanic steam would prevent him overhearing. The tearoom was full of chattering shoppers, but a nervous smile was all Julia could produce.

'Hope massage is working,' Julia replied tensely, not looking in David's direction.

Trudie continued. 'Amazing crossing paths again. Where's that tall, dark, handsome husband? Was that Warwickshire hotel good?'

Julia froze, quickly glancing at David staring at the floor, his eyes narrowing with concentration. She knew the signs.

'Please excuse me. I have a headache and my er... friend's getting juice so I can take a painkiller,' Julia told her shakily.

Trudie stood up. 'Hope it goes soon, next time I'll book a treatment perhaps, bye.'

As David approached, his glare said it all. Her headache was going to get worse.

Trudie exited into Church Street, crisp autumn air welcomed after the stuffy tearoom. Walking two hundred yards to Trinity Church, she thought of the woman she'd re-met, wondering if Stephen knew her, he gardened for a Julia.

As she entered, her attention was diverted near the west door, a history of the fourteenth century church. Sitting in a pew reading of barons and women they married over the centuries, she recognized names from Worcestershire and Warwickshire; Sheldon and Throckmorton, big landowners in Henry the Eighth's era. Money had married money, power the goal. One's daughter had to marry well to acquire wealth and land. She'd seen Cheshire names in Worcestershire churches.

Scanning the Requiem programme, she recalled Stephen saying behind choral music there was spiritual agony. On the cover was written, 'those that sing, pray twice'. Both, Trudie thought, were true.

She opened the old oak door to leave. In the distance, she could see Julia and a man approaching a black BMW, looking glum, like a couple after a tiff. Gaze slightly averted, she saw telling expressions.

Wandering into Stephen's garden later, she picked two half open roses from the Sir Edward Elgar bush she'd given Stephen, reminding him of his home county. Vibrant red stood out against the whitewashed brick wall. Inhaling the perfume stimulated memories of Laurie. He'd once scattered scarlet rose petals on her bed. They'd made love on top of them. He'd been the rose-covered wall keeping her safe; which had crumbled with his disappearance. Perhaps she was better alone, but there lurked a longing to find him.

***

It was Rex who'd recommended Trudie visit Cornwall in September 2008. She assisted him with his cashmere business, meeting two days a month. He'd gone in three years from counselling client to employer, explaining her attractiveness, intelligence, and warm personality were an asset. Extra money, and travel a bonus, raised Trudie from the depths when Laurie had gone. Rex was the epitome of an English gentleman. Late fifties, widowed, Colonial background, product of British public schools, he rarely showed emotion, upper lip stiff, brought up by nannies; parents in a perpetual round of cocktail parties and military functions.

Trudie would book two rooms in a hotel, he'd collect her, their days busy, companionship a comfort to both. Rex told her she'd brought happiness into his solitary existence, jolting him out of a serious outlook with her humour and intellect. Living in Berkshire, life was work and watching rugger; so he enjoyed Trudie's company enormously. Clients liked her, reflected in their goodwill.

Away on business, he'd confessed his feelings. Tactfully telling him she loved him in the brotherly sense and would he settle for that, he'd agreed, giving her head a doting kiss.

In August 2008 Trudie had travelled by train to London. As it snaked along the final half mile of track, she gathered up her carpetbag, slipping on her red silk jacket over her red and white shift dress. She wore flat shoes in London, even a short walk in heels was tiring. Trudging up familiar platform 13 at Euston, she spotted Rex. His white beard, once so dark, stood out a mile. When she'd met him, she'd noticed he resembled Tzar Nicholas. He'd gone into Sotheby's for a valuation on an enamel box, the receptionist fetching the valuer, who'd been astonished at this mirror image of the long dead Romanoff.

Seeing her weaving past other passengers, Rex waved from the top of the slope, greeting her with a discreet peck on the cheek. Taking her carpetbag, he escorted her to the taxi rank. She knew they were dining at The Royalty, from liveried doorman to the maitre d'hotel, the employees possessed old fashioned courtesy, no irritating music in the elegant dining-room; a rare relief.

With roast beef and charlotte russe eaten, Rex hailed a taxi for Sotheby's. Trudie was not required until next morning, so viewed their jewellery sale. At the hotel, she took an afternoon nap, until ten past five. Over dinner, Rex related holidays in Porthcurno, Cornwall, Trudie saying she wanted to visit a friend not seen for years. By the end of the evening Rex had persuaded her to go, insisting on paying, including a car service on her Toyota Corolla. A bonus for being worth her weight in gold, he'd said.

'Do gardens en route, stay one night at The Nobody Inn at Doddiscombleigh. It's spiffing.'

After their business appointment next morning, Rex waved her off at Euston. At Watford Junction, she'd abandoned the *Evening Standard*, thoughts full of holiday plans.

Holly's aloofness made Trudie chuckle. When prawns appeared, Holly forgot her annoyance at Trudie's absence. Weaving through her legs, miaowing plaintively in anticipation of her favourite dinner, she was at one with her mistress.

Pointing to a prawn Holly had missed, Trudie promised Cornish pilchards soon. Holly was unmoved, stretching legs up the freezer, giving an appealing silent miaow for more. Eating the rest of the prawns with salad, Trudie then went to bed. Thinking of her proposed trip, she snuggled down resolving to plan it tomorrow.

***

September Sunday fair weather was ideal for motoring to Knighthayes Court, a Somerset Burgess house and gardens.

Trudie stayed at a Victorian guest house near Tiverton, which didn't live up to its internet publicity; snail trails on the carpet and mosquitoes floating around the dining table chandelier. A meagre 8 a.m. breakfast disappointed, then finding bedding had gone, no chance for a rest before moving on at ten. The bedcover remained; her lip curled to think it hadn't been clean the previous night.

'The previous night.' Trudie thought, yawning. 'A nightmare.'

The proprietors had entertained friends to a bridge evening. From Trudie's room adjoining the hall, there'd been to-ing and fro-ing on floorboards, up and down, in and out, doors banging, people shouting. At ten-fifteen, the guests left – loudly. Luckily Trudie had packed ear plugs. When the ten o'clock TV news ended, in went the plugs, out went she. At 6.30 a.m. more noise, a toddler arriving with his mother, to be cared for by the proprietress, who shouldn't be running a guesthouse. Rush, noise and chaos; the last thing Trudie wanted.

Loading her travelbag into the car, she thought Hilltop a misnomer, Chaos Castle more accurate. Her mood improved heading for Hartland Point on the Northern Coast. Docton Mill Gardens had a best cream tea award, needed to make up for the awful breakfast.

Snaking through winding lanes under a slate sky, Trudie thought she'd never arrive. Realizing the map was in the boot, she pulled onto a grass verge, stretching to unstiffen from the uncomfortable bed. The hedge was low enough to view the sea, over the cornfield. A coastal breeze caressed, fragile poppies quivered, like Trudie holding onto life in all weathers.

Passing Hartland Abbey, a sign loomed for the tearooms. Trudie wandered down stony steps by a shallow stream. Aromatic smells emanated from the cottage kitchen. Trudie sat underneath a sheltered terrace, the waitress hoping the Labradors weren't being a nuisance. Watching people slithering down the slope, there'd evidently been an English soaking, rivulets trickling over cobbles.

Enjoying coffee, cream, and a cherry scone, Trudie realised no-one else was alone. Mostly couples, even two Labradors. It would have been pleasant to join someone, but no one looked in her direction. Seeing couples made her yearn for what they had, chatting, sharing, linking arms.

'How can I live without the love of my life?' she thought regretfully. 'Stop it.' she reprimanded. 'I have a talented son, friends, cat, lovely house, sufficient money, satisfying job, marvellous memories. Painful memories too, wanting what I had, having to do without it.' Deprivation made her hungrier for Laurie. Emotionally, disappearance was a powerful weapon.

Overhearing someone breathlessly saying they'd walked the slippery path to the waterfall, and seeing their exhaustion, Trudie did the gardens instead. Half an hour was enough, the ground squelchy, viewing lush greenery proving difficult. The sun broke through, flooding the valley en route to Boscastle.

Valency Valley Hotel was quality, privacy and peace. Trudie read information on the area. Valency meant millhouse, the stream had powered waterwheels, beeches used for charcoal in manufacturing gunpowder. The woods were full of oak, hazel, beech, holly, willow and ash, jays, deer, fritillary butterflies and a carpet of violets. Prints of dippers and wagtails graced the hotel staircase.

Dinner over, in her room she left the drapes open, as dusk descended. Whispering beech leaves and shivering pines surrounded the hotel, peace prevailed. Later a man trudged up the drive, a wagging torch lighting his path. Night had closed in.

Trudie remembered books she'd packed. In pyjamas, she unzipped her second bag, having searched for days, before discovering it languishing in the summerhouse. Zips had been fastened to prevent spiders emerging unannounced.

Kneeling on soft carpet, Trudie lifted out two biographies, one novel. She'd often begun novels, finding them boring, so had selected a Joanna Trollope to re-read. The holdall felt heavier than it should have been. Touching a bulge under a zip, she heard the crackle of paper.

113

Unzipping, grasping the wad, she shuddered, realising they were misplaced when moving house. Rocking, she clutched them to her breast. A door to a room full of sweet memories banged open.

'Praise God,' she uttered emotionally, 'I thought I'd never find them.' Sniffing, she read.

'Darling, let me remark on questions you raised. All my life I've waited to meet you, not imagining I could be so close to a woman. My commitments and love for you, tear me apart.

My desire for your happiness transcends my own, please be patient and wait for me. Laurie xxx'

With thumping heart, Trudie re-read the letter with a cocktail of emotions. The legacy of involvement with a married man; grief was the price she'd paid. Feeling Laurie's presence strongly, she read the second.

'Darling, I miss you, part of me ripped out, endurable because of our love. Bitter-sweet. Bitter as you're not with me and sweet because you're the loveliest soul.

I'm bound hand and foot, my inability to be with you has laid me low. I want to hold you, be strong for us. My situation prevents this. Please be patient until I'm back from the court case. Endless love, Laurie. xx'

She'd been forced to live without him, perhaps he'd ended everything. When his wife had died of a heart attack, Trudie supposed they'd meet frequently. Not so. He'd called round to say he wouldn't be in contact for a short while because of the funeral. They'd held each other nervously, neither mentioning the future. He was also devastated, that was apparent. No matter how discontented he'd been with Irene, they had children. Trudie told him she understood; he promised to call the day after the funeral, and did.

Ten days on he'd visited again, looking terrible. Wanting to hold him, wondering if he'd think it appropriate, she'd merely listened. He'd sombrely spoken of the funeral, having to sort Irene's things, insisting he needed 'to do all this now so I can concentrate on work I've had to put on ice.'

Laurie had received news so severe it prevented plans to see Trudie. Not having heard from him, she'd telephoned, his manner evasive; she'd felt like a stranger. He'd falteringly admitted he was weary, but couldn't bring himself to admit the very thing he should have.

'Are you ill, depression, what? Don't shut me out,' she'd pleaded, in vain. Irene's death had been heightened by a terrible discovery. Emotional pain wouldn't allow Laurie to share it.

Shivering, Trudie climbed under the duvet. Old wounds were being re-opened, but she read a serious letter from before Laurie's wife had died.

'Darling, have to cancel Wednesday. Irene has been questioning my whereabouts, saying she rang the golf club and I was absent, wondered if she should save dinner. I was wary, she never does that.

I pray this has nothing to do with the stalker. I haven't heard from obsessive Jean since she moved to Scotland.

This is hardly a love letter. Forgive my pessimism, I'm erring on the side of caution. Let's wait until next week, to alter the pattern of my "golf" evenings. I'll come during the day. I have to be cautious for our sakes. Laurie xx

Trudie realised this may have been a forewarning; Laurie could have been right to fear the stalker's involvement.

Amazingly she slept, in spite of complicated dreams. A ray of sun filtered through the drapes, pleasing on her face. Trudging from the bathroom at seven-fifteen, she plugged in the kettle. Nine hours rest had made up for poor sleep the night before. She was pleased to see a cafetiere and ground coffee, not instant packets.

Peeping through tulip-patterned curtains, she saw a clear day. Sunshine was forecast according to the dinner waitress. Trudie wanted to see Boscastle fully recovered from the flood devastation four years previously. At the Information Centre by the harbour, she'd be able to see the floods video and Thomas Hardy connections.

She slid into bed to watch local news on television. The waitress's forecast was correct, no rain. Trudie touched the sheaf of papers. 'Laurie, you're gone I know not where, your ghost haunting me. These precious letters, thought I'd lost those as well as you.' She read each one.

'Trudie, I meant it when I told you yesterday how you are – the most stunningly beautiful woman, the kindest gentlest person. Your beauty matches your spirit. I think of you in superlatives. Massaging your feet, I was filled with deepest love, knowing I'd have to go, always torture. I want to be by your side constantly. So as Philip Larkin put it, "we should be careful of each other. We should be kind whilst there is still time." Until Tuesday, your warmth surrounds me. Laurie.'

Laurie was far from dead and buried in her life. No escape, but she didn't want one. A change of scenery, new faces couldn't eradicate memories. Replacing the letters in the overnight bag, they'd resurrected unfinished business. A favourite poem of Laurie's by Edna St. Vincent Millay came to mind, 'total absence is so dreadful, time does not bring relief. You have all lied.'

Showering, she hummed 'I'm Gonna Wash That Man Right Out Of My Hair.' Not what she wanted, but like a wet animal, no matter how much she shook, droplets remained. Trudie likened this analogy to hope, knowing she'd always wonder where he was and if she'd ever get a sudden telephone call.

Putting the past away, she saw her reflection in the mirror. Losing weight when Laurie had disappeared, lately she'd neglected exercise, gaining half a stone. Aware exercise had an anti-depressant effect, she rued not taking it as medicine. In navy leggings and white tee-shirt, she brushed her blonde hair into a pony tail clip, resolving to begin after her holiday. For now, a Cornish breakfast awaited and Boscastle beckoned.

At the National Trust shop, Trudie purchased a miniature rose – Bodmin Beauty – and a Beningfield book on orchards for Lizzie. In the newly-built Harbour Lights café, she thought of their friendship, fractured somewhat when Lizzie hadn't passed her 11 Plus exam for a grammar school and Trudie had. Lizzie, influenced by her mother, had let jealousy mar their friendship, with hurtful words through inverted snobbery, for some time. Trudie's mother had made it worse, insisting she was better off without Lizzie. Trudie had been the peacemaker, diverting hurt into schoolwork, continuing to write lighthearted letters to Lizzie. After a few months, Lizzie had settled happily into her new school and the friendship had healed.

Stirring coffee, Trudie knew self-sacrifice was self-neglect. When we set aside our needs for the benefit of another, we can become doormats. When Laurie was stressed over their situation, especially the stalker, Trudie had put herself last. His happiness had become more important than hers, proving detrimental. A harrowing learning curve. The one who leaves is not the one enduring the silence. Laurie had said she was the most warm-hearted person he'd ever met. Kind words, but he'd still left.

An irritating couple from Melbourne joined her. Their incessant babble about Born Again Christians, thrusting pamphlets on sin, rankled. They quoted 'love thy neighbour as

117

thyself,' which she had no wish to hear after thoughts of self-sacrifice. What did these insensitive bigots know of her life? Spotting her gold cross around her neck, they'd assumed she was like them. She wasn't. Enduring ten minutes of their quoting Matthew this and Luke that, Trudie escaped.

Thomas Hardy had connections with Boscastle, re-designing one of the churches. Trudie bought a Hardy book, and saw a video of the flood restoration programme. Later, she began reading *The Girl With Blue Eyes*. Lamorna Birch, her favourite Cornish artist, wasn't represented locally, different part of Cornwall, but a vibrant oil of Strangles Beach tempted. Trudie resisted, the Dorset seascape Laurie had given her had real meaning.

At dinner Trudie read more Hardy, concerning a woman with two suitors. One would be wonderful, she thought ruefully. Full of crab and vegetables, she declined dessert; *From Here To Eternity* was on television. She'd watch for just one erotic scene, Deborah Kerr and Burt Lancaster coming out of the sea. Compulsive viewing, but would make her long for what she'd had.

As Deborah Kerr lay in abandonment amongst crashing foam, Burt Lancaster's hungry look was so arousing. When he laid his soaking body across hers, mouth raining hard down on her submissive lips, the scene made Trudie short of breath. Too overwhelming to deny, thinking of Laurie, she gave herself pleasure.

Next morning Trudie awoke from a deep rest, the sensual beach scene had ensured it. Driving to Pencarrow she'd reflected on its excitement, the actors having become Laurie and herself. In the grounds of the stately home, she'd met two women with their rescue dog, joining them for tea, discussing pets; a pleasant break from travelling alone. Reluctantly bidding them farewell, she proceeded to Lizzie's ten miles on.

13

Lizzie Stafford, one of Trudie's few friends still married, lived near Loswithiel. Her husband, Tom, had a successful sailing school, ill health making him retire at sixty-one. She was pleased he went on frequent coastal walks, it gave them breathing space; retirement could be a strain.

They'd resided in Fowey, Daphne de Maurier country, when Trudie had visited years before, but downsized since to a four bedroom bungalow with an uninterrupted view of rolling hills and the Bodmin railway. Approaching Wenford Road, Trudie imagined what Lizzie might look like now. Grey hair? Heavier? Smart casual and modern, or as other women of their age – beige and brown everything. Wonder if she has the tarty gold stilettos from the sixties? Don't suppose she hangs on to things as I do. Hm, or people either? How wrong she was to be.

Turning into the seventh entrance on the right, she saw a slender woman with short blonde hair, dressed in a pink and white tee-shirt and pink skirt. Almost jumping onto the pebbles, crunching towards her, arms wide, Trudie enveloped her warmly.

There were grins, uproarious laughs, and catch-ups that evening. From the moment they walked inside, conversation flowed. The house, Trudie said, was just her style, she loved modern even though her cottage was traditional. No matter how opposite they were emotionally, they had similar taste in design and fashion. The oblong kitchen was all white, appearing even larger with reflected light from the attached conservatory. It had been run down; they'd employed professionals to transform two bathrooms, kitchen, and install the conservatory overlooking the lawn and distant hills. Trudie admired sparkly granite worktops from a Camborne mine.

Settling on a bamboo sofa, the evening sun bathing the neat garden, Trudie saw dahlias standing to attention along the fence – orderly like Lizzie. A briar rose clung to the neat toolshed. Turning, she saw a framed piece of embroidery. It read 'By thy scent my soul is ravished' encircling a rose. Trudie knew the quotation by Persian poet Sadi, but had no idea Lizzie had done lovely embroidery and quiltwork.

As Lizzie made elderflower cordial, Trudie teased, 'To think I imagined you might be a grey, beige trousered, sensible-shoed pensioner.' She ducked as Lizzie gasped, throwing a cushion at her. They collapsed giggling.

'Perish the thought. I see you're still sexy.'

Trudie was genuinely surprised. 'Me, sexy? Chance would be a fine thing. You know of Laurie.'

'A little on the phone, but not in detail. I can hear it now we're on our own, Tom's in Aberdovey until tomorrow evening.'

'If it gets boring, tell me. Couples tend to find singles lives tedious.'

Lizzie kindly replied, 'I'm your friend with my own mind. I want to hear whatever you want to tell me. Over forty years married doesn't mean it's been plain sailing, 'scuse the pun. Sometimes I've envied your single status. You look surprised; Tom was possessive, no affairs I know of, but oh, his meddling, tempers, control. As for returning your letters, when I caught him tearing one up, I twigged he was trying to cause a rift. You wrote with your new address, he intercepted that too.'

Trudie admitted, 'Not wanting to cause trouble, I ceased contact.'

'That's why I rang, explaining his mid-life crisis, not admitting he was always like that.' Locking the conservatory doors, she noticed Trudie's amazement. 'Sure you don't want wine?'

'No thanks – alcohol brings on headaches. Surely life hasn't been so traumatic I'll need a stiff drink. I've been widowed, brought up Stephen, and when I did find happiness – a married man. When he was finally free... he vanished. Now YOU look surprised.'

Lizzie became less facetious. 'I know wifey died, not why Laurie vanished. What did he look like?'

Trudie sipped her drink. 'Think Robert De Niro. He...'

'Robert De Niro!? No wonder you want to find him!' She giggled. 'Shame he didn't look like Dirk Bogarde. You were mad on him, are you still?'

'Of course! Robert De Niro, but taller, dark hair, his build, and oh those eyes! I saw *Falling in Love*, that film with Meryl Streep, where they've picked up the wrong parcels in the book shop. If you haven't seen the film – believe me, it got into my soul.

Four years on I'm incomplete without him. Irene had died of a heart attack, so I expected our affair to continue. He may have felt responsible, I didn't dare ask, he looked broken. Three weeks on he was more depressed, saying there was nothing to discuss. Intimacy ceased as soon as he was bereaved,' Trudie shrugged. 'I never saw leaving on his face.

Rex and I went to Tenbury on business. He said Laurie would be round with red roses and lingerie soon. Rex's emotional level was peripheral, I knew he wouldn't understand.'

Lizzie shook her head, 'Oh how naïve.'

'Well Rex has been ruled by women, ayah in India, Matron at school, unemotional mother and wife, but he means well. Three days in Shropshire and no call from Laurie, so I rang both home and mobile number. No answer.' Trudie's speech faltered. 'I rang his office, told he was on holiday. Some holiday, he never came back.'

From looking down, Lizzie, touched by Trudie's revelation, slowly raised her head.

'When you said you'd split, I never knew it meant so much. You look like you've only just been told the bad news. Intriguing why you haven't been able to locate him. Or have you and he's with someone else?'

Trudie flicked a hovering tear. 'I was shocked and bewildered he hadn't told me of a holiday. As days passed and he hadn't answered his phone, my hurt increased. No replies a week later, I felt angry and confused. This wasn't the Laurie I knew. You sure you want me to go on? It's rather a saga.'

'Don't dare stop. This is déjà vu for me.'

'Oh, OK,' Trudie frowned, intrigued. 'I rang his office after ten days, told he'd left the practice and no forwarding address. I'd been to his house the previous week, no reply, then went again – A For Sale sign! I rang the estate agents for a viewing – surreal.'

Mesmerized, Lizzie uttered, 'I'll bet.'

'Dazed, I went from room to room. The retired viewing agent drank tea from his flask while I looked for clues. Everything was immaculate, polished, carpets pristine. Not the actions of a depressed man who'd lost his wife and walked out on his mistress. None of his personal things were evident.

'The agent said it wasn't in a good state when they did the valuation. The owner had it cleaned, within days he'd moved out.'

Lizzie spoke, wide-eyed. 'I can guess what you asked him next.'

'Yes, and he didn't know, the owner was widowed and needed a quick sale. The agent said, "I'm a widower meeself, I knows how he feels." The estate agents forwarded a letter to him, to no avail.'

'Surely he's been traceable?'

'You don't think I let it rest there? Didn't know where his son was in America, nor his daughter's married name. The internet proved fruitless, his old place appearing.'

Lizzie asked, 'A private detective?'

'Done that. Four months after Laurie vanished, I engaged a Worcester chap who said it would be a doddle; he was hopeless and I begrudged money wasted. Why didn't I keep my self-respect and forget Laurie's unforgiveable behaviour, scarcely loving.'

Lizzie nodded, thoughtfully.

'I was in shock at his estranged wife's death, his changed behaviour, then desertion. I tried to rationalize it and my reaction, but I'd lost my soul to him. I carried on with my job, and Paula in Cheltenham was so supportive. Stephen too, but he had his own life.

'I've avoided places where I went with Laurie. Kissing gates on walks; a pang when I encounter one. The missing, how awful it is, no sharing music, nature, humour, sex. The whole picture, once colourful, now a blank canvas before me. Perhaps he's committed suicide. I know someone who did, it brought as much destruction to his family as a bomb exploding. I'm facing a lifetime of confusion, in the dark.'

Lizzie shook her head, subdued. Usually contained, emotions tidy like the house, she moved to sit by Trudie. 'Terrible, from what you've said, he worshipped you. If only you had closure.'

'Closure, painful, but an ending. Relationships concern investment not bankruptcy. I'd mislaid his letters but ecstatic to find them in my holdall in Boscastle. Remember Barry Manilow's song "Somewhere Down The Road? Our roads are gonna cross again, it doesn't really matter when." I'll find him. I have to.' She frowned, 'Er… what did you mean by déjà vu?'

'Déjà vu…? Ah yes. You're not the only one to have lost a loved one.'

'But she lived till ninety nine and had a good life.'

'No, not Mum. Rick, the one I was engaged to before Tom. I was nineteen and Rick much older. We went separate ways when

I met Tom and married. Some years back Rick scoured the phone book, took a chance and rang. I was amazed, but excited, my marriage was going through a terrible patch. He rang my mobile every week when I was out walking, so no trace on the home phone, but eventually wanted to meet. What? Don't look at me like that Trudie Boyce!'

'You've never said, all stored in that neat brain. Exciting, carry on.'

Lizzie gave her a gentle push. 'Shush then and I will,' she laughed. 'Rick's job as a land agent brought him here, but he didn't know I was in Cornwall. The year before, he had to look at property three miles from Fowey, so I could have bumped into him getting petrol. Asking me on the phone to meet as he had to travel there again, I found myself agreeing. Can you imagine, me throwing caution to the wind?'

Trudie shook her head. 'Knowing you it would have been well planned.'

'It was, very. I'd carried Rick in my heart, occasionally wondering if he thought of me; drew him to me, as you'd say.'

'You did. The timing was right.'

'Mm, when Tom was late home, I'd wish he was having an affair, to salve my conscience. Selfish, but I loved Rick deeply.'

'Some are happy in a brother and sister way. I'd settle for that – friendship, mutual support, thought Laurie and I had it. I used to wish his wife wasn't in the equation, that she'd divorce him. I tell clients – you get what you expect. Well we did.'

Lizzie retrieved her Chardonay, continuing her confession. 'Tom was on a course. Rick and I lunched at a Fowey hotel, we gelled like we'd never been parted. He had grey hair, kind eyes, slim, big smile, but rather pale. He asked to see me again; when he kissed me against my car, I couldn't say no. Boldly I invited him to dinner. Shall I go on?'

Trudie's eyes widened. 'Ab... so... lutely.'

Lizzie took a glug of cold wine. 'I was nervous when he arrived next evening. Trying not to let things go further, wondering if they would. I'd been a faithful wife and Tom was often a real pig. Well, we didn't get to the pudding!' she confessed, eyes sparkling. 'I've been outwardly non-emotional; not this time. Floodgates burst. Before, during, and after, he told me he'd always loved me.'

Trudie was amazed at this admission of intimacy. With Paula she could discuss sex, but Lizzie was a closed book. 'Phew, how did you feel?'

'The same, told him too. Shouldn't make comparisons, but I hadn't had that with Tom, ever.'

Trudie asked, 'Was it as if you'd never been fully awakened?'

Lizzie brightened with realization. 'Exactly that!'

Trudie admitted, 'I went through most of my life the same.'

'He didn't want to go next morning, nor did I want him to. Realistically we telephoned as usual. Unrealistically he wanted me to visit; living in the Cotswolds wasn't ideal, but I knew I'd go. Made sure he knew I wouldn't leave Tom, he didn't push me either, saying he'd given up on relationships, wanting me. He'd thrown himself into his career, made money, finally working part-time. A heart weakness five years previously at fifty-one had made him slow down.'

'Did you see him again?'

Lizzie softly replied, 'For a while.'

'For a while?'

'Mm. I stayed for three days with Rick, having to plan it like a major crime, which I suppose it was. I told Tom I was visiting Open Gardens, knew he wouldn't want to come, hates gardening. Trudie, it was exciting with Rick, but confusing – I had no guilt, isn't that awful?!'

'No, I've been there. I wasn't married but Laurie was. Look, we're decent women; we didn't envisage this hitting us. I never saw myself as a mistress but that's what I became.'

'Yes. With Rick I was able to ignore Tom's grumpiness and criticism of me, accepting I could love two men. Tom and I were intimate so infrequently it wasn't difficult to switch off. Trudie it was bliss with Rick those two years.'

'Those two years, what… what do you mean? Did Tom find out?' Trudie enquired, mystified.

Lizzie gravely clasped her hands. 'No goodbyes. Having been unwell, Rick took a week off work and I drove up for two days in June. I made him rest, I cooked, we ate outdoors, swam in his pool, strolled in the woods. We lay down in the afternoon and early to bed at night. The last words he said to me were that he loved me totally and envied Tom.'

Trudie looked perplexed.

'The usual call didn't happen; I rang, no reply; not hearing for a week, I was worried.'

'So am I.'

Lizzie became solemn. 'I was desperate, rang the land agency and spoke to his partner. Rick didn't leave me willingly, he was taken, an embolism.'

Now it was a stunned Trudie embracing Lizzie. 'Oh I didn't expect that.' She paused. 'You said someone had gone, thought you meant left you. How appalling.'

Freeing herself from Trudie's compassionate hug, Lizzie regained her composure, resignedly telling Trudie it was the worst thing she'd ever faced. 'I went into myself, couldn't speak of it, the shock was monumental. If I believed in God, which as you know I don't, I'd say this was our punishment, Rick and me. We loved each other and ensured no-one knew. Tom was controlling, dogmatic, and worse when older. However, after by-pass surgery, he depended on me, so became more civil. I was in charge; the power had switched.

'I cried a lot, unusual for me. Previously, I didn't have stuff to cry about. Although Tom had always made it impossible to be really happy, when our daughter was born I was busy, then two miscarriages, hobbies, friends and… I got on with things.'

'Lizzie, I used to wonder how you stayed together. At least

you had someone special in your life. Er… I imagine it would have been difficult to attend Rick's funeral?'

'I went actually. His parents were dead and I didn't recognise anyone at the church near Stow-on-the-Wold. Just wanted to be there for him.'

'Difficult not being able to speak of Rick. Did you go to the house for the wake?'

'No, it would have been unreal.' She sighed. 'I'm glad Rick came to find me, giving me love to a depth I'd never experienced.'

'You must miss intimacy with Rick. It can't be the same with Tom.'

Lizzie ruefully shrugged her shoulders. 'I had a bond with Rick and deep passion. When he died I was devastated, and keeping it from Tom was a strain. Hmm, we've both lost our soulmates.'

'You know, we're more alike than I'd thought. Until I came here, I'd no knowledge of your life in any depth, nor you on mine with Laurie. We're different characters with different lifestyles, I show feelings, yours are hidden, but parallel experiences. Even for a short while Rick enriched your life. Laurie's not here for me, but I've never regretted love stored up and eventually given to someone with enough love to take it. One day I'll bump into him. Until then, memories, worth a lot.'

'You must miss your dad Trudie, you were close.'

Trudie softened at the mention of her late father. 'Yes. He didn't express well outwardly, but I felt treasured. The best thing he ever said to me was when I was rather broke a year before he died. He arranged to get new car tyres fitted for me, refusing my payment, saying it was a pleasure. When I saw the bill on the table I said, "Oh Daddy, new tyres, I get re-treads." He told me seriously, 'Re-treads are for other men's daughters, mine will have new.'" Trudie's voice quivered, recounting the meaningful sentence.

'What a memory. Hot chocolate time now.'

It took Trudie ages to fall asleep, awhirl with revelations. She realised they'd scarcely discussed parents. Trudie's mother,

Alice, had been neurotic, unable to express love; harsh words and criticism her middle names. Her father was 'under the thumb', but had endeavoured to make Trudie feel loved, despite disapproving looks from Alice. Lizzie's father was a different kettle of fish.

Trudie shivered, replaying how, aged fourteen at Lizzie's, he'd mauled her, when sending his daughter to the postbox. He'd pretended to be teasing, but in trying to avoid his embrace, Trudie had fallen. In seconds he'd taken advantage, pulling dress and petticoat up, twanging her suspenders, face aflame. Her struggles were in vain as big gnarled hands trailed roughly towards her crotch. She'd kicked him, resulting in a painful cry. Lizzie was heard coming in the back door; her father, wide-eyed, had dashed upstairs. By the time Lizzie had hung her coat in the hall, Trudie had been able to get herself together.

She hadn't seen him again until Lizzie's wedding to Tom, too crowded for a repeat. She'd wanted to tell her own parents, but doubted she'd have been believed. Perhaps Mr. Dean had touched Lizzie, though she'd claimed a perfect childhood?

At breakfast, like mischievous schoolgirls, Lizzie and Trudie shared humorous events. Trudie remarked on Lizzie's Cornish accent, thinking it sounded earthy.

'Mm, Rick said that, well... sexy anyway.'

Trudie giggled. 'A faux pas from Rex when we were in Cumbria staying on the Lorton Fells. The woman, Janet, who ran the guesthouse, did massage treatments. I'd had one when we stayed, and Rex asked about it. I said it was brilliant, Janet had been on a lymphatic drainage course.'

Trudie began to giggle, making Lizzie grin in anticipation.

'He blankly replied "Drainage? I thought her husband dealt with the plumbing."'

The two friends lost control. Damp-eyed, Trudie spluttered. 'You remember my mother was rather unworldly?'

'Yeeeerrrrsssss.'

'When I was married and plagued by small illnesses, Mum rang to ask what I was doing that evening. I replied, "Going to see Dr. Zhivago." She asked in an exasperated voice: "Now what's wrong with you?!"'

They both laughed loud and long.

'No funnies re my parents.' Lizzie admitted. 'Dad used to make furniture, mend cars, build walls, caravans, sheds. They were happy, Mum a housewife; devoted to Dad. He wore a stern look when I brought a boy home, frightening some off. Rick and Tom humoured him, bark worse than his bite.'

Trudie gave a weak smile, knowing otherwise. 'Remember when I met that fanciable chap on holiday and he wanted to write to me. I gave him your address cos Mum would have been furious, as I was practically engaged. You'd hand my post over when we met in Birmingham. All those envelopes and your mother thought you were cheating on Tom! What a hoot!' laughed Trudie, almost spilling her coffee.

'Hey I forgot to ask about Stephen? Remember, he's your son, you haven't mentioned him!'

'Gosh, neither have I. Same loving son; I told you on the phone of his Cheshire move. He recently did a series of Chopin concerts. Alison, his girlfriend is lovely, she's forty two. He needed an older woman, now he has a good one.'

Trudie gave Lizzie the rose Bodmin Beauty. They relaxed outdoors until Trudie journeyed to Devon that afternoon.

'We used to meet on Saturdays in Birmingham, you from Wolverhampton, me from Redditch. Go on, remind me.' Trudie invited.

In unison, they chorused. 'Watches of Switzerland, 11 a.m. under the clock!'

'Wasn't Rackhams fab, up in the lift to the top floor for Viennese coffee, listening to the pianist in the white tuxedo? We used to buy bargains for our bottom drawer in their sales.'

Fond reminiscences over, farewells were said at the gate,

Trudie sniffing, not wanting the reunion to end. Lizzie was stoical, not dropping her guard.

'Great to see you.' she managed.

Trudie sniffed. 'Every minute's been brilliant. Remember… sealed lips!'

'You too!'

She waved Trudie off, quickly flicking a stray tear. Both knew their bond had been renewed and wouldn't be broken.

Having taken a wrong turning, Trudie eventually joined the A38. Checking the map, she saw Saltash, Ivybridge, Buckfastleigh, Ashburton; all en route to Doddiscombleigh. Halting a few miles on to drink water, she noticed a sign for Hessenford.

'Why does that ring a bell?' noticing it led to Seaton on the coast. 'Oh… Hessenford. Laurie's birthplace.' Thoughts were arrested by a fly whizzing in, hitting the windscreen, buzzing uselessly on its back. Trudie scooped it in a tissue, shaking it into September air.

Laurie was born in Hessenford during World War Two. He'd told her of holidays with paternal grandparents, when the family had moved to Worcestershire. Describing cottages on the steep hill, pub, bridge over the river, woods, bus to the coast, he'd promised to take her – something else that hadn't transpired.

As the third movement of Brahms Symphony No. 4 on Classic FM played on, curiosity borne out of emotion ensued, rich resonance of double bases stirring her into action. 'Time takes care of all our aspirations.' she thought excitedly, signalling right.

In The Copley Arms enjoying a sandwich and coffee, Trudie should have been relaxed, but a nervous frisson invaded. Actually being where Laurie had his roots; surreal. From the window, viewing seventeenth and eighteen century cottages, St. Ann's Church where his grandfather was buried, Hessenford Mill and the bridge over the River Seaton, she felt an intruder on Laurie's 'patch'. His history, not hers. Chatting to a waitress, she gave Laurie

Martin's name. Trudie was told most weren't original villagers, and asking at the bar, people shook their heads.

Originally planning to see Talland Bay near Looe with its pink shale stone, now its charms had faded, Hessenford the replacement, afternoon sun giving a warm welcome. She stood on the bridge, light glinting on the chattering river below. In the churchyard, she wondered where Laurie's grandparents' grave was. He'd read Tennyson's In Memoriam to her, saying Victorians felt comfort from it, but it failed to console him when his parents had died. At the door, Trudie knew neither that poem nor any other could ease her loss of Laurie.

Taking in the stained glass, inhaling mellowed old oak, touching everything, knowing Laurie would have breathed, sung and prayed there, her footsteps echoed, bouncing off the barrel-vaulted roof as she walked the aisles.

She knelt in a pew on a beautifully worked kneeler. Alone, Trudie prayed for family and friends. She'd told God, although she wanted to pray 'Thy will not mine,' she couldn't believe she was meant to be without Laurie forever. No answer came but she'd continued. Occasionally, she'd felt she had no favour to ask for herself, imagining God wouldn't understand as she'd spent four years with another's husband and four years wanting him to reappear. Here she was in his church on his territory, praying, wringing her hands so hard, her body stiffened.

'Thank you, Lord, for directing me here. I try to forget Laurie, have many blessings… but… part of me died when he went.' Tears spilled onto her jacket; she reached into the pocket for a handkerchief. With a heavy sob, she wailed, breaking the stillness, 'Please bring him home to me.'

When she'd regained calm, Trudie walked to exit the aged building. Spotting the Visitors Book, she put on reading glasses, writing, 'Trudie Boyce, Little Arrow.' In the comments space, she wrote, 'Perfect Peace' knowing it wasn't quite.

Trudie noted overseas people, Texas, Berlin, Vancouver,

131

Rotterdam. Mainly British, Paula's Cheltenham, Swansea, Bromsgrove; the latter not far from Little Arrow. She leafed through 2008, smiling at a drawing of a grinning cat drawn by a child in July. Sitting on a pine chair, she read more.

It was fortuitous that she did. Browsing back to June 2007, an unbelievable entry – 'My Church' and a name – Laurence Martin.

14

Julia sat at her dressing table mirror, looking almost like a few months ago, dark brown shoulder length hair, good complexion, hazel eyes, ten stone in weight. Lately, she hadn't liked what she saw. Guilt stared at her; she'd winced, frowning, hands slouched in her lap.

At first she'd felt no guilt over Jonathan when David was being beastly. Poppy was her prime concern, she told Julia she hated David's behaviour, but had friends, school, and weekends with her father. Initially slamming doors and swearing, she'd improved since David was less volatile. However, Julia knew the explosive atmosphere could return after the café incident.

'David may not have heard. It's usually humming in there, you have to speak up above coffee machine and folks talking.' Alison suggested on the phone.

Unconvinced, Julia replied, 'I'm certain he overheard, his demeanour said it all. Since then he's scarcely spoken; glaring hatefully, his silence thunderous. As for that woman in the café, my manners were terrible; I pleaded a headache. Pleasant woman, she'd reminded me I'd recommended massaging her cat and she used Rescue Remedy too.'

Silence from Alison.

'Alison?'

'I heard, but wait… bells are ringing. Worcestershire, Rescue Remedy, cat, visiting her son. What was her name?'

'Hm, she told me at the exhibition. Begins with a T… Trudie. Oh… Trudie! D'you think it's…?'

Alison chuckled, 'Course it is. Stephen's mother puts Rescue Remedy in her cat's bowl. She's gorgeous, intelligent, a stress therapist. I met her last weekend, an amazing co-incidence!'

'Sure is, I didn't connect, too aware of Big Ears overhearing. She didn't know I was in Cheshire so no mention of her son living here. Don't tell Stephen will you?'

'No, when are you seeing Jonathan, have you told him?'

'Tonight, and no I haven't. At the risk of his running off, I should.'

'Running off? He won't. He loves you.'

'Alison, that's what he says, but I wonder if sex clouds things. If I was say… disabled… if he'd feel the same.'

Alison interjected sharply. 'Stop. I've had precisely that issue with Stephen. The break did us good, difficult though it was. You didn't begin sexually, but the attraction led to love. He wouldn't be taking risks if he didn't love you.'

'No, but my situation makes for insecurity. You once said no one can make you feel inferior without your consent, but mine's complicated. Any of us could quit, married or not couldn't we?'

'True, but be positive of a happy ending. Bet he's got a tan from Dubai, bound to have sunbathed as well as cataloguing Art Deco.'

'Thanks Alison. I'm supposed to be seeing a client so David's in with Poppy. I'll handle it, got to.'

Julia's relief, as a tanned Jonathan took her into his arms, was immense. She apologized for lateness; he silenced her with a deep kiss, leading her into the beamed sitting room for gin and tonic.

When she'd related the café conversation with Trudie, he'd agreed David mustn't know anything yet.

'He doesn't know who valued Mother's effects and the paperwork's here.' Julia told him. 'Gosh, your tan's deep, are you sure you worked in Dubai?'

'You'll want to see the rest, won't you?'

Julia took no persuading. She followed him up to the candle-lit bedroom.

'Missed you, Julia. I want to hold you, love you.' he said, discarding his clothes with obvious desire. Breathlessly whispering, 'I'll have to slow down or there won't be any actual lovemaking,' he held her, chatting about his trip.

'Jonathan, how lovely to be here with you, a haven for me, I can totally relax.' A tear spilled onto her cheeks. Jonathan kissed it, snuggling into her neck. Encircling his shoulders with her arm, she drew him to her breast, whispering, 'Love you, love you,' feeling ecstasy, that rare emotion real love brings.

They spoke of Dubai, antiques, their love. Jonathan had thought of everything, candles, water, matzos, even a damp flannel. 'You do realize we've blown out most of the candles?' Jonathan laughed later.

Julia smiled up at him. 'Poppy's had to get used to David, resents him now, but doubt she expects us to split up. If we're together in a couple of years it will be different.'

'No IF about it!' Jonathan proclaimed.

Julia confessed, 'I've never had an affair. Poppy's father didn't either. We drifted, divorced, but stayed friends, civilized. Ultimately I met David. Why I married him after ten months alone, I can't imagine. He moved in, a natural progression, no moods, fights, tension then.'

Jonathan sat up. 'Mine was similar, no quarrels, nor anything else. No passion nor children. She blamed it on that – no children, mattered to me, not her. She busied herself with committees, societies, bridge. I was the breadwinner, growing busier with my career. No highs, no lows, until she contracted cancer. A month later, I was arranging her funeral.'

Jonathan sighed. 'I moved to set up here. The solitude struck me with great force, work got me through, all I knew until I met you.'

'Terrible, no-one to share concerts... films... walks... no romance.'

'I hadn't had that with my wife though. Hope you're not bored staying in when we meet.'

Julia reassured him she knew the score. If he could wait, so could she.

15

Paula had learned to live without James. He'd been a workaholic, gradually becoming an alcoholic, warning signs recklessly unheeded. Small heart attacks, culminating in a fatal one six years later. After a lengthy marriage, Paula had come to terms with solitary living. Lack of confrontation with James so welcome, his drinking and ill health had left her frazzled, now she'd settled into a peaceful retirement. Driving again was freeing, visiting her daughter, grandchild and Trudie.

Paula had received a postcard from Boscastle, before going with neighbour Mary to Whitton Church near Tenbury, which had a Burne-Jones stained glass window.

At home on this rainy September day, Paula pondered on her trip two days before. She'd been the map reader, as Mary had driven along narrow lanes lush with ancient trees, tall hedges and covetable houses, village names quaint, Hope Bagot, Greete, Whitton.

Parking on the steep hill outside Whitton church, they puffed up steps leading to the wicket gate. Entering the twelfth century church, Paula saw Trudie hadn't exaggerated, it was a gem. Stroking polished pews, she walked to the famous window, rose and green glowing in the morning sun.

They viewed the Medieval Preaching Cross, the churchyard a conservation area, with two hundred plant species. Mary drove them to a garden centre, where Paula was tempted to buy Trudie a clematis, but no idea what she had. From there they headed to View FromThe Top, renowned for food.

Travelling up through the hamlet of Greete, they reached their destination. The pub had a large car park, affording a panoramic view of distant hills and patchwork fields below. Paula and Mary were shown to the restaurant overlooking the valley. On cue, the sun appeared from behind a cloud, bathing them in noonday warmth. After ordering local beef, they perused brochures.

Not managing without reading glasses she'd left in the car, Paula exited the restaurant, gleaming with oak and polished brass, noticing more cars next to Mary's. Retrieving her glasses and deciding to wash her hands, she passed through a narrower room where two men were propping up the bar discussing local beers. They looked up, the darker haired one saying 'Hello.'

'Mmm. Quite a catch, Italian looking.'

Exiting a few minutes later, she saw the room full of people chattering in high spirits. Passing the two men, she heard the younger mention the bowling club. The older one said, 'Music, I've been living with my son in America; he likes modern stuff, now I can play my choice. I love this area, peaceful, bought a cottage in Ashton. You're right to invest in modern collectables. seventies Troika pottery's fetching top money. Wish I'd bought some when I was in Cornwall in 2007. I collect glass paperweights.'

Paula walked through the bar, squeezing past customers to rejoin Mary. Dining, Paula's thoughts concentrated on the bar conversation.

Too full of main course, dessert was refused, as the room filled up with the lively group. Paula and Mary entered the bar en route to the Ladies. Exiting, Paula saw the younger man giving his card to the older one.

'Builders to the discerning and others!' he quipped. 'I'll ring you about that extension. If Dad's busy, I'll do it.'

The Italian look-alike thanked him, writing his telephone number, which Paula witnessed while Mary located car keys from her handbag's depths.

'No card, I don't practise law again yet, settling in first. Here's my mobile number, must go, I've inherited an unruly wilderness with the property. I'll ring you, Max. Bye.'

'Cheerio, Laurie.'

***

Paula caught her breath, goose-flesh rising at the memory of the overheard conversation two days before. Touching her cup, the liquid had gone cold. 'Like me when I heard that name,' she thought, finger absent-mindedly circling the rim of the Danish cup. Trudie had coveted the Dansk 1960s coffee set.

'What were the chances of encountering Laurie? It had to be him though.'

Mary had listened to the Radio 4 play, driving back. Paula's head had been elsewhere, awhirl from the name the dark-haired man had given.

Her brain didn't want to switch off from that moment. Extricating herself from the Italian leather chair, she flushed at the Laurie connection. 'God, I could do with a ciggie.' she thought frustratingly, but giving up when James had died, her coughs had become past history. In the lobby amongst junk mail, a splash of blue and green indicated another postcard from Trudie. Smiling, she read – 'Have news. Will tell in person. Trudie. x'

'Not as amazing as what I've got to tell you.' Taking coffee to the open-plan living room, she sat on the low-backed Corbusier leather sofa. She'd initially disliked its masculine lines with gleaming chrome arms, but James had insisted. Now she loved it, most afternoons resting there for a nap. She began to write notes.

Evidence – View From The Top. Bar. Two men. Dark-haired man – sixtyish, Italian looking. Told Max, younger man, had moved. Been living with son in America. In Cornwall last year. Collects paperweights. Said Hello. Soft voice. Lawyer. Heard Max call older man Laurie!

Paula finished writing with a flourish, raising the pen in the air, plonking it on the smoked glass table with a clank, imagining Trudie's shock when back from holiday.

***

Rex had accurately described The Nobody Inn, ancient beams, excellent food and service. At the bar, Trudie was amused to hear two different conversations. The first from a weathered-faced Devon farmer talking to his friend.

'Old Joe? Blimey 'ees dead, fell outer iz plum tree. Yers, that's what killed 'im.'

She then heard two county ladies discussing the cost of living.

'Selena, the price of Bath Olivers, two pounds a packet! Can you believe it? Oooh did I tell you, we're having the stables enlarged? Gin and chronic dear as per?'

To ensure she wouldn't forget both quotes, at dinner she wrote them in her notebook. At ten o'clock she'd left people chatting with her by the fireplace, for bed.

Sun distilled through the floral curtains next morning. Snuggled under the duvet, swallows twittering under the eaves, Trudie remembered the previous day's discovery in Hessenford church. If she'd read it in a novel, she'd have deemed it far fetched. Again, truth was stranger than fiction.

'Let mourning stop when your grief is fully expressed,' came to mind. Hers was ever present, the wound less open but not healed. Getting over it wasn't an option. She grieved as if Laurie was dead. It ambushed her, one day fine, next day raw. Life had continued with Stephen, friends, work and moving house. Happiness had returned in some measure, but still the long tunnel of longing for Laurie. Perhaps distance had lent enchantment to the view. Had she been wearing rose-coloured spectacles?

Her holiday diary hadn't been written since leaving Lizzie's the previous day. She drew the curtains, seeing a clear September day, an old man on a bicycle riding past. What life had he led, a simple rural one or had he experienced tragedy and loss? She wrote the sequence of events, including that prayer she plagued God with some days. The hardest line was the culmination in the visitors book. She wrote simply – Laurence Martin's signature found from June 2007. IT MUST BE LAURIE.

The journey home to Worcestershire loomed. She'd rung Georgina, next door. 'Marvellous time, home around two.' She mused, settling into the car, 'Perfectly true, beautiful scenery, reunion with Lizzie. That familiar signature though – surreal.'

She wanted to go home to her cat, job, friends. Trying not to let melancholia mar memories of a precious week, she turned the radio on. As soon as she heard the first two notes of the song, she knew it was Gladys Knight singing 'Part Time Love,' which she'd once liked, but now the lyrics stung. She'd told Laurie it reminded her of his promise to end his sham marriage to be with her. He'd looked ashamed and defeated.

At the motorway services she rested, drinking tea. The last few miles had been difficult, seething rain lashing the windscreen. With connections to Laurie that week, she felt a revelation was imminent. If she was with a client, she'd advise such signs were making them aware of new possibilities. Four years had made her a realist, increasingly difficult to practise what she preached.

Two middle-aged women with overladen trays shuffled towards the next table. Flustered, they crashed down, splashing tea, scraping chairs noisily, slumping heavily. The larger of the two called to someone in the queue so loudly, half of it turned.

'Ivy, get us a couple of them serviettes will yer luv, spilt 'arf o'this. Ta.'

'Ivy.' Trudie thought, 'that's what I've become, clinging to what I thought was an oak tree, solid and immovable. Turns out I put all my energy into a wavering spindle tree.'

Walking to the car, she knew the women would moan about their lives, but they'd have family at home. Trudie looked forward to reuniting with Holly in an hour and a half.

16

Julia's garden was finished, but Alison was asked by Clare if Stephen could tidy her friend's neglected one in September, where Clare was housesitting.

He'd cleared the jungle of tangled weeds on a warm evening. Wondering why Pink Floyd was playing, he felt Clare was watching. Having met her once since his relationship with Alison had begun in February, he'd felt uneasy, suspecting Clare was jealous. Depositing weeds in the bin, he'd gone to wash in the kitchen.

She'd suddenly appeared, startling him as he reached for a towel.

'This what you're looking for, Babes?'

Stephen had jumped. 'Oh, Clare, didn't see you there.'

Wearing shorts and crop top, she'd replied coquettishly, 'You are gonna stay for a glass of wine aren't yer?'

He'd made excuses and left, to the annoyance of Clare, who'd frowned, calling him a spoilsport.

Trying to relax with a gin and tonic in the bath at home with Delius in the background, Stephen grimaced at Clare's appearance, wearing little, reeking of booze. If only he could cancel pruning scratchy pyracantha on Friday. Pink Floyd, perhaps she knew Alison liked the group. On their first night, *Dark Side of the Moon* added to the eroticism. Odd Clare should be playing it.

On Friday, Stephen reluctantly returned to Clare's friend's house. Clare pretended she'd forgotten he was coming. He recognized the lie.

'Don't let me disturb you, Clare, I'll get on with the hedge.'

She winked, saying he could disturb her anytime. Stephen pretended not to have heard, tamed the monster hedge, binning the cuttings. Entering the kitchen, relieved Clare was absent, Pink Floyd wasn't. Before he could leave, she appeared in a robe.

'Ooh you've got bits of 'edge in yer 'air Stevie. Alison'll wonder what we've been up to.'

She leant on him unsteadily, stumbling against the table. Stephen caught her, informing her Alison would think no such thing. 'Clare, drink's made you say things you'll regret.' He led her into the sitting room, where she flopped onto the sofa, grinning hideously. As he began to leave, she grabbed his leg.

'Don't go, Stevie, don't. Mee boyfriend an' me 'ave 'ad a row. I'm desperate for sex. Purleez, Stevie. Pink Floyd for you, Babes.'

Stephen, hearing her slurred words, tried placating her. 'Look I'll put TV on so you can sleep here.'

'If you'll come Stevie. I could do with a young stud, Alison says you're dynamite! I played Pink Floyd cos you like makin' out to it. Fancy choosing 'er when you could 'ave me. 'Ere, look!'

Wildly, Clare flung open her robe offering her writhing naked body, fondling her breasts, throwing her head back. This was the final straw.

'Cover up you stupid girl. You won't compromise me! Wait for your own boyfriend to return, or do it yourself!' he shouted angrily. 'I'm off.'

Stephen needed to tell Alison, but was wary. He didn't want to believe Clare about Alison's intimate conversation, but she had too much information for it to be a lie. In Stephen's bed on the first Saturday in October, Alison had discussed her week. Stephen looked distracted.

'What? Alison, to avoid misunderstandings, we should talk.'

Alison nudged him conspiratorially 'You've been having a fling with Phoebe Cade, that's why she's got a spring in her step.' Seeing Stephen's serious expression, her grin faded. 'Oh, not that then.'

'It's been bothering me… about Clare.'

'Don't tell me she's not paid you the gardening money her friend left for you.'

'Not money. It's how she was when I was there. I went twice and…'

Alison interrupted, 'I can guess, she was drunk, always like that over men. Sobbing she may as well move to Norfolk to an ex, she'd split up with a divorced chap in Cheshire, but now they're together again. She'll have gone home now her friend's back from holiday. I don't know Clare's own address but I'll ring to get the money.'

'She was drunk. On Monday she had Pink Floyd belting out. When I went inside she was disappointed I wouldn't stay for wine, flirty she was too. When I did the hedge later that week, she appeared in a robe. When I'd finished, she was blotto. Can I tell you everything?'

Intrigued, Alison agreed. 'Er, please do.'

'She lunged at me, stumbling, so I guided her onto the sofa. Rambling re the boyfriend split and how she needed sex, she revealed something that rocked me. *Dark Side of the Moon* was playing, which she said was what we liked making out to – you and I! Said you'd told her I was dynamite in bed.'

Alison flushed, too appalled to speak.

'When she flung her robe open, I angrily left, hesitated to tell you, hurt you'd discussed our intimacy.'

Alison shamefully explained. 'It was the morning after we'd had our first passionate night. Clare called round, finding me overtired but full of girlish elation. It was indiscreet, but I'd had such depression from Phil's lies, then a wild night with you, so fantastic I mentioned *Dark Side of the Moon*. We didn't need it, but Stephen... I wasn't sure we'd see each other again and perhaps did say it was mind-blowing or dynamite. It's not my style to discuss partners, but you shouldn't have been such a sex bomb should you!?'

Alison giggled, changing Stephen's anxious expression to a nervous smile. 'OK, I thought you'd believe I'd led her on, you'd been so quiet.'

Alison kissed his bare shoulder. 'I know Clare, she's a minx, jealous of us. I don't care what boyfriend trouble she's got, I'll get your payment, then drop her. I was quiet on account of helping Mrs. Cade with a difficulty. I get weary, approaching middle-age.'

Stephen drew her into the well of the bed. 'Sshh, I'll pretend I didn't hear that. Middle-aged? I'm going nowhere, you'll need me soon to help you on with your support stockings.'

She giggled, reminding him how embarrassed he'd been when his mother had revealed after his first day at school, he'd announced, 'I've done it!' When informed he'd have to go again next day, he'd burst into tears.

Stephen grinned, yawning. 'Time for sleep now. Mum rang, home from Cornwall.'

17

Julia knew David had overheard the café conversation. It didn't need a genius to suspect she hadn't been alone in Warwick. She'd expected ructions at the brief, revealing café chat with Trudie. None, but he was more watchful since that early September Saturday. Guilt about Jonathan had evaporated, compared with a few months ago when it was immense. After a calm period, living with David was stressful again, he now stared and smirked with contempt.

'He seems to accept our breakdown,' she told Jonathan one late September evening. 'I can see anger in his eyes though, hoping I'll crack first. Yesterday he opened the kitchen door for me, a rare act, making me nervous. When I thanked him, he winked, bowing – psychological warfare.'

Jonathan frowned. 'I feel frustratingly powerless, hating the anxiety our situation gives you. Should we continue?'

Julia gave him an old-fashioned look. 'What a question! Have the Americans been on the moon?'

Jonathan chuckled. 'Well there's a question mark over that these days.'

Julia giggled, 'You get what I mean, Cleverclogs.'

As Julia drove home, she wasn't to know the situation would take an unexpected turn.

Recently, Poppy had become sulkily withdrawn. Julia had asked if there was anything wrong at school or was it period time? There'd been denial of both. Because the domestic situation was causing stress, Julia had offered a Shropshire spa day. Poppy's mood had instantly changed.

They enjoyed deep tissue massage, thalassotherapy, and healthy food among beautiful surroundings. Poppy's impish smile reappeared. Reluctantly leaving, wrapped up against October wind, they skipped to the car, giggling.

Poppy held Julia's hand on the steering wheel. 'Thanks, Mum,' she said fondly. 'It was fab, I don't deserve it.'

Julia frowned. 'Don't say that, you do.'

'I've been a pain lately, you know that.' Nervously, Poppy asked, 'Mum, have you ever had to say something, but not sure how?'

Alarmed, Julia feared what was coming, imagining rape or pregnancy. Looking at her fingers, Poppy told her, 'When you were out, my phone battery was low, so I tried to phone Angie on the house phone, not knowing David was on the extension talking about you.'

Julia stiffened.

'I should have put the phone down but I was shocked. The guy said he'd followed you to a woman's house in Rylands.'

Julia gasped. Poppy frowned. 'Mum, wait. David called the guy an effing loser. "I'll ring you when she's next due out." he told him, then rang off. So did I, hoping he hadn't heard my breathing, and turned the TV up pretending to watch Coronation Street.' She asked nervously, 'Mum, why is David having you followed? He's not having you killed is he? Tell me it's not that!' A choked plea escaped her mouth. 'Mum, say something!' she sobbed, burying herself in Julia's coat.

Julia comforted her. 'David won't be planning anything sinister. Probably employed someone to report on me. He's…'

Poppy retorted, wiping her eyes, 'I guessed that, but, Mum, why? Are you having an affair…? Oh Mum, you are!'

'Yes. I'm sorry,' Julia answered hotly.

'Bloody hell, who isn't?'

'Poppy, please. I'm unhappy with David, there are things you don't know. I didn't anticipate this and didn't tell you because… you're too young to be burdened with it. OK, I met a man six months ago. We love each other, he's stood by me when I thought I could stand David no more, but you're my priority.'

Poppy broke into a smile. 'Mum, I'm happy for you. Terrible, married to someone who treats you badly. David's vile, unhygienic – leaves the loo in a disgusting state, mucky underpants lying around. Ugh, I couldn't go to bed with that, no wonder you went off him!'

Julia gasped, smiling. 'Poppy Benedict, how dare you be so mature! At your age I only knew of my little world of school, hockey and pop music. You must have been so anxious.'

'Yes, watch it, Mum. You've seen what David's tempers are like. Can we go home, I'm starving?'

'Scarlet Woman, Pink Passion or Rose Pearl?' asked Julia at Alison's kitchen table.

'Rose Pearl, I've had enough passion for one weekend. Crumbs, I'll be getting headaches next!' quipped Alison.

Julia replied 'Scarlet Woman, that's me! Basecoat first.'

Alison saw Julia's worry. During the manicure, Poppy's conversation was discussed.

'Private detective? Scarlet Woman? David's a pig, he tried to rape you.'

Julia sighed. 'I felt awkward, but at least now Poppy realises my insecurities, flaws and needs.'

'If she wasn't in the picture, I doubt you'd stay with David.'

'True. She said she'd understand if I asked him to go. Yesterday she was doing homework, calling, "Mum, how do you spell hallelujah?" I told her not sure if a j or y was correct and couldn't she put "yippee" instead? I heard her groan, "Mum, I can't write The Yippee Chorus, silly."'

Alison laughed. 'Getting to the spy in the camp, why would David get a snoop on you, when it may be him having an affair?'

Julia looked surprised. 'Hadn't thought of him having one.'

'Best form of defence is attack, deflecting from himself.'

With a winsome smile, Alison said, 'What varying backgrounds my friends have had, yet similar emotions. Look at what I've told you about Trudie. You met her unexpectedly, and she turns out to be Stephen's Mother. You're decent women, with no intention of falling for the wrong men. Not forgetting my fling with a married vicar! Mrs. Cade's had a knock too. We're all similar, it's levelling I think.'

'Mm, my father quoted a saying when Mum was critical "There is so much bad in the best of us, so much good in the worst of us, it ill behoves any one of us, to find fault with the rest of us."'

Alison nodded. 'Speaking of men, Stephen's coming for dinner. The sky's a threatening shade, must get washing in, make a lentil curry, and alter a design.'

'I miss Stephen since he finished my garden. You wouldn't think he was thirty, he could be my contemporary.' Julia remarked.

Alison stood up. 'Mm, feels like he's older than me, even recommended herbal stuff for PMT! He's a gem.'

Julia warned, 'No gardening to wreck those nails.'

Alison replied smugly, 'Promise. I've got my own personal gardener.'

They exchanged a kiss as Bo, anxious to make it inside before the door closed, dashed to avoid the ominous storm brewing, elegantly sidling in as though she hadn't been in a hurry at all.

18

That butterfly rippling, as Trudie approached home, was always there. She'd relocated from a house in Evesham to an outlying village, Little Arrow, longing to live beside her childhood river, having paddled in it, picnicked by it, written poems near it, even skated on it one freezing winter in the fifties. Discovering it was serendipitous, location perfect – seven hundred yards from where she'd lived as a child. The *pièce de resistance* was beyond the garden, the River Arrow flowing into the Avon downstream. Both river and surrounding buttercupped fields embraced her cottage.

During the viewing, Trudie had asked to walk across the bridge along the riverbank. She'd seen red clay deposits from soil further up in Redditch. Peering into its depths, she'd wondered if there were white-clawed crayfish she'd fished out as a child.

Since moving into the idyllic property, she'd spent hours by her river, listening to it chattering over polished stones and moss-glazed rocks, treasuring its privacy and tranquillity. Whispering of the wind in the ash trees made their keys rattle and alder cones tremble. Freeze-framed, Trudie recalled seasons ebbing and flowing like the river, skeins of geese flying in formation, wildflower fields, her childhood playground near steep, terracotta claybanks, nature proving the best artist of all.

Driving down the lane, her heart did a joyous dance seeing sheep grazing in the sun-scorched field. Obviously fairer weather than Cornwall. She knew there'd be tangled bramble clumps smothered in huge blackberries at the river's bend, remembering vicious barbs when collecting them as a child.

With Holly weaving through her legs, Trudie made tea. Promising the cat Cornish pilchards, she let her out. Inhaling autumnal air, she closed the door to check the answerphone.

'Troods, ring me ASAP. Bye.'

Running the bath, Trudie rang Paula, who invited her to Sunday lunch, wanting to discuss something important. Soaking the motorway from her system, Trudie imagined Paula's daughter was pregnant or needed to borrow more money.

The journey to Paula's was delightful, whispy clouds feathering the sky over unspoilt farming countryside, roadside stalls near Evesham selling local produce. Trudie bought apples and plums. A lipstick-red clematis named Ever Paula had to be bought, serendipitous like Bodmin Beauty for Lizzie.

When Trudie knocked on the huge front doors of the nineteen-seventies house nestling under Cleeve Hill, she heard loud unbolting with lots of 'phewing'.

Hugging her, Trudie felt her frailty, suspecting since James' death, she may be struggling. The clematis sent Paula into raptures. 'I nearly bought you one in Tenbury but uncertain what you had. Sit down, got your favourite Dansk set ready. Cold out, coffee in the kitchen, at least we can see the roses.'

'Super. I got a rose for Lizzie.'

'How did you get on with her?'

'We talked ourselves hoarse, remembering hilarious incidents. I knew she'd mention my mother, so I recounted her faux pas years ago. Thought of another on the way home, want to hear it?'

Pouring steaming coffee, Paula giggled. 'Ooh, please.'

'We were at the cinema and Mum had rather a loud voice. I forget which film, but the actor was trying to indicate to an

152

attractive girl that he was an intellectual, saying he was a great collector of books. Mum announced loudly, "He collects rooks?! Can't stand dead birds, give me the creeps." Folks turned around staring. I tried telling Mum quietly it was books, but she hadn't got her hearing aid in. I had to stifle giggles at inappropriate moments.'

Paula bent double, laughing. Trudie joined in until tears sparkled.

'What a tonic. You look well, I'm pale. Have cream in your coffee.'

'Thanks. Mixed weather, sheets of drizzle and sunshine. Now Tenbury, did you go to that church?'

'Mm, all you said it would be. We went to that pub you recommended too.'

'The View From The Top? Was it ok?' Trudie interjected.

'Very. In an unexpected way.'

'Oh, intriguing.'

'Yes, you said you had something to tell.'

Trudie put her cup into the saucer. 'No, you first.'

Paula described the pub, excitedly revealing the man at the bar. Trudie felt a chill run through her, nose tingling. Listening to the sentence where the builder called him Laurie, she gasped, 'Ohhh… ohhhh… Laurie! It was, it was.'

Paula replied, eyes dancing. 'From what I heard, it has to be!'

Held close to Paula's nurturing warmth, Trudie wept. Several tissues later, she uttered, 'Driving back from Cornwall, that Moody Blues track was in my mind. "I Know I'll Find You Somewhere."' She paused. 'Phew, my news is an enigma too.'

'About Lizzie?'

Trudie dabbed her wet face. 'No, what I found in Cornwall. Unbelievable, but proves we shouldn't give up. I tell clients, thoughts are things, giving them affirmations to attain goals. I haven't always practised what I've preached.

'On holiday I was happy, sunny weather, rained a bit, felt sad a bit. The icing on the cake was staying with Lizzie. We talked, laughed, I revealed more of Laurie, she filled me in on her stuff. I thought, on the A38, how our paths have been so diverse. She's been married forever, feelings hidden, an orderly life.

'In letters and on the phone, we'd only discussed sketchy details in our lives. You and I live closer, we're each other's confidantes; Lizzie's unexpected secret was a revelation. I imagined it would be tricky telling her of Laurie, cos a real friend is one who knows why you act as you do, and she hardly knew about me. She empathized, a surprise; I knew nothing of her comparable situation. A relief not to have to pretend.'

Paula listened attentively. 'Is that the news then?'

Already thrilled with Paula's revelations, Trudie said, 'No, that was realization we're all on let's say... parallel lines. Diverse characters experiencing joy, sadness, elation, and loneliness – parallel lives. My revelation came when I was bold enough to turn off the A38 to Hessenford.'

Paula was riveted. Trudie slowed, reliving the church and visitors book.

'Laurence Martin. My church,' she uttered in a whisper.

The reaction was instant. Paula, eyes widened, shouted, 'Stone the crows!'

Trudie smiled at Paula's reaction, especially the old country saying. 'Stone the crows. Haven't heard that for years.'

'Well, my revelations, now yours, same subject. I need a dry martini.' At the drinks trolley, she asked, 'Orange juice OK for you?'

'Lovely.'

Eating roast pork, the conspirators laid plans. Discreet probings had to be done to locate Laurie. At two fifteen, Trudie fell in with what Paula practised, an afternoon rest listening to the Radio 4 play. Trudie curled into a foetal ball in the spare bedroom, one she'd occupied until James made it prohibitive for her to stay. She shuddered at his gropings and suggestions, relieved Paula had no knowledge of it.

When Trudie had driven home down the steep hill, Paula took *The Sunday Times* into the living room. She stretched out on the white leather sofa, musing on their day, newspaper remaining unopened. Trudie was beautifully groomed, younger than sixty five. They'd laughed and chatted, but the main topic had been Laurie.

Paula had a secret of her own. She couldn't tell Trudie what she'd unearthed concerning James. Trudie was part of the equation. Paula recalled discovering his briefcase in his den at the back of a cupboard, some months after his death. The case was locked; Paula, supposing there was nothing she shouldn't see, but men guarded their stuff to keep their egos intact. James only revealed what he wanted, until later years, admitting infidelity.

Paula had noticed a bunch of keys, feeling guilt trying them. Though James was dead, she'd felt an intruder on his personal property. The fourth try was successful and the bulging case burst open. Paula had removed half a dozen men's magazines, although not a man in them. No surprise, normal stuff. She'd smiled, spotting two notes from their daughter to James.

'Daddy, settling in. Made two friends. Thanks for money.
Stephie. Xxx'

She picked up the second note, sighing fondly at the crayoning by Stephie aged six.

'Daddy I luv yoo. Heer is a picher ov yoo in the gardun.
Luv Stephie x'

The third was not from Stephie or anyone. Rather it was TO someone. In James' spidery handwriting, dated eighteen years before. Lowering her glasses, she'd frozen, reading,
'Dear Trudie.'

'James writing to Trudie?'

'I hope I haven't frightened you off. Drink, I plead in my defence, I'd have explained at the motel, if you'd played ball! I'm sore at your rejection. Your beauty, voluptuous body, sharp wit like mine, intellect, you know what you are. I thought you'd welcome more than friendship.

'I was and am hungry for you. You know how long-married couples behave. Everyone has flings, no harm done if the little woman doesn't find out. This makes me sound a bastard; I haven't been the most faithful of husbands, but a good provider for Paula and our daughter.

'Apologies for drunken fumbling. Nerves. I thought you'd agree, looked forward to exploring you. You're correct, Paula is your best friend. Unlike you I don't see it as betrayal. A bit of fun and release of sexual tension. Oh the exciting things I wanted to do with you at the motel. For a start...'

The next sentences were like something out of Men Only.

'Please ring me at work. Forgive my clumsiness, re-consider. We'll stay in a distant hotel, have dinner with champagne, and... (see previous paragraph). I live in hope. James. x'

Paula had remained inert. The reason why James had the note became apparent – a reply on the reverse. Trudie had written in red script:

'I SEND THIS REPLY AS PAULA IS IN HOSPITAL AND WILL NOT SEE IT. FROM YOUR ACTIONS AND LETTER IT IS APPARENT THE ONLY PERSON YOU LOVE IS YOURSELF. BETRAYAL YOUR MIDDLE NAME. IT IS NOT MINE. ANY MORE AND YOU WILL HEAR FROM MY SOLICITOR. DESTROY THIS SO YOU DO NOT HURT PAULA.'

Paula's body had echoed her emotions. She'd scowled, shifting uncomfortably, tense and bewildered. Casting the letter onto the Berber carpet, fists clenched, she'd trudged into the adjacent kitchen. Pouring a dry martini, she'd gone to the fridge for ice, mesmerised by the discovery. The clunk of the central heating had startled her, causing her to spill the drink.

'Oh, blast,' she'd uttered frustratingly as cold liquid stained her gorgeous beige Joseph sweater. Irritated, she'd reached for kitchen roll to absorb the stain, peeling off the delicate garment, immersing it in cool soap flakes. Changing into a scarlet square-necked sweater she'd observed herself in the mirror. She'd smiled involuntarily, aware she was still slender, firm bustline, shapely legs and only a slightly lined face.

'I look all right. I DO! Even better when James sent Trudie that bloody letter. Trying it on with my best friend! Hell, how dare he!' Her anger had mounted. 'He knew Trudie would remain silent, not wanting to hurt me. Mean swine, not content with propositioning, he has to write to her too. Bastard.' she'd spat.

Downstairs, returning the letter to the briefcase, she'd wondered whether to tell Trudie. Pouring another drink, she'd concluded there was no point. 'Let sleeping dogs lie. Trudie's innocent, her reply proves that.'

In the sweater's final rinse, the martini stain had vanished. Paula had dried it flat over a rack on the patio, then watched TV absent mindedly. 'The rape of the soul disturbs the mind.' had filtered into her brain. She'd definitely been disturbed, and thought it ironic she'd usually shared revelations with Trudie. This one was the exception.

Checking the sweater to ensure the breeze hadn't dislodged it from the drying rack, she'd been able to remove that stain – others would be more difficult.

19

'I adore your home.' Alison told Stephen, lying in his bed.

'What made you think of that?' he murmured.

'Late Georgian and not ruined with the wrong décor. Restrained, that's what you've been, it's worked.'

Stephen turned around, stroking Alison's hair. 'I'm not always restrained,' he admitted, nuzzling her neck. 'I can't concentrate on piano practice thinking of you.'

Alison held him. 'Feels right doesn't it – us?'

'I never knew such happiness existed.' He paused, suddenly serious. 'You won't leave me will you, Alison?'

'Why would I do that?' she asked fervently, holding him tighter. 'Until we met, I was a mess, cheated on, sexual encounters with little love, and since Leo's father left when he was little… no one I've truly loved. I want you for keeps.'

'That means everything. I felt half a person, now life's us, not me. So happy I could burst!'

'Ooh no bursting,' Alison replied drowsily, kissing Stephen goodnight. 'Save that till we can burst together tomorrow. Sweet dreams… of me that is.'

He kissed her, whispering, 'Always of you.'

Next morning Alison called on Phoebe en route home.

Phoebe had seen her from upstairs, so was on the doorstep, arms outstretched. 'Alison how nice!' crushing her to her ample purple wool bosom.

'Just come from Stephen's. Is it OK?' Alison asked.

Phoebe led her in happily. 'Very OK, my clever detective,' voice echoing around the lofty hall. 'Coffee? I've had a sort out. No herbal tea, used to keep it for You-Know-Who. Even when he'd gone I used to buy it, habit. I buy what I want now.' she said with a naughty twinkle, shrugging her shoulders conspiratorially.

'In here. Sitting room, haven't touched it,' she affirmed busily. 'You can sort it out next week. Enough frivolity in one family, I'm off having seventies décor anywhere! This room was once full of friends, chinking glasses and conversation. Not now. Got plans to alter that.' she twinkled. 'When I've finished I'll be like a recycled teenager!' she proudly exclaimed, assuring Alison she was getting past the business of Gordon's misbehaviour.

'Most of our friends were joint, happens when you've been married ages. Hubby's the one at work, so brings business associates in for drinks, I don't recall ever inviting a couple I'd met to dinner. You modern women are liberated. Good thing too!'

Phoebe recounted their life. Alison said she missed her father. 'He steered without controlling. They had a Morris Minor, saved up for it, sacrificed to send me to grammar school. By then they had a better car and house. I sought similar in Leo's father, but became pregnant, scarcely knowing him. Given up finding a decent man, until Stephen.'

Phoebe beamed. 'The dear boy, so right for you.' She chuckled. 'Hark at me calling him a boy, more man than some twice his age. Pass your cup.'

Alison smiled at the boy bit, at Phoebe's age he'd seem like one. She watched her pour from the new cafetiere. 'This is new, super coffee it makes, with this plunger. Our ancient percolator's gone to the church jumble,' Phoebe announced proudly.

'Good for you. Stephen, although younger than me, is older

159

than his years, has my father's wisdom and sensitivity. Phoebe, he's the man for me, we're happy, ignoring comments about the age difference.'

Mrs. Cade clapped, affirming, 'Quite. Jealous bitches, wishing they could attract a young virile man like Stephen. They've no chance, you're beautiful, a stylish catch. They're not, boring lives and boring men in them. Carry on regardless I say!'

Alison welled up. 'Oh Phoebe, I will. We will. Let's give you a cuddle. I'll see you Tuesday. Fancy saying Stephen's virile. He is too,' she giggled. Phoebe giggled back loudly. 'Don't change everything though Phoebe. You're still wearing Tweed perfume, beautiful.'

Mrs. Cade stated confidently, 'Some things I won't change, but I'm not a shadow of someone else now.'

***

Stephen's concerts in Cardiff and Bristol on Thursday and Friday, gave Alison space to do overdue tasks – lists, filing, bank statements, room plans, diary.

She hadn't written her diary for days. Beginning the day taking Bo to the vet for annual jabs against feline ailments, she was back by ten, giving Bo salmon. Filing took ages, bank statements file sagged with their bulk.

Alison wanted to finish Phoebe's décor for her Edwardian sitting room. By noon, she'd ticked three tasks off the list. Satisfied, she adjusted the red kitchen blind, deciding to complete the rest there.

She laughed, watching Bo, low on the lawn, ears back, stealthily creeping towards a magpie hopping about, resembling a clockwork toy, having swooped like a pterodactyl. Alison knew Bo might come off worse if there was a skirmish, so knocked the door to shoo the noisy bird. The angry magpie shot into the hawthorn tree, cackling bird obscenities. Bo jumped, sending a fierce look in Alison's direction. Like all cats when they're confused and embarrassed, she began furious grooming. Paul Gallico had been correct in his book *The Silent Miaow*. 'When in doubt, wash!'

A sudden downpour made Alison dash to retrieve laundry. Bo, sheltering under the hawthorn, gave up 'hunt the magpie' and dashed into the kitchen, skidding. She shook, fine sprays of rain spattering the floor tiles, while Alison folded sweet smelling bedding upstairs. When she returned, Bo had squeezed behind a chair for a nap by the radiator. Leaving Bo twitching, Alison moved her work into the study. Propped up against a white silk cushion on the blue leather sofa, she read entries the week prior to meeting Stephen.

'Bought Julia's birthday present. Can't go to party, facing awkward questions.

Leo rang. Says I sound happier. I'm not.

February 9th. Freezing day. Bo, buffeted by strong wind, madly tore up trees. Indoors, fur tangled with dried leaves and bits of twig from silver birch. Licking, she coughed as debris got in the way, took pity and picked it off her fur. She let me brush her back to normal, purring loudly. Back to normal, will I ever be?!

February 12th. Mrs. C. asked me to do seventies decor in her sitting room! Gordon would turn in his grave! Clare rang in vino.

February 13th. Julia gave me herbal sleepers. Took two – worked!! If they work tonight shall come off anti-d's. Says David not coming to birthday party. Dislike him, gives her hassle. Still don't feel I can go. Perhaps I need anti-ds, herbal pills too weak.

February 14th. No Valentine's sent or received. Without love what's the point? Felt low this evening, played Roxy Music loudly. Poor Bo, alarmed, scarpered rapidly. When it stopped, she made me laugh, tentatively creeping back in, looking left and right to make sure Bryan Ferry had disappeared.

February 19th. Four days passed since writing. Should have written – Decided to go to Julia's party, deliver present, leave. Can't now. Met Stephen, musician. Invited him here, shameless hussy. Rockets, bells and poetry!

February 20th. Stephen went. Thought that would be it, despite promising a second visit. Sex magical, closeness wonderful, frightening. Too soon after last fiasco. Clare called, told her of S. Caught me unawares, vulnerable.

February 21st. Lots of sex. Miss him when not here.

February 22nd. Says he loves me. I'm cautious, love needs time. Stephen's intelligent, sensitive, loving. Don't want bubble to burst.

Alison looked up from the page, smiling. 'It hasn't, thank God.'

She'd put thoughts in a diary separate from her appointments one. Helpful to check on mistakes, plans realized, who'd been there, who'd left, who remained and why. Julia told her she envied her methodical coping, orderliness even amidst anguish. Alison had admitted it wasn't easy.

How could I think I loved him so soon. Sex, my drug, precluded rational thinking. When I missed him, it was as a child having lost my toy dog, emptiness. When he was found I was happy again. Good analogy. All that sex though, scared me, told Stephen we should have a break. No contact for ten days, after five I knew it wasn't lust. Confused with relationship so soon, I'd reflected on feelings.

Found Stephen trustworthy. Revealed our pasts. He thought Leo may resent him. Assured him Leo wants my happiness. In hindsight realize Phil is a sociopath, no conscience or compassion. Julia's David – same. No ability to give or receive love. Power mad, liar.

Stephen and I – similar views. He was worried hearing Henry's message – believing it was Phil. I was cross, thinking he didn't trust me.

He's a brilliant pianist, gardener, loving son to Trudie, whom I've met. We like each other too, important. Julia's fond of him and Mrs. C. has pronounced him a 'gem'. Praise indeed.

We talk about music, film, theatre, politics, philosophy. We had a debate on how old the world is, agreeing that those who believe the world to be less than ten thousand years old (as Henry did) are fools. Stephen said this denies science and archaeology.

Every day is precious with Stephen, when he's away, I'm confident he'll return. Gives me stability and confidence, respects me. Absolute contrast to previous men.

I wouldn't like S. to see this diary. Does that mean I'm deceptive? From experience, best not to reveal all. There has to be mystique and subtlety, not to be confused with deceit.

Achievements – Since Stephen, more work, more energy. Even exercising twice a week. Dealt with past, even though it re-appeared through Henry. Gave best advice I could with his recklessness.

Mrs. C. – shaken at revelations via internet re Gordon.

Taught me a lesson. Hidden depths in everyone, seeming to have perfect lives – an illusion. I suspect most folks are capable of 'living a lie'. Mrs. C. says I'm her rock. Glad to help.

Clare bolted to Norfolk. Mischief maker, tried to split up S and self. He thought I'd believe her lies. Definitely not, trust him, know her.

Not an achievement, but Julia and Jonathan together. Feel things will come to a head soon re David, am standing by for flack. She says such certainty about a man comes once in a lifetime. True.

The shriek of the telephone made Alison jump, releasing her from concentration and scribblings. She reluctantly leaned over the sofa to answer.

'Julia, lovely. I'm catching up on my life-diary.'

'Good idea making notes. Mine's in my maze of a brain, trying to find the exit for each problem. Can we have lunch tomorrow here, something's come up? I'm off to Mrs. Cade's at two-thirty. She's having a manicure and pedicure, already had her hair tinted. She'll be getting a toy boy next!'

Alison giggled. 'I'll bring apples, freshly picked.'

'Lovely. See you tomorrow.'

'Apples!' exclaimed Julia as Alison appeared with a wooden box.

'No, Alison's the name.'

'Sharp as ever, come in. I've made vegetable soup and we can eat it with my new rat-tailed soup spoons. Jonathan bought them, Birmingham hallmark for my birth year. Sit there.'

Alison sat at the table smelling a jug of late pink striped roses.

'Heavenly perfume. Are they Ferdinand Pichard?'

'Yes. I chose them on the net, Stephen planted them. Suppose he told you.' replied Julia, stirring thick aromatic soup.

Alison explained. 'Yes, but he bought one for me. I must look at your garden.'

'Stephen did a wonderful job. I do the lawn, weeding and deadheading. Stephen's busy with music, David refuses to cut hedges, so I need someone.' Julia replied, pouring the soup into two bowls.

'I could ask my cleaner if her husband would help. He does odd jobs to eke out their pensions. Shall I?' volunteered Alison.

'Please, I can hardly lift the cutter, let alone use it. That's another job I can cross off the list. How's your listmaking, did you finish it?'

'Ouch, soup's hot, delicious though. I cope doing lists, but the diary I'd neglected. Didn't you have something to discuss. Is David still on the spy?'

'Probably, but not that. It's Poppy.'

Alison took on a serious demeanour. Looking at Julia for some insight and receiving none, she uttered, 'Oh Julia. She's not...?'

Wide-eyed, Julia replied. 'At her age, God forbid! She has a way like most teenagers of making you fret before they've opened their mouths. David was doing the shopping on Saturday, we were baking lemon drizzle cake listening to Coldplay. She looked furtive so I asked what was wrong. Her reply was, "It's a bit diffi, Mum." You can imagine my face!'

'Julia, I'm on edge, what was it?'

'She's been to Cannes with Guy several times. He's a good daddy, she loves the area and he's relocating, busier there than here, leaving the Shropshire osteopathy practice for his assistant to manage at Christmas. Now for the crunch – she wants to go with him, attend the English/French school there. Bit of a shock.'

'I'll say. Why?'

Julia shrugged, looking wistful, but accepting. 'Says she loves the area and the language, wants to try it. Guy had told her to ask me but thought I wouldn't agree.'

'You don't surely?' Alison quizzed.

'Er, I didn't at first, a kick in the stomach. She's my only child, a pain the last six months, but I blame my situation. David's been beastly to me in front of her, no wonder she wants to clear off. When she told me her wishes, I could hardly speak and she started crying a bit, must have been an effort to tell me, brave even.'

'Mm. What did David say?'

Julia walked to the sink to fill the kettle. Leaning against the worktop, arms spread, she spat out 'Him! Sundays are a trial, even though he spends hours behind the *Mail*, providing a barrier between us. While I make Sunday roast, at least I can't see him. The few years we've been married, he seemed to like Poppy. When she'd gone to Guy's, I told David what she wanted to do. Thought he'd show concern, some kind of emotion. No. Over the motoring page, he looked up, sarcastically saying, "One down and one to go, then you can move lover boy in."'

Alison shrieked, falling back into the chair. 'My God!'

Julia nodded. 'His remarks were a shock, but I kept a poker face. Told him he was ridiculous and if he didn't want to discuss Poppy's situation, I'd decide. All I got was, "Get real. Bet she doesn't know you've been opening your legs in Warwick." He gave a triumphant smirk, threw the paper, knocking over his drink, soaking the rest of the Sundays. Shook me up, I was relieved hearing his car tearing off.'

'No way! One suspicious, twisted man, trying to catch you out.'

'I've lived with that too long, humiliation, snide remarks, unnerving silences. My self-esteem's fine when I'm with Jonathan, at home my morale's been annihilated. Recently I've smashed wine glasses, hearing his key in the door. It's like permanent premenstrual tension.'

Alison listened sympathetically. 'Hardly surprising. Julia, that book *Cosmic Ordering*, have you used it just once? It worked, Jonathan came as a result, despite my great scepticism.'

'Yes. Six weeks ago when things were worsening, I asked for a solution out of this mess. If Poppy goes to live with Guy in France, I can rid myself of David. Ideal in theory but her happiness is first, I'll talk to Guy.'

'Yes. Now before it rains, show me the results of Stephen's gardening.'

20

Julia had become used to sleeping in her treatment room. Once the futon had been folded up, no evidence, clients mustn't know of her private life. David occupied upstairs, insisting he was staying put. From her prison, her room was now her haven. She cleaned his, changed bed linen, and retrieved her clothes from upstairs.

Anxious about Poppy's recent bombshell, Julia rang Jonathan at 9.30 p.m.

'Are you ok?'

'Mm. I climbed into bed just as Poppy had gone to sleep, exhausted from her riding lesson. It's cosy in here reading. Jonathan, I need to see you.'

Jonathan's tone darkened. 'Oh, what's wrong?'

'I'd like your input on a matter. May I come tomorrow at ten-thirty?'

'Yes. Something to show from Boston.'

'I shall think of a bigger bed awaiting me,' was her inviting reply.

'Goodnight, your wish is my command.'

Once Julia had hidden the car at Jonathan's, she relaxed. He wanted to know what was wrong immediately.

'I'll tell you, but if you think I haven't missed you terribly…

Let me see what you wanted to show me, then you can show me what I want to see!' she suggested provocatively, drawing him into her arms.

He kissed her neck. 'My resolve's weakening. Let me get our drinks.'

Leading Julia to the sofa, he went into the den. Seeing the garden, she recalled the first time she'd walked down it with him. A magical moment, ethereal mist suspended around the pines beyond the fence.

He returned with coffee and a plate. 'Here's my find.'

Jonathan poured coffee into poppy-decorated china mugs. Julia had been touched he'd bought them to remind her of Poppy. He collected eighteenth century coffee cans but wouldn't use them. Julia read the motto. 'For age and want save while you may. No morning sun lasts a whole day.'

'You've heard of Benjamin Franklin? One of the Founding Fathers of America. Scientist, politician, writer, philanthropist, inventor of bifocal glasses, urinary catheters, et al. This is an ABC plate, to teach children to read. Some made in Staffordshire, some America.'

Julia kissed him soundly like a mother to her child. 'Your enthusiasm makes everything interesting. I'd no idea who Benjamin Franklin was.'

'One of his parents was English and at seventeen he worked as an apprentice printer in St. Bartholomew-the-Great Church in Smithfields, London. I learned from the Boston dealer that Rahere, a jester in Henry 1st's court, was cured of malaria by asking in the church for healing. It's said that prayers made there are answered. Your mother's Fabergé items are at Sotheby's next week. Why don't we go for the day to the auction and the church… what?'

'Our situation. That is what you mean isn't it?'

'Yes, I believe, and you're a don't know. I'll pray for both of us, say you'll come?' he implored.

'Yes please. Now, let me tell you about Poppy.'

***

Julia had prepared carefully for London, informing David she was attending a reflexology course. He'd grinned manically, not replying. His mouth had a permanent sneer. A sarcastic, unwashed slob, a large plaster was needed to heal Julia's wounds. Thank God she had kind, considerate Jonathan.

Julia had kept the catalogue at Jonathan's. David was vindictive and would cheerfully flatten him. Too much at stake not to be cautious, but if Poppy lived in France, the David situation would be resolved. Next day, Julia drove with jellied legs to Jonathan's. He took them to the station for the London journey. Travelling alone on a train she enjoyed landscape flashing by, today though would be an exciting adventure with a loved man.

Having lunch in Sotheby's café, when Jonathan paid the bill, she mused on how different he was to David. Jonathan returned. 'In twenty minutes we must allez up the stairs. Fair few Russians here by the accents, desiring your lots in the catalogue.'

Julia felt safe far from home, excited the Russian Sale would sell her parents' Fabergé animals. Passing a Bond Street jewellers, Jonathan had pointed out similar, nestling amongst Art Deco diamond brooches, rings and necklaces. Jonathan had swept her up as they left Sotheby's, ecstatic her lots had reached top prices.

They'd taken a cab for a quick look at St. Bartholomew's Church. With only fifteen minutes to spend in the old church, Jonathan had knelt, praying for healing of their situation. Julia hadn't, but visualised their future. At five twenty they'd boarded the train from Euston.

At Jonathan's, Julia had told him she hadn't relaxed so much for months. Someone she loved in equal measure, a selfless good man. Driving home through dark autumn lanes, she envisaged the brutish, selfish man there. She shuddered, the path wouldn't be smooth exchanging one for the other.

In bed, she went over the day. The house was quiet, Poppy

asleep, a changed girl since Julia had promised to consider her moving to Cannes. Earlier, in her bedroom, she'd patted the duvet, inviting Julia to join her. 'Mum, here's my list for France. In chemistry lesson I was bored, so wrote places we've visited with Daddy and what I want to see when I'm living there. If it's ok… with you.' she asked, looking up nervously.

Julia stroked Poppy's dark glossy hair, reading her list.

Vieux Nice has 19 museums
Le Bistro d'Antoine
The Maight Foundation, not far from St. Paul de Vence centre
Le Grimaldi Hotel
La Zucca Magica – veggie resto
Parfumerie Molinard
La Vague – need a new poster

'Ooh those fab houses in St. Paul. Daddy says he's selling the apartment and buying a house. You will come and stay won't you, Mum?' she asked emotionally. 'If you'll visit, I'll be OK.'

'Yes, but you'll need to be near Cannes for school, besides which, St. Paul is terribly expensive. I see you've written Parfumerie Molinard. I'm out of Jasmine perfume so I'll have to come ASAP won't I?' Julia twinkled. 'Vieux Nice has nineteen museums does it? Sleep, or you won't have energy for school tomorrow. Goodnight.'

'Night, Mum. I'm going to be vegetarian from now on. Red meat's toxic and carnivorous animals have a short bowel. We've got yards so don't get rid of our waste quickly enough.'

'Poppy! Vile! You shouldn't be going to France thinking like that. They're big meat eaters.'

The remembrance made Julia recall the desperate hug she'd received from her daughter. She was assured of her love, and France a flight away. La Vague – the wave poster familiar to student bedsits. Guy had given Poppy one but David had binned it because of the state of her room. She'd burst into tears, kicked him, calling him a cruel bastard, screaming he wasn't her dad and never would be.

Julia was certain she'd allow Guy to take Poppy to France, but lay awake, mind awhirl. 'Stop. Poppy wants to go, Guy's a brilliant father. She'll be happy. David's making her unhappy. What if she can't settle, hates it, oh why did I let him cause this?' Thoughts circled, body restless under the duvet. She squinted at the illuminated clock radio, turning the dial away, slipping into an uneasy sleep.

21

'See you next week.' Max Allen said, retrieving measuring tape and clipboard. 'Dad and meself'll come while weather's fine. M'Dad likes doing extensions, a brickie at heart. Gets fed up with conservatories, everybody's havin' em. Folks don't consider all that glass to clean. Cheerio then.'

Laurie shook his weathered hand. 'Thanks Max.'

He waved as Max climbed into the red Ford truck, emblazoned with bold lettering. 'Allen and Son – Building Specialists.'

Laurie had missed his four o'clock pot of tea. Used to the ritual at Trudie's, he'd reverted to it now. Filling the kettle, he strayed to those lovely times. Almost four years with Trudie, the discovery around his bereavement had floored him, He carried his tea into the oak-beamed room to sit in the new armchair. Marital home contents had been sold, so he'd bought a sofa, bed, and other necessities.

Drinking from the studio pottery mug he'd bought in Cornwall, he knew Trudie would have served tea in china cups and saucers. He wasn't used to that with his late wife, but Trudie had standards he liked. A pang of regret stabbed, hot tea burning his mouth, hardly noticed.

He'd acted whilst the pain of discovery was rife, no option, he'd become so ill. Giving notice at work on the grounds of mental strain from Irene's death, he'd put the house up for sale, within weeks flying to live with his son in North Carolina. He'd intended to rest a few months, then return to his daughter in Bamburgh, a beautiful coastal area in Northumbria, to recuperate. His grief while in America had been enormous, he'd suffered a breakdown and temporary amnesia. His son and daughter-in-law's care enabled him to gradually recover.

As the day faded, Laurie switched on the brass tablelamp. He drew emerald curtains, knowing they'd be Trudie's choice. 'Trudie... how I wish I could explain.'

Sorting a drawer, he found a copy-letter he'd sent to a local newspaper once, criticizing the parish church for not observing the two minutes silence at the eleventh hour on November 11th. He'd gone at ten to eleven into church, where a coffee morning was taking place. One of the ladies told him no direction had been given by the vicar. Laurie had been appalled at the stupidity of the statement. The library would be honouring the dead, so that's where he went.

The comments to the local rag had vented his spleen concerning the non-happening in the church, assuaging annoyance at his life then too. He'd wanted to honour those who had no choice but to do and die. His frustration with his situation, the lie he was living and not able to be with Trudie, had added to his internal grief.

Wondering if Trudie had spent her birthday on November 2nd with a new man, his mind rewound to tender moments. The brain was the world's finest computer, not easily switched off. The price he and Trudie had paid was immense. From living with his wife, seeing Trudie whenever he could, then with family in America, Laurie now lived alone.

He'd settled into the old cottage in Ashton, near Tenbury Wells, liking the remoteness, winding lanes. He'd joined the library, ventured into village pubs for company, walked on Catherton

Common above the beautiful Clee Hills, and visited his daughter in Bamburgh. She'd stored his belongings; he'd returned with a loaded car from a week's stay.

On some level he knew he deserved to be punished, but his actions had punished Trudie too. Abroad, he'd punished himself further, beating himself with his own stick of remorse. When amnesia had faded, he'd recalled surreptitious phone calls, clandestine meetings, vigilance that had to be kept. Recently he'd been in a Ludlow supermarket, hearing a man on the phone to his wife, explaining he was in the office and would be late. Noticing two bottles of wine in his basket, Laurie had grimaced at the deceit, his also in the past.

Until Trudie, he hadn't experienced total love. He'd believed one day they'd be a couple, entering a room together, friends knowing them as Trudie and Laurie. That hadn't happened, now he entered everywhere alone.

22

'*Celebrity Equinox* or *Queen Mary 2*?' wondered Phoebe. October sun highlighted cruise brochures on the window seat, a decision had to be made.

With Radio 3 playing Haydn, Phoebe had formed plans when Alison last called. Whilst Wilf the decorator worked on the outside window frames, Phoebe had proclaimed in loud Queen's English, 'I've selected from four William Morris wallpapers. Methinks Strawberry Thief's just the ticket, expensive, but worth it. Alison, what d'you think of these?' She'd shown Alison the holiday brochures.

'Phoebe, are you really going?'

'Spiffing idea don't you think? Next spring say, a cruise will help my arthritis.' She passed Alison a Cunard brochure. 'When I went on that confidence course, the lecturer told us to turn our attention to the present and see it as a present. That's what I'm doing. I could do with getting away from the waxed and waterproofed for a bit. County ladies, suppose I'm one meself. Have a browse, I'll see if the decorator wants coffee.'

She walked back to find Alison enthusing, 'Phoebe, new people, sea air. I'm excited and not even going. Which one do you fancy?'

Phoebe sat by Alison. 'One of the WI ladies has been to St. Petersburgh on a Baltic cruise, quite fancy that,' she twinkled. 'They keep you active on these cruises. I'll be OK, but don't know how anyone elderly would cope.'

Alison twinkled at the last comment.

'Gosh, me making all these plans. Decorating – thanks to you – a holiday, which one, where, when? Gordon always decided. If a stranger came to the door, he'd mutter "What do they want? Whatever it is, we haven't got it!" I've made another decision too.' Phoebe added.

Alison was agog. 'Crumbs!'

'I'm taking a paying guest, to share my house four nights a week. My cleaner has a teacher – he leaves on Fridays for Derbyshire and returns Monday evening.'

Alison was even more amazed. 'Brilliant, picking yourself up like this. A male lodger – could be your toy boy.' She squeezed Phoebe's wrist conspiratorialy, wrinkling her nose.

Phoebe chuckled. 'Hadn't thought of that!' she shrieked loudly, voice resounding around the walls. She turned towards Alison, voice quieter.

'Thank you for your assistance a while ago. Not decorating, you know to what I'm referring. Last month two folks at church died suddenly. I realized I'd got health, family, friends, money to enjoy the rest of my natural. Carpus Diem! Or is it Carpe? Anyway, making changes. Firstly, forget what the silly old fool did. Why let his behaviour make me miserable? I'll get re-decorated, get a cultured man to stay, see the family, then further afield on a cruise. What d'you think?'

Alison shook her head. 'I applaud you, excellent. Why don't we turn Gordon's study into the lodger's room. It would erase what you found there.'

Phoebe lit up. 'Ideal! When can we begin?' she asked excitedly.

Alison beamed, holding Phoebe's wrinkled hands. 'I haven't seen you so animated in months. I worried you'd struggle from that other business, but you're planning the future, what a trouper you are, strong and valiant.'

Phoebe smiled thankfully at the praise. 'It's how I was brought up. Parents, school, taught to get on with stuff. Valiant – attributed that to war heroes, nice of you to say it. You're a special friend to me. Real friendship when I was so broken. Ooh, meant to give you a jar of damson jam I made.' She grinned mischievously, 'Difficult making raspberry in August, those horrid wasps, little villains! Look like burglars in their striped tops don't they? When the children were small, I made one jar with a dead wasp trapped inside, labelled it wasp and raspberry jam. They found it hilarious.

'Let's make plans for the transformation.' she demanded feistily, leading Alison determinedly out of the room.

23

Trudie hadn't liked her own birthdays as a child. When she married, sadness she felt on November 2nd went, resurfacing when her husband died. She didn't want to celebrate at all, but as grief faded and Stephen could appreciate her day, she'd enjoyed it. When he moved to Manchester to study music, Trudie spent the day with Paula. When Laurie was there, she made birthday cakes, he was the icing on top.

Since his sudden exit, birthday melancholia had reappeared. Even with cards, presents, and telephone calls from Stephen, Paula, and Lizzie, Trudie became increasingly aware of time passing. Memories of Laurie resurfaced every year, albeit slightly out of focus.

Stephen and Alison had driven from Cheshire in lashing rain, but ten miles from Little Arrow, a rainbow had dazzled. After lunch at the village pub, they'd had a damp tramp by the riverbank, with tea and birthday cake at five o'clock.

Alison had made a fuss of Holly, Trudie's cat. As they owned tortoiseshells, they'd compared notes re markings, habits of the feminine breed. Trudie had expressed concern for Bo, Alison's cat, who had a forthcoming operation to remove a jaw carcinoma, worrying, but the one option to save her pet. Steroids, she'd told

Trudie, would delay the inevitable, so the vet would remove the affected part of the lower jaw.

'She's been acting strangely, eating Fuller's Earth from the cat tray. It contains magnesium oxide, a colon cleanser preventing toxins in the intestinal tract. Strange behaviour though, so I bought a mineral supplement to stop her craving. You wouldn't think there was anything wrong with her, Trudie, eats well, dashes about, so the vet says she should survive the op. She'll look a mess and they'll have to keep her a few days to feed her through a tube, before I bring her home. I have to give her this chance.'

Trudie had sympathetically put her arm around Alison. 'Of course.'

Whilst Alison was admiring the décor and discussing design, Stephen divided perennials. Alison admired Trudie's farmhouse-type hall, stripped pine, lime-washed walls, Cornish prints, stoneware jugs. The kitchen brought more praise.

'Mine's red and white sixties style so clients can see that setting, but I love your scumbled pine cupboards, terracotta tiles, white walls. I'm doing a client's cottage interior, may I replicate yours?' she'd asked enthusiastically.

Trudie said she'd be honoured. After chicken pie and a rice pudding with nutmeg-freckled skin, Stephen and Alison reluctantly left at 8.15.

Laurie wasn't mentioned. 'Thank God for Stephen.' she thought. Such a contrast to childhood birthdays, her mother stern and depressed, unlike Trudie's kind father, mentally battered by his wife. Better apart, but then most married couples weathered the storms and didn't divorce. Her father worked hard in heavy engineering, Alice a housewife and dressmaker. Their daughter was seen in pretty dresses, but Trudie would have preferred a loving family like her friends, rather than smart clothes and an unhappy fireside. It was not her father's fault, at least Trudie felt love from him, giving her life some purpose. In her mother's view, he was wrong, so was Trudie.

Her hypertense, negative mother made Trudie secretive. She could admit things to her father, but dramas ensued if Alice knew, explosions, fraught silences for days. Schoolfriends were ill at ease, confused by Alice checking they weren't making a mess, embarrassing Trudie. Trudie had been the polar opposite with Stephen. Her mother should have sought medical help. Her father had tried to placate her and avoid rows, but she wore the trousers.

For her tenth birthday, Trudie had asked for a stamp album. Excited, she'd opened the black, hardbacked loose-leaf album, gone to school happy, but as she didn't have parties, went home alone. Alice was at the sewing machine. Her father, at dinner, had given her a packet of Romanian stamps depicting animals. Sitting at the green baize card table, while her parents were washing up, she heard raised voices.

'Fifteen shillings! You spent that on her, what a waste. What was wrong with Woolworths? They'd only be five bob. She's spoilt enough.'

Trudie winced, frowning at the recall.

'Alice, it's her birthday, we can afford that, keep your voice down. Don't upset her today please,' her father pleaded.

The sound of saucepans crashing made Trudie shrink, hurt beyond measure.

Alice retorted spitefully. 'I don't see why she should have everything I didn't. We were too poor, do you realize how that felt? Do you?'

'Alice, yes, but we want our daughter to be happy. We're comfortably off, no debts, good jobs, why shouldn't she have a nice present? It won't spoil her, it's normal on her birthday.'

'Wish I was normal, the damage she did, pain, tearing and stitches. I couldn't sit properly for three months. How would you like it!'

'I wouldn't, but it's not Trudie's fault. Stop blaming her, I'm sick of it, and if you say anymore I... I don't know what I'll do.'

181

Enraged, her mother threw cutlery, slammed the door, thunderering upstairs. Trudie's father, aware she'd overheard, told her Alice didn't mean it, she was depressed. They'd hugged, father and daughter, but the damage was done. Trudie's sense of desolation had been overwhelming.

'Mother was mentally damaged, spoiling my childhood. It's taken me from an insecure child to a needy adult.'

In bed, reliving her day with Stephen and Alison, her body softened, and sleep claimed her.

24

November 4th was a day Alison wouldn't forget. Stephen had stayed at Alison's the night before. He had rehearsals in Chester and offered to take Bo for her jaw operation en route.

'Stephen, thanks, I want to be with her and have to sign the form. You go.'

Stephen picked up keys. 'Where is she? Don't want to let her out.'

'You won't, she's in the cat carrier.' Alison walked with him to the front door.

He hugged her, feeling her worry. 'Give her a head flattener from me, I'll see you this evening.'

Closing the stained glass door, its heaviness echoed Alison's heart. In fifteen minutes she had to set off with her constant companion. She knew Bo would purr as ever in the carrier, Mr. Edwards said Bo was one of the most amiable cats he'd encountered.

Fetching her fleece jacket from the cloakroom, Alison retrieved Bo from beneath the washbasin, touching her re-assuringly through the carrier's air vents, telling her she was very loved. The purring was deep. Handing her to the nurse at the vets, she prayed it would never stop.

It was five o'clock on 4th November when the vet had made the call, telling Alison the operation had gone well, that Bo was on morphine, with a feeding tube in her oesophagus. He'd ring her next morning to report on Bo's progress. Alison had an ominous feeling, spending two hours tossing from eleven o'clock until one. She awoke to discover it was ten minutes to eight next morning. Sluggish from shallow sleep, her first thoughts were of Bo.

Shuffling slowly downstairs, the shrill ring of the telephone made her bang her hip against the door. Mr. Edwards gently told her the grim news.

'I'm sorry Alison, but Bo passed away at eleven o'clock last night.'

Alison heard herself shout, 'No, no, oh no! God no – please!' she yelled at the heartbreaking call. Her whole body shook at the terrible news. 'Please, no. Don't say that. Don't. Don't!' she cried. Her sobs grew louder at the appalling outcome.

'I really am so sorry. Six hours after her operation, she miaowed and tried to stand up. I'm afraid her breathing became faint and she suffered a stroke. I didn't want to ring you then, but this call isn't any easier now. Ring me with what you'd like to do with her body.'

Alison had to sit down, but didn't want to let Tom Edwards go, repeating questions through choking sobs. Afterwards, she gazed inertly at the carpet, dampening her leggings with tears. Her call to Julia was almost unintelligible, voice racked with clots of sobs. As soon as Poppy had been driven to school Julia visited, comforting Alison. They'd discussed what to do with Bo.

'There's no way I could have an urn full of ashes on my mantelpiece, not an animal's nor a relative. I wouldn't want a reminder that someone I loved was grey ash. Don't want the pet cemetery either. I need to bury her in the garden. I need to say goodbye and… and… oh God, it's so awful I can't bear it.'

'When's Stephen home?'

Hearing his name, Alison wept again. 'Tonight. He's rehearsing for a concert.'

'You're not going to phone him are you?'

'I shan't do that, he'll be terribly upset too. God, why did I put my precious girl through that.' she cried, in Julia's arms.

Alison had rung Tom Edwards with her answer. Bo would be collected next morning. He'd re-assured her she'd be wrapped in a box and he'd explain what happened.'

That evening, Stephen had rung his mother, with the dreadful news of Bo. He told her Alison couldn't face ringing. Trudie was comforted when days later she received a typed letter.

'Dear Trudie,

As you know from Stephen, Bo is dead. I'm devastated. Forgive me, I can only type on my laptop, I'd break down on the phone.

Stephen dug a grave by the shed. The vet explained why she'd died six hours after her operation. A stroke. I opened up the box and unwrapped her from the towel. Heartbreakingly beautiful, and I cut some of her tortoiseshell fur to keep. I kissed her and told her she was so loved. We buried her, prayed at her grave amidst cascading tears. Put paving stones on top so foxes couldn't dig her up, and late roses in a stoneware vase. I loved her, a soulmate to me. I've felt a little better bringing her home.

Apparently, the carcinoma on her jaw was huge. I had to give her the chance of living through the operation, but no-one expected her to die. I feel immense regret, asking myself "what if?" I'm empty inside. I left her at the vet purring, telling her I'd see her next day. I should have been with her at her end, but it wasn't possible.

To think I'll never have her on my lap purring, playing

headbutting. I seem to have cried a million tears, refusing to accept she's gone.

I'm so broken. Stephen was wonderful, as he's been since we met nine months ago. You can be justifiably proud of your son, I bless the day we met. His compassion is sustaining me, so I'm able to cry until exhausted. Some men would be irritated, not Stephen. He's a credit to you, Trudie.

Love, Alison

p.s. When Stephen and I were burying Bo, a robin trilled beautifully in the hawthorn tree. Having never had a robin in the garden on account of Bo, it felt like a sign. I'll tell you what I think – she's gone to heaven. That robin's been here ever since. I try to emulate his song to show him I appreciate his message. I do that with the blackbird. Stephen knows me well enough not to run off.'

Trudie wept for Alison's loss of a loved pet. She should reply immediately but a client was due. Later she'd write a reply, more personal than an e-mail. Lunch came and went, but she couldn't convey what she wanted.

Two cups of tea and an hour on, she was no nearer, the notepaper full of crossings out. Trudie was a good writer, but a simple task was proving difficult. On the chaise longue, wrapped in a white throw, gazing through the roof, she hoped to doze. No noise, no washing machine whirring. No reason not to fall into a beneficial afternoon nap. Indecision though, that robber of rest, was present.

Rather than acting on vital clues gleaned from Paula, plus the Laurie revelation in Cornwall, she'd left them on ice. Inertia was evident in the kitchen, dishes languishing in the sink for days, worktops cluttered, resembling a scrapyard. Leafless Robinia's spindly branches wafted above in November wind, leaden clouds scudded across the sky, echoing her mood.

'How will I reveal the truth if I don't make a concerted effort? I'll be stuck with negative grief. I've tried in short spurts... then abandoned it.'

She winced at the disappointment, mystery. Under the throw, she drifted to what might have been. 'He'd languished unhappily with a wife who may as well have been on another planet. What if he'd left Irene? We might have been blissfully happy but we might not. He may have been consumed with guilt or she'd have made him feel it, which may have destroyed us. The stalker, would she have re-appeared? Would the split up and divorce have been destructive, he wasn't a man to hurt people. Perhaps our sexual relationship would have been affected. Exciting when we saw each other twice a week, perhaps if we'd been together constantly, everything would've been routine and boring.

I've wasted time grieving for this man. Judgement for not considering his wife; nobody forced me to love a married man. It felt right, but I should have been content with what I had. I won't find happiness until I've located the lost pieces to this jigsaw.'

Doing what was necessary would be a mighty leap. Conscious of her own mortality and irked for not using time she had left, she was ashamed of her inertia. Hessenford church and Paula's discovery in that pub; if they weren't an answer to her prayers. Procrastination, that cruel thief of time had won again.

Drifting for forty minutes, finding winter sky almost dark upon waking, she resolved to begin positive steps.

25

Laurie Martin was pleased with Max's work, the kitchen extended for dining, a brighter outlook and full view of the garden. Laurie had scythed grasses and choking weeds, uncovering perennials, gooseberries and rhubarb. The dining room, he'd made into a study.

Since re-arranging the kitchen, he'd eaten there every day. Even on dull days he'd felt buoyant with the open aspect, instead of the dark room with no view. He'd bought bird feeders, hanging them high in pear trees, safe from cats fancying extra dinner.

He observed hungry tits, wrens, chaffinches, blackbirds, robins, even greedy quarrelling starlings. In late summer he'd seen something resembling an oversized chaffinch. Going into the newly-named study to fetch his British bird book, he resolved to unpack.

Since October, the bird, a Whitethroat, had flown. Books too, from the study. Laurie had made a concerted effort to unpack, dust and put them on pine shelves each side of the fireplace. As he was dusting *Swallows and Amazons*, a postcard from his daughter youth hostelling in Cumbria, aged fifteen, spilled onto the rug. Her earnest plea, 'only eaten Kendal Mint Cake and half a wasp since breakfast PLEASE SEND MONEY TO NEXT

HOSTEL, Helena. xxx' His children loved him, but no complete happiness away from Trudie, whom he'd abandoned without explanation.

That evening he'd unpacked LPs, EPs, tapes, and CD's. Sitting on the floor too long, his back felt like a creaking gate, hunched shoulders ached. His life was in these boxes, unopened since he'd departed England's shores in confused melancholic haste four years previously.

Sorting a box of rock 'n' roll, his tea went cold. It was fascinating going through dog-eared shiny covers of Eddie Cochran LP's, Cliff Richard, The Shadows, Elvis, The Everly Brothers, The Platters, Tommy Steele. One extended player stood out. 'Twist and Shout' by The Beatles. He'd held it, knowing it was Trudie's. She'd lent it to him, telling how in 1963, she and Lizzie had gone to Brixham on holiday. Lizzie had bought 'Sweets For My Sweet' by The Searchers. Trudie had listened to 'Twist and Shout' in the shop's booth. She'd told Laurie how they'd spontaneously performed the twist to the records, customers clapping and smiling at the sight of them giggling, falling into each other.

'Beautiful remembrances.' he thought, holding the sleeve, inhaling the musky plastic smell, wondering when he'd be able to return it. If ever.

Memories in every box – Nat King Cole, Frank Sinatra, Johnny Mathis, John Dankworth, Cleo Laine, Miles Davis, Pink Floyd, Moody Blues, Dire Straits. When he met Trudie, their music co-incided. Trudie liked bitter-sweet ballads, raunchy rock 'n' roll, jazz and classical. Laurie had been amazed at her knowledge of composers, artists, orchestras. They'd snuggled up to Sinatra's albums. He'd seen in Trudie's collection, *Wee Small Hours*. The lyrics mirrored his feelings. He'd told her, in his opinion, Frank was the greatest exponent of lyrics ever.

An apt song drifted into Laurie's head. 'The Other Woman, The Other Man'. Words so apt to his situation.

189

Getting up, he stepped over piles of music to put the kettle on, gazing vacantly at the garden, rinsing his mug more than necessary, oblivious of weather, garden, birds. Miles Davis's *Once Upon A Summertime* filled his brain. He and Trudie had listened during dinner, danced to it, made love with it in the background. These watercolour pictures swooped without warning, the click of the kettle halting his memory. He made tea, these days not in a tea pot as Trudie would.

Arranging music into alphabetical order, he pushed the boxes into the corner, then watched television, switching to *Judge Judy*. He smiled at how he and Trudie viewed her programme in bed, eating rich tea biscuits, drinking hot chocolate, wincing at Judy's waspish comments. They'd laughed at her clever analogies and put downs. People in the courtroom were often trailer trash, no chance against the Judge's intellect and quick appraisals. Over the top but good entertainment.

Laurie went for a slice of cake bought from the WI market. In his armchair, he saw the second case was their favourite. Now he'd laugh by himself, no alternative. The courtroom had erupted with raucous laughter, people collapsing into each other. Laurie and Trudie had too. Trudie's biscuit had sunk into her drink, making them giggle more. The door had opened to reveal Holly wondering what the hilarity was about. Her shocked expression had made them laugh again.

The episode now had made Laurie merely smirk. He switched to an episode of *Round The Horne*. He and Trudie had laughed at the brilliant script and particularly Kenneth Williams hilarious antics and comments.

Laurie grinned, but with Trudie it would have been hilarious. On a book programme, a panel were debating *Forever Amber*. He'd once told Trudie he felt like an insect trapped inside amber. She'd been hurt, until he'd explained he meant his marriage. These days he felt like a snail without its shell – vulnerable.

Sorting the music into categories, before placing records

onto shelves below the books, he dusted them, noticing the odd spider. An image of Trudie recoiling made him sigh at the sweet memory.

Two Rachmaninov piano concerto albums seemed stuck together. Separating them, a cascade of papers spiralled to the carpet. Reaching for reading specs, he recognised Trudie's handwriting immediately, heart lurching at her backward sloping script. When he discovered memories, butterfly fluttering caused happiness, becoming his oxygen. Pictures in his mind, whenever he wanted to recall them, he'd flick through pages of his mind so Trudie would always be there.

'Oh, Trudie suggested these when I hadn't the guts to leave Irene. Scared of change, upsetting my wife, kids, job, that bloody stalker, whole damn business.'

On the first page Trudie had written, 'I'm remarkably at one with the universe, a calmness reaching out from you. We must persevere with a positive attitude, so… Von Goethe wrote – "Unless one is committed there is hesitancy." He read on. "Boldness has genius, power and magic."

Laurie wished he'd taken heed; serious events had prevented this. Holding more affirmations Trudie used, scarcely noticing his blank reflection in the TV screen, looking down, he traced her script with his finger.

'We change affirmations as our lives unfold, so here are new ones, also mine. "I allow my life to change for the better. I go straight to what I need. I have, give and receive love. I am in the right place at the right time."'

Laurie had asked, 'How do we project happy if we're so down?'

Gazing into anxious eyes, she'd firmly emphasised, 'We have to try. I will if you will.'

26

'That's Showbusiness' was Alison's choice for interior design. Her scarlet and white kitchen/dining set had been purchased there, with discount as a valued regular customer. If Alison's clients wanted modern, this is where she came. Quality, supplying British showhomes, and twice a year opening to the public, offering surplus stock and returned furniture. Alison had planned to take Julia, whose cold had worsened.

Shaking raindrops off her hair, Alison was glad she was early. Even at nine-thirty people were leaving with rugs, lamps, material and cushions. She hoped there'd be a Barcelona chair.

'Hi Jennie.' she called, approaching the manageress at her desk.

'Alison you came. Phew, mad already, where's your friend?'

'She's developed a chill; I need items for clients. Don't suppose there's a Barcelona chair?'

Jennie lowered her voice, beckoning Alison. 'One back yesterday, £200 to you. Want to see it?'

'Oh thanks, a pale colour?'

'Mm, ivory, no stool though.'

'Fine.'

'I can't leave the desk, go through to the storeroom.'

Alison spent five minutes inspecting the designer chair,

famous and copied by many. It had soft leather, statement chrome, untarnished, leather buttons intact.

When Alison emerged, Jennie was with a customer. She caught her eye, giving thumbs up for the deal, then selected a white round table on a chrome stand, and a leather-topped desk. The assistant put a sold sticker on them, directing her to Jennie, in conversation on the telephone.

'Won't be a minute,' she confided, covering the mouthpiece. 'Have a seat.'

Alison scanned a brochure, hearing Jennie say, 'I remember your unusual name from a previous order. Reduced to £20, remind me of the address Mrs.de Mar.'

Alison, adrenaline racing, stiffened.

'Wednesday morning, £30 including delivery, pay the driver please.'

'Alison, popping to the loo. Back in a mo.'

Flushing, Alison swivelled towards the desk. Bewildered, she knew it wouldn't be Julia. Shakily scribbling the address onto the brochure, she stuffed it into her handbag.

***

With her mind full of 'should I, shouldn't I tell?' the answer came. 'Would I want to know?' she thought, absent-mindedly watching *Flog It* at home. A resounding YES! This was not tittle-tattle, but vital evidence for Julia.

Next day, Julia angrily flopped onto a kitchen chair, totally shocked. 'The hypocrite! The punishment I've given myself for being with Jonathan. Hell!' She stared at coffee dregs, uncurling from her slumped position. 'I've tried until I'm worn out. Determined not to develop second wife syndrome, bringing baggage from the first, I trusted him.'

Alison sympathised. 'Don't know how you've lived under the same roof for three years.'

Julia sighed heavily. 'He was too attentive, I should have detected his falsehood, I was needy, ignoring the signs.'

Alison nodded regretfully. 'What about me? Repeated mistakes. I'd got rid of Phil and his deceptions, vowing I wouldn't start an affair again with sex. Ha, fell at the first fence with Stephen. Sorry Jools, I must go over to Phoebe's now, but had to tell you what I heard.'

'Glad you did. I've been worrying if David can read me when I've been with Jonathan. I thought he was a workaholic, looks like he had someone well before I met Jonathan. Lashing out with cruel remarks, putting guilt onto me, but planning his own exit, what a nerve!'

'Mendacity. I had that with Phil and Henry.'

Julia frowned, 'Remind me what it means.'

Alison flinched, uneasy at how she let Phil and Henry deceive her. 'When a man paints a picture of what he wants us to know and withholds what he doesn't want us to discover, that's mendacity. Not little white lies, big fat ones from the start, the truth being the opposite scenario from the one he's presented. So convincing we don't question it.'

'That's exactly it, bet there's other stuff I'm unaware of. Now I'll be observing him.'

***

The night before David de Mar's forty-third birthday on a freezing day in December, he casually revealed he had a meeting in Yorkshire. Julia's mouth twisted, emotions near the surface. She guessed there may be a different meeting, but kept a blank expression, difficult with knowledge gleaned from Alison. Next morning she wished him a happy birthday.

'Yeah, while the cat's away, the mouse can play,' he sneered, steaming through the hall, slamming the front door.

Each time his BMW disappeared, Julia felt emotionally freer, as if a heavy overcoat had been shed. David never felt guilt so continued to taunt. She mustn't let him suspect she had knowledge of Dolphin Avenue.

Although he'd employed a detective, Julia could do her own sleuthing. Armed with directions, she set off at ten-thirty, nerves attacking. Driving seven miles to Sandstone village, she drew into a layby to check directions. Her hands quivered, reading the last direction to turn into Dolphin Avenue, number seventeen being on the right. David's car could be outside, despite the Yorkshire story, with him in the house. She had to take the risk.

Parking to look at what lay ahead, Julia noticed aisles of lime trees, making her less visible. During her childhood in a working class street, there were no drives or garages; her father infuriated with people parking outside their terraced house. Now Julia had a detached home with a double drive she didn't have that problem, but since David, much greater concerns had loomed.

Julia cruised down the sleepy avenue, counting odd numbers of semi-detached properties. Passing number seventeen her pulse quickened as she parked opposite. Her mouth dried. David's car was absent but the garage to No. 17 was open. A yellow Mini was there, matching the yellow front door. Julia drove further down and re-parked. Seeing the Dolphin Avenue sign, she wondered about the name. Perhaps an Alderman called Dolphin? Irritated for straying off the point, she drank water, took deep breaths and exited the car. As nervous as if she were about to rob a bank, she gazed around. No one, just ranks of semis. Walking across the road, her legs as wobbly as when she'd taken her driving test, a black cat sauntered past. Julia hoped it would bring her luck.

The high privet hedge was an advantage, tatty with gaping holes; she dipped to peer through one. A woman could be seen near the window. Seconds later the door opened, the woman shuffling to the garage. Dragging a box along the path, she heaved it into the porch. The door closed.

She was wearing a dark robe, slippers and a towel over her head.

The dull December day gave no clues as to what David's 'squeeze' looked like. Julia pursed her lips with frustration. 'Damn, damn.' she muttered under her breath. She hugged the thickly padded coat to her, trudging to the car, shuddering from remaining an undiscovered voyeur. At least she'd had a brief glimpse of David's mistress.

She tried to freeze those seconds, as December frost had done to the hedge. That David was unfaithful ages before she'd met Jonathan, was painful, all the while acting on a different stage. Clenching the steering wheel, anger welled as she wiped the misted windscreen. 'The flack I've taken, accusations, guilt re Jonathan, when David's been keeping a mistress. Even tried to rape me. Wasn't he getting enough from the tart with the yellow door?!'

Julia cast a last glance at David's secret home, now no such thing. It had, in effect freed her. Pleased her detective work had been successful, she shivered, re-joining the main road. On the way home, a plan was formulated.

Relieved to be back in her own house, Julia made a hot toddy, pondering on the surreal visit. I-Spy had previously been a game with Poppy. Julia had played the grown up version. Caressing the steaming drink, body thawed out, her mind was taking longer. Annoyed she hadn't been able to see the mistress's face – whoever it was, she was welcome to David. He never cleaned his car, Julia did. Now she'd stop, laundry too. 'Ha, once he returned home with shirt buttoned up wrongly and tie askew; suspicious, but I let it go.'

Putting the morning's revelations aside, she spent a few minutes skimming through the local newspaper. A Disneyland advertisement depicting Minnie Mouse appeared, reminding her of the yellow Mini. The next page featured an article on sexual predators. 'Would that apply to David? Depends on how many others he's zoned in on.' She read on, making mental notes.

'Receives thrills from disrespecting boundaries. Shallow, charming, flattering, enjoying prey's confusion. Cruel, self-centred, manipulative, exploiter. Sociopath – incapable of empathy or remorse, feels he's untouchable.'

'Absolutely him. Alison's ex had these symptoms too.' Discarding the newspaper, she knew she and Poppy were living amongst this.

A sprinkling of snow had fallen overnight, the beech hedge silvered with frost under a leaden sky. After a client appointment, Julia drove slowly to Alison's, the car slithering on thin ice.

'Is he still in Yorkshire?' asked Alison, ushering Julia into the study, the table covered with sketches, fabric and catalogues.

Julia sank in Alison's white Barcelona chair, legs up on the footstool. 'Don't know, don't care. Oooh, coffee thanks. Didn't expect snow and ice, freezing playing I-Spy in Dolphin Avenue. Wow, I like those fabric swatches.'

'Thanks, natural fibres for a gorgeous house with a panoramic view overlooking Buxton. Right, spill the beans.'

Within ten minutes Julia had related her detective work, describing the house, yellow door and matching Mini car.

'Is there any point waiting to confront him?' Alison asked.

'None. He's been sending messages for ages, unwashed, nasty, violent.' She shivered. 'I dread it, no idea whether he'll lie, deny or... no idea.'

'It's best Julia. I have to finish this project, come for lunch tomorrow.'

Resuming work, Alison lost concentration thinking of the yellow Mini.

On Friday morning the sky was thick with winter mist, no thaw. The hawthorn tree had branches brittle with ice, grass beneath them stiff with frost.

Alison heard Julia's VW creeping onto the drive.

'Come in, roads bad?'

'Not half.' Julia said, shrugging off damp boots.

Alison saw her strained face. 'Come in here, all toastie.'

Julia padded in winter socks, sinking wearily on the sofa.

Alison tentatively asked, 'What happened, imagine it was awful?'

'Mm, After a rare shower, he came downstairs ranting about callers not putting their names at the end of a text. "How the fuck am I supposed to guess who they are? Arrogant shits!" Spat the words out. I took a deep breath and asked him if he was cheating. He looked up from his beer, sneering, admitting it. I didn't expect that!'

Alison's eyes widened. 'No.'

'I've heard him whispering on the phone. In September we were in the garden. His phone was in his shorts pocket, he must have clicked on when mistress was ringing. She'd heard our conversation and gave him an earful. He said he was at the paper shop admiring roses. Once, I came out of the bathroom with noisy mules click-clacking on the tiles. He had his back to me, on the phone to her. In a loud voice, I heard her say "Who the bloody ell's that?" Quick as a flash he said, "My neighbour, wearing flip flops." I thought it was an office girl he'd flirted with. Stupid me!'

'Who is it I wonder?'

'Said he met her in a bar, hadn't slept with her yet, a lie probably. I told him I wasn't remotely interested in whether he had or hadn't. That, he didn't want to hear. Said she was intelligent and well spoken, another lie. Still, as long as she puts out… following so far?'

'Yes, but there must be more.'

'There is. Said he's told her he's divorced. She's insecure and checks up on him constantly, had lots of rejection. As if I haven't! No wonder she suspects him of lying. Everyone has a past, I told him, why can't he admit the truth? Replied he was scared of losing her and having no-one.'

Alison looked astounded. 'To think he imagined you wouldn't notice.'

'But I didn't! You gave me the clues, even though I caught him out in lies. On the phone, I could tell he was smoking a ciggie, hearing him drawing in breath. Once home, he reeked like an ashtray; I asked if he smoked. He said someone at work smoked heavily, then I saw Benson and Hedges packs in the car glove compartment. Thank goodness you overheard that showroom conversation. Well done Holmes.' she smiled at last.

'Incidentally, he asked me how I knew. I said, "I didn't, you just told me." Her name's Clare, moved from Cheshire to an ex boyfriend's, but he dumped her quite quickly. David said he felt sorry for her cos... Alison?'

Stunned, Alison slowly uttered, 'Jooooliaaa! I know who she is!'

'Eh? How?'

'She was crying in the church porch up the lane. I took her home, made her tea while she told me she'd split from someone. Then we met in the library, and for two months became friendly, although I wondered if she was for real. I was going through the mill with Phil's deceptions, so in no state to judge. Told her about Phil, which I regretted.

'Then at your party I met Stephen and took him home. He went to your house next morning for gardening; I went back to bed. Dog-tired, I answered the door to Clare, asked her in, stupidly telling her of Stephen. When she was housesitting and Stephen did the garden, she drunkenly tried to seduce him. Took him ages to tell me, fearing I'd believe her. That did it, I dropped her.'

'What a nerve! But... why would she be David's mistress? Did she have a broad Northern accent?'

Alison slowly nodded, lips pursed. 'She also had a yellow Mini.'

'Oh! Wouldn't she realise by his surname that he was my husband?'

'No, I only mentioned your first name once, re your birthday party. Clare was full on that evening Stephen did her friend's garden. Unfortunately, she told him she knew my favourite music, even played it – "Pink Floyd – *Dark Side of the Moon*," informing him what I'd said about his performance in bed. You may look shocked. It was girl talk, but she twisted the knife all right. I apologised to Stephen, she's a little minx.'

Julia sighed, nodding. 'IF David's telling me the truth, he's told her he's divorced, but not my name. According to what you heard at the design place, he's had a house in Dolphin Avenue or she has, for ages. Anyway, he'll be going soon, I made that clear. Surely if she thinks David's divorced, she'd wonder why she wasn't invited home.'

'Hm, probably invented living miles off. Dolphin Avenue's seven from here, so he'd bank on her not bumping into him. No doubt he'd have had a ready answer.'

Julia concurred resignedly. 'Definitely. Look, can I skip lunch today and come on Sunday? I can't bear being with HIM all day without Poppy.'

'Come, I'll get lamb and make bread and butter pudding, comfort food. Julia, are you ok?'

Julia pulled on her boots and coat in the hall. 'Are you? Is something else wrong?'

'Does there need to be!?' Julia snapped. 'Haven't I had enough misery?'

Alison flushed. 'It's… I can't bear to see you unhappy… I… '

'No, no… sorry…' Two hovering teardrops balanced precariously on Julia's lashes.

Alison dabbed her face. 'There is something isn't there?'

Julia leant against the door. 'I'm angry and want to confront this tart.' She raised her voice, spitting, 'I want to reveal what a bloody liar David is. It's not spite, I need to hear what he's told her, tell her the real story, get rid of the lying cheat and put the whole mess to bed. Ha, bed!' she fumed.

'Julia, don't. She's bound to be furious at his lies and confront him; he'll go mental.'

Julia turned, giving a weak smile. 'I'll end this nightmare by finding the truth, to stop living on a knife-edge.' Looking up at the gloomy winter sky, she crunched heavily on frosted pea gravel, knowing there'd be darker clouds to come. The storms would be faced.

27

Saturday morning changed everything. David's regional manager collected him in his four-by-four for an Edinburgh exhibition.

'In the shower?' Geoff asked. Julia liked Geoff, but not enough to admit David and showers were incompatible. 'Sorry it's short notice, I need more staff on the stand. Train would have been best, but picking up colleagues further north, so driving it is. Ah, there you are David, we must get going. Julia, promise I'll deliver him home on Sunday.'

Waving them off cheerfully, Julia knew the pretence had to be maintained until she was ready.

Washing up, she mapped out her plan. David's departure had made it easier to visit Clare. Slithering on icy roads, Julia parked outside David's second abode, car hidden by the high privet hedge. She'd rehearsed what she'd say at the door. If invited in, adrenalin would take over.

This time she didn't feel nervous, determination for answers paramount. She walked past the yellow Mini, noticing showroom boxes, a workbench with David's distinctive toolbox on top, and curiously, a pushchair box in the garage.

The Hollies could be heard – probably Radio 2's *Sounds of*

the Sixties, Julia surmised, ringing the doorbell. Glimpsing Clare through the dimpled glass door, her plan of what to say proved unnecessary. Clare beckoned her in with a cheery, 'Hiya, 'scuse the mess, mee 'usband's 'alfway through paintin' this room.' She ushered Julia towards a sofa, moving newspapers. 'Plonk yerself on the settee luv.' Clare sat on an old battered Parker Knoll, instantly recogniseable as one David had supposedly dumped at the tip months before. The room reeked of stale nicotine; Julia hid her expression, head awash with questions.

'Just put one out, trying to give up. Dave mee fellar, 'ee is an' all.' Clare gushed. 'I'm Clare de Mar, Shirley. Coffee? Did you bring the brochures? Sorry, too many questions. 'Ormones.'

Julia studied Clare. Black unkempt hair, overweight, nervous smile.

'Terrible driving from Stafford in this weather eh? Give us your coat. Ooh The Kinks – Mee Mum likes them. Er... I'll turn the radio off.'

Julia stood up, noticing chipped red nails and a plain band on Clare's left hand. As Clare put the coat on the sofa, Julia boldly spoke. 'I don't want a drink, but information. You were apparently expecting someone else. I'm not that person.'

Clare flopped down, flushing, smile vanishing. 'Ay?'

Looking straight at her, Julia said 'You don't know me, but you should. My name is Mrs. de Mar, David's wife.'

Clare, horrified, gripped the chair's arms. 'Whaaat? You mean Dave's EX-wife? What yer doing 'ere? Bloody 'ell! What's goin' on? I don't...'

'You don't do you? There is no EX-wife, just wife – ME. If you're innocent of knowing of me or guilty, I want to learn a few truths and tell you some too.'

Extremely agitated, Clare reached for the phone.

'No! We'll talk before you ring my husband. To your credit you look shocked. I don't want to upset you but I can't get the truth unless we compare notes on the same man in our lives. You call yourself Mrs. De Mar. You aren't really married to my husband are you? Is he a bigamist as well as a liar?'

Clare shook her head. 'Eh? We've been an item eighteen months. 'Ee lives miles away and works abroad sometimes. Ex-wife's causin' problems with money, so we're using my savings to do up my 'ouse, cos 'ee 'as to pay towards 'is daughter.'

'Really? Eighteen months? You've been living here all that time?'

'Yeah, I bought this before I met Dave. We split up and I went to Norfolk to live with an ex-boyfriend, but Dave came to get me. I took the 'ouse off the market, and moved back in. Dunno why we're 'avin' this conversation. Think you'd better go lady.'

Julia coldly leant forward. 'Be prepared to forget all you've been told by David. If you think this is unpleasant, it certainly is for me.'

Clare scowled with disbelief, face burning at what might come next. She could throw out this strong-willed intruder, but needed to know. Sulkily shrugging her shoulders, she stared down, not wanting to face Julia, then jerking her head up, icily demanded. 'What's 'is mobile number then? If you're 'is wife you'd 'ave that.'

'Oh that's easy.' Julia fumbled in her handbag. 'Here's his business card.'

Clare turned. 'Ha. You could 'ave picked that up from an exhibition. 'Ee's at one now.'

'Edinburgh would it be? I have his home number too, the one I already had before we married.'

Clare's neck veins bulged thick as rope. 'Whaaat? Are you on summut?'

Julia quietly asked, 'Hasn't it occurred to you why you've never been to his home?'

'You don't gerrit do you? My Dave's in this country so little, 'ee lodges with a mate in Yorkshire near the office.'

'And you're OK with that are you Clare?'

'Yeah. My 'ouse, but 'ee pays bills. I keep it nice, cook, give 'im sex. Dave loves me, doesn't care I don't 'ave a posh Cheshire accent. 'Old on, 'ow d'you get this address? Anyway, the David you're looking for isn't my Dave. Either that, or you're 'is ex-wife. Won't be best pleased, 'ee's got a temper.'

'I'm well aware of that. I'm not blaming you, but you rang, overhearing him talking to a woman about roses. When you asked where he was, he said the paper shop. A lie, he was in our garden. I can see you recognise it. Once, when you rang, I was wearing mules on the tiled floor, you wondered who it was. He said a neighbour, which you didn't buy. How else would I know all this?'

Clare's body crumpled. Biting her lip, she folded like a rag doll, crying.

Julia held her hand. 'I had to know, it's been driving me mad living as I do. We're not a couple now, his behaviour's been foul. I need to free myself of his deceptions. Surely you want to know the real David too?'

The telephone rang and a message heard. 'Mrs. de Mar, this is Shirley Daniels from Stafford Kitchens. There's a build up of traffic on the M6, I'll be half an hour, thank you.'

Julia handed Clare a tissue. 'Yesterday Alison was doing the same for me.' she thought, sitting down.

Clare was bewildered. 'OK, you know lots about Dave, but you're 'is ex. Maybe 'ee's not told me you're friends cos of 'is daughter. Why would 'ee stay with Geoff in Yorkshire, 'ee lives 'ere wi' me. I can't grasp this at all.'

Julia replied. 'Let me correct you. Poppy is my daughter, she lives with us and sees her father, my ex-husband, whenever she likes. Geoff Green is David's area manager and doesn't live in Yorkshire, but Cheshire near us. He called for David this morning for an Edinburgh exhibition.'

Clare looked even more broken.

Julia continued. 'David's away on business, but not abroad. When he returns, it's to our house, or so I thought. Don't you see he's built an elaborate web of lies, while married to me, deceiving both of us.'

Clare blew her nose noisily. 'Bloody 'ell, I'll kill 'im. God knows what you think o'me.'

'I'm not blaming you, David's the deceiver. You can't have had reason to doubt him. He's been clever, covered his tracks.'

Clare, dazed with the enormity of the revelations, asked shakily, 'What's 'ee gonna say when you tell 'im?'

'Oh we're past that. I confronted him recently.'

'Eh? 'Ee told you about me?'

'Admitted it. Said he'd told you he was divorced, hadn't slept with you yet, you were insecure, constantly ringing him. He didn't say he was supporting you or where you lived and I didn't ask. I knew you were here.'

'Not slept together? Never 'ad so much sex. As for supportin' me, it's my 'ouse. Dave's bought some stuff, but I'm payin' for a new kitchen 'I need a drink. Not alcohol, 'ad to give that up. Would you like a coffee?'

'I would thanks. Shall I make it?' Julia offered.

'Er no, I know where stuff is.'

Clare plodded into the kitchen, Julia followed out of curiosity.

'Plonk yourself there, move them newspapers.'

Julia stood by the messy table, angry cigarette burns indenting the scarred top. She remarked, 'Pretty garden.'

'Dave did it.' Spooning coffee into mugs, Clare didn't see Julia's face.

'He doesn't do any at ours. What I can't manage, a gardener does.' Carefully not saying who, Julia put crumpled newspapers onto the floor. Sitting opposite a cork noticeboard containing trade cards and a photograph of David in baggy red shorts leaning on a spade, she felt revulsion.

Clare trudged over. 'Forgot sugar.'

'Not for me thanks.' Pointing towards the photograph, Julia asked when it was taken.

To her credit, Clare blushed. 'Er, a year ago – August 2007. Laid a lawn an borders. I… you don't want to 'ere that do you? Look, can I ask somethin'?'

'Yes, then we both have clarity.' Julia replied kindly.

''Ow come your marriage went wrong?'

'We were happy for a while. He made an effort with my daughter and my wheelchair-bound mother. Then moods and rages, increasing eighteen months ago, so a relief he was away more. My daughter was upset, slamming doors, outbursts. Mum died this year, at the funeral he played the dutiful husband, by then I feared him. Incidentally, he rarely showers, wears underwear for days, and used to pester me for sex. I say sex, that's all it was. I began sleeping downstairs, so I wouldn't be with an unwashed, sweaty man, subjecting me to cruelty. The crux came when he burst into my room, attempting to rape me. I had to fight him off.'

Clare sneered, saying she didn't believe her.

Gripping the table edge, pursing her lips with frustration, Julia gave Clare a stony look. Banging her fist she said, 'If you think it's easy to confront you, you're mistaken. David's put me through hell, my daughter too, she's going to live in France with my ex-husband soon. You're welcome to David, unwashed, uncouth liar that he is. The Great Pretender – he's all yours!'

'Yer 'ee is.' Clare's eyes narrowed. 'You're makin' this up. I 'aven't noticed 'im smellin. Never tried to rape me, no need,' she smirked sarcastically, 'I love sex, especially forbidden fruit. Anybody's boyfriend or 'usband, if they want me – their choice. I didn't know Dave was married though. Can't wait to see what 'ee says about you,' she sneered.

Julia pushed the chair back and stood up. Giving Clare a pitying look, she said, ' I wouldn't make up anything as disgusting as rape. David wants what he wants in the way that he wants it and if he doesn't get it, fireworks. He's selfish, dirty, and a deceiver. A sociopath only gives if there's something in it for him. He's also a misogynist.'

Clare's eyes widened. She slammed her mug down splashing hot liquid on her hand, wincing. 'Mis what? I've listened enough, nearly believed it an all. Ha, if 'ee's married and you divorce, 'ee'll get 'alf of everythin'. You'll be without a man, no woman wants that, luv.'

Julia sighed wearily. 'After all I've revealed, you accept his fairy tales. You'll get an Academy Award performance from him, he's constantly rehearsing his part. Incidentally, he won't be getting half of anything.'

With a thunderous glare, Clare led the way through the cluttered living room. Julia picked up her coat, hardly having time to put it on as Clare banged open the front door, snarling she'd be ringing David immediately.

'He won't thank you while he's working.' Julia suggested.

Grinning manically, Clare affirmed, 'Don't need advice from you, yer toffee-nosed Cheshire cow. Lookin' down on me cos o'mee Northern voice. Dave'll want to see 'ow I am.' With a superior look she told Julia. 'In fact 'ow we both are.' Opening her navy cardigan, she proudly stroked her stomach. 'That's summut you didn't know – Sherlock bloody 'Olmes!'

The door slammed, making the letterbox rattle. Reeling at Clare's parting shot, Julia walked, dazed to her frosted black VW. Digging into her bag for keys, she observed a grey Vauxhall crawling onto the tarmac. A frantic woman got out.

'Am I at the correct house? Does Mrs. de Mar live here?'

Julia answered, 'No, but her disillusioned understudy's in there expecting you.'

28

Two miles from home Julia pulled into a layby to vomit. Slumped in the seat, churning over the tableau she'd just witnessed, she felt wrecked from the necessary ordeal. Clare had been in denial, but willing to accept David no matter what. The final news imparted had been a shock, Julia annoyed she minded. 'Don't want him, why do I mind he's made her pregnant?' dabbing her mouth with a tissue.

Indoors, she stripped off clothes for the washing machine, coat in a carrier for the cleaners, then shampooed her hair. 'I don't want any trace of the bloody mistress.'

Dressed in a fleecy tracksuit, Julia turned up the radiator and made tea, unable to face food. Entering the sitting room, she tripped on something by the coffee table. Putting her tea down, she picked the mobile phone up, aware it was David's. 'Hell, nine messages, all from Clare. If I open them up, he'll know.'

Alison rang to see if Julia was OK. By then David's phone had rung a dozen times.

'I did go to see Clare. David's boss arrived this morning for an exhibition in Edinburgh, leaving me free to drive to Dolphin Avenue. Also, David's left his mobile behind, so he won't know I've been to see her, unless he rings from someone else's phone.

Don't think so, dozens of messages from Clare. And no, I haven't listened, tempting though it is. He's due back tomorrow afternoon.'

'Why don't you come earlier, I'd be happier if you did.'

Julia felt comforted. 'Thanks, I've got to face him tomorrow, but although the balloon will go up, I don't want to be here when he accesses Clare's texts. Be prepared, lots to tell.'

Sparkling snow dazzled next morning. Julia's boots squeakily crunched as she ducked under overhanging trees loaded with haw. After lunch they let the dishes soak. Looking beyond frosty windows at the garden, Alison remarked, 'Looks abandoned. You wouldn't think a resurrection would occur in spring.'

'Mm, new beginnings, for me too. That was delicious food, haven't eaten properly for days. Best bread and butter pud ever, my stomach looks like I've swallowed a balloon. Hm, just what will be bursting at home soon.'

Alison was concerned. 'Poppy won't be there will she?'

Julia gasped. 'Poppy! Oh heck, I don't want her to witness a monumental row. I'll ask Guy to keep her, he can drop her at school tomorrow. Hope they're in.'

While Alison drew the curtains to hide the drab December Sunday, Julia rang her ex-husband.

'Hello Guy… Could you keep Poppy tonight? Tell you why when it's sorted… thanks… It concerns David – I don't want her around… you've got her school uniform… Thanks darling. Bye.'

Alison could be heard rattling pots and pans. Julia took her cup to the kitchen. 'It's OK.'

'I heard. To call him that name, he is though, a darling, isn't he?'

Julia picked up the tea towel. 'I'll wipe. He's brilliant, knows of David's behaviour from Poppy, glad they're close.'

When Geoff Green's car crunched up her drive at quarter past three, Julia's heart pounded. The dreaded return. She waved to Geoff. David stomped towards the front door, clutching briefcase, bag and a carrier. Julia walked shakily into the hall, searching his face for clues.

Scowling, he slung everything down, stomped into the sitting room, swore loudly at the sight of his mobile, glaring at Julia accusingly. 'Where the fuck was this?'

'There.' she replied, trying not to sound defensive.

He grunted. 'Thought you were playing games, hiding it.' he smirked.

Julia bridled. 'I'm not the one playing games.'

'I'm bursting for a slash.' he crudely announced. Leaving the phone on the hall table, he tramped heavily upstairs.

Making tea, Julia dreaded the inevitable explosion. He shuffled in. 'One for me then?' he asked, turning his phone on.

Julia replied nervously, 'Mm.'

Reaching for the tea canister, she jumped as he exclaimed, 'I'll have it later!'

Julia turned hotly, seeing him shaken, having noticed Clare's message stream. 'OK.'

'Er left something in Geoff's car. Gotta go.'

His manic look, blundering into the hall, dragging on scruffy navy anorak, snatching keys, told Julia everything. Seeing him stumble on bags he'd discarded, she pushed them under the table.

Watching snowflakes descending from the darkening winter sky, Julia knew he hadn't left anything in Geoff's car. Anxiously, she feared his return. 'She'll have told him all. Having an unexpected period's making this worse.' Stress had taken a toll on her monthly cycle; tension making pain worse. No point going to the doctor, too complicated to explain.

Realising David would listen to the many messages, then go to Clare, she needed a bath to relax, but didn't want to be undressed, half-dressed or in the bath when he reappeared. Taking painkillers with water, then rinsing the glass, she smashed a chunk on the mixer tap. Although she hadn't cut her hand, tears trickled down her face. A PMT moment she'd experienced before, breaking a glass or banging into furniture, but this wasn't menstrual behaviour.

An hour later the balloon burst with an almighty bang. Her stomach lurched when she saw him tear up, skidding to a halt in the big BMW. Ramming keys noisily into the lock, storming through the house, he burst in on Julia in the sitting room. Standing, legs apart, hands on hips directly in front of her, he delivered a snarling tirade.

'You bloody bitch!' he spat, leaning over her, paunch throbbing with rage. 'You had to go uninvited and harass the poor girl didn't you? Whatever I told her was my business. But snoopy wifey, she's havin' none o'that is she? Goes round uninvited, grills an innocent woman. What's all this about me trying to rape you? As if!'

Julia stood up shakily. 'You did, you were drunk.'

He smirked. 'Well you probably made me snap from denying me sex.'

Julia scowled at his excuse. 'That makes it OK does it?'

'You're my wife, it's your duty. No wonder I found somebody else eventually.'

'Eventually? Clare said more than a year. The cocoon of lies you've spun, lied to me, lied to her. If she loved you, she'd have understood. Don't you feel any guilt?'

David sneered. 'Nah, never have. Clare loves me, wants me, up to me what I admit. When I met you my business was failing, you had money, house, beauty business, let me move in, seemed a great plan to marry you for security. It was a business arrangement for me, took months of planning, pretending to be interested in stuff I'd never heard of. Thought you'd be impressed by the surname De Mar I'd adopted to attract women with money.'

Julia flopped, bewildered, scarcely able to speak. 'Name change? Business arrangement? I thought you loved me… I loved you.' She looked down at her hands, not wanting to see him.

He tore off his anorak, casting it onto the carpet. 'Yup. Got me out of a tight hole, made me solvent. Poppy was part of the deal, but she's a chip off the old block. Shit, how you let her get away with stuff. Surly looks when I tell her to get off the phone. Who does she think pays the bill, Alexander Graham Bell? I've always been a user and unfaithful, lie to get out of situations, to get what I want.'

Amazed to hear him actually admitting it, Julia glared. 'And now you've used Clare, telling her a complete fabrication. What an imagination! I was going to say poor girl, but she's only herself to blame. Apparently, you split for a while, she went to live in Norfolk with an ex-boyfriend.'

David shrugged. 'So? We got back together once she'd realised her mistake.'

'Ha, what about her drunkenly propositioning Alison's boyfriend before Norfolk?'

'Ay? Alison, how does she know Clare?' he asked, flushing.

'They met by chance months ago. When Stephen revealed Clare's drunken advances, Alison ceased contact. She realised Clare was your affair.'

David adopted a superior look, saying Clare would be waiting. Julia ordered, 'Go!'

He smirked. 'I bet lover boy's waiting to fill my shoes.'

Julia rose, giving a hard stare. 'He fills his own very well, house, money and business; doesn't leech off women. Doesn't lie, saying he lives miles off, stays with his boss in Yorkshire when not abroad. Yes, Clare told me everything, so pack your bags and get out!' she exploded.

He made a mock bow. 'With pleasure your majesty.' strutting out, tearing upstairs.

After three trips to the car, he strode back in. 'The rest, I'll pick up.' he snarled, showing neglected teeth.

'Fine. Oh congratulations on the baby.'

David froze. 'What baby? Get real!'

Julia was mystified. 'Clare's baby. She told me as a parting shot, stroked her stomach to show me. I saw a pushchair box. She… '

'A kid. Nah. Bloody hope not. Bad enough having your spoilt brat. I like sex, not babies.'

Julia was disgusted. 'She was desperate to tell me.'

'Yeah, she bought the pushchair, it's going back to the shop. She weaves these fantasies. Ha, bit like me.' he told her, smirking.

'Go please.' Julia stiffly ordered, following him to the front door. 'Keys.' she demanded, holding out her hand. Ignoring it, he cockily tossed them onto the carpet.

'The word sorry isn't in your vocabulary, David. You're both sociopaths and deserve each other, good riddance!'

With a supercilious smile he turned, saying, 'I wanted you to be my golden goose, but you turned out to be an old duck.' He snarled, 'Ha, now an old fuck!'

***

'Self-centred child! Arrogant liar!' Alison spat out. 'Wanting to believe the best, you weren't prepared for this corruption, now you have clearer sight.'

Julia blushed, embarrassed. 'I'm not without fault, but thanks.'

'Look, warmth radiates from you, unlike him. He was jealous of you, of our friendship, undermining your confidence.'

Julia, surprised to hear Alison speak so plainly, calmly listened.

'Another thing, that beauty client who said not one of her family or friends is divorced – it's not the nineteen thirties, it's the twenty-first century. Sometimes people have to get divorced, not suffer forever.'

Julia was impressed. 'You should do counselling. You know I tried with David, but he wasn't worth it. I should have suspected when he came home in sprayed on leather trousers, saying a colleague had gained weight and given them to him. With the weight David had gained, they didn't fit him either. Then smoking,

I knew he did cos his breath was foul, teeth decaying. When he drove me to Tesco, I noticed the passenger seat in his BMW was pushed right back; I had to move it forward. He said a colleague had long legs; I realise now it was much too horizontal. Yuk. Married me for money, then pursued Clare for that reason and sex on tap. She accepted his bad character traits cos she's the same.'

Julia shrugged. 'When Mum died I was pre-occupied with arrangements and grief, assumed furtive calls were business. His treatment clouded my thinking, a gradual erosion, I wasn't on the lookout for signs. I've had to be devious too because of him.'

Alison agreed. 'You've been living with that brute's hostility and treachery, probably why his parents and brother dropped him.'

Julia stretched, reflecting. 'I did love him once, he had some good qualities.'

Alison sighed cynically. 'Very few. He's cheated on you in every respect.'

'Now I've dealt with it, I can shut the door. I was so treasured as a child, I thought I'd choose well. Hm, I chose Guy but that didn't last, if only he hadn't been a workaholic. Look who I gave my heart to next – David! Gosh, Poppy will be home soon, she's baking mince pies at school tomorrow, must buy mincemeat.'

She walked to the front door, linking arms with Alison, who helped her on with her coat.

Julia shrugged. 'David used to do that, opening the car door, running me a bath. Falling in love's easy, staying's harder. Jonathan's home from Dubai soon, going to see him on Thursday, Poppy's staying with a schoolfriend.'

Faint winter sunshine appeared. 'Forgotten what the sun was like. Jools, come here for a hug, you've been brilliantly brave, buy yourself a cream cake too.'

Julia grinned. 'Cream cake? I've gained pounds snacking through stress, Jonathan won't want a fatty on Thursday.'

'He wouldn't bother if you'd put a stone on. Careful, icy. Bye sweetheart.'

29

Phoebe Cade's excitement didn't end when she left her cruise. Returning home in the courtesy coach, she looked forward to telling Alison, who'd been transforming Gordon's den for a prospective lodger, having finished the Edwardian sitting room at the end of January.

Mauve wallpaper had been erased in the sitting room. William Morris Strawberry Thief had replaced it on the main wall; mint green adorned the others. Phoebe had seen a programme on television. 'Morris had seen thrushes stealing berries from his garden, which gave him inspiration,' she informed Alison brightly. 'You see I'm not a complete Philistine.'

'Phoebe, you've educated me. Willow pattern was from trees by the Thames near his house, I knew that.'

'Blue and white wallpaper, Chinese men on bridges? Not for me, Strawberry Thief will do nicely.' Phoebe affirmed.

Alison twinkled at Phoebe's innocent faux pas. 'I quite agree.' she smiled benevolently.

Family photographs within a mount of wallpaper had been put in frames. They stood out against the pale mint wall opposite the fireplace, floor length curtains matching the wallpaper. Mahogany furniture gleamed from re-polishing, fifties stick leg tables and paper rack given to Oxfam, room de-cluttered from dusty bric-a-brac. A rose carpet had been chosen by Phoebe.

Alison received approval when Phoebe returned from staying with her daughter. She'd phoned ecstatic about the transformation, asking where her sagging old armchair was.

'In the garage, it didn't do your back any favours. I've ordered on sale or return a Forest Green Stressless chair, footstool included. Your osteopath recommended them remember? I'll pop round tomorrow at eleven.'

'Oh my old chair, had its day. Yes, come tomorrow. I adore my new room, beautiful.'

That was four weeks ago and Phoebe had departed for Norway, trusting Alison to erase Gordon from the den. The discoveries within had shaken her. Her children were not told what had caused her low mood, but had suggested a cruise. It would, they felt, let her meet new people, see wonderful sights. Hugo had asked if she'd offer temporary lodgings to a colleague for two months, beginning in March. Daniel was divorced, a non-smoker and trustworthy. His company would lift her spirits, she'd met him over Christmas at Hugo's, and had a great rapport, both being *Last of the Summer Wine* fans. He'd amused her on Boxing Day with quotations from the series.

Phoebe was ebullient, telling Alison of her holiday. 'Seafood and mouthwatering puds, then we hurried on deck to see the magnificent aurora borealis, jade flickers growing into dancing ribbons, incredibly emotional. Norway's far north is haunting, peaks, fjords and magical Northern Lights.' Phoebe wrung her hands excitedly.

'Had to wear a hat and coat on deck, chilly. We went near the Russian border, air pure, Gulf Stream warming the Arctic Ocean. Listen to this! I went on the husky adventure, the sledge took me around the frozen lake with the doggies. Minus 15, so I had on m'harvest knickers – you know – all is safely gathered in.'

Alison beamed benevolently at Phoebe recounting the scene and the quaint saying.

'Saw reindeer and,' she gushed, 'we went to that ice hotel. I wanted to go cos that actress, Joanna, did a film on it. When we sailed up fjords, they played a CD of Peer Gynt, so moving. Even had a hot tub on board, lay gazing at millions of stars.'

She clasped her hands tightly, shrugging shoulders. 'Old Phoebe having an adventure at this age, I ask you. Ha, I bet Gordon with all his shenanigans didn't have as much fun as I! When he was dying he said, "Time to give God his ticket back methinks." When I unearthed his affair, I wanted to hand mine back too.' Her voice softened. 'Not now… dealt with and dropped overboard outside Tromso.

'I read a quote on death, "You've been asked to leave the party, but the problem is the party will carry on without you." That's why I'll carry on as if it's my last, so I can enjoy the party each day I'm spared by God Almighty.'

Alison hugged her. 'Phoebe, that's the spirit.'

Unclasping her hands, Phoebe rubbed them together. 'Anyway, how are you? Brought you a troll from m'hols.'

30

'March winds and April showers bring forth sweet May flowers' – Trudie's calendar announced, as she turned over from February 2009. 'March already.'

She wanted to go for gloves and trowel from the summerhouse. Gardening was a soothing occupation, looking for new beginnings. She would touch the soil with the flat of her hand to see if it felt warm enough for seed sowing.

As a child, she'd clutch two shillings pocket money on a Saturday morning to go to Woolworths, racing across wooden floorboards to dazzling Bees seed packets of nigella, nasturtiums, Californian poppy. Her father warned against African marigolds, earwigs liked them. She'd meet him in De Greys café for a knickerbocker glory – 'Don't tell your mother.' Their secret, hidden from Alice's disapproving scowl.

Trudie stepped outside, noticing variegated ceanothus finally coming through. Swathes of wood anemones, cowslips, primrose cushions, pulmonarias – new creation usually making her thankful to be living. Not this spring, her mood echoed bleeding heart coming into leaf. She returned indoors. Symptomatic depression had been around since before Christmas, even after Paula spotting Laurie in Shropshire.

Since Christmas Trudie was certain she'd seen him. In January, Ugg boots had been reduced at Crane's. Exiting with a beautiful pink pair, a surge of adrenalin shot through her. A man stood near the window, slowing his pace to look at sweaters. Her sharp gasp made an audible 'Huuuuur'. She edged closer to cast a sidelong glance at the dark-haired man, convinced it was Laurie. Willing him to raise his head above the turned up coat collar and scarf, he dropped his carrier, bending to retrieve it. Excitement quickly became disappointment. In a DIY store he was seen again, as he'd have been in his youth.

When these sightings were made, Trudie would lie in her evening bath listening to *The Stylistics Greatest Hits*. One track stood out. 'You Are Everything And Everything Is You.' The falsetto voices echoed what had been happening to her, melody beautiful, words heartbreaking.

In March she'd found a poem written to her father upon his retirement from industry. Paula had rung whilst she was reading it, Trudie had answered sniffing. At Paula's request she'd read it out.

What thoughts has a man, when his working span,
Ultimately and finally ends,
When sad to relate, he makes for the gate,
Having said goodbye to his friends.
The noise of the shops, the smoke in the bays,
The shift change, nights and then days,
A world of endeavour, all left behind,
The know-how learnt through the ways
Of dealing with problems, both manufacturing and men
All part of his working life.
Did the dummy look good, was the part press OK,
Did I turn off the gas for the wife?
Journeys abroad to Otto Fuchs plant,
Supervise work to his skill,
Cut out the cackle, on with the job,

Then back to the 'run of the mill'.
Smethwick on nights, Smethwick on days,
Weekends as duly required.
Feeling the pace, no time at home, a little jaded and tired.
Now put aside your tongs, the pinch-bars, the slings,
The grabs, batch cards and grease.
Filling in this, and noting that, let working
Activities cease.
When weather allows, a spell on the green,
A quiet nap on some pleasant beach,
A noggin or two enjoyed when you will, the
Ashtray within easy reach.
We will certainly miss you, many years having spent
In giving HDA of your best,
Look after the missus, look after yourself, and
Enjoy a bloody good rest.

'Oh now I'm sniffy too. It's beautiful and just your dad.'

Trudie's floodgates had opened. She'd sobbed, overwrought. 'I… I can't go on like this.'

'This doesn't concern the poem does it? I've seen it coming, you need a shoulder and a plan to sort this agonising unholy mess.'

Trudie could not stop crying. She blew her nose, breathing erratically. 'I… I can't go on… it's awful… day and night… . I'm on automatic pilot, a robot, that's what I am th… these days. Some th-therapist I am – can't cope – c … can't.' she'd sobbed desperately. 'I used to fear death… now I'd welcome it.'

Paula had been alarmed. 'I'll come Saturday, weekends are worse alone.'

Trudie's sobs had quietened. 'Oh yes, that w… would be grand.'

Paula had replied, 'I'll come at three, I'll bring food too.'

'No no… No need. Oh crumbs I sound like that chap from *The Vicar of Dibley*.'

'So you do! There, you giggled a bit, good girl. Send me the poem, it will make you walk to the postbox up the lane. I'll reply, then Saturday will be here and so will I.'

True to her word, Trudie had posted the poem.

Paula replied, 'The poem. Amazingly touching, generosity of their words, these men respected your father so, having had a huge impact on them. Above some of them in stature and experience, but understood he was part of their working lives in a permanent fashion. He'd integrated himself so thoroughly with them and the job, he was part of the factory itself. Remarkable qualities of humility and brilliance. Generous and gentle, he gave on such a consistent basis, his men had come to love and depend on him. Some make an imprint, altering our lives, bringing honour to the workplace. Your dad was all of that. You've forgiven him for not being strong with your mother; he had a lot to cope with. Paula xxx'

Trudie had tidied the house for Paula's visit, spirits rising to an extent they hadn't been all winter.

Over coffee, Paula began. 'Trudie, you were a loveable child and channelled that goodness to Stephen, giving it in spite of isolation from your childhood. You've transformed pain into generosity, taking love your father gave, making it into more. He gave you what he could in spite of your mother pulling his strings. You loved him back, he was all you had.'

Trudie concentrated on the emerald ring Laurie had given her, twisting it backwards and forwards. Not looking up, she solemnly replied, 'With Mother sapping my confidence as a child, I became passive you know. I learned not to retaliate, which made me accept hurt too readily, remaining docile, burying it, no choice at the time. Losing Laurie, part of my identity going with his leaving, my foundations fell in. The idea of giving him up was like an operation without anaesthetic – unthinkable. How rare it is to have someone we truly love.' She raised her head, whispering, 'He… was the one.'

'Yes and you've tried hard to find him.'

'Paula, I don't deserve to, I was living a lie with a married man. Where was the integrity? He used to ask why should he suffer the indignity of a barren marriage? Platitudes came from both of us. I wasn't the one that made the commitment to his wife, so I wasn't the one lying. On TV yesterday a woman said she didn't regret being a mistress because she learned a lot. She won't take blame, she said. I feel though, when someone cheats, they treat the third person badly, disrespecting them. You see, our intentions were good, the results disastrous.'

Paula's brow furrowed. 'Sure you want to go on?'

Giving an almost imperceptible sigh, Trudie admitted. 'I have to. The breakthrough came last September on holiday, then your Shropshire sighting. I used to wish our lives were twice the size. Not since Laurie's departure. If I feel low, I think of the Jews in the holocaust while I was safe in my cot in England. Nevertheless, my hurt's real to me, but what have I done about it? Zilch.'

Paula took Trudie's hand. 'Difficult after so long.'

'I'm scared Paula. I-I-I don't know how to tackle it. No beautiful love, but no great disappointment. You may not agree.'

'But I do!' Paula emphasised. 'Stephen has a really loving mother. You have a generous spirit and came from an unaccepting family – yet you give love. Your mother was technically one, but spiritually could have been on Mars. I need you to listen, don't look like that, it's all good.

'You have backbone, vitality and humour. People love you for who you are. Stephen for one. What was that text you told me he'd sent? "Thanks for doing that Mum. You really are the most wonderful person, I'm lucky to have you." See? We're intact because of your love.

'When I felt despair after James died, you wrote to me. He could be difficult, but nursing him it was devastating, watching him fade. I bought new clothes, but the dopamine feeling soon wore off. What you wrote soothed when I felt empty, saying our

223

nervous system benefits by kindness, what we do and is done to us. Energy through prayer makes things grow and change, you said. My horizon was bleak, your kindness let me see some of the mist evaporate.'

The hall clock struck four, reminding Trudie of her parents Westminster chime clock from the thirties.

Paula paused. 'Do you want to hear my views on moving forward?'

'Yes I need input. Er, fancy an Italian for dinner?' She saw mock-astonishment on Paula's face and giggled.

'You know what I mean. The village restaurant delivers.'

'OK. I came to sort this once and for all. What you have to do can't be as bad as your fear of water and heights.'

Trudie smirked. 'Mm, nor did I learn to ride a bike.'

Paula stood up, leant across the table, twinkling fondly. 'Yes, but you've got me riding tandem now so you won't fall off. That brings me to your guilt re Laurie's wife. Depression intrudes on good times, believe they will change. Say what you like, let it out, we'll sort the pieces and make up the jigsaw.'

Trudie smiled, gratefully. 'You're more of a therapist than I am. Strange how I can sort out clients, keeps my mind off my own inertia. At Christmas I nearly gave up my therapy practice, I felt a hypocrite.'

'Why?'

'Well, for instance, I do male psycho-sexual counselling. I can't say their wives are sexually unawakened. That implies they're at fault, sometimes they are, but they're with their wives, good or bad. I couldn't even hold onto my man. Laurie married Irene, his first romance. Said he should have just been friends but his own insecurity made him stay, no confidence with women then. Straight out of law school, married the girl he was engaged to. I asked him why he didn't admit his change of heart. He said he was too dutiful, insecure, pleased parents, fiancé and himself briefly. He wasn't courageous then,' Trudie shrugged her shoulders. 'Ha, still isn't.'

Paula took Trudie's hand. 'Well that's your pain talking. How can we know what made him leave? He's across the county, but no phone call. It's beyond me – what enigmas men are. When I saw him in that pub, I'm certain he didn't recognise me, so perhaps he's had amnesia.

'Troods, my weakness used to be, when someone was nice to me, I was nice. I felt your pain, I've had similar. When someone close hurts us, it's hard to erase; we forgive and continue giving while they inflict more, making us vulnerable.'

'True, I'm mindful of what my father used to say. God would punish the world by fire, flood or something else. I spoke with a church minister once, who said he didn't believe God sends illness to us, but admitted he hadn't any answers. Laurie had terrible misery when Irene died, blaming himself, but to disappear, heartbreakingly drastic.

'Paula, my brain's too loaded, causing me to forget things, like leaving rhubarb simmering on the stove. Today I forgot I'd left the hot tap filling the sink. A shock, even the overflow was overflowing. I quickly soaked up the water with stuff to be washed – robe, tea towels, socks.'

She saw Paula trying not to laugh. 'Hey don't laugh. Jack, the odd job man I use, came on Thursday to replace the cloakroom tap washer. I had to smile, he told me his ex-wife was a terrible cook. He left for good after the worst Sunday roast ever. So disgusted, he got in the car and drove three hundred miles to Lands End. My remark was, "That must have been some dinner!" It was the last straw, but he tells it so deadpan, I crack up.'

'Hilarious. I'd like to have been a fly on the wall, but you'd have swatted me!'

Trudie sniggered. 'Yes. Let's look at the menu in the sitting room. Shall we eat at seven?'

Paula linked Trudie's arm. 'Perfect, then we'll make plans.'

Next morning, over breakfast Trudie discussed the dream she'd had. 'So vivid, can I tell you?'

'Yes please.'

'As a child during winter there were frozen filigree patterned windows, icicles hanging from the guttering, fascinating me. The dream begins there, me in bed, thinking of our house. The plaster Whistling Boy, the dresser's shelves housing Bakelite napkin rings, a plastic donkey with a magnetic carrot, assorted thirties plates, orange and green. Coronation table mats, ration books in the sideboard, an Ultra radio in my bedroom. Our Standard 10 in the garage. A comforting coal fire, seeing things in the flames. Winter though – brr – dressing in the cold, breath condensing, milk bottles freezing.

'In the dream, I go to the kitchen door leading to a lawn, beyond which Dad had planted cabbages, peas, Aran Pilot potatoes and a plum tree. The heady scent of phlox vied with McGredy's roses in summer. River clay soil, but Dad added a product to make it into workable stuff.

'As it was then, though I heard the current owners have let the garden go, plums rotting, discarded bikes, newspapers impaled on the hedge. Neat in my dreams, cabbages in rows, the sun on them even though winter. One corner unplanted by the field fence, I'm keen to plant so it will be complete. Probably means something's missing, not ignoring opportunities before it's too late.'

Paula spoke slowly and deliberately. 'Beautiful, comforting, vivid memories. You don't need me to tell you what they're urging you to do.'

Trudie nodded. 'Same dream for years, urging me to grab that spade and dig. See, if a client had told me, I'd suggest she was solving issues in her sleep, but it's me, and recurring since Cornwall and your visit to Shropshire. I've dragged my heels – scared to death.'

Paula cleared breakfast crockery. 'Shall I make more coffee? Don't mean to go off the subject, I just…'

'Yes.' Trudie replied tersely, gripping the napkin tightly,

wringing it like a dishcloth. 'I'm so bloody angry. Took risks, welcomed him in my home, my bed. How dare he leave me, how dare he!' she shouted, forcefully throwing the chewed up napkin across the floor.

'I should have said, "If you don't want me, I don't want you." Paula, I've held on, to what? Memories of a man I was sure would always be here. He is, dominating my every day, an interloper, and by my refusal to give up, I'm allowing him to do it. Oh damn the man!'

31

Alison attempted to concentrate on plans for her Derbyshire client. Sitting on the floor surrounded by the project, she'd worried about Leo suffering gastric flu, recuperating on his balcony overlooking the Alpes Maritimes; clear air and sunshine. Alison would hear him rasping with croup as a baby, watchful nights by his cot, steaming his room with a boiling kettle. On her own, worry immense.

At Christmas, she'd given him a thick navy bathrobe when he flew home to Antibes on December 30th. Having visited him twice in the past year, the first telling him of Stephen, he'd hugged her saying how happy he was.

Alison, eight weeks into dating, had realised she was pregnant. Having fallen for Mark's boyish charm, she'd believed his promises. When Leo was two months old they'd rented a flat in a poor area. For five years, in between lengthy spells working in the Middle East, Mark saw Alison and Leo twice a year, for a few weeks. He'd stayed with his parents in Kent, drinking heavily upon return, picking arguments with Alison. Eventually confessing he'd met someone, he'd promised to send money, which quickly ceased. When Mark returned to Saudi permanently, Leo was happier, his disobedience from being sidelined by him, over.

Alison had interior design work, so didn't need to chase Mark for child support. She wanted complete severance, they'd manage and they did, her parents in South Cumbria helping when they could. After a year, they'd emigrated to Perth, Australia, to join Alison's brother's travel business. Since her father had died, they'd remained there.

Alison had dates, a few relationships. Sex became her passport to approval, ending in disappointment, not wanted for herself. She'd naively gone to bed to get to know them, thinking sex was the path to love. 'Needy, that's how they see me,' she'd told Julia. 'Insecurity makes me put out, scarcely knowing them. Good intentions with the next one, but... my parents were so happy, I felt I couldn't match up. I'm not blaming them, my childhood was OK.'

Julia had remarked she wasn't surprised after Mark's letdown. When Alison had begun dating Phil, she was adamant he was different. Julia knew his police position was causing Alison to believe he was looking out for her.

'This one really cares, honestly.'

Julia had been dubious. 'You go the extra mile for the wrong men.'

Alison had naively replied, 'He's working tiring shifts, hasn't time for cheating.'

It took months to realise his treachery, resulting in anxiety, panic attacks and depression. Only when Stephen came into her life did she find real happiness.

With late February watery light streaking the carpet, Alison sat back against the view, too tempting to gaze out of the window. Scanning notes for the client wanting a Swedish influence, she ticked each suggestion, putting illustrations into a folder.

Fir green, birch greys, white painted furniture, reflecting light. Bleached floorboards, cream curtains and blackout blind.

Phoning That's Showbusiness, where she'd discovered Clare's address, she ordered a curved beechwood Cassina armchair with

229

an aluminium and grey lacquered frame. Alison hoped the weather would improve for her journey into Derbyshire.

She'd have to work all afternoon to bring a feel of the garden into the room. Stephen had suggested ivy stencilling. Seeing Alison's horror, he'd stick to removing it from brickwork, he'd promised, tugging his forelock and bowing. 'Sorry, milady, I knows mee place.'

'Keep to it in future, Boyce, and get back to the compost heap!' she'd replied imperiously, breaking into giggles.

Alison had told him of Julia, David and Clare. He'd remarked, 'Julia seemed like a gazelle running from David the lion.'

'True. When Clare was housesitting while her friend was on holiday, and you did that garden, I didn't know where Clare herself lived, only that she was moving to Norfolk to live with an ex cos she'd split with a divorcee in Cheshire. No idea she'd returned here, nor got involved with David. Little minx.'

'Glad you believed me when she drunkenly threw herself at me.'

'Course. I offered your services, knowing her briefly, and Julia had never met her. It was when Julia revealed the yellow Mini that I connected the two.'

'What a mess.' Stephen responded. 'What complications folks have in their lives.'

Alison replied sharply, 'That's not fair, we all do! My parents emigrated to Australia, I was a single-mother. What about your mother? If that's not complicated…'

'Ouch, didn't think.' Stephen replied apologetically. 'Mum had a difficult childhood, dominant mother, hen-pecked father, often at war.'

'Sorry, you sounded smug.'

Stephen kissed her cheek. 'It came out wrongly, let's make you giggle. Mum said when her father had been relegated to the spare room, she asked him why. He wryly replied he wasn't sure, but wouldn't be getting out until they next had visitors.'

Closing the curtains, Alison laughed.

Stephen grinned. 'Mum laughed telling me, although she felt sorry for her father.'

'I like your mum, so upfront, told me she had an orphan psychology, which made you free of trying to please parents when you grew up. She said she'd carried on though, pleasing others instead of herself most of the time.'

'Really? She's never mentioned that. Don't we all try to please those we love, wanting their happiness?'

'Not to the extent we become doormats. When our insecurities are profound, we let that happen. I was like that because I hadn't dealt with it from the past. My childhood wasn't as insecure as your mother's, but I didn't feel special, attracting men who saw my neediness and capitalised on it.'

She saw Stephen's serious face. 'Let's get to what we needed an hour ago, dinner. Pass me that menu please.'

32

The month of March had come in like a lion but not gone out like a lamb. Alison had finished the Buxton project. All month there'd been unforgiving rain, squally winds bringing down trees and tipping wheelie bins over. The roads were steep and winding up to the remote house. She'd been fortunate on two days she'd worked there, clear visibility.

At the end of March, fog had descended – a thin grey blanket. After three hours with her Buxton client, Alison's anxiety had increased about returning. Refusing lunch, she'd explained she should leave as fog made visibility difficult in unfamiliar territory.

Arranging a date for final finishes, including lemon spring plants for pastel window boxes, she'd been relieved to be driving back. Anxiously crawling down sharp chicanes in patchy fog, when cars appeared round a bend, she had to dip headlights to avoid dazzling, making visibility worse as grass verges melted into the tarmac. The terrain so opposite to the flat Cheshire plains, Alison drove at a snail's pace. Guessing drivers behind were irritated by her slow progress, she'd ignored them, concentrating on descending treacherous slopes. She'd shivered seeing Macclesfield streetlights emerge and fog becoming mere mist.

At breakfast next day, Alison imagined her extreme fatigue was from the previous day. Pouring coffee into the sink yet again, she opened the kitchen door. A wave of dizziness attacked, making her sway into the frame, stumbling towards a chair, falling clumsily onto it.

She'd enjoyed good health, apart from the mental challenge of unsuccessful affairs, leaving her anxious and depressed. Periods had caused problems, but most women had that issue. The contraceptive pill had alleviated excruciating cramps.

By lunchtime she'd made an appointment at the Well Woman Clinic, where her pill had been changed the month before. Stephen had rung from Sussex, he was a worrier and couldn't have helped, so Alison kept quiet. She saw the same female doctor, anxiously revealing her symptoms.

'You may be having an early menopause. I don't think it can be the pills I prescribed last month. Let's do your blood pressure. I'll give you a note for a blood test for your surgery, take a urine sample too.'

Alison called at the surgery for an appointment. The telephone was ringing upon her return. Usually she'd drop keys and handbag, dashing to answer it. Rubbing her hands wearily over her face, she picked up the receiver, hearing Julia.

'I'm here, wait.'

'You're out of breath.'

'Just come in.'

'Won't keep you. I'm going next week to see Poppy in France. Would you like to come?'

'Can't, feel dreadful, insomnia and nausea.'

Julia was concerned. 'Get checked out.'

'Done that, been to the Well Woman Clinic. Blood test tomorrow.'

'Maybe another virus.'

Alison sighed. 'Yes. Coming down in that blanket of fog from Buxton, I was already drained, but my nerves were jangled when I got home. Everything's an effort.'

'Could be early menopause. It's possible.'

'Ha. That's what the doctor suggested,' Alison replied anxiously.

'Periods, how are they?'

'Scarcely there. I dunno, probably this new pill.'

'Which?'

'THE PILL, contraceptive. It was changed, but this one's worse. Julia, do you think it could be ME? You had that.'

'That was the stress of David and ghastly Clare. Within two weeks my nerves had settled, slept better, periods regulated. Not seeing him, dreading the scrunch of tyres, thunderous face, key in the lock quickening my pulse. The mental state's bound to cause physical symptoms. Look, soon you'll hear blood results… have you told Stephen?'

'Not until I know the outcome and he's home. Hope it's not the pill, don't want to resort to condoms, men don't like them, neither do I.'

'True. At half term in Feb, seeing Poppy in situ made me happier. Now I'm rambling… let me know results.'

'Mm, thanks Julia.'

'What for?'

'Being there.'

Julia affirmed, 'Always will be. Oh, my three thirty appointment's here, must go, bye.'

Alison drove into Lower Birches to the health shop. Reasoning she needed a tonic, she bought Agnus Castus for women's health. Opposite was Trinity Tearooms. The aromatic smell of coffee beans swamped her as she joined the queue.

Within minutes she had to leave. Noisy machines with steamy heat overpowered her. Reluctantly, she left queue and café, a young man steadying her as she stumbled onto the pavement. In the car she glanced at the mirror. 'Phew I look hot.' With no water in the glove compartment, she headed home.

That had been five days ago, constant nausea. Work had been

put on hold, her brain wouldn't let her. She put on an act for Stephen when he rang, saying she was recovering from a cold. Julia had popped round, bringing soup and pizza. Alison had no trouble keeping it down, she hadn't been sick, but no let up with the nausea.

Alison's garden was therapeutic, two days blessed with a balmy spring breeze. On a recliner observing blackbirds and blue tits, she wished Bo, her late cat, could rise up from her grave to watch with her. She longed for her fragrant fur and mighty whiskers tickling her arm. Uneasy re her health, to focus she began re-reading Jeffrey Archer's short stories, the intriguing A *Quiver Full of Arrows*. Not taxing, but attention holding.

Monday morning, a call from the surgery with an appointment. The female locum she saw was new and pleasant, but Alison didn't anticipate being so long in the surgery, or the diagnosis.

At home, still dazed, she made tea, managed to pour without spilling it, and finally ceased staring at the wall. The diagnosis imparted an hour before, was a complete shock. She should have been relieved, even elated, but could hardly believe the result. The major anxiety was how it would affect Stephen.

She had two days until his return. It would be a shock to him too when she revealed there'd be three of them in their relationship by Christmas.

33

Laurie pondered, on a wet March Sunday, whether it was worth driving to the car boot sale near Tenbury Wells. The wintry morning didn't beckon him out, steady drizzle had produced a clinging dampness. He'd been most Sundays, to be part of the crowd and not the loner he'd become. 'Loneliness can be a self-inflicted wound,' he was told by a therapist. He'd had no choice.

Back from living with his son in North Carolina, it had been a hard quiet road. Quiet, moving to live on a remote Ashton lane a few months before, peaceful in some measure too, but incomplete without the woman who could fill his heart with happiness.

Car boots occasionally produced gems, like American yard sales. Despite driving rain, there were plenty of people wrapped up, sloshing over the muddy field. Laurie thought he'd arrived at a cagoule convention. Two hours later, he'd bought a Victorian jam pan, a book of Spike Milligan's jokes and a CD. The jam pan was for French lavender on a wrought iron garden table. He and Trudie liked Spike Milligan. The CD made the slushy trudge worthwhile.

Indoors, he donned a black tracksuit, padding in thick socks around the extended kitchen, making coffee and toast. Sitting at the dining table, feet up on a chair, crossing his ankles, browsing the paperback, he laughed. Seeing Spike's sketches and cartoons, he thought of what Trudie said. 'Books are old friends and teachers.'

Refilling his mug, he took the CD with him, pulse quickening as he inserted it into the player. *Home Thoughts From Abroad* by Clifford T. Ward. He hadn't heard the title track until his son played it one hot day on the deck in North Carolina.

It had hit him in the solar plexus, words so apt, a Worcestershire girl's lover missing her from abroad. The singer almost spoke, asking her if she still read Browning, reminiscing about their love. It stirred up what he'd abandoned in Worcestershire – Trudie. When the family were out he'd listened, anguishing for what he'd lost, feeling cowardly, guilt having caused his breakdown, rendering him powerless, scarcely able to move. His daughter had travelled with him to North Carolina. He'd lived with his son and wife for four years, then back to England permanently.

There'd been much to do settling into his cottage, taming the garden, sorting his few possessions. The CD had been waiting for him that morning. Looking blankly out of the picture window, Laurie recalled Trudie saying you had to be brave in a relationship, aware your heart could be broken. He'd assured her that wouldn't happen. Wincing at his naievety, he stopped the CD, his mood had changed. The nostalgia of the song reminded him he'd thrown away his security blanket four years previously.

Even after therapy in America, he felt in limbo. Unfinished business. One therapist had explained we need closure, but cannot always get it. He hadn't needed the explanation. 'Let grief come,' she'd advised. Until meeting Trudie he'd been emotionally disconnected, then transformed by her affection. Their intense romantic collision had overwhelmed him with joy, but ultimately broken him.

Cognitive therapy was useful, but he'd only told half the story, pretending his grief was for his wife. He'd ceased praying, told one therapist that religion was to assuage the fear

237

of death – God had abandoned him. Subsequently he knew he'd abandoned God and his commandments, felt he needed aversion therapy for the twenty-first century. Irrational, but he was in a dark place. He took anti-depressants as directed, settled with his son and made friends with God again. It took time, but he had plenty of that.

He watched a discussion on BBC2 on Sigmund Freud. Hearing an egghead say, 'All of us want to sleep with our mothers and talk about it until we feel better,' Laurie wrinkled his nose with a disgusted look, uttering, 'Tosh, utter tosh!' There was just one person he wanted to sleep with, walk with, talk with, be with, hold, love.

Knowing his daughter had laryngitis and wasn't online, Laurie decided to send a notelet. Rifling through the desk, he selected one depicting spring flowers. The drawer was untidy. Noticing a card, edges curled like a stale sandwich, which his daughter had sent when her mother had died, he re-read it.

Mum's in heaven, she's still with us, don't worry.

Irritated, he crumpled it, angry for lies he'd been forced to tell in the barren years away from Trudie. Helena believed he'd been happily married to her mother – another deceit. He unclenched his hands, picked up the notelet and walked to the kitchen to write.

'Dug up buttercups, split forget-me-nots. Female robin flew onto my spade. Been to car boot today. Get well soon. Dad. Xx' Sealing the envelope, he longed to be chatting with Trudie, sharing simple pleasures.

The weather improved, buds were bursting to welcome a warmer spring afternoon. Sooty had wolfed his food while Laurie changed his blanket. Sooty not venturing indoors, Laurie had left the shed open, having made the jet cat a cosy bed there. Winter had been hard, so the bed had been lined with foil, a blanket and hot water bottle. Refusing to accept such luxury, Sooty had slept under a variegated holly bush. When snow came in mid-January, Laurie found him in the bed one morning.

Checking the outside of the cottage, Laurie saw rain and frost had dislodged the guttering from the downpipe of the extension. He spent twenty minutes dislodging compacted leaves. Blackbirds and thrushes swooped with assorted bedding for their nests. Laurie observed where they were taking it, hoping Sooty was elsewhere. Within seconds he arrived at Laurie's feet, turning and twisting, miaowing loudly. Laurie bent to stroke him. He allowed that, but picking up was out, he was nobody's pet.

Laurie's fingers felt warm sun on Sooty's winter coat. He went indoors to spoon tuna into Sooty's bowl, he'd warmed milk for him some freezing mornings. Sooty had drunk it like there was no tomorrow. Laurie had never owned a cat. Owned – he supposed he now did, as Sooty had decided to stay, on his terms. Cats – an investment in grief. You're aware they'll die before you, but no easier when it happens, Trudie had said, but she'd always given a stray a home. As he'd done – the black cat came, saw and had conquered.

Laurie had mostly black trousers, sweaters and shoes. Leaving Sooty to polish off his food, he went indoors. Turning on the television, an advertisement for Black and Decker was showing. In the last hour he'd thought of 'black' three times. Black cat, black clothes, Black and Decker. Trudie used to tell him things cross our path for a purpose. Observing Sooty vigorously grooming, Laurie was trying to locate what significance the word 'black' had. By five o'clock he'd have the answer.

Up the dark lane, Laurie quickened his step to reach the post box half a mile down. Spring sun which had warmed Sooty, Laurie and the garden, had retreated. He turned his anorak collar up, hunching shoulders against chilly afternoon air. He could have posted his daughter's letter next day, but needed to sort out what was puzzling him. He didn't practise law now, but was still orderly; couldn't stand living in chaos. Moving in, traces of depression kept him from being efficient. Coping alone was challenging in a new area, with the ever present memory of a beautiful woman probably in the same county. It had taken time and courage to unpack his memories, put them on shelves and in cupboards. The bijou cottage was tidy, Laurie's head wasn't.

Once the letter was posted, he journeyed back. The breeze was stronger, blowing hard at him. He bent against pinhead rain, digging hands deep into anorak pockets, striding out, quickening his pace. He didn't mind wind and rain, but once he'd had Trudie to link arms with, laughing together, shrieking as a squall attacked them. It had no appeal to him now. His lips pursed, irritated at the increased strength of the shower, making him stagger.

Inside, he made hot chocolate, shining a torch to see if Sooty was in the shed. He was. Laurie turned on the television, seeing *Countdown* advertised on Channel 4. Wasn't that the programme Trudie said Paula loved? Laurie found it mind-numbingly boring. Paula, Trudie's confidante and soulmate, Laurie met her once. Tall, slim, elegant, beautifully spoken. 'What was her surname? Same initial as Trudie.'

Getting up to draw curtains against the black March evening, he exclaimed. 'That's it – Black. Black!' It was the push he needed. By five o'clock he'd located Paula's telephone number online. According to the listing, she lived in Cheltenham, alone.

His heart thumped. 'What if she rings off?'

With nervous trepidation he dialled, hearing Paula's soft voice asking the caller to leave their number. Words wouldn't come. With a wobbly wrist and sweating palm, he replaced the receiver. 'Damn.' he uttered, but only the room heard it.

Two days on, the call hadn't been made. In a Tenbury café, Laurie stirred chocolate flakes into cappuccino, idly watching them melt through foam into hot liquid beneath. Soft muffled chatter was relaxing, rather than irritating pop music in other cafés. Inertia, since knowing Paula Black's number, was cowardice.

He winced, even before illness he hadn't the guts to tell Irene the truth.

In a rare moment of irritation, Trudie had accused him of 'wanting a housekeeper wife, plus a lover who satisfies other wishes – wanting your bun and your halfpenny.' Laurie had been hurt, explaining his position with the law firm, his wife's neurotic state, his imminent retirement. He'd be free of the heavy workload and could make plans with Trudie.

'Give me a few more months,' he'd pleaded. He scooped the foam from the steaming drink. 'She did. What did I give her? Disappearance.' He noticed a middle-aged couple exchanging doting looks. He'd had that once and blown it. Now he was a bystander observing love instead of experiencing it. No one's fault but his own.

Embarking on a romance later in life, was not like someone you've known when younger, had children with, shared a loving home. Loving? Until Trudie, he'd been resigned to frustrating boredom, the rest was work. Then an angel appeared, transforming it, before ecstasy became agony.

Procrastination, days turning into weeks, no move to find Trudie. The longer he left it, the more reclusive he became, the cottage his refuge, a safe nest from responsibility and reality. Sooty, garden, library and acquaintances at the pub were now his world.

His mental health in America had taken ages to heal. Family and much counselling and pills had been required. His son's furniture restoration business prevented him obsessing about former life. After two years, a more physical illness attacked him, requiring lengthy specialised treatment. Eventually he was well enough to return to Worcestershire. The plan had been to buy a cottage, retrieve belongings from his daughter, settle in, then find Trudie. The most important of these, he'd postponed.

He shrugged on his overcoat against the March wind. The café manageress gave him a large smile.

'OK Mr. Martin? One fifty please. How's that stray cat?'

'Sooty, he's a survivor, gets five star treatment now. He won't come inside, but likes the shed, food, and me.'

Miriam smiled. 'My husband rescued a ginger kitten once, injured in a ditch, starving. We nearly called him Rogers, after the dancer, but it was November so he became Scorpio.'

Laurie smiled. 'Very apt. See you soon.'

Outside the café, the cat's name struck a chord. Scorpio, Trudie's birth sign. Signs – plenty of those prodding him, too apparent to ignore.

At home, Sooty was at the door with an immovable look – Laurie saw it each day. Bolt upright, paws neatly together, he stared to catch his master's eye. If no move was made to the kitchen cupboard, he'd give an Oscar winning performance with the silent miaow. Oblivious to cold drizzle falling, Sooty quickly trailed his dinner into the shed. Laurie stroked the dense fur, Sooty hardly noticed, food was what the next three minutes concerned. 'Slow down, Sooty. Bad old days have gone,' he told him, going indoors for the important call.

'Bad old days,' he muttered by the telephone. 'Not all good ones for me either.' He daren't move, resolve might go, he had to take the risk. Scanning notes so he didn't slip up, he dialled Paula's number. This time he didn't hang up.

'I'm not able to answer your call at the moment, please leave your message after the tone.' Paula's beautiful English voice announced.

Laurie swallowed. 'Hello, um Paula. It's Laurie, I've hesitated phoning. You may not welcome this but...' The answerphone switched itself off.

Laurie tensed hotly. 'Damn and blast.' He redialled, speaking slowly. 'I'd appreciate your call.' Carefully giving his phone number, he nervously continued. 'My name is Laurie, I suspect you'll have gathered that. Thank you.'

He replaced the receiver, moist from nervous hands, mouth

dry from anxiety. Scribbled prompts had helped, imperative to get the message correct. Now it was a waiting game, one he'd been playing for too long.

***

Paula returned from town, grateful for the taxi service she'd engaged since James' death. She'd passed her driving test before marriage, but not encouraged to drive; James' ploy to keep her dependent on him. Part of his controlling nature, but Paula's was slightly subservient, seeing her role as homemaker, so compliant; James the breadwinner and head of the household.

When they moved to Cheltenham, high up near Cleeve Hill, it was impossible to shop without transport. Buses stopped a mile off, so James had arranged taxis to collect and deliver Paula to and from town. On Saturdays James took them in his Jaguar for heavier shopping at Sainsbury. When he retired, he drove them everywhere. When he became ill, he saw a Paula he hadn't known. Unable to walk as far as the gate, he reluctantly had to let her take charge of his total welfare.

When he died, Paula used the maroon Jaguar, mainly to visit Trudie, but occasionally used the local taxi service, the driver carrying her shopping in, making her feel secure. She could certainly afford it, James had left Paula well set up.

She emptied carrier bags, made tea, ate rhubarb yoghurt and dozed to Radio 4. The five o'clock news awoke her. Feeling chilly, she got up to increase the wall thermostat, noticing the telephone flashing.

The first message was a call urging her to renew something she hadn't got. Then a second. In the kitchen she'd run the tap, so couldn't hear it all, only the name. She froze, turned the tap off quickly, moving to stare at the phone. As if her movements would erase the message, she slowly crept towards the machine. Her nervous body sat by it.

'Laurie? Can't be. Not Trudie's Laurie? Oh why did I have the tap on?' Her hands shook as she clicked delicately, so nails didn't press Delete instead of Repeat, then committed the information to paper in case the message became wiped. Shaken, she pondered what to do, couldn't ignore it, imperative to do the correct thing. Her head, whilst bathing, was full of the big question – should she tell Trudie? Despite warm bathwater, her skin tingled with trepidation.

Donning a robe, she heated up a chicken pasta for dinner. She'd planned something else but chose the easiest option with no preparation, her mind elsewhere. With Laurie, wherever he was. With Trudie, should she phone her first? Should she phone Laurie at all? She poured a small dry martini, desiring a large one, but needing a clear head. Deciding she wouldn't tell Trudie in case Laurie disappeared as soon as he'd re-appeared, she read the newspaper.

The simple task of ringing back had become a lead weight. This was no ordinary message, nor ordinary person, but Laurie who'd caused huge pain to Trudie. She screwed up her mouth in distaste, but ring him she must. He answered within five.

'This is Paula Black returning your call as requested,' she began quietly, trying not to sound offhand, but guessing she was coming over like that.

She heard him draw in breath. 'Thank you, Paula. My apologies for contacting you, I have no right, but need to talk about... er... Trudie. I wanted to find her months ago, but feared the consequences.'

Paula arched her eyebrow, telling him sharply, 'Fear is the oxygen of negativity.' She flinched. 'Sorry, this is awkward for me too.'

'I appreciate that. You're right, and what Trudie would have said.'

'Would have said? She is alive you know.'

Laurie's voice broke up. 'Thank God. Paula, I really need your help please. I live not far from you and...'

244

'I've seen you actually.'

Taken aback, he asked, 'Oh… where? I've been home months, scarcely been anywhere.'

'Last year at View From The Top. I didn't twig until I heard your name mentioned. I hesitated telling Trudie, but best she knew.'

He asked cautiously. 'Didn't she want to find me?'

Paula exploded. 'You arrogant man! The affair ending for her was brutal. Don't you realise the severity of what you did with repercussions ever since?' she spat out.

Laurie meekly replied, 'Oh I do.' Trying not to crack, he begged her to meet with him.

Paula knew she should see him. 'Tomorrow here, we can speak privately.'

'Oh thank you. Will you tell Trudie? I…'

Paula hastily spoke. 'Not at the moment, depends what happens tomorrow. I sound cold, but last year I told her, "Tackle your addiction to this man, he's ruined your self-esteem. Don't let him ruin the rest of your personality. Summon up your dignity, stop being his victim."'

Laurie winced. 'I deserve that. Trudie said you were a generous loyal friend. Would ten-thirty be all right?'

Paula gave her address. She did not say she was looking forward to seeing him.

34

Paula remained inert. Laurie, a ghost in the shadows, re-appearing in human form. The secret she'd keep from Trudie for now, weighed heavily.

Laurie paced the floor, the call had been a strain. He stretched, releasing tension, running his fingers through his hair, puffing. He needed a stiff drink. Pouring a gin, and out of orange juice, he loaded the glass with ice. From the second gin, his head ached. 'What a faux pas, asking her if Trudie had looked for me. Decent of her to see me tomorrow; I need an early night.'

Rinsing his glass at the sink, he saw two amber headlamps lighting up the dark path. He tapped the window, sending Sooty scampering towards the door. Laurie scooped dried meat into the bowl. Outside, Sooty wove around Laurie's legs, miaowing manically.

'Here boy, this what you want?'

Sooty wolfed dinner. Laurie stroked him, getting the usual 'perroop' sound of satisfaction. Within ten minutes, both were in bed. With a brief wash, Sooty slept deeply, no worries on his mind. Laurie took longer; plenty on his.

Next morning pinheads of hail splattered the windscreen until the sky became harebell, changing into a deeper love-in-a-mist approaching Cheltenham. On Paula's steep road, Laurie parked underneath chestnut trees for composure. This was a big step, for Paula too. Five minutes later he was in her beautiful open-plan house.

She was as he'd first seen her. Tall, slender, elegant and beautifully spoken, wearing cream trousers, black v-necked sweater and a double row of pearls. He was glad he'd dressed well, black trousers and cornflower sweater. His hair was greyer, still thickly layered.

In the vast cathedral-ceilinged living room, Laurie admired the Dansk coffee set. 'I know Trudie loves it,' he smiled shyly.

Paula poured coffee, watching him stir cream into his cup. He had a quiet boyish charm and sensitivity, she could see why Trudie had fallen for him.

He saw Paula's equally nervous face. 'I need to reveal why I vanished, but should be telling Trudie,' he said, apologetically.

'Yes you should.' Paula affirmed.

He placed his cup down, putting his hands over Paula's. 'How grateful I am for this generous opportunity.'

'It's OK Laurie, really.'

Looking serious, he settled into the chair. 'Paula, here's what happened. Trudie and I loved each other, circumstances made it necessary to hide our affair. When Irene died, we thought we could give up our cloak and dagger existence. The death was a shock, but I cannot pretend I loved Irene, the marriage was boring and stressful. May I tell you everything? I also want to hear how Trudie's been and if she'll want to meet me. I could have gone to her house, but she's suffered enough. Excuse my putting it this way, but I realised you could be the catalyst.'

Paula saw his desperation. 'Whatever I can do, I will. I found this photograph Trudie copied for me.' She handed it to him, depicting Laurie and Trudie hugging at Lulworth Cove, surrounded by shrieking seagulls.

He smiled fondly, telling Paula it was wonderful to see. He

247

recalled their Dorset break, beaches with dunes and marram grass, Durdle Door, the hotel's privacy.

'Trudie said it was the happiest she'd ever been. Laurie what went wrong?'

'Everything,' he replied gravely. 'Firstly, may I use your cloakroom? The one with the photograph of Mighty Moth snoozing in the basin.'

Paula raised her eyebrows. 'You've heard of my old cat? Bet Trudie told you he caught that hawkshead moth. She was terrified, named him Mighty Moth. I'll show you the way, then top up our coffee.'

Laurie saw the British Blue cat in the frame on the cloakroom wall. En route back to the living room, he noticed a framed photograph of James. Laurie had imagined he'd be a handsome devil, but he wasn't. 'Piggy eyes, thin lips, knew he had little to offer my Trudie except a quickie in an expensive hotel, pathetic swine. My Trudie, wonder if she is? Doubtful.' Altering his expression, he joined Paula in the kitchen.

'I see you like my keys, Trudie bought that one at the top.'

'Yes, she described them on the white brick wall. I used to collect paperweights.'

Carrying the tray, Paula replied. 'Yes. Gosh, we seem to know a lot about each other, hope you don't believe all of it!' she giggled.

He smiled broadly. 'I do, all good I assure you.' He couldn't admit awareness of James propositioning Trudie. Paula had no knowledge herself.

'Whatever you want me to tell Trudie I will, and whatever you don't, I won't.'

A relaxed Laurie asked. 'May I share some feelings?'

'Absolutely.' Paula replied, sitting, legs elegantly placed like a nineteen fifties model.

'I read in America, when you're grown up you get fewer scabs on your knees, but more internal injuries. America. That's where I've been, staying with my son. I'd known my shortcomings, but

Trudie was my love, so I carried on wrongdoing. When you hear people say, "I wouldn't change a thing," they're liars.' He reached for his drink.

Paula empathised. 'Yes. it's remarkable how the presence of someone you love can make life beautiful. We've all had a past, married or not.'

'Yes. Now my leaving, you must be wondering – Trudie too… I dare to hope she is.'

Paula nodded. 'Definitely.'

'Thanks. When I met Trudie, I loved her immediately. As our feelings deepened, I saw the significance of the deception it necessitated. A beautiful fantasy, but Trudie was cautious. Although Irene was oblivious, after three years with Trudie and my marriage an empty shell, it became unbearable to continue in the same manner, so a divorce seemed inevitable.'

Paula listened attentively, privileged to be a confidante. 'Oh the phone, the answerphone's on.'

The voice was one Laurie hadn't heard in years.

'Paula. Are you there…? No? I'll phone later. Bye.'

Placing his cup slowly in the saucer, Laurie, fighting a cauldron of emotions, was visibly shaken.

Paula said sympathetically. 'Yes, that's our girl, must be strange hearing her voice again.'

Laurie uttered vacantly, 'Surreal.' Paula went into the kitchen so he could recover. Bringing a highball glass of water, she advised, 'Drink this, bit early for brandy. She has no idea you're here.'

'What joy, I've actually heard her voice… she sounds normal. Sorry, talking rubbish.'

'You're not, she is normal, happy sometimes, but it's been a struggle not knowing, loss, anger too. I stayed with her recently; she was rock bottom.'

Laurie, shamefaced, narrated the complex tale. 'When Irene died, I intended to be with Trudie after a decent period. What I found when I sorted Irene's clothes, jewellery, and cards she'd saved... I... er...' his voice trembled. 'I... may I relate that later?'

Paula looked puzzled. 'If you like.'

Perturbed, he continued. 'My discovery brought massive pain. Migraine and high blood pressure, sleepless nights and anxious days. The doctor gave me anti-depressants, but within ten days I'd lost weight. Three weeks on I could hardly put one foot in front of the other, off work with nervous exhaustion, didn't answer the phone, ate little, then my daughter came. If it hadn't been for her, liaising with my son in North Carolina, I dread to think what I'd have done. He insisted I stay with him to recover.

The solicitors practice couldn't have been more supportive, believing it was Irene's death that had caused my breakdown. If they'd known of Trudie I doubt they'd have been so kind. I gave Helena my car, she packed my stuff to store at her house and drove us to her home in the North East. I was there two days before we flew from Newcastle to the US. Tell me if I'm not making sense won't you?'

'I'm relieved to solve the four year enigma.'

'I was out of it, so my daughter made decisions, the right ones for me. The wrong ones for Trudie.'

'Yes, wrong and terrible. Could you not have telephoned or written? Were you really too ill?'

Laurie affirmed, 'I was, had amnesia, regained memory, lost some again. I was on heavy medication, the doctor recommended a psychologist. I ask you, a psychologist? Oh... by your face you think I was mistaken?'

'I do.' she replied decisively. 'A breakdown calls for it. Some can't get that on the NHS., or have to wait ages for an appointment. It would have been an opportunity to open up in a confidential non-judgemental environment.'

'True.' he responded. 'Too ill to face strangers. I didn't tell my children about Trudie. They knew their mother was difficult, but I daren't risk admitting my deceit.'

Paula suddenly stood up. 'I'm sorry, Laurie, the postman's here with a parcel. He bangs hard on the door, it's so thick, he thinks I won't hear him.' She hurried up steps to another level, hoping to reach the solid oak doors before he knocked. Too late.

Laurie heard Paula hadn't exaggerated. 'Blam, blam, blam.' The postman's fists rained down on the solid door. Laurie jumped, seeing outside, birch branches shiver, as startled starlings flew to a safer perch. He hadn't been aware of them, concentration had been on Paula.

She returned with the parcel, apologising. 'I've put off getting the doorbell repaired.' She saw Laurie smiling.

'George, feel I know that man. Trudie spoke of your postmen, Hubert and George, first and second post. She used to do their Gloucestershire accent a treat.'

Paula laughed. 'Trudie's impersonations, I encourage her. When your health improved, didn't you think of coming back?'

Laurie's expression morphed from animated to regretful. 'It took ages to be relatively normal. I helped my son with his furniture restoring business, gradually liaised with clients, building up confidence, nil in England when I had the breakdown. I relied on anti-depressants though,' he said, sipping water. 'As I improved, I felt less guilt, but pills kept that at bay. I weaned myself off, then planned to fly home to find Trudie. I doubted she'd want to see me, but I'd have to try. Pathetic, but…'

'No, all that time you must have been terribly ill,' she sympathised.

'Unrecognisable. Not the Laurie that Trudie nor anyone knew. My son and wife were brilliant, I let them look after me, had to. Luckily they're quiet types, friends constantly calling would have been stressful.'

Paula smiled benevolently. 'Glad you had good care, but I too have been mystified, pained watching Trudie struggle. You say you planned to come to England to see her. Did you?' she asked, knowing from what Trudie had seen in Hessenford, that he had.

'Oh I planned and did it, once I'd reduced my anti-depressants.

I was going to contact Trudie but only got as far as Cornwall, I was born there in Hessenford. I went to the churchyard to view family graves next day, then inside to pray. I signed the visitors book and left,' he told her, regretfully. 'Paula you look cross.'

With a penetrating glare, she replied curtly, 'I am. Don't tell me you lost your way to Worcestershire so decided not to bother?'

Laurie's face betrayed his pain. 'You have every right to use that tone.' He touched Paula's hand, clenched with tension, her demeanour cold and stiff.

She withdrew her hand. 'Forgive my sarcasm. I've seen and felt Trudie's anguish and disappointment. You finally made the effort, yet only got as far as Hessenford. What good did that do? You could have stayed in America.'

'Please hear me out. I did visit Cornwall.'

'I know you did.' she replied firmly.

Laurie, perplexed, said, 'I can't prove this either, but I rang Trudie. A discontinued sound.'

'Laurie, she'd moved by then and her new number was ex-directory.'

'I didn't know. Trudie probably wouldn't want to see me but I planned to go to Worcestershire. That morning, when I was packing, my son's wife rang with shocking news, he'd been in a collision with a motorbike and was seriously ill in hospital.'

'Oh how terrible, forgive me. I presume you had to return?'

'No option, his condition was serious. Instead of driving to find Trudie, I had to fly to North Carolina. No time to think, only act. It took months for him to recover in hospital, operations, physio, etc., we almost lost him. I managed the furniture business with his wife. I couldn't phone Trudie, number still unobtainable. At last I know why.'

'Is he fully recovered?' Paula enquired sympathetically.

Laurie responded croakily. 'Yes, thank God, but took ages until he could take over himself.'

Paula frowned. 'If your love was so great for Trudie, surely you could have written to her, and if no reply, telephoned the local post office for her whereabouts? You weren't aware she'd moved house and she only began using a computer recently, so no e-mail contact for her then. In Cornwall though, and no reply on the phone, didn't you ask Directory Enquiries?'

'Paula, yes of course, all of these things and more. I was told she was ex-directory, so I wrote to her old address in case she'd moved, asking the occupants to forward a letter to her. Obviously, they didn't. When my health improved somewhat, I tried several ways to seek a solution to the problem, even a psychic medium, who told me Trudie lived close to water. I was cynical, most people in England live not far from a river, a lake or the sea. Then something else occurred, wasn't sure whether to mention it, but since you've asked, here it is.'

With a dry throat, Laurie drained his glass, stumblingly admitting, 'When I visited Cornwall in June 2007, intending to drive up to Trudie's, I'd been having treatment for prostate cancer for two years.' Witnessing Paula's immense shock, he told her, 'On medication, I was coping, but after Cornwall, the worry of my son's terrible car accident laid me low again. I was helping run the business while he was in hospital and recuperating, but it took many months for him to be back to normal. Attending hospital appointments for radiotherapy etc, and popping pills, my recovery took ages too. Thinking I'd be no use to Trudie with cancer and the depression it brought, I ceased searching for her.

'My cancer went into remission, as it was caught early. Stronger and more confident, I felt I could come home to Worcestershire. I knew Tenbury, beautiful countryside, so bought a place in Ashton. I like Worcestershire and want to die there. People say they want to die in their own bed; I want that too, but want to love in it first.' He sighed solemnly. 'Morbid, but you get my drift.'

'Yes. Laurie, I'm staggered to hear of your cancer, no wonder you were absent for so long, with all you've had to contend with, your own mental and physical stress, plus your son's. I'm amazed you look so well.' She stood up.

'Thanks. Can we speak of how Trudie's been? I'll then tell you what tipped me over the edge.'

'Yes.'

'Thanks. I came here for help, don't deserve it.'

'Sit back – much to tell.'

Laurie remained silent while Paula spoke. Too afraid of losing it, lest Paula think him the weak man he was.

'That's it. She's soldiered on. Now anger's set in and she's been desolate. When I stayed with her, she said that to live in the heart we leave behind is not to die. She'd been doing bereavement counselling, re-assuring the client with those words. She said she may as well be dead, doubting she was on your mind.'

Laurie looked grave. 'I tried to handle it, my condition laid me so low. To let my lover suffer, terrible.'

Paula sighed. 'The one that's abandoned suffers more, especially when they don't know why.' She tilted her head to one side. 'Well, are you going to reveal what made you disappear?'

Laurie began hesitantly. 'A cliché, but I was in a dead marriage. I buried myself in work, accepted a brother and sister existence. Scarcely that, we weren't even friends. Our relationship had eroded, intellects hugely different, little in common, except the children.

'Irene was happy keeping house, knitting, sewing. She'd mock my middle class values, spitefully, for holding my knife properly, calling serviettes napkins, buying quality clothes, even shopping at Waitrose. She was uptight about her working class roots, I couldn't have cared less. When I became a senior partner in the firm, she became worse, refusing to accompany me to law society functions, saying I was getting above myself.'

Paula asked, 'Do you think she was unhappy then?'

'She insisted she was contented. Finally she told me, years before Trudie, she didn't need sex, suggesting we live separate lives. Although she'd put me off lovemaking, I did try to be caring, but she didn't want that either. I asked if she'd like a separation? Horrified she was, saying she loved her home, and wasn't going to suffer financially when I was earning an excellent salary. It sounds mercenary, but I'd worked hard and didn't want to lose the house, savings etc. so I accepted we'd live in the house separately.'

Paula told him. 'An unhappy state, one I can relate to actually.'

Laurie knew Paula's circumstances, but looked suitably blank. 'When we began our relationship, deceit set in immediately, inventing absences from home, all that goes with an illicit liaison, easy to lie when you're trusted. Going from credits of euphoria to sometimes debits of despair, we halted our liaison for a while, but couldn't stand it. The missing was terrible, like anaemia of the brain. In the desert with Irene, Trudie was an oasis for me. You'll know most of this.'

'I understand how it was, except why you vanished when you were eventually free to be with Trudie and no pretence.'

Laurie cleared his throat. 'Trudie and I had played cat and mouse long enough. Determined to end the deception, we discussed options, planned final moves. A month prior to Irene dying, I'd promised Trudie I'd finish the contracts I had, resign from the law firm, then set up independently elsewhere. I'd grown to love Worcestershire, even though I'm a Cornishman by birth. We fancied living in the Tenbury area.

'I'd stayed at Trudie's, going home at six thirty next evening. Irene was drunker than usual, slurring words, stumbling against furniture, slumping onto the sofa. Ornaments were askew, magazines scattered, washing up left undone and rubbish overflowing the waste bin. This was unusual, she always washed up immediately. Mrs. Atkins, the cleaning lady, should have been in the day prior. I rang her, she told me Irene had phoned to cancel, saying she had a chill. She thought Irene would have said, but I couldn't tell her she was drunk.'

'Gosh, intriguing.' Paula said.

'There's worse. A strong perfume, Irene never wore it. Wasn't alcohol.

'I was ignored next day. It seems preposterous to say no one knew, but we'd been discreet. Apart from a woman stalking me, no one was suspicious. You're aware of the stress she gave us, and her move to Scotland?'

Laurie wrung his hands, informing Paula that two days later Mrs. Atkins had found Irene collapsed. Despite efforts of paramedics she was pronounced dead, a heart attack.

'Now, why I became ill after the funeral. Within three weeks, I'd cleared Irene's belongings for charity and our children, then tackled her chaotic bedroom. Dusty clutter under the bed, on top of the wardrobe, everywhere. Inside a mahogany box in the wardrobe...' Laurie stared at the table, swallowing hard. 'A letter. Five pages from... the stalker.'

Paula gasped loudly. 'Oh no!'

'From Jean, dated the day Irene got so blotto, thanking Irene for letting her in to tell of my affair. Wanted her to know more details, places we'd been spotted and when I'd made a play for her at the office. Wrote disgusting sexual things that I supposedly did to her. All absolute lies.'

'Devastating. Is that what caused Irene's heart attack?'

Solemnly, Laurie told her. 'That aroma when Jean had visited, the letter smelled of it too, and dated the same day, so another blow for Irene the following morning. She'd have been destroyed.'

Paula moved near Laurie, putting her arm around his sunken shoulders.

'I haven't told anyone. If I'd had courage to tell Irene, none of this... Illicit love,' he uttered sadly, 'has to be paid for.'

'I think you're courageous to come here. The pain you must have endured.'

'Enormous, it floored me. Irene dying after that evil woman called out of nowhere.'

'I... I'm almost speechless.'

'So was I, sitting inert for ages re-reading the letter. Irene, letting in a stranger, announcing she used to work for me, injecting poison, a complete shock. She'd have thrown Jean out, then hit the bottle. To receive terrible lies next morning would have been much worse. Although Irene didn't want me, she wouldn't have wanted another to have me.'

'Laurie what action did you take?'

He shrugged. 'Devastated, I put the vile letter in my desk, not knowing where Jean lived, but the damage had been done. I couldn't sleep, went through shame, guilt for causing Irene's death,' he confessed, frowning.

'You didn't. You'd agreed to live together, she'd have expected you to seek love elsewhere surely?' She saw Laurie's eyebrows raise, mouth puckering.

'Not Irene. Wouldn't have wanted me to enjoy happiness elsewhere, definitely not.'

Paula raised her voice. 'It was vicious Jean who did the damage. You'd planned to tell Irene you were leaving. She'd have been furious, given you hell, but ultimately accepted it. What Jean did was cruel, she's to blame. Did Irene have a heart condition?'

'Yes. Partly why I kept Trudie a secret and waited until I knew I'd have to face the truth. Irene liked me as breadwinner and life as she wanted it. Paula, you know the rest, how my health deteriorated rapidly. No matter how unhappy I'd been with Irene, the trauma of her death circumstance was immense,' he confessed sadly. He stretched his arms and back. 'Hm, what do we do now?'

Paula saw Laurie's bewilderment. 'Trudie must be told.' she replied definitely. 'No matter how she reacts, there'll be closure, which she's desperately needed. I'll go to see her. Is that OK with you?'

Laurie's relief was apparent. 'Oh that would be marvellous. If you think I should do it though, I will.'

Paula shook her head, standing up. 'It should be me. Forgive yourself, what you've revealed is forgivable and not all your own doing. Others have played their part, including Trudie. The only bad person is the stalker. You and Trudie didn't deliberately set out to ruin Irene's happiness. Jean did.'

With a flourish, Laurie rose to his feet, walking towards Paula, surprising her with a bear hug, thanking her profusely. 'You really are the best friend anyone could have,' he beamed, holding her arms, kissing her soundly on both cheeks, making her giggle.

She waved Laurie off, promising she'd inform him what transpired.

35

The telephone rang as soon as Trudie returned from the village.

'Mum. How are you?'

'Stephen, hello. Just came in, I'll put you on loudspeak. Let me get my reading specs, so I don't cut you off pressing the wrong button.'

'OK. I've got exciting news.'

'Concerts going OK?' she enthused.

'Yes, well attended. My news is connected with someone you've admired for years.'

Trudie's face lit up.

'When we went for rehearsal in Sussex, I saw the church wasn't far from the cottage Dirk Bogarde and his sister used to stay in with their nanny.' He heard Trudie shriek. 'Alfriston, we performed in the church. Staying in the adjoining village, I hadn't connected until I drove there. Amazing.'

Trudie was elated. 'Wonderful. I'd love to go.'

'I took photographs of the church, walked over the white bridge, and up Great Meadow to the tiny church above – wait for it – THE COTTAGE!!' He heard Trudie shriek again.

'How marvellous. It's inhabited, can you see into the garden?'

'Afraid not. Took a picture of the cobbled stone wall and one down the valley with Great Meadow in front. Out of sight you may be, not out of mind.'

'Can't wait to see them,' she told him excitedly. 'The tiny church was where Dirk and Elizabeth put jam jars of bluebells on the altar.'

'Turn the heating up, Mum. It's chilly here in the South, wind and rain.'

Trudie couldn't tell Stephen how low she'd been, he had his happiness with Alison. 'I'm OK. Love you.'

'Love you. Bye.'

Trudie saw her reflection, smiling for a change. 'Out of sight, but not out of mind.' Stephen had said. She wondered if that applied to Laurie, wherever he was.

36

Alison had managed to eat, drink and rest a little. Two days until Stephen returned, she had to compose herself to impart breathtaking news. Her concentration was poor, subject always the surgery scenario. The shock of the doctor's words, her own at hearing them. 'Blood and urine tests have solved the mystery of your health worries.'

Alison, in disbelief, was given a glass of water, which she robotically drank, hands shaking, head reeling at the startling outcome. After a brief discussion, she drove home dazed, scarcely remembering the surgery conversation. Only 'Six weeks pregnant.'

Requesting a phone call from the doctor next morning, she sheepishly admitted little had registered the day before.

'That's all right, Alison, I could see you weren't expecting my diagnosis,' she was told kindly.

'Phew no, I've been on the pill.'

'Yes and what I explained yesterday was how this could have happened. You said you had three days of diarrhoea and sickness six weeks ago. Severe vomiting could account for the contraceptive pill not working. Recall?'

'Hardly. In between bouts, I had a day when I felt better, that's when we must have made love. Two days later, gastric symptoms reappeared. Yesterday's news was a bombshell.'

'Your partner, will it be good news for him?' she enquired.

'Honestly, I'm not sure. I have a son in his twenties in France. Stephen and I have been a couple over a year and love each other, happy as we are, although he likes children. Did I say this yesterday?'

'No we didn't go into details, except he's a concert pianist. Tell him, then we can make plans, if that's what you want.'

Cleaning worktops, Alison reflected on the phrase 'if that's what you want.' The doctor meant if Stephen rejects being a father, there wouldn't be ante-natal plans, but those of another kind. She flushed hotly at the possibility.

Expecting Leo more than twenty years ago, she'd experienced twenty-four-hour nausea, as now. Pregnancy was the last thing she'd anticipated, even the Well Woman Clinic hadn't suggested that. Stephen was due, so she changed into black leggings, stretchy but tighter, early expansion. She didn't want Stephen to see the little bump until she'd told him. Merely a thickened waistline, but she dragged on a loose floral sweater.

A thrill of excitement invaded, but didn't last. Preparing shepherds pie, she fancied rosehip tea.

'Damn,' she gasped, waiting for the kettle to boil. 'The strip light's gone off.'

'I'll see to it tomorrow,' she heard from behind. Startled, she whirled around to see Stephen at the door, holding out his arms. 'A beautiful splash of colour on a grey day.' He threw down his bags, rushing to enfold her. 'God I've missed you.'

'Me too. Ouch you're crushing me,' she laughed coyly.

Pulling back a little, he nuzzled Alison's neck. 'Ooh what's that delicious aroma?'

She grinned mischievously. 'Shepherds pie.'

'I meant you, silly. Let me put the table lamp on. Is the kettle boiling, I've visualised tea for hours? I'm travel worn, need a shower.'

She grimaced. 'You do smell a bit whiffy. I'll make tea and finish the pie. You are staying tonight?'

Stephen kissed her glowing cheeks. 'If I'm still required.'

'Oh you're definitely required,' was the reply, as Stephen picked up his luggage.

At nine o'clock, snuggling up with Stephen on the sofa, Alison's butterflies had increased, more like moths whirling inside. To impart the diagnosis should have been simple, but not knowing how he'd react, scared her.

'Darling, you've hardly spoken. You're glowing, is that from shepherd's pie?' he enquired cheekily.

'Glowing? Recently I've been the opposite.'

Stephen frowned. 'You didn't say on the phone.'

Falteringly, she mentioned nausea, weakness, and irritability. He asked if it was a repeat of the sickness bug.

'That's what I thought. I went to the clinic in case it was the new contraceptive pill. They advised blood tests at the surgery, which I had.' Alison fiddled with her silver ring, clearing her throat.

Stephen felt fear, head awash with questions. 'Whatever the diagnosis, we'll face it together.'

The remark let Alison relax. 'It's nothing terrible,' she nervously replied, welling up.

'Thank God. What is it then?' he asked urgently.

'I've been wondering how to explain, not wanting to lose you. I can see I'm not making sense.'

'Lose me? Never, tell me please!'

Anxiously, she began. 'Deep breath. The symptoms I've experienced have been ghastly, I couldn't function properly and didn't say on the phone because you'd have worried. I'm not seriously ill.' With a shaky whisper, she revealed, 'I'm pregnant. I'm carrying your baby.'

The reaction was unexpected, Stephen like a wide-eyed child on Christmas Day. Endlessly hugging and kissing, confessing how happy she'd made him, he'd be there for whatever she needed. Alison said she'd explain how it had happened, which made Stephen laugh.

'I think we both know that! When you were poorly, throwing up, the pill didn't have a prayer. We'll make good parents won't we? I've no experience but you have and we'll love it to bits,' he told her, wide-eyed with joy.

Alison chuckled. 'Your face! I thought you were going to faint. That's what I'm meant to do.'

Stephen beamed. 'To think you were afraid to tell me. You don't realise how I love you, I mean it.' His expression altered, worriedly asking, 'You do want to have the baby don't you?'

Alison kissed him warmly. 'Stephen, I was nervous, but hoping you'd want our child. I love you and thrilled there'll be toys under the tree at Christmas.'

For days the lovers scarcely ceased smiling. Alison assured the doctor there was no question of not having the child, was re-examined, given the due date, ante-natal care, and as an older mother, an amniocentesis appointment.

She told Stephen it had taken time to accept he loved her. 'Alien to me, you must have thought my insecurity would never alter. It has and the baby's the icing on the cake. Since telling you, tension and some nausea's gone.'

With pregnancy confirmation definite, Stephen rang Trudie.

'Mum, I have fabulous news, not Dirk Bogarde this time.'

'Stephen, what else can there be?'

'You're going to be a grandmother!' he exclaimed in a rush.

Trudie's ears rang, fingers tingled, a tear hovered.

Incredulous, she uttered quietly, 'A baby? I… I'd no idea that was what you wanted, but… oh how lovely.'

'It wasn't planned, and Alison's had constant nausea. We're delighted though, thank goodness you are too, it matters.'

264

'Oh I am! I'm delirious with joy, but Alison's an older mother, she will take extra care?'

Stephen re-assured Trudie, putting Alison on the phone so she could hear how thrilled she was.

'I can't think of two more compatible people to give life and love to a little one.'

Alison's voice broke. 'Oh that's a super thing to say. I can't think of a better grandmother.'

The call exhilerated Trudie, heartbeat like percussion; adrenalin zipping through her. Paula would be delighted, it would give Trudie something happy to report.

***

'Fancy that, just going to phone you Troods.'

'Paula, I've been given some brilliant news, had to see if you were up.'

'Slow down. Brilliant? Haven't heard you so animated for years. Do tell.'

'Shush then and I will! Stephen rang with marvellous news.'

'Concerts a success? Royal Albert Hall next!'

'Paula, no, shush!' she implored impatiently. 'Something I want to shout from the rooftops! Alison and Stephen are expecting a baby. I'm going to be a grandmother! Whee Hee!'

She heard Paula shout. 'Whaaaaaaat?! Fanbloodytastic and… unexpected surely?'

'Yes very. Paula, my Stephen a father, me a grandmother, Alison's Leo a brother or sister! It wasn't planned, a beautiful accident. I'm ecstatic.'

'Oh so am I. Thank God for something joyful.'

'Absolutely. Why were you going to phone me?'

Paula was cagey. 'I feel like popping over, are you free?'

'Yes please. Tomorrow?'

'OK. I'll bring that old magazine with Dirk Bogarde in it.'

'Brilliant.'

'I'll be there at twelve. Going to pour myself a martini to celebrate. Night.'

'Night, love.'

37

For the first night in ages Trudie slept immediately. Paula took longer, wondering how Trudie would react when told of Laurie's visit. Upon waking, Trudie had remembered Stephen's news. She'd brightened and a measure of joy had returned. Some mislaid jigsaw pieces had been located.

Trudie often strolled near the river, this morning no exception. Exiting the garden gate, she trod carefully over the bridge straddling the whispering river. Sun streaked across dewy meadows, the sky less threatening than when she'd walked to stave off depression. Today, warmth penetrated her red fleece, the wind's sigh flicking her blonde pony tail. The deepest point of the river was without a wrinkle, danger lurking darkly beneath. She shuddered, childhood fear of water ever present.

Startled by warring magpies up in the giant ash tree, Trudie jumped. They argued, shrieking wildly, outdoing each other with their loud rattle.

'Rattle,' she smiled at the connection. She and Laurie had listened to Sir Simon's CD of Mahler's Resurrection Symphony, a mindblowing piece. 'Come on, something beautiful to look forward to,' she told herself. The baby wouldn't be the sole revelation.

Paula, en route to Little Arrow, rehearsed how she was going to impart Laurie's visit. It would be a giant shock. At quarter to twelve she arrived at the cottage by the chattering river. The long-time friends embraced, Trudie bright-eyed. 'Let's eat in the conservatory, the sun's on it today. Quiche and salad OK?'

Paula smiled, handing her the 70s magazine, *Films and Filming.* 'You-Know-Who's half way through, looking gorgeous.'

Trudie's eyes shone, thumbing pages until she came to Dirk's. 'What a photograph! He said the camera can photograph thought. Bet I haven't read the article, I'd have been immersed in child rearing then. Unlike now, endless time on my hands.'

Paula saw Trudie's expression alter, twinkling eyes gone. 'Hey ditch that look, you've reason to be happy. The baby's fabulous news.'

'Mm, c'mon, let's eat. I'll save the magazine for bedtime.'

Conversation flowed easily, unlike Paula's last visit when Trudie had been very low. She brought tea into the conservatory. 'Oh, sun's gone in, let's have this in the sitting room.'

Paula thought it fortuitous, safer to faint on soft furnishings. The opportunity arose.

'Paula, saw one of our favourite films on TV. *Room at the Top* with gorgeous Laurence Harvey. Alison thinks Stephen resembles him.'

'He does too.' Her stomach lurched. 'Er speaking of Laurence, er Laurie...'

'Laurie?' Trudie's face lost its sparkle.

'Yes, Laurie. He has a lookalike too, De Niro. No word from him...? Actually, I know you haven't.' Watching Trudie flush, she took her hand. 'I have information.'

Trudie's grip tightened. 'You've seen him again! That pub?'

'Not there. Prepare yourself and don't shoot the messenger. Laurie rang me. In fact came to see me yesterday.'

Paula's gaze swept over Trudie's shocked body. 'He rang out

of nowhere, saying he needed to find you.' She hesitated. 'Are you OK? I need to relate, warts and all.'

Wide-eyed, dry-mouthed and very shaken, Trudie slowly puffed out, 'Warts... and... all. Don't know whether to be excited or worried.'

In chronological order Paula related most of what Laurie told her of his disappearance, why, what he'd been doing and what he wanted to do next.

Trudie, trying not to interrupt; almost managed it. With feverish impatience, she surprised Paula with an angry announcement. 'Huh, if he thinks he can just slither back into my life, he can think again!'

'You don't mean that,' Paula said, sitting at Trudie's feet. 'I was pretty frosty with him on the phone. Something else, wasn't sure if I should reveal it, but explains why he was gone nearly four years.'

Paula told of Laurie's prostate cancer, a massive shock, Trudie distraught. Crying like her heart would break, she falteringly uttered, 'Terrible, but I'll have to consider this. I didn't feel so guilty during our affair; since he went I've felt it greatly. Now I know what Jean spitefully told his wife, I feel worse. Because of me his wife's dead,' she said solemnly.

'Laurie feels that. You're not to blame and now have explanations for his unfathomable actions. Wonderful becoming a grandmother, now this. I think Laurie was brave to contact me, a vulnerable action.'

Trudie bent to hug Paula. 'I'm stunned, so grateful. Good job he contacted you first, if he'd come here, I'd have hit him!'

'You're bound to feel anger, take time to digest it. If you want to contact him, I have his number.'

Trudie shook her head emphatically. 'Uh uh, no. When I've come to terms with it, I'll phone you.'

'OK. You haven't asked me how he looks, I was closer than in that pub.'

Trudie brightened up. 'Not bald with a beard is he?'

Paula laughed. 'Few more lines, but still Robert De Niro.'

That night Trudie snuggled under the duvet rejoicing in its weight. She felt like a bear cub, protected by the mother's warmth. As a child she loved Rupert Bear, each Christmas receiving his annual, her escape when the atmosphere became tense with her mother's outbursts. Rupert's mother was entirely the opposite. Mrs. Bear cheerfully let her little son have chums to tea. An idyllic family life, which Trudie had coveted. When she became widowed, Stephen could bring friends home, build dens, make a noise. Feeling mental wounds from her upbringing, she never belittled him, ensuring he felt loved. Paula had told her she was a prime example of 'you can give what you haven't received.'

Smiling, she recalled when she bought the picturesque cottage, Paula saying, 'Now Mrs. Bear, you've got the annuals and the cottage. Hope you've made raspberry buns and lemonade.' Imagining what Laurie would think of it, her heart fluttered. Needing sleep, she prayed. Reaching 'thy will be done,' she sank into the night.

By seven-thirty her head was full of yesterday. At breakfast, she'd spent ages reliving it. Fiona Monroe, a therapy client, was due at ten. Trudie's own life must be set aside. Within half an hour she was dressed, moisturized, made up, reading her client's notes in the conservatory. In the folder was a Christmas card. 'Thanks for the support. Fiona.' Looking up, Trudie saw condensation on the panes. She dried them each morning, but this was no ordinary morning, more important items on the agenda.

At eleven-thirty, when Fiona thanked Trudie for her guidance, Trudie had replied. 'With these pointers I've printed, visualise the outcome.'

Realising Holly was absent, Trudie opened the door. Steaming in with plaintive cries, Holly nuzzled Trudie then the fridge.

'Thank heavens you were only gone a couple of hours. Some people were absent much longer.'

Trudie decided to ring Paula after the radio play. They loved discussing good, poor and riveting ones. Feet up on the chaise, Holly snoozing, Trudie thought of advice she'd given Fiona.

'We get through guilt and misdemeanours by doing other things, putting a barrier in between – what you've been doing. You're capable of forgiving your husband, who hasn't inflicted harm deliberately. Step towards, forgive him.' Trudie knew the advice was what she needed herself.

Holly snoozed on, twitching, nothing on her mind. Trudie had plenty on hers. The telephone's shrill ring made Holly stretch as Trudie took the call.

'Hi it's me.'

The Cornish voice was Lizzie's, the tone unfamiliar.

'Lizzie?'

'Yes. How are you?'

Trudie sensed a false lightness. 'What's the matter?'

Lizzie quietened. 'Er… I'm hopeless at offloading, sorry.'

'Stop being sorry, I'm sitting here frowning, enough anxiety lines as it is.'

Lizzie faltered. 'Tom's in hospital with a stroke, hit his head on the bathroom basin. He kept grasping for words recently, I should have realised.'

'Oh, that's terrible. How is he now?'

'Not good. We've got private health insurance, but the NHS hospital's all right. He's…' she began to cry.

'You're bound to be upset, have you anyone to help you?'

'A friend took me to the hospital this morning. Fancy needing someone to drive me? My brain was foggy, felt silly accepting her offer.'

'Don't we all need people at times like this? You've given it to others haven't you?'

She heard a sigh. 'Regretfully, nobody ever asked me, suppose they saw a hard nut. It didn't occur to me to offer, not having been through great traumas, I didn't appreciate theirs. Even kept it to myself when the love of my life, Rick died; first time I'd experienced heartache. I've been a selfish cow, wish I could have been like you.'

'Ha! The pain I've had, you wouldn't want that. Lean on your friend, she cares.'

'Thanks, must go – got my sewing class here in half an hour. Can't cancel that.'

Trudie smiled wryly. 'What an orderly person you are, keep me informed. Bye.'

Lizzie's life had been very orderly, Tom too. Trudie wondered how they'd managed to let passion in. She'd asked in Cornwall. 'Don't you ever let go?'

She'd replied enigmatically, 'Only when I think of Rick.'

Visiting a year ago, she knew how Lizzie had loved Rick, her childhood sweetheart. No matter what differences in character between the two friends, there were parallels in their lives. Parallel lives, parallel loves.

Tom was a difficult person, like many lengthy partnerships they'd survived through having their own interests, the occasional blow up and finally acceptance. Tom had worn the trousers, but since his health issues, she'd been in control. She'd cope with the present situation, Trudie knew, no matter what.

'Hope I can cope with mine too.' Preparing for the important call.

By six-thirty, three calls had been made. Trudie to Paula. Paula to Laurie. Paula back to Trudie. The first was easy. She agreed to Paula telling Laurie he could phone the following day. When Paula rang Laurie within the hour, he answered as though waiting by the phone. To say he was delighted was an understatement. Paula then rang Trudie with his reaction.

'Have his number in case you decide to phone him.'

'No, I need to relax this evening. Let him wait, another day won't hurt him – nor me for that matter.'

Trudie's brain was in overdrive, Laurie punctuating the day. At quarter to six she dragged on a fleece, night air would clear her mind. She trudged up the slope towards the farm at the top of the lane, farmhouse lights and the street lamp illuminating the dark verge. Wishing her heart could be lightened so easily, at seven she struggled to eat an omelette. Nausea was rife since the phone call from Paula; ginger and lemon cordial soothed. Nerves adrift, easy crossword clues tricky, she tuned in to Jazz FM for the *Dinner Jazz* programme, usually calming. All through 'Take The A Train,' 'Summertime,' and Miles Davis, tension remained. Straying into corners of her unconscious, rattling half-closed doors, bathing in the pain again.

Halfway through Chris Barber playing 'Petite Fleur,' Holly leapt onto Trudie's lap, getting claws caught in the curly throw. Frowning with irritation she snapped, 'Holly, silly girl.' The old cat looked uncertain whether to remain or jump off. It was uncharacteristic to be shouted at. 'Let's feed you.'

Holly followed Trudie into the kitchen, steaming towards the door where dishes and tasty tins were.

'Here, everything comes to she who waits. Move then,' she urged, as Holly manically twisted and twirled. As the cat gobbled as if she hadn't been fed for days, Trudie poured another ginger cordial, knowing what she'd told Holly was true. She'd waited overlong, had to ensure it ended well.

By quarter to nine, she knew she simply couldn't speak to Laurie directly. Wondering what he'd say, what she'd tell him, arranging to meet, too stressful. Lateral thinking – a better plan. She rang Paula. 'He ought to come here, rather than stilted phone conversations. I'm uptight about the call, would you ask him to come here on Sunday at eleven o'clock. What do you think?'

'I bet he'd prefer it too, I'll give him your address.'

'Thanks for being the go-between. If he can't make Sunday, Monday will do.'

'Oh he'll make Sunday – you can bet on that.'

At nine-thirty the last call was made. Paula's tone was light.

'Sunday eleven o'clock. Laurie said he was dreading the phone call too. Said he'll spend the rest of his life trying to make amends, if he's allowed. Let him, he loves you completely, I heard it from his soul.'

Trudie sighed. 'You have to endure a lot to enjoy the views – after the longing and despair, I'm not losing sight of them. Without him there wasn't much on the horizon, but now…' her voice trembled, 'Who knows what we might see together.' She giggled, 'I sound like a self-help book. You see what I'm saying though?'

'I'm getting sniffy. What a few days!'

'Few years! Hey, he might not fancy me, or he might have had a romance in North Carolina.'

Paula re-assured her that wasn't so. 'Won't be long until Mr. De Niro's back, then you can put winceyette jamas away and dig out beautiful nighties.'

Trudie giggled. 'Hadn't thought about that. Paula, I'm here largely thanks to you. Gosh, I was forgetting. The baby! Herbal sleepers for me, or I'll be awake all night!'

38

Laurie hadn't bought smart clothes for years, only sweaters and jeans in North Carolina He had an anorak, but couldn't wear that, Trudie must see him in a suit or smart casual, not struggling with a cumbersome anorak messing up his hair, leaving him flustered.

By afternoon, he'd shopped in Ludlow. A black cashmere jacket, black trousers with an Italian coral and black cotton mix sweater had been purchased from one shop, the sort of gear he used to wear. Realising trainers wouldn't do, he bought black German loafers. The sweater lightened the outfit, and having a v-neck, could be worn with a crisp white shirt underneath.

His reflection in the wardrobe mirror showed a confident man. A misnomer. Excited but anxious at the enormity of Sunday's meeting, hoping Trudie would accept how things had been, if she'd be forgiving. Would she still want him? Doubtful, but he hoped for an opportunity to prove his love.

By Saturday evening, having fed himself and Sooty, he listened to Mahler's 2nd Symphony, 'The Resurrection,' feeling it a positive sign. He and Trudie loved it. His spirit soared during the massive finale, confident the bond between Trudie and himself could be repaired.

Trudie snuggled into the duvet's cosiness, glad to have made the decision. Before dawn on Sunday morning she'd been standing at her bedroom window. There'd been a storm overnight, flooding the field, pouring torrents down the Arrow's red banks, muddying the river beneath the bridge. Volleys of thunder had woken her at three o'clock. Peering at the river's inky depths, she'd witnessed lightning forks and thunderous percussion.

Sheets of rain angrily slammed against panes. Until Laurie had gone, Trudie hadn't minded. Security, warmth and sharing it had disappeared, with him to blame. Irritated, she'd thought, 'I shouldn't be angry, he's returning – if I want him.'

She'd slept again, stumbling from her bed at six, watching a shiver of light trickle across the field, illuminating the damage. Torrents had cascaded down the Arrow's bursting banks, crashing over boulders to dash downstream. Opening the window to inhale fresh air, she could see daffodil stems flattened, the shed roof glossy with rain. The field beyond the river bank had flooded, fallen ash branches strewn across the river, none on the garden or house. Wisteria fronds had been ripped, but fleece from half-hardy Salvia clung on. Nothing wrecked blackthorn hedges on the bank, she'd picked their fruits for her father to make sloe gin.

Letting past hurts haemorrhage into the river, she went downstairs. She liked taking coffee through the silent house, sensing peace, wanting to discover Laurie there. Squeezing into the sapphire jersey dress she'd chosen, unaware it wouldn't fit, she grimaced. 'Blast, I'll have to wear another.' She struggled out of it, knowing when you're wanting what you don't have, a day can seem like an eternity. She'd sought solace in food, a poor replacement for love. Night cream had been applied, hoping she could turn back four years of face and life.

'Damn, I should have exercised. This isn't how I want Laurie to see me,' she frowned, frustrated. 'He used to say I reminded him of Grace Kelly. My face might be similar, but she was never this size.'

Putting on a looser dress in deep pink, she told the mirror, 'That's better.' Blonde hair was swept up with two silver and pearl combs, and a little make up. Wearing sheepskin slippers, she giggled, kicking them off, stepping into navy suede wedgies, glancing outside. Lavender clouds parted slightly, revealing drenched meadows a brighter shade of green. A hopeful sign.

Little Arrow Lane was three hundred yards long. From the main road out of the village, street lights grew scarcer, only the lamp near the farm defining the turn into the lane. The farm took up a lot of land at the top near the river's bend, further down Georgina's detached house, and Trudie's detached cottage tucked at the end, hugging the river bank. The shallowest part of the river was directly behind both homes. A bowing weeping willow embraced the old stone bridge.

The lane was a dead end, a thicket of sycamore, a garage and spacious area for two cars, in a quiet, private location. Beyond Trudie's garden, patchwork fields belonged to the farmer, with a few acres of crops, a flock of sheep and no pigs or cows. She'd investigated fully before buying the property, wanting peace and a sweet smelling environment. Having the conservatory connected her through to the garden, the bridge to the opposite river bank, old hedges, trees and clear views of the seasons.

Plaintive cries from Holly fragmented Trudie's thought pattern. Letting her in, Trudie wiped her fur. 'You're soaking wet.' Anxious not to miss Laurie, she put Holly into the laundry room. Alarmed, she noticed a white Volkswagen Golf had drawn up. No driver.

Realising Laurie was at the door, she nervously entered the hallway. Her heart thudded, catching sight of his dark head through pebbled glass. She never invited strangers in; this one was the exception.

Trembling, she opened the door. Gazing at Laurie for the

first time in four years, she wanted to fall on him. She must not. Woodenly, she beckoned him in. Acutely aware of his unease as he stood against the door, shakily she managed to utter 'Hello Laurie.'

Her words hung in the air until Laurie, legs trembling, eyes misty, managed a weak smile. 'My Trudie, may I kiss your cheek?'

Trudie half-smiled, nodding.

Laurie unbuttoned his jacket, beckoning her towards him. Trudie saw he'd aged, but she probably had too. He kissed her lightly, nervously holding her hands, gazing into deep green eyes. 'You're wearing Je Reviens. Even when I lost my memory, the perfume stayed with me.'

'Yes darling.'

'You called me darling, that gives me some kind of hope.'

'Well, Paula told me a lot, but you need to hear how it's been for me. What are you looking at?'

'Lamorna Birch, that painting. It was at your old house, that Stanhope Forbes print too. A Cornishman has to recognise his county's artists.'

'I never forgot you're a Cornishman. You were there a couple of years ago, Hessenford,' she told him knowingly.

'Paula told you why I didn't make it up to Worcestershire, my son's accident?'

Trudie stroked the soft jacket. 'Yes, but I already knew you'd been there. Let me fetch Holly from the laundry room, we had a storm overnight; got drenched this morning, she's in there drying off. Tea or coffee?' She took him into the conservatory. He told her he loved the garden, especially the River Arrow below.

In the kitchen, Trudie's hands shook as she filled the kettle. Laurie, who had not been seen or heard for four years, was only a few yards away in the conservatory, surreal. As she spooned coffee into the cafetiere, she shuddered with both excitement and apprehension. Five minutes later, she put down the tray.

'May I sit facing you?' Laurie asked, as she poured coffee. 'I want to look at you… breathtakingly beautiful. Sorry, had to say it.'

'Don't apologise. It's wonderful to hear, honestly. We have to discuss the years in between. Paula told me of Irene, the stalker, your breakdown, amnesia, cancer. I need to tell you how it's been for me. Seeing you is surreal, I can't promise not to get cross.'

He nervously reached to hold her hands tenderly. 'I want to hear it all.'

Trudie sat on the chaise, bamboo table separating them. Shakily, she began. 'When someone dies, a space remains. Part of my stress was grieving for someone living. You crossed my path for a fraction of life, but left an indelible mark. I lost a friend, lover, shared past, shared future.' She sighed. 'Also lost part of me, who I was when we were together. Facing aloneness, I lost confidence, asking myself, "What's wrong with me that he should leave me. Thank you and goodbye."' She shrugged. 'Not even that.'

Laurie looked crushed. 'You see…'

Trudie interrupted. 'Let me talk until I run out of breath. I need you to hear what I did, what I didn't do. Remove your hands, I can't concentrate if you touch me.'

Laurie, taken aback, complied.

'For four years I occasionally knew I was wasting my life with a married man, but happy with our stolen times; loved and cherished. I was able to return that love, despite restraints. I should have expected the unexpected. When you disappeared, I wished I'd been brave enough to find the exit at the beginning. If the first four were tricky, the following four were more challenging. Fierce intimacy had been replaced by savage despair.'

Laurie flushed, shamefaced.

'Ours was an unreal situation, wonderful highs but inevitable lows. From being honest, I had out of necessity, become dishonest. Only Paula knew of us. Not able to speak of you openly was a regret, but one I had to accept.

'When I thought it was behind me, it was in front; my situation when you'd gone. Ghosts everywhere. Kept thinking I saw you in a crowd. Like The Stylistics song 'You Are Everything and Everything Is You', where the lover mistakenly imagines they see their ex. I ran up to a man once, certain it was you. Embarrassing, like being caught with a milk bottle on the breakfast table.

'When we were together regularly, spending hours doing nothing in particular was bliss. When you live alone you have no one to do nothing with. Passing houses, I wondered if the inhabitants were happy. Once, I slowed my pace to watch a man enter the room with a pot of tea, a woman smiling up at him. Envy filled me, desiring that scene for myself. In a heartbeat I'd have exchanged my life for theirs.'

Laurie's expression grew grave.

'Laurie, I was in a café hearing a woman advising her companion, "Never put off seeing someone who is ill, one goodbye may be the last." I sighed, aware I didn't have that opportunity, viewed as an unnecessary hindrance.'

Overwhelmed with guilt, face contorted, he lowered his head.

She continued. 'Mother was difficult to please. I became an addict to approval and acceptance. I'd love to have discussed her behaviour with my father, but we muddled through dark days. There were some idyllic episodes, but mother spoiled so many, barbed jibes that stung me like a wasp's dart. My self-belief was extinguished by her sparse affection. Longing for approval, I could have taken the wrong path. I didn't, but denied those painful memories. Denial doesn't work. Some days were better, both then, and when you, like my mother, discarded me. When you're older you have more of a past than a future, making what you've got in front more intense. I concentrated on that to avoid complete depression.'

Laurie's screwed up face said it all. 'Terrible, I know depression,' he responded lamely. 'With my breakdown, it was like a trapdoor had opened beneath me. At my son's in USA, I didn't have the attention span to read the newspaper.'

Trudie shrugged, trying not to sound bitter. 'You, the one who went, had family. I was the one left behind. Paula hauled me out of despondency when I was utterly dejected. I knew you couldn't possibly understand what pain I was going through or you'd have contacted me. I realised the clock was ticking and I should make the break or be stuck forever with toxic indecision. I didn't want to seek the right man, I'd found him. Oh why did I have to wait so long to find you weren't an uncomplicated widower?' she growled.

'I advised my clients, "Visualise your dream, use affirmations, things will gradually change." Ha, some therapist I was! I knew the answers, couldn't get them right myself. They moved on, I didn't. I dreamt of a light shining through a curtain. When I awoke I knew if I was bold enough to continue searching, I could draw the curtain aside to see someone with the key to your disappearance, or you.'

Laurie went to interrupt.

'I'll hear your explanation later. The tumour of doubt became increasingly toxic. Since Paula had seen you, and my visit to Hessenford, I knew the last piece of the jigsaw could be slotted in. I could make the picture complete, like the poem I composed. You may recall I read it to you –

I am the unfinished woman
Trying to make the pieces fit
With some finesse – without success

The lover I thought would complete the picture
Only makes the shapes even more irregular
Destroying the built up pattern
So carefully blocked out for survival

I keep losing the image of the puzzle
So life's difficult to follow
Perhaps it was crumpled too long ago
To make any headway…
So I'll settle for joining the edges
Secure amongst the familiar jumble on the inside.'

Laurie's serious look turned into a loving smile. He told her she read it beautifully; it was how he'd felt too.

'Something else. I did love my late husband, but death claimed him when Stephen was three. A friend said then, happiness comes when you're doing other stuff, like earning a living. I had to earn mine, but real happiness didn't happen until I met you. One of my schoolfriends didn't marry because her family was so loving, she never wanted to leave. I didn't have that and married too soon because of it. When he died I felt guilty and missed him terribly. It kept me celibate, disappearing when I met you. Another kind of guilt set in when you'd gone. Deep down I knew we didn't deserve to be together after our deceit. We'd caused our own karma. Thought I was being punished, God the Father had abandoned his child. Ultimately, I saw I'd abandoned him by choosing infidelity, causing my own heartache.'

She saw Laurie's shame, but continued. 'Monogamous love is trusting completely. I did, but should have felt guilt about Irene. We practised selective morality, selfish feelings overtook us. You reminded me of my father, kind, wise, loving, with a strength he didn't have. You won't like my saying this, but when you'd gone, I realised you weren't so strong, or you'd have parted from Irene. The thrill of secret trysts came to an end and there'd been no permanency in illicit love, only pain. Infidelity, that awful virus, I'd caught it and was continuing to suffer.'

Sighing, she told him, 'Relationships leave wounds from vulnerability of love. Some let things slide, resulting in misery, becoming victims like us, dreams becoming nightmares. I'm not sure how we managed four years, nor how I survived the rest alone. In the midst of chaos, routine kept me sane. Moving here I was seduced by sunlight streaming in through conservatory windows, flooding me with happiness, yet tinged with regret having to experience it alone.

'One day when hoeing the garden I saw a shadow on the lawn. My heart throbbed, thinking it was you. Looking round, I saw it was a delivery man with a parcel. The hole was deep, but occasionally I had hope.'

Trudie took a sip of water. 'Life slowed – an understatement. Undignified, wanting you, but blown away like a dandelion clock. Real love is when you want the other person to be happy, even if it excludes yourself. I tried to think like that but…' her voice became raised, 'damn it, Laurie, I wanted happiness too. With you. WITH YOU!'

He joined her on the chaise, rocking her as she wept against him.

'Laurie don't you realise how I've wanted your hands on my skin, your body against mine? I have a recurring dream where I'm drowning. You jump into the Arrow to rescue me, but when we get to the bank, you disappear.'

He choked back heightened emotions.

'In cafés when waitresses told me to "enjoy" their words were wasted. So many good days with you, but not enough years. I wanted to write a book, *The Dark Side of Paradise*. How alive do we feel when we're living a lie? Death seems the ultimate rejection, despite my faith in God. Not needed here, no choice, gave me nightmares.'

Shakily, Laurie moved to hold her. 'I don't deserve forgiveness, causing intense hurt to the person who loved me most.'

Trudie broke away. 'I had to tell you how it's been for me, the anguish, loneliness, abandonment. It felt like a life sentence imposed on me, payment for what I loved, having to give it up, no choice, made for me. My stomach used to knot when I thought of my new home, new coat, beautiful garden with an idyllic view. I could show none of them to you.'

She gazed at Laurie's strained face. 'If ever this moment came, I thought I'd fall into your arms, difficult not to earlier in my hall. You see, I took strength from memories, letting me survive. I couldn't help embracing our love, accepting it can bring loss, but what we'd had couldn't be demeaned.'

Trudie managed to smile a little. Laurie's eyes didn't. 'My darling, I was aware of my shortcomings, but carried on nonetheless. A profound difference between alone and lonely, I was both until I loved you, so special I couldn't turn away.' He paused, face serious. 'Until my illness. Before that it was heaven and hell to be in love, ecstasy and misery. Such joy, but parting, agony. I came today to ask forgiveness and expand upon what I'd told Paula. I prayed you still cared, although I had no right. If I hadn't been so ill, we'd never have been parted. I… would…' his velvety voice broke up, breathing in staccato bursts. Clearing his throat, he buried his head in strong brown hands. Trudie put her arm around his shoulders.

'Yes, I know what we were going to do, also I never stopped loving you. It's taken courage to re-build your life from massive illness, return to England, buy a house, try to find me. Incidentally, this isn't Trudie the counsellor speaking. It's Trudie who loves you, who's prayed for this every day, even amongst despair.' Her voice fell to a whisper, 'I've said what was necessary, wonder if we can build on what we had and may still have? A leading question and I don't expect an answer straight…'

'Darling…' emotions escaping.

Trudie clung to his once familiar body. 'Gosh your sweater's damp.'

'I don't care. You took my breath away when we first met, I'm still trying to get it back.' With half-closed eyes, he softly told her, 'I love you.'

Trudie told him through tears. 'You've got more Trudie now, voluptuous.'

'Voluptuous? I like that, rather than cuddly,' he laughed lightly.

Trudie gave him a dig. 'Cuddly indeed, stick with voluptuous.'

'Darling, there's not been anyone else, I want you to know that. If you reject me today I'll return to Ashton heartbroken and there'd be just Sooty and me.'

Trudie quietly told him, 'You can go home to Sooty, whom I assume is your pet, but you can invite me to meet him.'

Laurie's face morphed from one of regret and angst to relief and joy. Embracing Trudie, planting warm kisses on her face, hair, mouth, he passionately told her he loved her. Breathlessly, she told him she knew.

39

Upon Julia's return from France, she'd been relieved Alison wasn't ill and delighted about the baby. Without David, Julia was relaxed, years younger. She'd re-arranged the house; cleaner, tidier, welcoming, impossible with him there. Her smile at Alison's happiness lit up the kitchen. Questions came out in a rush. 'What did Stephen think, how did you tell him, are you OK?'

After an hour of chat, Alison drove to Phoebe's. Important people had been informed, Stephen's mother first, Leo, now Julia. Alison's family in Australia were surprised, but accepting. Phoebe's reaction would be a sight to see.

By mid-morning, nausea had escalated. Pulling into a layby, Alison spent ten minutes with the window down, listening to Radio 2, drinking barley water. 'Stay With Me Till Dawn' by Judy Tzuke was being played. Alison loved the track. In the early months she'd hoped Stephen would stay longer than that. He had. The previous evening she'd voiced her insecurity, asking him if he felt trapped. Stephen had re-assured her he was going nowhere. Forever was the word he'd used.

Motoring down the avenue of pleached limes, lit up with underplanted daffodils, Alison felt satisfaction visiting a beautifully transformed home. Phoebe had changed too, brighter of spirit having come to terms with Gordon's dalliance. She'd told Alison it was time she put herself first, make plans and fulfil them. She'd been on a wonderful Northern Lights cruise, bought new clothes, lost weight through the church walking group, and taken a temporary lodger, Daniel, her son's friend, for company, making her bother to cook properly. He'd relucantly departed after five weeks, when his Chester project had finished.

Her voice was different, booming speech gone. Welcoming Alison in, she remarked how well she looked. Rattling crockery, she told her, 'Positively blooming because Stephen's home from musical travels.'

'That's right.'

'Speaking of travels, Daniel said I'd like St. Petersburg, there's an event in June and July. Tell you in a mo, let's take our refreshments into my super sitting room. Would you carry the tray? My wrists are arthritic today.'

In the restored room, while Alison poured, Phoebe asked if she wanted to hear her plans.

'Mm, then I'll give you my news.'

Phoebe queried. 'Good, I hope?' settling into her new chair.

'Daniel – decent boy – man really. In St. Petersburg between June and July they have White Nights. Because it's the most northern city in the world, the sun stays above the horizon so broad daylight nearly all day. They have an arts festival, ballet, drama, music, even a carnival. White Nights stars at the Marinsky Theatre, which is splendid apparently.' Phoebe excitedly related. 'I long to go, will go.'

'That's fabulous. Makes me want to go too.'

'Daniel sent me details, come too if you're free.' Phoebe exclaimed enthusiastically. She saw Alison's expression. 'Oh why would you want to go on hols with me? You've got Stephen and...'

'Phoebe, it's not that. I won't be able to, that's what I came to say.'

Phoebe was concerned. 'Not had bad news have you? I've been telling you my plans and forgetting to ask about you.'

Alison sat beside her. 'I felt terrible for weeks. Now worry's been replaced by joy.' Eyes dancing, Alison announced. 'I wasn't ill, but pregnant.'

Phoebe was bewildered. 'Wait a moment. Pregnant, is that what you said dear? Surely you're too old for that. Not the sexual bit, the getting pregnant,' she blushingly admitted. 'Are you really having one yourself?'

Alison burst out laughing. 'Yes I'm only forty-two, it does happen. A surprise, but we're thrilled.'

Phoebe's eyes lit up. 'Sorry, I thought I'd misheard you.' She gave a gentle hug. 'I say, d'you fancy a sherry to celebrate? Ah, bit early.'

'It is, and I'm driving, but I have constant nausea. I felt wretched following gastric flu, thought it was that again. When I had tests at my doctor's, the pregnancy was discovered.'

Reaching into her cardigan pocket for her handkerchief, Phoebe blotted an approaching tear. 'What a visit this is! It's made my day honestly. I'll knit... matinee coats or cardigans? No idea what babies wear these days.'

Alison laughed. 'Whatever you like, I'm out of touch too.'

'So exciting, can't wait to begin!' Phoebe exclaimed.

'Our child won't have close grandparents on my side, only mother in Australia. Stephen's mother's delighted, but not local. Phoebe, would you consider being a surrogate grandmother?'

A sharp intake of breath and a dazzling smile ensued from Phoebe. Tingling, she slowly replied. 'Oh... I... would, what an honour. It's going to be a marvellous year.'

Driving home, Alison reflected on Phoebe's words, a marvellous year. Trudie had been thrilled at their baby news too. Alison was unaware Trudie had her own shock to deal with. For her it could also be a marvellous year – if she was brave enough to allow it.

Julia's life had altered too since David had gone in December. She didn't miss one thing about him. He'd contributed little, but caused enormous heartache. Gradual erosion of her self-confidence had built to huge proportions. Through his rejection, she'd found a better path, no longer having to comply with his controlling ways. Alison had told her. 'He lives for himself, you're important. A wonder when you met Jonathan that he found any of the real Julia.'

'Jonathan,' she mused, in the bath one June evening, 'coming when I was at my lowest, I'd have cracked up without him.' She smiled. 'Even Poppy approves, and settled in France.' She stretched out in the buoyant bath, thinking of her last trip. They'd gone on Le Grand Nice Tour, a hop-on, hop-off bus. Poppy, not a lover of classical music, had been riveted by Tchaikovsky's Violin Concerto soundtrack, played when commentary ceased, enthusiastic about Chagall and Matisse museums. Julia had felt happier about her daughter's move.

'Just over a year since meeting Stephen, Alison's carrying his baby. How our lives have transformed because we've met decent partners. Although, if I hadn't met Jonathan, I'd still have had to eliminate David.'

David's possessions were placed outside the garage in January, Julia not trusting him to take only his. Jonathan had offered to be there, but Julia didn't want to invoke a scene. Not wanting David to see her nervousness, she'd remained on the doorstep, despite the bitingly cold afternoon. He'd glared sullenly, giving a feral snarl, showing teeth like a row of condemned houses, slamming boxes into the car boot. Issuing his parting shot, 'Good riddance bitch,' he manically gave two fingers, roaring off, tyres spinning, splattering frosty shingle onto the lawns.

Topping up the bathwater, she sighed, relieved she had no

need to see him again. In February this year Jonathan had asked her to live with him. She wasn't ready for it, unnecessary when they lived not far from each other. Aware their relationship may fail by jumping in too quickly, she'd revealed her fears. He'd understood her desire to stay in her home, keeping it for Poppy. If he'd not suggested the move, Julia may have believed he wasn't serious. She'd admitted she'd thought the same thing.

Now in mid-June, life was bliss without antagonistic liar David. She'd visited Poppy twice since, happy she'd settled with Guy near Cannes. They'd called on Leo in Antibes. Julia's relationship with Jonathan was secure, no need to plan clandestine trips, invent smokescreens.

In her bedroom, she dropped the bathtowel, analysing herself. As stress had decreased, so had her desire to snack, resulting in a stone lost. At five foot three she'd felt dumpy, making her depressed. Clothes hadn't fitted, self-esteem low, extra pounds hidden by loose tops. Concealer had been used to disguise shadows beneath her eyes. Jonathan had met her at the height of her problems, but had loved her as she was. Try as she might then, her resolve to shed much weight was overshadowed by the burden of David's treachery.

Now in sunny June, she'd worn summer clothes, abandoned on hangers two years ago. They had a new lease of life and so did she.

40

When Laurie had driven from Trudie's, they hadn't arranged another firm date, much to his disappointment. He'd looked at her searchingly, to no avail.

That evening while washing up, the overwhelming reunion became unbearable, hitting Trudie like a brick wall. Hot tears sprang up as the hugely emotional day was recalled. Heavily sobbing, vision blurred, she quickly wiped her hands on a teatowel. With a tremendous howl, she sank heavily onto the sitting room sofa. Being with Laurie had taken its toll – what she wanted, but a huge strain. She thanked God for the miracle, praying 'Thy will, not mine.' She knew and so did God, that HER will was what she wanted. She often asked for forgiveness for uttering that prayer half-heartedly.

Trudie knew Paula needed to know the outcome, but she couldn't phone. A kind of peace had set in, an inertness, unable to emerge from her surreal mood, gazing out at changing weather, emotions shut down.

Groping her way out of sleep on Monday, Trudie saw thick mist hanging above the river after punishing rain, a shadow of the previous day. By mid-afternoon lasers of sunlight between trees made them shimmer and birds sing again. Trudie could hear the flooded river gurgling past boulders, ash keys shivering in the gentle breeze. Holly sprang up, miaowing to be let out. Trudie opened the sliding door, watching a flash of tortoiseshell dash to her haunts, sniffing aromatic shrubs and prancing over puddles. Immediately making punctuation marks on the lawn, she seemed satisfied her territory was safe. Wildly sharpening claws on willow bark, then chasing her tail, she sedately walked to the door.

Trudie thought of the many days since Laurie's absence. Optimism lasting a few hours, then realising the day wasn't yielding anything positive. Spring planting was therapeutic, a positive step, jewelled bulbs and perennials shooting from barren earth, echoing the hope Laurie wasn't entirely gone. Shrivelled winter trees were reborn in spring, an optimism Trudie coveted. She'd sown, pruned, watered, nurtured, raising seratonin levels. Early mornings were sometimes spent in pyjamas, weeding. When autumn came, hope would fade and abandonment re-appear, her mood echoing the sky's cobalt denseness.

Observing Holly's antics in the garden, she felt anaesthetized. Making tea, feeding Holly, watching TV, nothing registered, a drugged tranquillity. On Tuesday it was still present. Most of the afternoon she sat cradling ginger tea, appreciating the river's beauty, spring bulbs, wrinkled leaved cowslips, twittering birds, distant bleatings of newborn lambs up at the farm.

Though not wanting to move, later she had to phone Paula, who'd made it possible for Laurie's visit. Hearing someone on the radio speaking of their acting career, stating 'A dream deferred is a dream lost' ended her lethargy. Paula was relieved to hear, Trudie relieved to tell. Relating the reunion, the phone call proved the catalyst to end the impasse.

'Thanks for your support with and without Laurie. When he disappeared, I almost rang The Samaritans, but didn't have the will to talk to a stranger. Being able to lean on you in the terrible down times – bless you.'

'Trudie, bless you for standing by me when James died. You're a jewel, I admire your ability to deal with reality, raising Stephen brilliantly.'

Trudie flinched, aware she hadn't dealt with reality well regarding Laurie.

'You're vivacious, intelligent, intent on doing good, no wonder men love you. That photograph Laurie took of you in the red dress is beautiful. I feel privileged to share your life, now it's given you this chance, take it and phone Laurie. Heal each other's scars, don't waste another minute.'

***

Nervously, Laurie had prayed for a positive phone call, hugely relieved when Trudie rang him.

The following Saturday, Trudie had awoken as morning broke from an indigo sky. Driving to Ashton she was nervous. Laurie had confessed he wasn't the best of cooks; Trudie didn't care, this wasn't about food. Nourishment, yes. Acceptance must be manifested, a lot had been explained and forgiveness promised. It mattered immensely that certainty had replaced the unknown.

She drove slowly along narrow winding lanes, lest a fast vehicle appeared. She pulled into a layby, checked directions, then realising the cottage was ahead, smiled to check for lipsticked teeth, asking God to give her courage to renew her relationship.

The Victorian building had old brick, white shutters and a small front garden. Laurie waved from upstairs. A song came to her. 'Not Waving But Drowning' by Clifford T. Ward. Hoping it wasn't an omen, she walked down the path. Laurie at the white front door greeted her with a tentative kiss. 'Let me take this scarlet coat, you look gorgeous in it.' Arm around her waist, he led Trudie into the sitting room.

'What a relaxing room, I like the curtains, did they come with the cottage?' Trudie asked trembling.

'An auction… oh gosh, I'm more nervous than I thought I'd be.'

Trudie smiled weakly. 'Um, me too.' She walked towards him, 'A hug first.' Ice broken, they clung, warmth of once familiar bodies at one. 'I have a present for Sooty.' From her handbag she produced a catnip-stuffed fabric mouse with a silly facial expression.

Laurie gave a rich, infectious laugh. 'Oh he'll love it.' He took her hand, leading her into the kitchen.

'Gorgeous, what a huge window.'

Laurie pulled out a chair for Trudie to sit at the table, asking if he should close the blind against the sun's dazzle.

'No, a treat after recent bleak days. It's bliss here, warm and peaceful.'

'It is now,' he smiled. 'In the few months here I've made alterations. This kitchen was too small; local chap extended it. The back garden's sizeable, so haven't lost much land. Sooty sleeps in the shed, came this winter and stayed. He won't come in, panics and I end up with torn clothes and arms.' Laurie saw Trudie's reaction.

'Don't worry. He hasn't a mean bone in his body for me, he reserves that for mice.'

Laurie opened the cupboard. 'Mugs, china though, not thick crock ones we hate. I'll buy cups and saucers for the future.' He flushed, 'If you want there to be one of course.'

'Laurie, let's be positive. We've been grieving, proof we've loved well.'

He spoke softly, 'Yes, thank you for your forgiveness.' He poured from the coffee machine. 'This is new, like most things.' He opened the fridge for milk. Trudie watched him closely, noticing his profile, expressive mouth, curve of calves in narrow jeans. A déjà vu emotion seeped into her, recognising it as the moment she fell in love eight years before.

Laurie seriously asked, 'Darling, what is it?'

Trudie uttered slowly. 'I love you. I DO. Getting milk from the fridge, a simple act, I saw you as I did when we met, that first magical rush. In the lost years I haven't felt that; I want it to stay.'

Ecstatic, Laurie held her, kissing her brow. 'It's rare, I felt it at your home last week but daren't say so. My beautiful Trudie, I'll do my best to atone for everything.'

He spoke of the cottage, people and locations he knew. Trudie had questions, but they'd unfold gradually, she didn't want to put Laurie or herself under pressure, their relationship had to be rekindled slowly. Laurie had asked her to trust him, to prove commitment; she would.

'Why did it take so long to unpack?' she enquired, holding his hand.

'Let's say I did a lot of ignoring boxes, anaesthetized.'

Trudie told him, 'I understand that feeling.'

'Falling over the damn boxes again, I opened one, gradually did the rest, placing them on pine shelves. Then I dusted Eddie Cochran records, Cliff and The Shadows, Elvis, Everly Brothers, The Platters, Tommy Steele and assorted romantic EP's of Nat King Cole and Frank Sinatra. Some of your fifties records too. You won't guess what I found in my EP's.'

Trudie twinkled. 'That's where you'd be wrong. My 'Twist and Shout' EP, you do mean that?'

Laughing, Laurie replied, 'Ten out of ten. I remembered where you bought it. Brixham 1963? Listening in the record shop, bopping to applause from customers.' He chuckled, seeing Trudie's mild embarrassment. 'Holding the record's shiny cover was surreal. Wondering when I'd return it, if ever.'

'Have you worn it out then?'

Laurie shook his head emphatically. 'God no. Daren't, I'd have bawled.' He brightened. 'What I found and did play was 'Once upon a Summertime' by Miles Davis, the scratched single I had. We listened, making love. Beautiful.'

Trudie attempted to stifle a giggle. 'Sublime, must have been a quickie though.' she grinned.

He chuckled. 'Mm, I don't recall complaining.'

Trudie blushed. 'Bet you've filed your collection in alphabetical order.'

He laughed. 'Relieved to sort them, so some order here. Your records and CDs are in a box for you.' He got up, taking Trudie's hand.

She stood up, drawing him towards her. 'My music – I will take it home, but only if we can listen together.'

Laurie hugged her tightly, his face speaking volumes. He led her towards the door. 'Come and meet my big black boy. I don't get many visitors so he may be shy.'

Scooping sardines into Sooty's dish, Laurie gestured, 'There he is.'

Trudie looked down on the glossy black cat snoozing by the shed. 'Gosh he's beautiful, a cuddly bear.'

Laurie chuckled. 'Eats like one too, making up for when he had to fend for himself. Let me go first, watch from here for now.'

As soon as Laurie opened the door, Sooty sprang into action – alert for what was on offer. His barn dance, weaving in and out of Laurie's legs, almost preventing food from being given, amused Trudie. Laurie put it on the lawn near the shed, signalling to Trudie after Sooty had wolfed it. Sooty halted the washing ceremony abruptly, yellow orbs staring suspiciously. Trudie crept towards him, placing the mouse down.

'Let's walk off and let him play.' suggested Laurie.

Trudie was shown fruit trees, shrubs, and told of the wilderness he'd inherited. She admired fiery ribbons of scarlet tulips, brightening the borders. Spring sunshine filtered through pear trees as they sat on the garden bench. A pink clematis montana was scrambling through a dead tree. Laurie asked her how to prune it.

She rested her head against Laurie's shoulder, feeling his breath on her face. 'Leave it to smother the dead branches, it will tangle itself beautifully over the whole tree by next year. Er... about the cancer, you said you're in remission, how is it affecting you?'

'Hardly at all. I go for regular checkups at the hospital... er... do you mean sexually?'

Trudie flushed. 'Gosh no, I meant can you go for walks, garden, do housework ... not sex, I certainly didn't mean that.'

Laurie appeared nervous. 'I'm rather worried full lovemaking may be difficult. Probably jumping the gun, but it does bother me.'

Shaking her head, Trudie told him it didn't matter, together they could get through anything. Lightening the conversation, she admitted 'Wish I was the same, have to wear reading specs now.'

'Oh I've had those ages, and for driving. There is an upside, without specs, when I look in the mirror I seem OK, when I actually look like hell.'

Trudie laughed, 'You seem fine to me, not scary at all.'

Looking over his shoulder, she exclaimed, 'Sooty!'

They giggled at his antics with the catnip mouse. He sat upright, concentrating intently, wiggling his strong body, pouncing on the toy, tearing round to dive on it again. Trudie shrieked when, wild-eyed, he tore up the cherry tree, inched down to further plague the mouse, then rolled on it, miaowing plaintively.

'Holly does that, even at her age,' spluttered Trudie. 'Who needs television with cats?'

'Quite.' Laurie said. 'Except he won't come inside. Let's eat.'

'Go ahead. I want to see if he'll let me stroke him.'

Walking casually up to the mouse, she waggled it in front of Sooty. Sharp eyes tracked it back and forth. Trudie threw it, amazed when he caught it, equally surprised when he sat, paws neatly placed, wanting more play. When it landed in a daffodil clump, Sooty dived into the middle, flattening trumpets. Laurie, at the window, was smiling.

Each time Sooty caught the mouse, he dropped it near Trudie. She stroked his head, scratching his chin, feeling him purring softly. Seeing Laurie signalling, she tossed the mouse and walked across the lawn. Turning, she saw Sooty peeping from a clump of ferns. He discarded the mouse and followed.

'My turn to eat, see you later.' Sooty's furry head gave her legs a nuzzling before she went indoors.

Trudie filled in gaps, her visit to Hessenford Church, emotions it had engendered.

Laurie told her. 'I was truthful when I said I'd been there.'

Trudie held his hand. 'There's no question I believed you, even if I hadn't seen the visitors book. A magical moment exactly where you'd been, even traced your neat writing with my finger. An enigma, why you'd been there, if you lived nearby, why no contact. Then Paula saw you in the pub, both had evidence within the same week.'

'Darling,' he said, voice low, 'I did phone, unaware you had a new ex-directory number and another house. When that failed, I was ready to drive to Worcestershire. Unfortunately, I had the sudden news of my son's accident.'

'I know. Excellent lunch, I adore fresh pasta, you always were a good cook.'

'I wanted to spend time with you, not cooking. You know darling, once I saw a man in the supermarket telling his wife on the phone he was in the office, working late. With two bottles of wine in his basket, I knew a mistress was waiting somewhere. Branding him a creep, I then realised I'd done similar, inventing reasons not to go home.'

'Well, I felt a paralysis about my situation, renewed hope mixed with apprehension. My own fault – values had become distorted when I met you. I survived through Paula's friendship. Because our love was so extraordinary, isolation of the ordinary was devastating. Sharing my anguish with Paula, when absence became unbearable, was life saving. Look, we said we'd put everything behind us, so let's not punish ourselves further.'

'Yes, go through, I need to top up Sooty's water.'

Trudie browsed the bookshelves, noticing how tidily they were arranged against the midnight blue wall. A Peggy Lee album attracted her. 'Mr. Wonderful' featured, she used to sing it in the fifties. Also 'Is That All There Is?' a cynic's view of life. So many selected it for funerals; a bitter-sweet song. She softly sang a few lines.

'Beautifully sung.' Laurie announced, appearing with the tea tray. 'Oh, damn, Sooty's water, back in two tics.'

Laurie replenished the bowl and opened the door. A woolly flash darted into the kitchen, mouse in mouth. Laurie was staggered, Sooty had never ventured inside.

'Hi boy. What are you doing in here? Drink? Here it is then.'

That was not what Sooty wanted. He headbutted Laurie's legs, determinedly padding to the sitting room. Trudie nearly spilled the milk. 'Oh Sooty! Thought you didn't come in.'

Astonished, Laurie appeared behind the cat. 'He doesn't. Ever.'

Sooty sat at Trudie's feet, gazing up with yellow foglamps, dropping the mouse.

'Perhaps he wanted milk?' Trudie asked, stroking Sooty's velvety coat.

Laurie shook his head. 'I know what's happened, you gave him the mouse, played with him without me. He saw you love him and loves you back – rather like me.'

Trudie beamed at Sooty and Laurie. 'I'm honoured.' Throwing the mouse along the carpet, she laughed as Sooty dived on his prey. Putting her cup down, she jumped when he leapt onto her lap, washing her hands with rasping licks. Another first.

Eventually, he was content to pick up his mouse, en route to the shed. Both lovers saw it as an omen. Slowly they'd get back on track. During the afternoon, they curled up listening to music, talking a little of the past, and a lot of the future. The warm thrill of love coursed through Trudie's veins. Laurie played the Clifford

T. Ward CD he'd bought from the boot sale – 'Home Thoughts From Abroad' – 'for my Worcestershire girl.'

Trudie decisively replied. 'That's true, I am.'

41

Casting off stitches of the four-ply white cardigan, Phoebe sighed with satisfaction at beginning four weeks ago in May; now third week in June, it was finished. She'd thought she may have forgotten how, but casting on, knit and purl were there at the end of her fingers. 'Like riding a bike.'

She put the sleeve into the knitting bag. Closing the nineteen sixties magazine featuring the pattern, she admired the cover, Princess Margaret in a yellow cocktail dress. Settling in her recliner, shielding eyes from the June sun, she was grateful her life hadn't been spent in the glare of headlights. To have been happily married with two successful children was preferable.

Drifting off for an afternoon nap, she shuddered. 'Happy marriage? Suppose it was, until I unearthed his naughty secret.' She shrugged. 'Not forgotten, but I'm surviving, thank God the old devil left me financially sound. Super holiday, pleasant lodger for a while, and now Alison's news.' Phoebe contentedly drifted, thinking of names for the baby.

***

With nausea having disappeared at the end of May, Alison was relieved to feel well again, able to invite Trudie to visit.

'Stephen, I want her to come. I'll do lunch, if the weather holds we can eat outdoors.'

'All right but… you're pregnant. I'll do it.' Stephen offered. He finished ironing the last pillowcase.

'I'll make it, you can finish it, OK? Gosh you're an ace ironer.'

'I've been doing laundry for years. Dying for a cuppa.'

At dinner, Stephen told her how his mother and Laurie had reunited.

'You're being cautious, bet she is too.'

'Mm, she's been through a lot; he caused it. I want her happiness and protection; he took them from her. Mum knows why he disappeared, but I'm anxious. You think I'm being too concerned?'

'A little. Your mum, if she wasn't happy, wouldn't be with him.'

Stephen looked doubtful. 'I knew of him and the complications, met him when Mum had known him two years. He was quietly charming and seemed to love her. I stayed for dinner and chatted for a while.'

'Why didn't you meet him again?'

'Work mainly, I was here and when I visited Mum, he wasn't there. I was working, before that, studying. When he disappeared, I rang and visited more.'

Alison cleared the table. 'Shall we invite Laurie when Trudie comes?'

She saw Stephen's immediate frown. 'I don't want that and Mum won't, they've been apart four years. In the honeymoon period life probably seems rosy, they need to make certain.'

He walked into the kitchen to wash up. Alison followed. 'I'll dry.'

'Thanks. I'll say I want to see her without Laurie. She'll agree.'

'We can show her the scan photo.' He dried his hands and held Alison excitedly, feeling overwhelming happiness.

Alison too. 'Hey, you're squashing our offspring. Oh no, I need the loo again.'

Trudie's journey up the M6 to Cheshire was eagerly anticipated. Meeting Alison last year, she'd squashed melancholia, not mentioning Laurie. Now a heavy weight had been lifted.

Nearly at Alison's, Trudie felt flutterings of happiness, having rung Stephen to say she was almost there. Passing elegant plane trees on the verges, she guessed he'd be outside. He was, arm around Alison, two Cheshire cats in late morning sun. Before he had chance to open the car door, Trudie was hurrying towards them, embracing both excitedly.

There was non-stop talk, how Alison was, the scan, date due, which hospital. Trudie discussed Stephen's concerts, especially the Dirk Bogarde connection at Alfriston. Stephen gave photographs of the church and cottage where her favourite actor had stayed with his sister in the twenties. Trudie produced a photograph album featuring Stephen's childhood. Alison squealed, moving closer to Trudie on the sofa.

'Ooh, what skinny legs!'

'Hey, Mum was proud of that little blonde boy.'

Trudie giggled at their humour, reminiscent of Laurie and herself.

Stephen took out the coffee tray. Alison remarked how happy Trudie appeared.

'To know you two are happy, and the bonus of a child. That's why.'

Alison smiled. 'Thanks, we're thrilled, so glad the dreaded nausea's gone.'

'Good, you look blooming.'

'We'll show you the scan.'

Trudie gasped, 'Wonderful!'

'Exciting isn't it? I had the full works cos of my age. Nervous, but the baby's normal. I hear Laurie's back, a cause for celebration too.'

Trudie smiled kindly. 'I didn't want to mention it, I've come to hear of your lives.'

'Yes, but you matter. Is it really OK? You're so forgiving, Stephen told me the reasons Laurie disappeared. But four years – an eternity.'

'You're telling me, I almost caved in at my front door. He was polite, nervous, so was I. He'd asked for forgiveness when we'd both had our say. If I didn't give it wholeheartedly there'd be no future.' Trudie shrugged her shoulders. 'I adore him and vice versa.'

'Trudie, it's a great story of forgiveness, resurrected from pain and loss. It would make a riveting book – don't worry, I haven't time to write it.'

Trudie laughed. 'It would sound far fetched, truth's stranger than fiction isn't it? I wondered why he'd gone without a word, shattering our plans. I remembered that poem by John Clare, finding no welcome at home when he returned. "I am homeless at home." Though I had a comfortable one, that's how I felt. Once I knew what had led to his breakdown, I could see he wasn't fit to think or do anything rational then. Alone, I'd endeavoured to enjoy life; now I rejoice in it.'

'Suppose it's too early to move in?'

'Yes, I won't leave my cottage. If ever we do live together, Laurie will rent his out and move to Little Arrow. Gosh, Stephen's been ages, a sandwich would have done.'

'No it wouldn't. I made it, he's heating it up. Like most men, he's noisy in the kitchen, crashing around. For a classical pianist, he's no pianist!'

Trudie grinned conspiratorially.

The two women spoke of religion. Alison told her she was brought up Catholic, but upon leaving home, dabbled with Church of England. 'I'd never return, that burden of irrational control they have over you. I am, like you, a believer, but actions speak louder than words. I'm not close to my folks in Australia; our baby's going to need Granny Trudie a lot.'

They beamed at each other, like schoolgirls given permission to miss hockey on a freezing winter's day.

'Thank you Alison. I had a dominant mother, so no real support. You can depend on me to be there. Incidentally, can I pay my respects at your cat's grave?'

'Yes, she's where she spied on birds. I was thinking of going to the rescue for another, but I'll have my hands full with pregnancy, birth, feeds, nappies and nights up. Oh help! You get what I mean though.'

Trudie smiled. 'Absolutely. Is Stephen moving in when the baby arrives?'

'Yes, his Georgian cottage is sweet, but rather bijou.' She walked towards the door. 'I'll see if lunch is ready.'

Stephen appeared, making her jump. 'Lunch. We're in here, bit windy out.'

'Super, I adore your kitchen, Alison.'

'Thanks. I'll show you the cloakroom so you can wash your hands.' She laughed, 'Sounds like a mother and child situation. Ooh, I've got to get used to that.'

Both women giggled and made their way along the hall.

42

It was a chilly October day when Stephen took the mysterious call, having moved in with Alison in September. He'd been in the garden raking wind-whipped leaves; Alison resting on the sofa, Saturday afternoon sun streaming in on her.

Entering the kitchen, he heard the phone, shaking off boots, hopping to the table. Alison said Julia may ring. She didn't – a stranger did. Puzzled, Stephen said he'd take a message.

'She won't know me. I've been phoning people from my husband's address book.'

'Erm, who is your husband?'

'He is, or rather was Henry, who died three days ago. I'm his wife, Collette, with funeral details.'

Stephen, perplexed, expressed sympathy for her loss.

'It wasn't unexpected; we'd been separated, but I'm organising things. He used to be a vicar so perhaps Alison was a parishioner. I'll give you my number.'

Stephen came off the phone having no clue who the deceased was.

As the kettle was boiling, Alison asked drowsily. 'Has that tea got my name on it?'

Stephen broke into a smile. 'Definitely. Two minutes.'

Pondering the mysterious call, he carried the tea in to Alison. 'Have you and the bump had a lovely rest? Sorry, forgotten to kiss him too.'

Alison enquired, 'Who was on the phone? Not Julia from your expression.'

'A woman; knew your name and number. Let's have tea and I'll tell you.'

As Stephen spoke, Alison's face went from warm to hot, pink to carmine.

'Was he someone you designed for?'

Alison put down her tea. 'Just after we met, you heard an answerphone message, assuming it was Phil, but it was Henry, needing my advice. I hadn't heard from him for many years.'

'I was insecure and suspicious then. How old was he?'

Alison shrugged. 'Forgotten. Henry had massive problems. I heard his concerns, advised he ditch his obsession and build on his marriage. Guessed he'd go from bad to worse, reckless even when he was a vicar. No clue what happened since then.' She sighed, puffing. 'Phew, now he's dead.'

'Collette said he'd been ill some time. From what you've said you won't want to ring back will you?'

Alison frowned. 'Emphatically not.' She gave a weak smile, her deep flush reverting to a healthy pink.

Stephen looked relieved. 'Good. You and our child are precious, I'll always keep you safe. I'm going for a shower then I'll make dinner. Are you... really OK?'

She smiled. 'Yes, it's lovely to feel so protected, baby. Speaking of baby, pass my vitamins. My book too, sorry.'

'Don't apologise. It's an honour to look after you.'

Alison opened her book, but despite not wanting to dwell on Henry's death, she did. For the first time since he'd revealed his surprising problems last year, she wondered how he'd gone on. Something Henry had said came to mind. 'The greatest gift to give someone is to listen to their story. Be with them, sympathise, empathise.' She'd done that. It had been up to him to heed her advice or continue in the same reckless fashion. She guessed which one he'd chosen.

Hearing Stephen coming downstairs humming Brahm's Lullaby made her smile, lighting up her whole being. Henry's life and death were nothing to do with her. Though he hadn't merited it, she'd gone the extra mile for this cowardly, shallow man. Lovely Stephen, soulmate and father of her forthcoming child, later entered the room looking as pleased to see her as if he'd been gone for days. Alison knew she'd found everlasting happiness.

43

On her birthday, November 2nd, Trudie awoke to a freezing Monday. Hoary frost hugged the fields. Turning the heating up, she opened cards, looking forward to Stephen's call after she'd visited Paula with Laurie. At nine-thirty a bouquet was received with a card, 'Happy Birthday from nearly three of us!'

Laurie arrived at ten for their Cheltenham journey, ecstatic to be sharing Trudie's birthday. Embracing Paula at her home, he thanked her profusely yet again for acting as go-between with Trudie. With Paula's lamb casserole, Trudie was given a subscription to *The Lady* magazine and a chocolate brownie with a candle for the traditional rendition of Happy Birthday. With the weather worsening, they reluctantly returned earlier than planned.

Back home, Trudie suggested a brief walk to her old haunts. She pulled on a woollen scarf and hat, coat collar turned up, linking arms with Laurie, thrilled to be spending her day with him. 'Those clouds look ominous, careful, the bridge will be slippery.'

Huddled against November chill, they passed the blackthorn hedge festooned with Old Man's Beard, shrouded in mist. Hugging the bank was the ancient ash tree where Trudie had gathered its keys to make ear-rings. She quoted the country saying, 'Oak before ash, we're in for a splash, ash before oak, we're in for a soak.' Laurie said he'd never known an ash tree come into leaf before an oak. Trudie smugly replied, 'Ah, but centuries ago springs were warmer.' Laurie nudged her, 'Trust you to have the answer.'

She giggled. 'Let's quickly walk to the millpond, where there used to be two swans, Jack and Jill. Herons patrolling too, eyeing up fish and tadpoles. I'll show you the haunted paper mill, where they made cases for needle firms in Redditch upstream. A schoolfriend and I scared ourselves witless, creeping in at five one morning. Taking torches, we saw blue dye in abandoned open tins, creaking floorboards and pitted tables.' Laurie felt her shudder. 'Tattered remains of Victorian Factory Acts on stone walls. In the torchlight, tangled webs cascaded from rafters, huge spiders in them. We ran home, terrified.'

Laurie laughed. After a quick look, he urged, 'The wind was whispering when we started, now it's beginning to shriek. Stephen's phoning too.'

'Ouch, didn't take my phone to Paula's.' Trudie realised, unaware Stephen and Alison's day had begun with great drama.

***

Sleeping at ten on Sunday November 1st, Alison awoke at six. Thankful she hadn't made nocturnal trips to the bathroom, she slipped out of bed, not disturbing Stephen. Six nationwide concerts had ended, the following week virtually free, enabling him to be at the birth. Hungry, Alison trudged downstairs, holding the handrail. The bump was tightening, making her walk ducklike. She heard the throb of the central heating.

She pushed the kitchen door open so the stair's light would be sufficient to see by. Yawning, she took two Rich Tea biscuits from the tin. Frowning, she sniffed an unfamiliar smell. Taking a deeper breath to identify it, nausea hit sharply. Unwisely she sniffed again, swaying with the sickening smell – immediately realising it was gas.

Alerting Stephen, he rang the emergency number, an engineer arrived quickly to investigate. While the man banged and clanged downstairs, Stephen, worried she'd been affected by gas, insisted Alison ate biscuits to stave off nausea. When the engineer left, Alison was vomiting in the bathroom.

'If you're like this in an hour, I'm phoning the hospital. Don't look like that, I'd rather do it now.'

Alison protested, wiping her mouth. 'Think I'll sleep again.'

Stephen tried to disguise his anxiety. 'I'll bring tea and toast later.'

At eight o'clock, he carried breakfast in. 'Alison what is it?' putting the tray down.

'Ooh, really sharp pains.'

Stephen looked alarmed. 'I'm no expert, but surely they're labour pains?'

Alison sat up, clutching her stomach. 'Mm, my back aches too.'

'Time to phone the hospital.'

Admittance was advised, a bag hastily packed. Alison wept with fear. 'I'm not due for ten days. Let me sort myself out, so I don't forget anything.'

At the hospital, ten miles off, she was examined thoroughly on account of the gas leak, and in early labour, transferred to an en-suite room. Stephen felt helpless. Jo, their maternity nurse, explained procedures. He'd told her it was a second child for Alison, she'd endured a protracted labour with Leo.

'Each delivery's different. She's having pain relief, go to her, I'll bring you tea.'

At twelve-thirty Alison's pains had halted. Stephen dozed in a recliner. A senior midwife examined her at one forty-five, informing Stephen it could be hours until established labour ensued. He assured Alison he'd stay.

'I'll ring Mum to wish her happy birthday.'

Alison smiled wearily. 'Give her my love.'

311

'I'll eat in the restaurant. You've had soup, d'you want anything else, sweetheart?'

Alison drowsily said no.

Disappointed Trudie couldn't answer his call, Stephen put a message on both phones, not mentioning the gas leak.

As dark descended, Trudie and Laurie slithered over the frosty bridge to the cottage. It was while Laurie was slicing Guinness cake he'd made, Trudie saw the telephone flashing. Upon hearing her shriek, Laurie dashed in from the kitchen, alarmed. Trudie falteringly told him the news. 'What? I thought…'

'Yes, he left that message earlier. I'm so excited!' she gushed breathlessly.

'Gosh you'll soon be a grannie!'

Trudie grimaced. 'No, not Grannie. Too… elderly. Not Nana either. I'm going to be Ga Ga. Hey, stop laughing. Not Gar Gar, Ga Ga with a flat a. Paula's grand-daughter calls her that. I love it.'

Laurie held her, sharing her elation. 'Did Stephen say anything else?'

'He'll phone when the baby's born.'

Trudie asked Laurie to cancel their reservation at the pub. 'We'll have a chicken dish from the freezer. I'm anxious for Stephen, he's all I have.'

A wide smile emanated from Laurie. 'No, you've got me too. Anyhow, Ga Ga, he's not the one about to give birth.'

Trudie giggled. 'You know what I mean. Would you make a fire and I'll defrost the chicken? It'll be cosy eating in here, let's watch episodes of Tinker Tailor you bought me.'

'Perfect. This is the second fire I've made since our reunion. I could get used to it.'

From the kitchen, Trudie called, 'You'd better!'

Later, locking the conservatory, Trudie saw the frost was fierce, night thick with fog. She shivered with happiness; in this warm den with the man she loved, walls flickering from firelight's glow.

Watching the DVD, Trudie told him it was occupying her mind. 'I get lost in spy films though.'

Laurie kissed her hair. 'Well now you have me, you won't be confused,' he said tenderly. Trudie looked up; they both laughed. 'Life's gone from despair to ecstasy. Being here on your birthday, your grandchild nearly born... what else could we want? From famine, it's now feast.'

With nothing evident by ten o'clock, Trudie asked Laurie to stay overnight.

'I want to be here for you.' he told her definitely.

Trudie told him convincingly, 'The spare bed's made up.' seeing Laurie's disappointment. She began to laugh. 'But you won't be in it. That is if you want to be with me.'

He softly drew her towards him. 'Try stopping me, thought I'd never be allowed back.'

'I can't promise anything, but want to share my happiness with you.'

Laurie gave her a bear hug. 'Heaven, thank you.'

At ten-thirty, Laurie and Trudie lay, warm against winter night's chill. Neither felt awkward. After drifting to sleep, the call came at ten to twelve, Trudie waking quickly. Fumbling for the bedside lamp, she answered anxiously, hearing Stephen's voice.

'Mum...' Trudie interrupted. 'Stephen.' She felt Laurie stir.

'It's taken many hours, but two people I love are celebrating a birthday today.' He heard Trudie gasp. 'Baby Boyce arrived an hour ago. Alison's had a bumpy ride.'

Trudie sniffed a little. 'Fabulous, the baby I mean. Erm, you might like to tell me what sex?'

'Oh yes, a little girl. Not so little, eight pounds and two weeks early. Alison's been so brave. Baby was back to back so labour longer, with shocking pain. Terrible to watch her going through that.'

'Awful. Did she have an epidural? Darling, we'll talk tomorrow.'

Shakily Stephen said, 'It's OK. Huge relief Alison's ordeal's

313

ended and our little girl's here.' Stephen cleared his throat. 'Towards the end of the labour they gave an epidural, nothing else worked. The baby was stuck cos of her position, and Alison's small, so they put something called a ventouse extractor on the head. As she pushed, they pulled, many stitches and a scab on baby's blonde scalp.'

'Oh thank heavens you were there. How long was she in labour?'

'From seven this morning, something triggered it. I'm off home now, really tired. They've advised Alison stay in hospital for two days to be monitored. You and Laurie could visit when she's home. Goodnight, love you.'

Trudie switched off the lamp, snuggling into Laurie, utterly relieved. 'Gosh, she's had a difficult birth.'

'I heard. Darling, this is a dream. Barren years, my illnesses, stress it caused you. Finding you, your absolute forgiveness and… here I am sharing your joy. I'm so happy I could burst.'

'Not in this bed you don't!' She giggled. 'That reminds me when I was in a café with Paula. We overheard a conversation between two women. One was complaining of her husband's snoring. Paula and I were riveted. The woman said, "I resort to throwing paperbacks at him, although hardbacks are tempting." Her friend replied with an equally poker face, "Oh my mum hit my dad with a hot water bottle once cos of his loud snoring. With each hit she shouted 'WILL… YOU… SHUT… UP?!! The hot water bottle burst and my dad jumped out of bed screaming." Deadpan, the first said, "Blimey, good job it was only rubber and not one of them stone things!"'

Laurie erupted with laughter, Trudie felt him shaking. 'Neither of the women even smiled. We had to go to the ladies room to recover.'

Laurie gave another loud laugh. 'Absolutely priceless. Only you would think of that at a time like this. My adorable, funny, gorgeous little Trudie.'

44

Choosing a name for their daughter had been the easy part; settling on a christening date a challenge. The traumatic birth had taken its toll on Alison. Stephen had been busy with concerts, so Julia had helped with the child. By Christmas, Alison was less sore in the 'undercarriage' as Phoebe called it. Mrs. C. had winced at Alison's discomfort, saying she could barely remember her confinements, but had a maternity nurse. She'd visited Alison, done chores, shopping, cradling the child close to her ample bosom, humming 'rock a bye baby.' On the first occasion she'd welled up, 'Hello little one, old Phoebe's come to see you. What a beauty you are. Alison, lovely you're on the mend and baby's an absolute corker. Any names yet?'

Alison smiled, twinkling. 'Ah, yes we have. She's to be Phoebe Rose.'

Phoebe flushed with pleasure, eyes sparkling.

'I like your name, Phoebe, and you are her surrogate grandmother. Pleased?'

'Oh my, I'm honoured, you've made this old girl very happy indeed.'

The day of her grand-daughter's christening in April, Trudie stood outside the conservatory door, inhaling freshness after the night's rain. Holly appeared from nowhere, dashing between her legs, leaping over a terracotta pot. She hid under the golden holly, peeping skywards, hoping for a fledgling dropping from its nest. Not as fleet of foot nowadays, more of a watcher than catcher.

Laurie had stayed overnight. He'd thought Trudie would have wanted him to move in. She was cautious; it was, after all, as if they'd just met. He'd accepted her wisdom, they needed time. There was also Sooty to consider, he was settled with Laurie, and Holly would be upset. In any case, Trudie was happy at last. At Christmas they'd fully resumed their relationship. Joy filled both their houses.

Watching dawn blocking out indigo sky on this April day, Trudie and Laurie hugged. Whilst Laurie was showering, Trudie sat outside. Climbing rose buds snaked up trees, early clematis scrambling through them. Aromatic hawthorn blossom was already cascading in drifts like a frothy bridal bouquet. A glut of plums promised. The garden gave her hope, something to nurture. Now Laurie was experiencing the spectacle of the seasons with her, observing birds and fish from the stone bridge, strolling along the sinuous river's banks, gazing down at the clear gravelly bed where minnows laid their eggs, and laughing at Holly attempting to snatch dancing gnats.

Trudie had been elated two days before when Stephen had revealed on the phone that he and Alison were planning to marry in September. This lovely news was followed by an unexpected call from Paula, mysteriously saying she was sorry she now couldn't attend the christening, having received a shock. 'Look I'll bring the Steiff teddy bear next time we meet. Forgive me, I'll ring you on Wednesday,' she'd shakily explained, sounding tense and distracted. Trudie had been hurt Paula had offered no explanation. They'd been soulmates for years and Paula felt part of the family. She and Trudie had shared their lives and been each other's 'rocks' through thick and thin. Even asking 'Why

Wednesday?,' she'd received no answer, only a hasty wish for a happy christening day. Worriedly ringing Paula back twice since the call, no reply. The second time she'd left a message, telling Paula she was very concerned, re-assuring her no matter what, she would help – again no reply. Now on her granddaughter's christening day, Trudie must put the mystery aside. She must not allow the enigma to spoil this joyous event.

***

Two hours on, Laurie and Trudie were in Phoebe Cade's church watching Phoebe Rose, in Petit Bateau pink velour, gurgling at the vicar as he christened her from the ancient font. Phoebe Cade, resplendent in violet, pronounced her 'good as gold' to Jonathan, next to her. Trudie looked on proudly as her handsome son in a cream linen suit, and Alison in ivory dress and hat, stood with the godparents, Julia and Leo, making their promises for baby Phoebe Rose.

Anglo-Saxon Ryelands Church was bijou, ideal for the small congregation. Trudie glowed at Laurie in the pew beside her, dressed in the black cashmere jacket and trousers she liked. She'd fitted into the sapphire dress she'd intended to wear that nervous reunion day. Julia, in lemon, gave Trudie a hug and an apology for being so furtive in the Regency Café the year before. She greeted a tanned Leo warmly, saying he looked the bees knees in navy chinos and jacket.

At the reception at Alison's, people were delighted to see Poppy, mingling confidently, vibrant in an emerald mini dress, poppies threaded into her upswept dark hair. She'd flown in from Nice with Leo. As Godmother, Julia was pleased Leo could attend as Godfather. She eavesdropped as Phoebe Cade asked Poppy if she'd settled into her French school.

She nodded, telling of a girl in her class called Fido. Phoebe was baffled, pronouncing it a strange name.

'Only a nickname,' admitted Poppy devilishly.

'Oh, what's her real name?' queried Phoebe, rather tipsy.

Poppy spluttered, replying 'Spot.'

Phoebe erupted, spilling her sherry. 'Good heavens, what odd names girls are given in France.'

Laurie laughed uproariously with a deep throaty voice, letting Phoebe understand it was a joke. She nudged Laurie, twinkling, calling him an absolute 'card'. Trudie's eyes shone, cradling Phoebe Rose adoringly, like the proud grandmother she was.

Leo gave a short speech, praising Alison for his upbringing and steadfast love. He proposed a champagne toast: 'To friends old and new, Mum, Stephen, and sister, Phoebe Rose Boyce.'

Following an hour of happy chat, drinks, buffet and cake made by Julia, Stephen wandered to the piano. Beginning to play Brahm's Lullaby, he was joined by Phoebe.

Her eyes lit up. 'Ooh beautiful. "As I bid thee goodnight, bright stars shed their light, the roses dew deep, their heads hide in sleep. When the dawning shall break, all the earth shall awake, when the dawning shall break, all the earrrrrrth shall awake."' Everyone clapped, amazed by her clear soprano voice.

'Phoebe, I didn't know you could sing so beautifully.' Alison admitted, kissing her.

'Ah, life's full of surprises, not to mention shocks.' she winked.

Jonathan smiled, holding Julia's hand. 'You can say that again.' Laurie nearby, admitted 'Same for Trudie and me. This time last year I certainly didn't imagine standing beside the love of my life, at a gathering of her family and friends.'

Trudie blushed happily, feeling her hand being squeezed. Alison approached, beaming at both.

'Thankfully you're part of the family Laurie, where you should be. May I take Phoebe from you Trudie, for her bottle and a nap? She's been so contented, no tears at the font gazing up at that old bearded vicar. Have more refreshments won't you?'

Passing Mrs. Cade, she paused. 'Are you enjoying yourself Phoebe?'

Kissing baby Phoebe, she beamed, 'Oh I am, being with these lovely people, especially my little namesake. Stephen's kindly giving me a lift home, er... hope that's all right.'

'Of course.'

Leo fed his sister and took her for a nap, while Alison and Stephen opened christening presents. Trudie made pots of tea, Laurie and Jonathan discussed antiques, and Poppy washed dishes voluntarily, telling Julia, Jonathan was 'formidaaaaaaaable!'

When Julia and Jonathan took Poppy home, Leo, staying at Alison's, reminded Poppy she'd be collected by Alison for their airport trip back to Nice. Trudie and Laurie prepared to drive back to Worcestershire.

Kissing Stephen, Alison and baby, Trudie promised to ring when home. While Laurie drove, she pondered on the day, ecstatic that Stephen and Alison's happiness was complete with their child, Julia's world had been transformed with Jonathan, and hers with Laurie. He silently thanked God for Trudie and her forgiveness for his vanishing act, telling Trudie the day had been 'an unparalleled joyous success.'

Trudie blissfully agreed, recalling the phrase she'd coined – parallel lives, parallel loves. Paula infiltrated her thoughts; disconcerting she hadn't chosen to attend this lovely happy day, knowing it meant so much to Trudie, enigmatically saying she'd received 'a shock' and would ring her on Wednesday. After Friday's call, Trudie had shared it with Laurie, who was equally perplexed. She'd managed to put the call at the back of her mind, determined to enjoy the fulfilment of everyone's dreams at the joyous christening. Only two days now until Wednesday. As Laurie signalled to turn onto the M6 motorway, Trudie, shuddering, hoped Paula's shock had no connection with late husband James...

***

About the Author

Joy was born in London, but grew up in Redditch, Worcestershire, attending grammar school there, living alongside the lovely River Arrow and wildflower fields. Her diverse career has included public relations, employment agent, interior design, voice-over artist, scriptwriter, antiques, Shelter for the homeless, animal charities, Esther Rantzen's helplines for children and the elderly and counselling and stress therapies.

Interests include the arts, music, films, theatre, gardening, animals, genealogy, British social history, concerts and literary festivals. She has acted in both serious and comedic plays.

Adopted as a baby, Joy voluntarily now helps others to trace their roots. She has two sons, who live both in France and England.

Now residing in Cheshire, she has written and published poetry, comic verse, and her autobiography. *Untangling The Webs* is her first novel.